CRACK

D E McCluskey

DE McCluskey

CRACK
Copyright © 2018 by D E McCluskey

The moral right of the author has been asserted.
*All characters and events in this publication,
other than those clearly in the public domain,
are fictitious, and any resemblance to real persons,
living or dead, is purely coincidental.*

All rights are reserved.

No part of this publication may be reproduced,
stored in a retrieval system, or transmitted in any form
by any means, without the prior permission, in writing, of
the publisher, nor be otherwise circulated in any form of binding or
cover other than that of which it was
published and without a similar condition including this
condition being imposed on the subsequent purchaser.

ISBN: 9781986367820

Dammaged Production

www.dammaged.com

Crack

For Annmarie and Helen
The two most supportive sisters a younger brother could ask for.
Remember Tinkerbell?
Paid off, didn't she?

TRIGGER WARNINGS:
graphic violence
sexual situations
animal violence*
3 instances – all of them integral to the story
DON'T HATE ME

DE McCluskey

Crack

PROLOGUE

CRACK!!!

Joe's head hit the cracked leather of the headrest behind him, as a noise, that could have either been a moan of pleasure or a cry of pain, escaped him. The shout was coupled with a violent spasm, a reaction that released bolts of adrenaline through him, ones that left almost every nerve ending in his body alive in a sweet tingle. He pushed his body back into the tattered driver's seat of the van, his reactions out of his control for at least the next few moments. His toes flexed inside his heavy boots, and his stomach muscles, deftly hidden beneath the onset of his middle-aged spread, contracted as the sensation that started in his feet climbed its way towards his stomach. With it came delectable shivers that helter-skeltered through his legs, twining around of his thighs, before turning inwards towards his crotch. There, the individual threads of the ecstasy culminated in a sweet release as they surged through the rigid shaft of his penis.

As the orgasm flowed, his fingers seized the steering wheel so tightly that the skin of his knuckles turned from pink to white in the blink of an eye. He shuddered for a few blessed seconds. 'Holy shit,' he whispered before it was all over, far too swiftly for his liking. Then his body relaxed. His stomach, his toes, his fingers, and, finally, his throbbing cock. His head, slick and cold with sweat, fell back into the already clammy seat as another, shaky sigh escaped him.

This time, there was no mistaking it. It was a deep sigh of relief.

Eventually, he opened an eye.

Everything was blurred for a moment, but acuity quickly returned as his post-ejaculate attention focused on his passenger. He knew he wasn't looking his best right now; he knew his hair would be sweaty and flat, pushed over his forehead, giving him what his kids sometimes, affectionately referred to as a *paedophile look*, but today, he didn't care about that.

He wasn't here to impress anyone.

He caught his reflection in the dark, curved glass covering his passenger's face and a laugh escaped him. *Is this how Karen sees me after sex?* he thought as he studied his distorted image in the black glass.

'You need to sort your mess out,' his passenger said. The muffle of the motorcycle helmet distorted the deep, male voice almost as much as it had distorted his image, but not enough for him not to understand every word.

He pulled his gaze away from his mesmerising reflection and looked out of the window. He rolled his eyes and released another sigh. He rolled his eyes as he regarded the mess outside.

As he shifted his position, he became instantly aware of the thick wetness inside his trousers, the wetness that had started warm, but was already starting to cool. With the cooling came the itch. Gritting his teeth, he pulled at his crotch, moving the wetness this way and that. Tutting, he opened his door and climbed out. He grimaced again when he realised that all he'd managed to do was move the uncomfortable, cold damp from one leg to the other.

He stepped outside, stretched, and scrabbled at his clammy crotch again. He then surveyed the grim scene before him.

There was blood everywhere.

It wasn't just blood, there was bone, grey matter, and pink gristle too, all of it decorating the plumage that surrounded him.

The dirty mustard paintwork of the van door was spattered in crimson. The driver's side wing was covered too, as was the wheel and the corresponding arch. The whole of the front of the van was coated in thick, slimy gore that dripped onto the tarmac below it in wet, steaming clumps.

Crack

He smiled. He exhaled through his nose and basked in the afterglow of the exquisite relief that came post-ejaculation and, of course, the larger relief of what he had just done.

Still struggling with his damp underwear, he waddled towards the small shed at the side of the road. The itch was annoying him now, as he envisioned the tops of his thighs turning red and sore as they rubbed together.

Tissues in the van next time, he thought.

Opening the shed, he removed the hose and the spade he'd placed within arm's reach earlier, before turning his attentions to a little further down the road from where his van was currently idling. He looked at the ruined, headless body of the scantily clad woman who was lying in a deep pool of her own blood. He only saw her as a chore now, something to clean up rather than the complex human being she'd once been. The mess where her head had been, was extensive and—dare he even think it- Beautiful?

His gaze returned to the interior of the van where he hoped to catch a glimpse of his helmeted passenger, maybe even shoot him a small wave, or a thumbs-up to the success of their little venture. He shrugged his shoulders, shaking his head when he saw the empty cab.

Fuck him, he thought. *I never needed him afterwards anyway.*

He scanned the area around him. The whole of the building site, making doubly sure there was nobody around, nobody who might have witnessed his gruesome little secret.

Happy that there was no one about, exactly how he liked it, he dragged the large tarpaulin and began the rigorous, disgusting, but completely necessary clean up task.

He was whistling a jaunty little tune as he did.

1.

'TAKE IT EASY, you guys, eh?' Joe shouted as he exited the security porta cabin. The guys from the day shift were beginning to filter through the gates, signalling the end of his shift.

'Yeah, you too. We wouldn't want you to go sleeping too hard.'

'I wish. She'll have me running around the house fixing things in an hour; you watch.'

'You need to show her who's the boss, man. Show her who wears the trousers,' the big man in the hard hat hollered back as Joe grabbed his coat, flask, and sandwich box.

'She knows who the boss is already,' he laughed as he trudged towards his car.

Joe O'Hara had waved goodbye to his forties. His thick head of hair was losing the battle with the greys, or the silvers as he liked to joke. The youthful look that he liked it styled worked a little to undo what the advancing years were doing to the rest of him, but he couldn't style his eyes. They were tired, aged eyes. This wasn't because he *was* tired; his eyes just looked it; they had done since he was a kid.

Right now, however, his eyes *were* tired. They were pink and the pupils were dilated, obviously trying to keep the light of the day from penetrating his brain. These, together with the two-day-old, salt and pepper stubble, that was currently caressing his chin, he looked, and indeed, felt every day of his fifty-one years.

His hands fumbled in his trouser pockets, eventually retrieving a small key fob, that he pressed a button on. The yellow indicator lights of a family car that, like him, had seen better days, flashed, and emitted two robotic clucks. With a deep sigh, he climbed in and closed the door behind him. Another sigh escaped him as the end of a long night of security work, that he had just endured, was finally here.

Crack

He flicked his eyes up towards the rear-view mirror where the reflection of some dishevelled, old, homeless man gazed back at him. He ran a hand over the stubble on his chin before moving on through his hair. Finally, he gave himself a little slap in the face. It woke the homeless man up a little, and a spark of life, small and timid, illuminated his eyes. 'Come on, Joe. Get home and get some sleep,' he croaked, surprising himself with how tired his voice was.

He turned the ignition, hit the radio, and pulled out of the car park.

His job as a night security guard wasn't fantastic, or even taxing employment, but it paid enough to get him and his family by. He'd been telling himself for the last ten years that it was only a temporary stop in his career progression, and that by next year, he would be in a cushy, nine-to-five, with a nice office and a sexy, flirty secretary.

It was a nice dream.

He released a short breath of air through his nose and hit the button for the CD player to start. 'One of These Nights' by The Eagles was already halfway through. This song was up there on the list of his favourite songs, so he pressed another button and it started again.

Tapping his fingers to the beat, he turned out of the building site, onto the ramp that slipped into the main road. Indicating, he checked his mirrors, hoping not to catch a glimpse of himself again, and looked for any oncoming vehicles. There were none, so, singing along to his favourite tune, he pulled out onto the three-lane road.

As he gripped the wheel, his foot searched for the accelerator, and he ended up oversteering. A blast from a horn from a vehicle behind him snapped him awake, instantly. The roar of the blood, suddenly pumping through his ears, bashed in time with the song coming from the speakers, and his heart. He watched as a motorcycle, one he'd not noticed, swerved into the middle lane.

'Shit,' he muttered as all the moisture in his mouth felt as if it had evaporated. He oversteered again, the opposite way this time, and the car skidded into the ditch at the side of the road.

He watched, his face soaked in sweat, with a feeling like his heart was attempting to escape the confines of his chest. The motorcycle corrected itself and accelerated off at speed, but not before the rider turned and flipped Joe a middle-fingered salute.

'Fucking idiot,' he shouted out of the window as the bike, and its rider, disappeared into the distance.

An SUV slowed down next to him. Joe turned. The woman driver offered him one of the dirtiest looks he'd seen in a long time. He offered her *his* middle finger in response to the glare, prompting another scowl, before she drove off.

Now one hundred percent awake and almost hyper-aware, Joe reached out a shaking hand and flicked the stereo off. He gripped the steering wheel tight with both hands, allowing the shivers that were coursing through him, to run their course. When he felt as if he were in some semblance of control, he turned the keys in the ignition of the stalled vehicle and pumped the accelerator. This time, he checked his mirrors correctly before pulling out of the ditch and heading home.

Crack

2.

'GOOD MORNING, DETECTIVE Ashton,' the hushed male voice from just above her head whispered. 'I made you some breakfast.'

Paula Ashton opened an eye and turned it in the direction of the voice. The small stream of sunlight that was beaming into the room from the half-opened curtain hit her light-sensitive organ, and she closed it again. She breathed in deeply, attempting to build up the courage to open it again. When she did, a silhouette was looming in a dust-mote-filled shaft of light. It was a large male, and he was wearing a uniform. It took a few moments before her sleep ravaged brain could register that the silhouette was a policeman, and that he was carrying a tray. She sniffed as the delicious smells caused a rumble to announce itself, from somewhere deep within her stomach. The smell was hot buttered toast, one of the best smells in the whole of the world. With a slow smile, she pulled herself up in the bed and regarded the man and his gifts.

On the tray, accompanying the toast, was a tall glass of orange juice and a single red rose.

'Always one for the romantic gestures,' she mumbled through lips that were still thick with sleep.

'You know me. I just wanted to make sure you got a nice bit of breakfast before Sally got up. Don't get used to it, though. I don't fancy the idea of a chubby wife.'

Ian Locke's handsome face grinned as his soon-to-be-wife raised her eyebrows to look at him. 'Why, thank you for your concern.' She reached out to accept the tray. 'I think.'

'Listen, I've got to run. The life of a motorcycle cop is never quiet for long.' He leaned over the bed and planted a kiss on her forehead. 'Remember, three months today and you become Detective Locke.'

As his lips left her, she laughed. 'We talked about that. I'm not changing my name.'

'Yeah? Well, whatever,' he said, rolling his eyes. 'I've got to go. I'll see you later tonight. Give Sally a kiss for me.'

With that, the big, romantic man was gone. Paula listened to the sound of him sneaking down the stairs before exiting through the front door. These small sounds were followed by another, even smaller one. The sound of Sally's bedroom door brushing open along the landing carpet.

A sleepy four-year-old girl appeared in the doorway holding a battered, brown teddy bear and rubbing her eyes. 'Did I miss Daddy again?' she asked, the disappointment in her voice mingling with the thickness of her sleep.

'Yeah, he's just left.' Paula patted the crumpled mattress next to her as a signal for the girl to get into the bed, which she did eagerly. 'He said he wanted to hug you too, and asked me to give you this …' She wrapped her arms around the little girl and gave her a tight hug and a little tickle, planting a big kiss on her forehead. Sally laughed and giggled, kicking her feet playfully. 'Do you want some toast and a huggle with Mummy before nursery?'

'Yes, please,' the little girl squealed before diving under the covers.

Paula wasted no time before diving underneath with her.

3.

JOE TURNED INTO his street. This house was there, at the end of the cul-de-sac, looking like all the others in the small close. He closed his eyes as he came to a stop. The slow, exhausted breath he exhaled caused his shoulders to slump. 'Fuck,' he whispered as he saw his wife's car still on the drive, meaning she was still home, and that meant the kids would be too. 'Oh, please don't let the kids be sick,' he continued, instantly feeling a little guilty at the thought. 'All I want is to get some sleep,' he said, as if attempting to make up for being so selfish.

He manoeuvred the car next to his wife's small, red one on their gateless driveway and stepped out onto the weed trimmed paving. As he stretched, his wife walked out of the house. She had once been stunning, gorgeous, however now she was a tired, slightly overweight, middle-aged woman. She was still beautiful to him though. Wearing a dark green blouse with the emblem of the supermarket she worked in, that bulged where each button battled to stay connected to the fabric. Her hair looked like she hadn't had the time to finish it, and her face was flushed red.

'Oh, thank God you're home.' She said this without even looking at him. 'Martin's sick, he's not going to school, and I haven't had time to get Annmarie to the bus, so she's missed it. Can you take her?'

'Karen, I've just finished a twelve-hour shift.'

'I know, and I'm sorry but he's the colour of death. I'm hoping it's not the flu; I really don't have time to catch it, and Annmarie can't miss any more school. Can you just do this for me, now? I really need to go.'

Joe's eyes rolled to the back of his head. The prospect of driving Annmarie to school was daunting, his shoulders dropped even further at the thought of not climbing straight into bed for another two hours, at least.

'Aw thanks, love. I know you're tired, but it's been one of those mornings,' she shouted, blowing him a kiss. 'I'll see you later. Have a nice day.' Without any further preamble, she was in her car and diving off with a small wave.

He watched her go. He would have replied to her goodbye if his arms hadn't been too tired to lift.

'Dad, I've got to get to school now. I've got drama this morning, and I can't miss it.' A young, pretty girl of fifteen appeared at the door. She was nearly wearing a school uniform, made up of a very short skirt and a blouse that had far too many buttons not doing their job. She was also caked in makeup.

'You're not going to school dressed like that!' he snapped as he looked at her.

Her face spoke volumes about what she might have said, but the words that came out of her mouth were, 'Like what, Dad?'

'You know like what. With that skirt on, and all that muck on your face. Come on Annmarie, get back in and put your proper skirt on. You know the rules.'

'Mum would've let me wear this,' she sniped back, her face frozen in the snarl she offered him almost constantly these days.

'Maybe so, but your mum's not here. Now, get changed.'

It hadn't seemed possible for Annmarie's face to contort any further, but it did, and an almost inaudible growl escaped her as she turned and stomped back into the house.

Joe followed, his despair, not to mention contempt for the day, was showing in his gait. 'Get a hurry on and ask your brother if he needs anything from the shop on the way back.'

'I'm not going in there,' she shouted. 'I've got a party next week, and I don't want to catch his yuck.'

'I'm all right, Dad,' a scratchy reply from somewhere up the stairs filtered down towards him. 'Although, if you're going to the shop, can you get me a comic?'

'Son, if you're well enough to read comics, then you're well enough to do homework. I'll see you when I get back. Annmarie, I'll be in the car.' He turned to make his way out of the madness. He raised his head towards the weak warmth from the sun. He closed his

Crack

eyes, enjoying the cooling breeze on his brow, relishing the freshness of the moment. He climbed into the car and opened both front windows. The breeze washed over his tired body, raising small goosebumps. Annmarie climbed in, and the smell of her perfume ruined the moment and snapped him back into reality. 'Whoa, how much of that shit have you got on?'

Annmarie looked at him as if he were dirt, then shook her head as she turned to fasten her seatbelt. 'First you tell me to get changed, then you call my perfume shit. What is this, Dad? Pick on Annmarie day?'

Joe shook his head and fired up the engine. 'One of those days,' he mumbled. Annmarie continued her dirty look as he reversed out of the driveway.

4.

THE TRAFFIC ON the way to Annmarie's school was heavy. It was flowing but tightly packed, filled with angry horns, and unhappy drivers. Joe was working the brakes harder than usual, and his tired muscles were screaming. Annmarie had picked a radio station that was blaring something nonsensical from the speakers as she sat back, nodding her head.

The pulse of the rhythmless music was in perfect tandem with the throb happening in Joe's head. The stop lights of the car in front pulled his attention from the irritating music and back to the road ahead. A sharp blast of a horn behind did nothing to help his fraying nerves. One obscene gesture later, he was moving again.

Eventually, he pulled up outside the school, and relaxed his grip on the steering wheel. 'Anywhere here, Dad,' Annmarie said, unbuckling her seatbelt and jumping out of the car the very moment it stopped. He shook his head as he watched her run to a group of girls who all turned to greet her with hugs and smiles.

'You're welcome,' he replied to his already empty car before indicating to pull back out into the busy road.

Crack

5.

HE HOPED THE journey home would be plain sailing, but in reality, he didn't hold out *much* hope of that. The rule of his life seemed to be, once he began to have a bad day, very little would change. He waited, for what felt like an age, for a gap large enough for him to get onto the road to open up. It seemed that *everyone* was colluding to make his day as bad as possible. 'Come on, come on,' he mumbled banging his hand on the steering wheel. About thirty yards behind him, a space he identified as his, opened and he began to edge forward, gaining enough momentum to take advantage of it.

The space did indeed open up, and he took it.

Immediately, he regretted his decision.

A smaller car was hiding in the gap. He hadn't seen it until the very last second, and by that time, it was too late. He'd already committed to the manoeuvre. The blaring horns came from everywhere. All he could do was watch as the smaller car swerved into the middle lane, causing the vehicle behind it to swerve into the—thankfully empty—outside lane.

Sweat beaded on his brow as he watched the events unfold via his mirrors. Luckily, no one was hurt no damage was done to any of the parties involved. All he got for his troubles were a few *wanker* signals and some angry horn blasts. These he could live with, as he was guilty of the *dick-head* mime himself a few times—quite a few times.

The beads of moisture on his brow cooled as normality began to wash over him. He stopped taunting all the other drivers and passed his attention back to the road ahead.

It was a straightforward drive home now, enhanced by a little bit of Motley Crue on his stereo, taking him back to his youth.

They, were all singing about smoking in the boy's room, when a motorcycle, it could have been the same motorcycle that caused him to swerve earlier, it all happened to fast for him to tell, cut in front of him. The powerful machine clipped his side mirror, missing the front of his car by less than an inch.

Joe's automatic reaction was to slam on the brakes. 'Fuck,' he spat as the bike wobbled in front of him. It looked as if the rider was just about to regain control when its back wheel spun out underneath it and the bike went into a skid.

From this moment, everything happened in slow motion.

Joe watched as the bike spun out of control and the rider had no other option than to let go of the handlebars. Reduced to a mere spectator, he watched the rider fall from the machine and bounce once on the tarmac in front of him.

That was the last time he saw the rider alive.

The momentum of his car continued, and he—or she, as Joe couldn't tell the sex of the person beneath the full leather jumpsuit—disappeared from his view, swallowed by his car.

The slow motion continued. The steering wheel twisted from his control, and he had to let go of it for fear of snapping his wrists. The suspension buckled and bounced, horribly.

Then he heard the noise.

He couldn't tell if the sound was real, or if he had only imagined it, misinterpreting it as something else, but he *did* hear it, nonetheless. It was loud, it was wet, and it was sickening.

CRACK!!!

Suddenly, as if being slammed by a moving wall, everything sped back up to real time again, and he found himself sitting in the driver's seat of a spinning vehicle.

He was calm, and collected as he took in everything that was happening in his environment.

The car was out of control, but luckily it had taken the direction of the side of the road and was currently skidding up a small embankment. It had lost quite a bit of velocity as it hit the grass and climbed, eventually stopping half on the side of the road, and halfway up the grassy slope. With a shaking, cold, and clammy hand, he unbuckled his seatbelt and flopped back into the driver's seat. He closed his eyes, giving himself a moment to contemplate, to come to terms with what had just happened. He took a number of deep breaths in a vain attempt to slow the rapid thrashing of his heart.

There were vehicles all over the road, all of them stopped. The people inside were either looking directly at him or their stares were directed towards the aftermath of the *incident* that had occurred on the road.

As reality hit, his stomach churned, and flipped; everything inside his stomach shifted. He sat forward as more cold sweat beading on his forehead. His mouth filled with saliva, a precursor to the bitter vomit that erupted from his mouth shortly after.

6.

'A LIKELY TO prove on the A552. A possible fatal RTC, Borough Road, Birkenhead area, ambo on route. This sounds messy!' the electronic voice cut through the police radio.

'All received; 8490 responding. I'm in the area. Send coordinates?' Officer Ian Locke tapped the intercom on his shoulder, put his bike in gear, and flicked on his sirens and lights before taking off along the tarmac at full speed.

7.

ABOUT A MILE from the designated coordinates sent to his on-board satnav, the traffic began to slow down and back up. Ian was experienced enough as a motorcycle cop to recognise the signs of an incident in the area, even if he hadn't received the exact location from dispatch. The cars in the queue were stationary, and there were several irritated blasts of horns as he passed through the mess as best he could.

None of the drivers showed much concern for what might have happened up ahead, or who might have been involved, all he could see were angry, frustrated faces, seething out of their windows.

Eventually, he arrived at ground zero, and what he saw there, he knew would stick with him the rest of the week, if not his life.

Several people had abandoned their vehicles and were standing around on the road. He could see people holding their children, clinging them close, as if to stop them from seeing something they didn't need to, at their young and impressionable age. A tangled motorcycle lay on its side on the second lane of the road, and there was a car parked haphazardly, half on the embankment, half on the side of the road. Ian could just about make out someone inside the vehicle, in the driver's seat.

As he removed his helmet, he saw that the person inside was still moving, he raised his eyes above, and thanked whoever might be listening.

He climbed off his own motorcycle and clicked his radio, reporting his arrival to dispatch, but something made him stop. Something that everyone was looking at, half hidden by the cars stopped on the tarmac.

Then he saw it for himself.

A thick, wet, red line trailed from the road. It followed the direction the unfortunate car must have taken. The words he was ready to report dried in his mouth as he stepped forward, his eyes following the line of blood. The sight that greeted him on the other side of the car guaranteed that this case would stick with him for the rest of his life. He just knew that every time he closed his eyes, every time he was half asleep, this would be the vision hiding in his subconscious, ready to jump out and grab him, like every villain in cheesy horror films.

There was a deep pool of crimson. The brightness of the blood was in true contrast with the dull greys, and blacks, of the road. It made it stark and horribly vivid. The corpse, covered in ripped black leather, was sprawled in the centre of the spreading pool. Blood still poured from the meaty welts of flesh protruding from the tears in the outfit. There was a thick, cloying stink, it was exhaust fumes mixing with the coppery tang of fresh blood.

Fighting a natural revulsion of the sight of a bleeding, lifeless human body, and the gag he could feel building in the pit of his stomach, Ian stepped closer, knowing he would be expected to examine the scene. A lump formed in his throat as a threatening nausea rose. It was his turn for his mouth to fill with thick saliva, and with a rising panic, he regarded the bystanders and rubberneckers who had gathered at the grisly scene. Some in shock, others just there to catch a glimpse of a dead body, and maybe take a few snaps to send off to their friends. He knew from years of it being drummed into him in training, he couldn't allow them to see the first responding officer vomiting on the scene. But it was difficult to keep the gag down.

The victim was lying on what was left of his, or her, stomach, their arms pointing at ten-to-three. The twisted, motionless, leaking body was languishing in a deep pool of its own coagulating blood. Gingerly, Ian edged over to the scene. He had to make the initial inspection before the paramedics turned up with their blatant disregard for incident scenes in their rush to attempt to save someone's life. There was not going to be any saving of this poor soul's life today; the paramedics were good, but they were not Gods.

He closed his eyes and mouthed a small 'thank fuck' under his breath as the ambulance sirens announced their imminent arrival in the distance.

On his first glance, without the tears blurring his vision, he assumed the rider had tried to protect his or her head during the impact, and it would be curled underneath the rider's arms, close to the torso. As he, almost unwillingly, bent closer, he got a much better image of the sustained injuries. That was when he noticed that something important, something very important, was missing.

There was *no* head.

Ian blinked, fighting his natural instincts to flee from such a sight; he found himself again combating the urge to vomit. His head began to spin. He stood, and putting his arms on his waist, he welcomed a few deep breaths of fresh-ish air. He needed to get his world, and his vision, straight again.

He needed to comb the scene for the victim's head.

He followed the bloody trail from the location of the body, all the way to where the car was stopped on the embankment. He gritted his teeth as he concluded that the car must have run over the victim's head, pulling it away from the body in the process. There were traces of motorcycle helmet scattered around the road, mingled with the gore. He'd missed them in his initial assessment, as they were made of red plastic and had camouflaged themselves within the drying blood.

The sirens in the distance were getting closer, and Ian, content with his initial evaluation, began to make his way up the embankment towards the car and the person who was still in the driver's seat. He balled his sweaty palms into fists inside his black leather gloves, and steeled himself for what he was about to witness. As he got closer, he had to double-check if the driver was still alive. His lack of movement was almost complete, and his expressionless face was as ashen as a corpse.

'Sir?' he asked tentatively, feeling a little silly talking to a dead body. 'Are you OK, sir?' he asked again on approach.

There was no response.

This guy looked alive when I arrived at the scene, he thought, second-guessing himself. He watched, as if he were a third person, as his own hand reached out to open the car door. There were spatters of red over the handles, and not for the first time this morning, he was thankful for his gloves.

'Sir, can you please respond? Are you hurt?'

The man's eyes flickered open, and he slowly turned his head. His eyes were vague, almost vacant.

Thank God, Ian thought as the man's eyes focused and then unfocused in his direction. He lifted his head and took a sniff of the interior, searching for a hint of alcohol. There was none, just a strong smell of vomit; that, he could deal with. 'Sir, an ambulance is on the way. Can you tell me if you're injured at all?' The man's dead eyes regarded him with a complete lack of emotion, or even recognition. If he'd understood what Ian had just said, there was no indication visible.

Slowly, the man shook his head. 'No!' The voice was dry, broken somehow, like a sound travelling from somewhere else. *Maybe from beyond the grave.* Ian hated himself for this thought.

A cacophony of lights and sounds attracted Ian's attention. Whispering a silent prayer, he backed away from the car to flag the ambulance over. 'Don't you worry now, sir, the paramedics are here; they'll take care of you now.'

As he stepped away from the scene, turning towards the flashing blue lights, he was relieved. It was the first time he'd ever felt like this at a scene, yet there was so much happening, and so quickly, he just wanted, no, he needed, to get away.

8.

KAREN BLUSTERED INTO the hospital main doors and bustled over to the small, manned reception desk. 'Joseph O'Hara,' she stated breathlessly. The news of what had happened, plus the near sprint from the car park, had taken its toll on her. 'Please, can you tell me what room Joseph O'Hara is in?' She gasped, wiping sweat from her face.

The receptionist regarded her computer for a few seconds, tapping her pen to her teeth as she typed, one fingered, on the keyboard. 'Here he is. Ward eight, room twelve A. It looks like the police are with him right now,' she replied with a courteous, but bored, smile.

Karen half walked, half ran through the confusion of corridors in the large building, attempting to follow the signs for ward eight. Twice, she got lost before finally arriving at the corridor where two large, uniformed policemen, and two detectives were gathered.

She eyed them suspiciously as she walked into room twelve A. Joe was in the bed. His neck was in a brace and his mouth was twisted as if he were in pain. A small smile crept over his lips, as she entered the sole occupancy room.

'Excuse me, I need to see my husband,' she announced, trying her best to sound calmer than she felt. 'Can these questions wait another half an hour or so? Can't you see he's exhausted?'

The policemen looked at each other. The uniformed officers nodded and exited the room, closely followed by the detectives.

Karen watched them leave and waited until the door was closed between them before turning and looking at Joe. She held her arms out to him in an attempt to sooth his ills. 'Oh, Joe, what happened to you?'

He just stared at her, his dark eyes blank, emotionless, and cold. There was an emotional distance between them, she could sense it, but felt she couldn't do anything to close it, not right now anyway.

'CRACK, Karen,' he whispered. His voice sounding like dry paper being torn in half. 'All I heard was CRACK!'

Karen shook her head. 'What?'

Joe's voice was slow and thick, like he was speaking from behind a heavy curtain. She guessed it was from whatever drugs he'd had pumped into him. 'The man's head. It went CRACK!'

She didn't like where this conversation was going, so she began to fuss about the bed, making sure the blankets were tucked in correctly, and the pillows were fluffed to her liking. 'Don't you go thinking about any of that right now, Joe. Just get yourself better and get your rest.'

'I can't close my eyes,' he sobbed. 'Every time I do, I can see it.' The words were drawing out of him, slow and deliberate, and he was trying to gesticulate, but his arms were obviously not behaving in the manner he intended them to. 'I can see the bike. It's wobbling in front of me, then I hear… that noise.' He swallowed hard, Karen watched, wincing, as his face changed, contorted, as if the pain, and the agony were fresh. 'CRACK!' he shouted. The word was loud, louder than anything he'd said since she got there, and it caused her to jump a little.

To avoid upsetting him any further, she turned her attentions towards the four policemen standing outside the door. She didn't know why they were there. Joe wasn't a criminal; he'd been involved an accident, that was all. She touched her husband's hand, giving it a little squeeze, before she left the room.

The four men regarded her as she approached them.

'I'm sorry,' she said, addressing them all. 'I don't think my husband is feeling up to answering any more questions today. Is there any chance you could come back tomorrow? Let him get some rest?'

The two uniformed officers looked more than a little relieved as they shrugged and began to walk away. One of the detectives leaned in and handed her a business card.

'Ma'am, if he remembers anything of any interest, just ring this number and ask for me; my name's right there on the card.'

She smiled a cold smile towards the man—that said, 'don't hold your breath'—before dismissing them all by turning her back on them. She walked back into the room, towards her husband, her face softening when she saw he was asleep. She waited until the men outside had gone before venturing back out herself, looking for a nurse. She grabbed the first one she saw walking by.

'Excuse me, Nurse, I'm Karen O'Hara; my husband is Joe, in this room. I need some answers, and no one had told me anything. Is he OK?' The question was frantic, rushed, but the nurse seemed to understand everything she was asked.

She looked past the desperate woman and regarded the number on the door of the room. She smiled; it was a professional one. 'Mr O'Hara is *physically* fine. There are no broken bones, he possibly just has a little whiplash, which we are monitoring. He is exhausted, though.' She smiled again. 'It's nothing a few days of complete rest won't cure.'

'He's *physically* fine?' Karen asked, cocking her head to one side, picking up on the words the nurse used.

The woman's eyes shifted to either side of the corridor, before she pulled Karen just inside the room. 'Yes, he's *physically* fine. Emotionally? Well, that'll be a different story. He has, through no fault of his own, killed another person. That's going to take a lot of getting used to. Now, I'm not by any stretch of the imagination a psychologist, but I've seen this same scenario before. There's going to be a lot of soul searching and more than his fair share of ups and downs, some with seemingly no light at the end of the tunnel, I'm afraid. There'll be times where there'll be no consoling him, but with the right help, the right encouragement, and his family around him, supporting him, then I'm sure, in time, he'll come to terms with what has happened.'

Karen eased, her shoulders sunk, and she rubbed her moist hands through her hair. It was only then she realised she was still shaking, but she could feel a determination growing within her. 'Will he be going home soon?' she asked, looking for a little hope.

The nurse smiled and took her hand. They were cold, but soft. 'I'm thinking, but it's not up to me, he could be home tomorrow. We'll keep him for twenty-four hours, just for observations, but I can't see him still being here much after that.'

Karen eased again. 'Thank God,' she sighed.

The nurse offered her a smile before walking off. Karen turned to look into Joe's room. He was still sleeping. She entered, kissed him on the forehead, and left the hospital.

Crack

9.

THE SUN WAS shining through the windshield, and the band on the radio were singing some nonsense about a 'Horse With No Name.' Joe knew all the words and was singing along with the gentle voice. His voice wasn't anywhere near as good, and he kept on wavering on the notes, but he was alone, and didn't really care.

He didn't recognise the car. The interior was leather, and it felt good, and smelt expensive. The dashboard looked like something out of Star Trek, that was how he knew the car wasn't his. His old banger was made up of analogue dials, dust, and scratches.

Feeling good about himself, he turned to look into the rear-view mirror, what he saw there almost caused him to swerve the car. He rubbed his hands through his immaculately cut, salt-and-pepper hair before continuing down towards his short, cultivated, smart beard. The hair had just a hint of grey in it. He liked it; it gave him what he thought of as an *interesting look*.

It wasn't the hair, or the beard that caught his attention, it was his eyes. They were the crystal blue of a much younger man. A man with lesser responsibilities than he had, and someone with a vibrance for life itself.

He nodded and smiled. He was loving this version of himself.

In the background of his reflection, against the backdrop of some, unknown mountains, he could see dust rising on the road, indicating a vehicle some distance behind him. As he watched it, intermittently flicking his attention from the road to the mirror, the vehicle moved into the overtaking lane. The dust cloud behind it was getting bigger, and Joe could only guess it was accelerating, gearing up to overtake him.

It was an SUV, a pretty nice one, and it slowed when it pulled up next to him. He glanced over and saw a young, very attractive girl in the driver's seat. She had long, dark hair that was blowing in the wind caused by her open window. The bikini top she was wearing barely covered her brown, tanned body. She was slim, and her toned curves gave off all the charms of youth. Joe's heart was speeding, as she removed the large sunglasses that had been hiding her beautiful face.

She offered him a smile. It wasn't *just* a smile though. To him it promised mystery, eroticism, carefree fun.

Then she shifted a gear and the car sped off.

Joe nodded to himself, a wolfish grin spreading across his face. 'Today is a good day,' he mused before reaching down and turning the radio up loud.

Without warning, the day began to darken. He leaned over the driver's wheel and squinted as he looked up towards the strange clouds that had just gathered overhead. They were ugly, ominous, and malevolent. His brow creased as they spoilt the beautiful day. As they began to merge, the heavy stench of ozone filled the air; it was the stink of an oncoming storm.

He closed his window, checked his mirrors, and continued driving.

In the rear view mirror, he saw a motorbike in the distance. This wasn't kicking up any dust, but the rate it was gaining on him, he guessed it was doing some speed. He ignored it and continued driving, his thoughts on the young girl in the SUV.

A large splat of rain spread across his windshield. It was a huge, summery blob. He flicked his wipers and checked his mirror again.

The bike was closer now.

Much closer.

More blobs spattered; large, intermittent globules of water hit, and spread, over the greasy, dusty glass. Then something darker splattered onto his windshield. It was intermingled with the rain. It was almost black, but not quite. He leaned forward, attempting to see what it was before the wipers spread it across the rest of the windshield. They kicked into life, and the dark blob was indeed spread over the width of the glass. The darkness began to dilute with the rainwater, and he was surprised to see his windshield was suddenly… pink.

Crack

He frowned as the wipers continued their work while more dark drops fell. Bemused by this phenomenon, he checked his rear view mirror again.

This time, the bike was nowhere to be seen.

He did a double take before looking out the side window. The bike was right there, next to him on the road. It had slowed, matching his speed, and the helmeted rider was looking in at him.

With one hand still on the handlebars, whoever it was began to unbuckle the black helmet. All the time, more and more dark drops fell onto his windshield before being wiped off leaving a thick pink smear. His heart was thudding as he flicked the lever to set the wipers onto a faster speed to combat the downpour.

A low-level panic was growing, flowering somewhere deep inside him, and he spared another look at the biker. The helmet was gone now, revealing the rider as the same young woman who had passed him in the SUV.

How is that possible?

He looked a little closer, before jerking his head back, his mouth and eyes aghast at what happened. Her flesh began to flay from her face, exposing pink, raw flesh, that quickly peeled away in the wind, like leaves in a gale.

What he could only think of as gore began to wash over his car. Reluctantly, he pulled his eyes away from the horror show he was witnessing as the filth splattered over the windshield caused his visibility to become something next to nothing. Thick, bite-sized morsels of what looked like raw meat clung to the glass. The wipers were on the fastest setting, and were still struggling to deal with it, only succeeding in moving from one side, to the other as it was instantly replaced with more.

He looked back at the girl on the motorcycle.

She was no longer a girl.

Her head was gone. It had been replaced with an erupting volcano of thick, dark blood that spat and dripped down her leather body suit, casting greasy morsels all over his car.

He tightened his grip on the steering wheel, attempting to stem the panic and nausea rising like hot-air balloons inside him.

Then suddenly, she was gone.

He found himself fighting the steering wheel as a familiar bumping from beneath caused the suspension to buck. He removed his hands to stop them from getting caught in the grips and snapping as the car span out of control.

A vile feeling of sickening déjà vu washed over him.

He felt himself go cold, as all the blood drained from his face. The world outside his bloody window began to spin and spiral.

CRACK!!!

He knew that noise. It hit him full in the chest, like a medicine ball thrown at him by a Physical Education teacher. It was a tinny noise that sounded far away, but the way the car was bucking and spinning, he knew it wasn't. It was close; very close. It was right beneath him. It was the same noise that had been plaguing his dreams and even some of his waking moments. It was a ghost sound, and it was hunting him, haunting him.

Eventually, the car stopped spinning, and he allowed himself to open his eyes. He looked down at his body, checking for cuts or abrasions; thankfully, miraculously, there were none. He looked up at the spiderwebbed windshield just as the only working wiper took another attempt at clearing the blood and gore away.

He heard himself scream; it was a funny noise, not something he thought he could get used to.

Before him, crouched on all fours, was the headless rider. Her body spewing blood and gristle over the front of the car.

The gushing corpse reached forward and punched a bloodied, gloved hand on the already cracked windshield.

More strands of gossamer spiderweb cracks appeared. As they widened, allowing the ghoul on the car access to him, Joe closed his eyes and began to scream.

Crack

10.

HE WOKE IN the twilight of a gloomy, strange room; the noise he could hear was the sound of himself screaming. Someone ran in, flicking the lights on as she did.

It revealed a stark room with little decoration, and a small TV on the opposite wall. His disorientation span, until he smelt the antiseptic.

He was in a hospital bed, and the woman, who he had assumed was either Karen, or Annmarie, was a nurse.

'Mr O'Hara. Joe, please, calm yourself. You're safe. You're in the hospital.'

He could see other patients through the open door of his sole occupancy room sitting up in their beds, lighting the lights on their bedside cupboards as they tried to see what, or who was causing all the fuss.

Anything to relieve the boredom.

Eventually, he sat up; his fingers were white, clutching at the metal rails on the sides of his bed. His wide eyes looked at the nurse. His eyes told him that she was a nurse, but his brain was playing tricks on him. It gave him the image of a headless torso wearing a bloodied and ripped leather suit.

In his mind, the corpse reached for him, gripping him by both his arms.

CRACK!!!

He screamed again. The scene was exactly the same as moments ago, only this time the nurse *was* just a nurse. There were no blood-soaked hands reaching out for him and no headless torso with gore spewing from its neck.

'Mr O'Hara, you're having a nightmare; that's all. Come on now, snap out of it,' the nurse soothed.

He swallowed, hard, and rubbing his fingers together on both hands, he flopped onto his bed. The sheets were soaking wet, and his clammy skin crawled as they made contact with the cold linen. It had been all been so real. He'd been there, the headless body had reached out and grabbed him. She had touched him.

It couldn't have been a dream.

Could it?

He let loose a deep sigh and sat up in the bed. His sweaty hospital tunic was beginning to cool and was sticking to his skin. He looked out through the open door of his single-occupancy room. The anonymous people in the beds outside were sat up and looking in his direction. He could feel scorn directed towards him, mostly for waking them up in the middle of the night, but he could also feel their amusement, and sick gratitude for giving them something to talk about for the next few days.

He was reminded of a scene from a horror film he'd watched once, possibly when he was a young boy and they didn't seem so scary, especially in the daytime. All the dead in the hospital had come back to life, awakening with a taste for human flesh.

A shiver tickled through him as the nurse returned with a fresh tunic and a plastic cup containing two white pills. His breathing relaxed as he accepted the cup, the medication, and the sweet relief they promised.

Crack

11.

'ARE YOU OK, love? Are you sure?'

'Stop fussing,' Joe snapped. 'I'm not a frigging invalid. I'm perfectly capable of making it up a flight of stairs on my own.'

'Oh, well, I'm sorry for caring.' Karen pulled a face and stepped off the bottom stair, but continued fussing as Joe commenced his slow ascent.

'Well, why don't you care all the way back to the kitchen and get me something to eat?' he replied, all the harshness slipped from his voice as the ghost of a smile broke on his face.

'Yeah, why don't I?' she mocked and made her way back towards the kitchen.

Eventually, he made it to their bedroom, and Martin popped his head around his door. His eyes were red, and his unruly hair was sticking up every which way it could.

'Dad,' he whispered. His eyes were all over the room, everywhere except at him. 'Are you OK? I... I heard ...'

Joe held his hand up to his son and offered him a theatrical grimace. 'I'm fine. I'm just really, really tired,' he soothed.

Ignoring his father's hint that he wanted to be alone, Martin stepped into the room, his eyes were wide. He sat on the edge of the bed and leaned in. The father and son looked like co-conspirators. 'Did you get to see the body, Dad? Did you?'

'*MARTIN*! Leave Dad alone. Can't you see he's tired?' Annmarie snapped from somewhere in the house, most probably her room. Martin rolled his eyes, got up off the bed, and slunk out the bedroom door.

Joe let out a long sigh and silently thanked his daughter as he leaned over on the edge of his bed and began to untie his shoelaces. He'd noticed Karen had changed the linen. He loved the feeling of climbing into fresh sheets, but the freshness was ruined by Nixon, the dog, who ran into the room and jumped up on the bed, stretching out on top of the crisp sheets. He lay there looking at him, panting.

Joe tensed his body and let out a low growl. 'Nixon, get down,' he scolded.

The Labrador's mouth was wide open, and his long tongue lolled as his tail wagged.

'NOW!' Joe spat, and the dog jumped off the bed and ran past him without a glance back up. 'Stupid dog,' he mumbled.

He kicked off his shoes and lay back on the bed, a long sigh escaped him as his body sank into the clean sheets.

Karen made her way back into the room holding a plate of sandwiches. The look on her face Joe instantly disliked. He suddenly felt as if he was as exhibit in a zoo, an exotic animal being looked after by his wife, the zookeeper.

Her face was filled with sympathy, something that he couldn't stomach. He tried to smile as he took the offered plate, and he reached over and took her other hand in his. He smiled at her, it was a thank you for everything she was doing for him, but one that he hoped she would read as *you can stop it now.*

'The doctor said you'll need to see this therapist,' she whispered, slipping a small card into his hand.

He looked at it, he squinted as he attempted to read what it said. He held it out at arm's length as he tried to decipher the squiggles. 'Dr Saunders,' he mused reading the name out loud. 'Psychiatrist. MD, PhD, LCSW, MFT. What do these letters even mean?'

'They mean she can help,' Karen replied, getting up off the bed and fussing around him. 'She'll help you readjust back into your normal routine. You *will* be able to put all of this behind you, but you're going to need help doing it. I've booked for you to go and see her the day after tomorrow.'

'She?' he asked, his whole face was squinting now. 'Is she even a real doctor?'

The look Karen shot him told him that the time for jokes was not right now.

He looked at her, his face melted into a little boy's who'd been told that he was going to the dentist for a filling the very next day. 'Do I really need to do this?' he pleaded.

Crack

Karen nodded as she folded his clothes that had been in a basket on the floor. 'Yes, you do. Now, I'm going to make a pot of tea; do you want one to go with your sandwich?'

He nodded; his small smile was genuine.

Ten minutes later, when she came back to the room with a steaming cup, he was fast asleep and snoring. She put the tray down at the side of the bed, kissed his forehead, and left, closing the door silently behind her.

12.

IAN WAS SITTING in the interview room in the police station where he was based. He was slumped forward in the chair, leaning on a small table, with his head his hands. His wife-to-be was sitting opposite him. She was dressed in a casual pantsuit, her long blond hair pulled back in a professional ponytail, and her Detective badge was hanging off her lapel. Ian was dressed in his full motorcycle uniform, apart from the helmet. The four-day-old stubble on his chin, and mussed up hair, along with his bloodshot eyes were red, reflected his state of mind.

'Thanks for your help with this,' he mumbled, lifting his head to look at the yellow pad and pencil before him.

'What else am I going to do? You're becoming a nightmare at home. A proper miserable bastard.'

Ian looked up at her. His smile almost made it to his lips.

'Come on, just write it all down, exactly what you saw and the states of the driver and the victim when you got there.'

He picked up the pencil and pulled the legal pad towards him as if he were about to write something. But he couldn't do it. He slammed the pencil back on the table and put his head back in his hands. A sigh hissed through his fingers, sounding more like a moan, or maybe even a sob. 'Christ, Paula,' he croaked. 'It was so fucked up. The guy was just sat in his car staring out of the fucking window. I'm serious. I thought he was dead. I really did. It was like an abattoir out there. There was blood everywhere. I mean fucking *EVERYWHERE.*'

'Once it's written down, it's done, then you won't have to think about it again.' Paula sidled up to him and rubbed her hands through his hair. 'Then all we need to think about is our big day,' she whispered in his ear.

Crack

Ian closed his eyes and stretched his fingers as she rubbed hers through his head. 'That feels good. Can we just blow this and go home?'

Paula smiled, there was something wicked/sexy in her eye, and what she whispered salaciously into his ear made him smile, just a little. 'What about if I just blow you?'

He gripped the arms of the chair and turned to face her, his face a mixture of excitement and confusion. 'In here?'

She turned his chair around to face her. 'Really,' she replied and leant over to kiss him. Her hands roamed down towards his belt and began unbuckling it.

'Paula ...' he sighed, pushing her away but there was no real conviction, or strength to it.

'Don't worry; the door's locked, the camera's off, and it's not like it's our first time, is it?'

He leaned back in his chair and let her go to work on him; he knew she was good at her job.

Just as it was getting interesting a rap on the door killed the moment. 'Detective Ashton,' a male voice asked from the other side. 'We've got to go. There's a lead on the body in the laundry truck.'

Paula, looked up and raised her eyebrows. 'Shit. I've got to go to this. If that body turns out to be the pawnbroker's wife, then we've got the bastard,' she said, shaking her head.

Ian was already pulling his trousers up, chuckling as he did.

'Oh well, at least I got a smile out of you, never mind the rise.' She laughed, fixing her hair as she made her way to the door.

'That you did,' he chuffed. 'Should we carry this on later?'

'We'll see, eh?' she said, tipping him a wink as she opened the door.

The detective on the other side double-took the situation as he looked at Paula and then at Ian, who was now standing next to the small interview table, nervously shuffling the yellow legal pad on top of it. 'Am I disturbing something?' he asked with more than a little hint of a smile.

Ian checked the fly of his leather motorcycle issue trousers.

'Yes, Al, actually, you are,' Paula said as she walked past the newcomer.

13.

JOE WAS IN his chair in the living room. Some whining old fart was on the TV spouting off, trying to convince everyone that he knew everything about everything. Joe hated this programme and the boring old fart on it, but the remote control was over the other side of the room next to Annmarie, who had her headphones on, and he was far too comfortable to get up and get it for himself.

'Annmarie, pass me the remote, will you?' he asked.

He was ignored, as he knew he would be. His voice was drowned out by the tinny music coming from her headphones. He leaned forward and looked directly at her. 'Annmarie,' he shouted.

There was still nothing.

He began to wave his arms at her. '*ANNMARIE ...*'

She removed her earbuds and looked at him like he'd told her the end of the world would be happening in fifteen minutes, and she was grounded for the whole of it. 'Are you shouting me?' she asked.

'Oh, for Christ's sake,' he snapped.

'Whatever,' she replied, holding her hand up to him while she got up and left the room.

He loved their intellectual conversations. He tutted as he eased himself up. 'What does a parent have to do to get any respect around here? Kill someone?' he muttered, wincing at his own bad joke.

'Dad, will you give me a lift to Brian's house?' Martin shouted from outside the room.

Joe picked up the remote control and sat back in his chair with a small groan. His body was just about getting back to normal from his ordeal, but every now and then, there was a twinge to remind him of the whiplash.

'Dad, can you, or can't you? I need to know.'

Crack

'Oh, if you're giving Martin a lift, can you call into the shop and get some milk and bread?' Karen chirped from the kitchen.

Joe gripped the arms of the chair and closed his eyes. All he wanted to do was to be left alone for a few moments. Was that too much to ask?

'Joe, did you hear me?'

'Dad, did you hear me?'

'Joe!' … 'Dad!'

'WHAT THE FUCK? WILL YOU LEAVE ME ALONE? THE LOT OF YOU!'

Joe suddenly found himself standing in the middle of the living room. He was gripping the remote control so tight that he fancied he could feel the plastic bending in his grip. He looked around the room, embarrassed by his sudden outburst. With a sigh, he slumped back into the chair and put his hands to his head. *What the hell is going on with me?* he thought.

Then he heard the noise.

CRACK!!!

He lifted his head and ruffled his brow as he scanned the room, his eyes flicking erratically from wall to wall.

CRACK!!!

It came again.

He stood up, turning towards the door. His heart pounding like he'd just finished a marathon, the rush of blood was throbbing in his ears.

CRACK!!!

The noise was familiar. Hearing it caused an odd smile to spread across his face. 'Karen, are you OK, love? What was that noise?'

There was no answer.

'Martin, Martin, is your mum OK?'

There was still no answer.

Suddenly, Nixon burst from the kitchen. His ears were lowered across his head, and his tail was tucked firmly between his legs. With a sense of bewilderment, Joe watched as the normally attentive pet passed him by without even acknowledging he was there.

'Nixon, come here, boy. What's up with you?' The dog stopped as he heard his master's voice. A pathetic whine, not suited to his size, escaped him, and he lay down, resting his head on his front paws, cowering at Joe's feet. He began licking at Joe's hand as it was offered to him, for comfort. Joe could feel the dog's body shaking beneath him. He bent and comforted the good boy. 'Hey, come on, boy. What's the matter, eh?' He stood back up straight and looked towards the door. '*ANNMARIE!*' he shouted.

There was still no answer.

With his heart contemplating escape from the jail of his chest, he edged out of the room, leaving Nixon cowering behind him. He glanced back, just the once, as he heard the low sound of Nixon growling. It wasn't a fierce, dangerous growl, more the bravado of a badly scared animal.

Joe didn't like it one bit.

Reluctantly, he left the dog in the living room and made his way towards the kitchen.

This was the moment everything went wrong.

Karen, Martin, and Annmarie were lying on the kitchen floor. The white floor tiles and the cupboard doors were awash with wet, dripping claret. The TV remote control fell from his hands, clattering unnoticed, and broken, onto the floor. All he could do was stare at his deceased family. His frazzled brain tried to absorb the terrible scene before him, but it failed, miserably. In the few moments of clarity, or sanity, that he had left, he attempted to recognize them but found the task almost impossible. The only distinguishing features left of any of them were the clothes they were wearing.

The crimson graffiti splattered over the walls, and the white kitchen goods, was their blood. The small dining table where they had shared many a morning meal, was now covered in dark, solidifying gore. There were shards of bone and pinkish, unidentifiable clumps intermixed in it. One of the kitchen chairs was overturned next to the body he identified as Karen's. She was on her back, her face next to one of the chair's legs, blood pouring from it

Crack

expanding the pool below. What he thought of as his daughter lay face down next to her, and Martin's body was splayed next to the large red and white splattered fridge-freezer in the corner of the room.

Not one of them had their head attached.

All three bodies ended in the same thick, grisly stump. A small, sane part of Joe's mind registered some of the grey in the gore to be brains, although he'd never actually seen one in real life, only on stupid television shows.

In a daydream, or day-nightmare, he stepped towards his family. Something soft squashed under his foot. With his stomach rolling like dark clouds before a storm, he looked down to see what it was.

A human eyeball stared up at him, a blue one.

It was the last horror he could withstand, and he fell to his knees, breaking the surface skin of the coagulating pools of blood. His hands covered his eyes, and he pulled at his hair. *The cracks,* he thought, it was nothing more than a maddening voice in his head, *the very same as when I ran the motorcyclist over.*

Behind his hands, he counted to ten before removing them. The doctor in the hospital had told him of this little trick in case he found himself having any reoccurring 'episodes.' He hoped this was an episode right now, or maybe a hallucination. His heart broke as a pathetic, mournful mewling sound escaped him. He opened his eyes and looked about the large kitchen; the three bodies were still there.

He then noticed something else, something he hadn't seen in his first assessment of the scene.

Between the pools of blood, there was a kind of pattern on the linoleum. In a herculean effort to attempt to block out the gruesome scene all around him, he fixated on this odd pattern. He crawled on his hands and knees to try to get a closer look. Ignoring the fact that he was wading through his family's cooling blood.

The patterns were tyre marks. Motorcycle tyre marks. The bizarre treads connected all three of the bodies, from head-to-head.

A noise from somewhere behind him made him jump. His brain registered it as a scream, but he couldn't be sure of his senses anymore. He turned, just in time to see bright headlights, impossible in his kitchen but nonetheless there, bearing down upon him.

43

Before he could scream, before he put his hands up to his head to protect it from the impact of the oncoming car, he just had time to see his own grinning face sitting behind the steering wheel.

Crack

14.

HE SHOT UPRIGHT in a damp, sweat-moistened bed. Karen was leaning over him, shaking him. Her eyes were wide, and her mouth turned down. 'Joe, wake up. *WAKE UP*. You're dreaming.'

Joe's eyes were wild; his pupils were dilated, and he was having trouble focusing on anything. He was screaming. It was an ugly high-pitched sound.

After a few maddening seconds the room had begun to swim back into focus. His face was as confused as his soaking wet hair. 'What? What … What's happening? Karen … the kids. Where are the kids?' As he spat the question, thick drips from his brow and lips dribbled down his face.

'Everyone's fine, Joe, everyone's fine. You're having another episode; that's all.'

Joe was up and out of the bed in a flash. He was hobbling over towards the closed bedroom door. As he gripped it and flung it open, he was shocked to see Martin and Annmarie standing outside, looking in. He jumped as the horrific dream broke all around him. His kids were white, pale, and covered in blood. One blink of his stinging eyes later, he saw them as they really were. Annmarie had an arm wrapped around her brother, who, despite the fact that he was taller than her, was on the verge of tears.

Karen looked swiftly from her children to her husband, and then finally back to the children. She didn't know who needed her attention first. She figured it was the kids. 'It's OK. Your dad was just having another nightmare. Everything's fine now. Go on, back to bed,' she soothed as she ushered the young spectators from the doorway.

After a few moments, watching the kids go back to their rooms, she closed the door and came back to the bed, where Joe was sitting,

45

looking very sorry for himself. 'Same dream?' she asked, her voice quiet and dripping in sympathy.

He nodded his head, unable to raise his eyes to look at her.

'Me and the kids again?'

'Yeah, same tyre tracks, same injuries, same old me driving the fucking car. Different location this time, though. The kitchen, if you can believe that. It's just so, so fucking real.'

Karen screwed her lips together, biting the inside of her cheeks. 'Joe,' she said, her tone one of someone tiptoeing around a question they so desperately want, or need, to ask. 'Maybe it's time you saw someone about all this. It's happening every night now.'

Eventually, he looked at her; his eyes were pink, his skin pasty, and the stubble around his face made things look even worse. 'I know, it's every night now. I also know I'm not going to be able to go back to sleep tonight. I'm supposed to be in work tomorrow night.'

'I'll make some warm milk and sit up with you. OK?'

He nodded again and climbed back under the sheets.

As she slipped on her housecoat, she turned to look at her husband. A sad smile clouded her features. He knew the questions running through her head, the accusations, but there was nothing he could do about them. He knew he looked pathetic, small, especially wrapped in the blankets, and waiting for his hot milk. *Am I still the man she fell in love with? The strong father figure?* Right now, he didn't know, but he did know that he was going to do everything in his power to bring the good, strong man he used to be, back again.

As he watched her leave, he recalled how vivid the dream was. He gripped his arms tightly, leaving red welts on his skin, as a shiver rippled through him.

He closed his eyes and lay back on his pillow.

Crack

15.

JOE WAS TWITCHING and pulling at the collar of the shirt Karen had made him wear. They were sitting in a posh reception room, surrounded by large windows and expensive furniture. She had insisted he wear his best clothes for this appointment, hence why he was wearing trousers, a white shirt, and a tie that he usually only wore for funerals. He was uncomfortable, irritable, and the collar kept pinching his neck.

'Leave it alone; you'll give yourself a rash,' she scolded him and slapped at his hand.

'I can't help it. You know I hate things around my neck. It feels like a noose.'

After another scowl from his wife, he dropped his hands to his lap and looked nervously around the office. The walls were magnolia and decorated with a few, what he thought of as bland, pieces of art. A large light oak desk, with a very attractive young lady behind it, was against one wall. Other than the receptionist, they were the only other people in the room.

'I feel like I'm in a hotel, one where they make you feel like you've got no right to be there,' Joe hissed.

Karen's smile looked fake. 'Don't be daft. We've got every right to be here. I think it's nice,' she replied with a girlish giggle.

'Mr O'Hara,' the overly attractive youngster behind the desk announced, making Joe jump a little. 'Dr Saunders will see you now.' He never liked being called Mr O'Hara. He much preferred Joe. Mr O'Hara made him feel like his dad.

The receptionist indicated towards a door at the other end of the room and ushered them inside.

A lady—Joe estimated she was in her late thirties and very attractive for it—stood to greet them as they entered. 'Mr and Mrs

O'Hara, I'm *so* glad you could make it,' she purred with a warmth that made Joe instantly uncomfortable.

'Please call me Joe. I'd rather Joe.'

'OK then, as it's my intention to make you as comfortable as possible, Joe it is. Please sit down.'

Joe and Karen sat down next to each other on the obviously expensive, black leather couch. Karen fussed at her dress.

'Mrs O'Hara …' Dr Saunders began.

'Oh, please. Karen, if you would.'

Dr Saunders smiled another irritatingly comforting smile. 'Karen, are you OK? Do you want me to get you anything? A glass of water or a cup of tea?'

Karen's smile was polite, the kind of smile a scullery maid gave her mistress. 'No, thank you, I'm fine.'

'OK then, good. Well, if we're all on first name terms, I'm Penny, Penny Saunders.' She beamed another smile, flashing her expensively maintained, and perfectly straight teeth. 'So, we're here today to get you, Joe, to reflect on the incident a few weeks ago. To help you come to terms with what happened and to guide you towards acceptance. For you to believe there was nothing you could have done that day. Are we all agreed?'

Joe fingered his collar again. Karen scowled at him before turning back towards Penny, smiling. 'Yes, Doctor, we are.'

Penny then proceeded to inform them both on the prescribed forms of therapy that were normally offered for traumatic situations, such as this, including relaxation techniques, breathing exercises, and hypnosis.

'So, Karen. Could I ask you to wait out in the reception for maybe forty-five minutes? Lucy will look after all your needs. What I propose to do is to allow Mr—sorry—Joe to relax on the couch while I put him under a very light hypnosis. It will be ever so light, just to explore his feelings and maybe understand his anxieties just that little bit little more.' Penny had stood and opened the door for Karen to leave. It wasn't entirely a request.

Karen looked at her husband and took his hand, giving it a little squeeze. She smiled. 'Are you OK?' she whispered, her voice giving away how sheepish she must have felt.

Crack

Joe winked and nodded, returning her squeeze. Karen stood, fixed her skirt, and walked towards the offered door.

'Thank you, Karen, everything will be fine,' Penny whispered her assurances as she passed.

She offered the doctor another sheepish, wan smile, then left.

Once she was gone and the door was closed behind her, Penny turned her full attentions onto Joe. 'So, Joe, I need you to take off your shoes, lie back on the couch, and make yourself as comfortable as you can.'

Joe did as he was instructed without question. The couch was hard, but it gave in exactly the right places. It didn't take much wriggling to find a nice, relaxed spot. Penny sat back on her chair and wheeled it closer towards him.

'Now, I want you to clear your mind.'

'That won't be difficult,' Joe quipped. Penny didn't react; it was an old joke, and she had probably heard it before.

'Just listen to my voice, Joe. Concentrate not on what I'm saying but on the way I'm saying it. Follow the flow of my voice. There is nothing else in the room, nothing except my voice.' Her words were becoming a breathy whisper, quieter and there was a lulling quality to them.

'Now, Joe, you're in your car. You're driving. It's a nice day, you have the window open. Fresh air is blowing over your face. Now, tell me what you can see.'

Penny had broken his dream; Joe truly was somewhere else. He was back in the nice car driving along the empty, mountainous road. He could feel the vibrations beneath him; the way the leather steering wheel caressed his skin. A cool wind was blowing through his hair, and the breeze caressing him through the open window felt fantastic.

He looked around, nodding as he recalled the surroundings from his dream. He remembered the hot girl in the SUV. He shook his head, attempting to clear those thoughts, as he remembered how that dream had ended. He reached down and turned the radio on. He was expecting One of These Nights by The Eagles again but was pleasantly surprised to hear This Old Heart of Mine by the Isley Brothers. He turned it up and began singing along with it.

About halfway through, his eyes began to tire, and he swerved a little on the road. This scared him out of his reverie, and he readjusted the steering wheel to correct his position. He overcompensated the readjustment and found himself half on the tarmac and half in the dirt at the side of the road.

An angry blast of a horn heralded the end of the song. He looked at his mirror and saw an SUV was overtaking him. The woman driver was shouting something at him, something he couldn't quite hear as the piano opening to Bat Out of Hell by Meatloaf began blasting out of the speakers.

He corrected his position, offered the SUV driver an appropriate—or rather, inappropriate—gesture of appreciation for her help in the matter. He turned up the radio and continued on his way.

His eyes flicked towards his rear view mirror. As he reached to adjust it, what he saw caused him to emit a shout, and the car swerved back over to the wrong side of the road. Once more, he fought the steering wheel for control as the vehicle threatened to skid. He remembered what his old driving instructor had told him to do in the event of losing control of the car. He'd told him to turn *into* the skid, not away from it. He did this without taking his eyes from the mirror.

In the circumstances, that was not an easy thing to do.

Sat in the back seat of his car, sitting motionless in the centre of the rear view mirror, was a man, or what he assumed was a man due to the size and shape of his body. He was wearing a large black motorcycle helmet. The centre of the blackout visor had a crack in it from the top to the bottom.

'What the fuck?' Joe managed to utter, as from nowhere, a motorcycle, with the rider wearing the same full-length leather suit and black helmet as his unwelcome passenger, came screaming from behind. The motorcycle swerved in front of his car before disappearing from view.

Joe looked in the rear view mirror again. The helmeted man was gone.

CRACK!!!

Crack

The car began to buck beneath him. He'd felt something exactly like it before, not that long ago. He gripped the steering wheel so tight that the joints in his knuckles cracked, only adding to the surreal situation.

From out of nowhere, a tide of crimson washed over his windshield. It was dark, and it was thick. He had the presence of mind to flick on his wipers, but they did little to alleviate the wave coating the glass. The vehicle was now out of his control; he could feel it spinning beneath him but could no longer see anything out of the window.

A scream broke from him.

'Don't panic. Just touch the brakes, turn lightly to the left, and you'll be fine.'

The soothing voice came from nowhere, yet everywhere at the same time. His eyes flicked to his mirror, to the back seat where he wasn't at all surprised to find the helmeted man sitting.

Joe opened his mouth to emit another scream, but no sound was forthcoming. All that happened was a strange kind of calm settled over him, and he turned the car slightly to the left and touched the brakes.

The vehicle responded. It slowed, eventually stopping on the side of the road as the wipers flicked the last of the blood from his window. The beautiful road that he had been driving on was gone, and he found himself on the layby at the edge of the A552, the exact location where his accident had occurred. He rested his head on the steering wheel, allowing his tensed shoulders to relax.

'You're safe, Joe, for now, but I saw you then. I saw the want, and the need in that face.' The helmeted man leaned forward closer to the rear-view mirror. 'You need me, Joe. I'll be back!'

He closed his eyes. He could feel the scream again as the horror of what had just happened dawned on him, when the world began to shimmy all around him. Everything looked to be under water, only for a brief moment, maybe two, then he was back driving on the sunny highway, where this had all begun. The song, Bat Out of Hell, had just finished, and the funky drum and guitar riff that was the into to a song Joe remembered from his youth, began. His mind instantly recalled its name, The Future's So Bright, I Gotta Wear Shades, by an obscure band called Timbuk 3.

51

With a shaky breath, he looked around him. Relief washed over him, much like the way the blood had washed over the windshield. He readjusted his grip on the steering wheel and looked into the rear view mirror. He didn't want to, as he dreaded what he would see there, but he knew he had no choice.

To his relief, there was no helmeted man. But to his utter confusion, Dr Penny Saunders was sitting in the back seat. She was wearing a light-yellow bikini and holding a green cocktail with sparklers in. She smiled, revealing her expensive teeth.

'It's time to come back, Joe,' she said, taking a sip of her drink.

He shook his head at this not unpleasant image and mouthed, 'What?'

'You can hear my voice, and you're now back in my office. You're safe and warm, and lying on my couch.'

Joe opened his eyes. He didn't even realise that they'd been closed until he saw the décor of the posh office.

'Good, Joe. Welcome back.' Penny's voice was no longer lulling; she was once again all business. 'We took our first step into your psyche. You're fully awake now.'

Joe sat up and was a little disappointed that Penny wasn't wearing a yellow bikini.

16.

'SO, HOW DO you feel after your first step back into how you view the incident?'

Penny was sat on the chair opposite him with her legs crossed. There was a large pad on her lap, and a pen in her hand. She was looking at him, her eyes boring into his head.

He took a moment to absorb the question before even attempting to answer it. 'Pretty freaked out, actually.'

Her eyes squinted, and her stare became somewhat more inquisitive. She leaned forward, getting a little, closer to him, as if to hear the answer to her next question a little better.

Her perfume was lovely. *Nice and expensive,* he thought from out of nowhere.

'Freaked out? Why do you feel freaked out, Joe?'

He turned to look at Karen, sitting next to him on the couch. He grabbed her hand and squeezed it; she responded with a small squeeze of her own. Joe's eyes darted around the room, looking for something, anything to focus on other than the beautiful smelling woman leaning into him. 'Well, the whole ... incident!' He stumbled looking for something to say that sounded like he fully understood the question.

'Yes?'

'It freaked me out, you know, reliving it like that.'

'Like what?' Penny asked, leaning into Joe again, creating a more intimate space between them.

'Like running that poor guy over again like that, plus the man in the back seat. The one with the motorcycle helmet on.'

Penny leaned back, she was still looking at him, her eyes questioning as she shook her head. 'You didn't relive the incident. All we did was set you off on a journey *towards* reliving it. It would be far too dangerous, not to mention unprofessional, of me to take you in that deep on your first session.'

Joe's brain felt as if it was cooking in his head. A frantic and fuzzy feeling was building inside him, and he was feeling dizzy. It was his turn to quiz the doctor, with his intense stare. 'But I did. There was a tidal wave of blood and a man in my back seat. He said he was coming back for me, for more of the same. What kind of tricks are you trying to pull on me here, Doc?' he asked, the anger suddenly filling every little bit of space within him. He felt violated, as if he'd been touched somewhere no one should ever touch him, not even Karen. He stood and began pacing the room, running his hands through his already messed up hair.

Penny looked at her watch; a small frown framed her features. 'Joe, it looks like your time here is up. Let's arrange to meet up again very soon for another session. I think you might have actually fallen into a deeper sleep then was intended. The images I was attempting to instil into you have somehow manifested themselves into a nightmarish scenario, complete with nightmare characters.' She was scribbling notes on her pad as she talked, Joe was impressed with the speed of her writing. 'The term PTSD is banded around quite a bit these days, and I am sometime loath to use it, but it might have some legitimacy here. The manifestation of the man in the motorcycle helmet could actually be a good thing, like you're giving the incident meaning, almost a life of its own. It's your psyche. It's making you better equipped to deal with your life. If you see your trauma as a person, with a personality, then you can deal with it on your own terms.' She was nodding as she looked at him, her eyes flicking between him and Karen. 'Let's run with that for now. I want you to try to develop this motorcycle helmet persona. I want you to talk to him, find out what he wants, befriend him even. Then, when you no longer need him, you can send him off on his way.'

Joe and Karen were staring at her from the couch, both of their faces were blank. Neither of them had understood a single word of what Penny had just said. Smiling again, Penny took a prescription pad from her desk and began to write on it. 'I'll sign you off work for another two weeks. I want you to relax and come back in and see me again in one week. Does that sound good?'

Crack

Joe looked at Karen, who was looking back at him, her face was ashen but there was a small smile resting on her lips. He turned back to Penny and nodded. 'OK, Doc. In a week?'

Penny smiled and ripped the little sheet of paper she was writing on before handing it to him. 'Give this to your employer, and …' she wrote another slip out, '…give this to the pharmacy. I'm recommending Nytrodol. It's strong, but it should allow you a restful sleep and block any unwanted dreams.'

Karen looked at the note, her smile was still not entirely convincing. Pleasantries were passed, and they left the office, making an appointment with the receptionist for the next week.

17.

'THERE'S NO WAY I'm going back there. You know that don't you?' Joe said, breaking the silence between them.

Karen took her eyes off the road and looked at him for a moment, before returning them to the road. 'But, Joe, you have to. Penny said—'

'I don't care what Penny said,' he snapped. 'You didn't see the dream I had. I don't know what hypno-mumbo-jumbo she did to me in there, but there's no way I'm doing that again. And you can forget the Rohypnol or whatever the fuck she wanted to give me. I'm not taking any of that crap either.' He folded his arms and stared through the windshield from the passenger side.

Karen sighed, repositioned her fingers on the steering wheel, and continued to drive.

'And I'm fucked if I'm taking any more time off work either. It's OK for her, in her plush office with all sorts of sick benefits, but I'm a working man. I don't get paid if I don't work. Nope, you can put money on that I'll be back in work come Monday.'

'Joe, she knows what she's talking about. Just think about it. Do you really think you're well enough to go back to work?'

Joe shook his head; a familiar fuzziness was growing inside him. 'I have to, Karen. I can't let this beat me. I won't let it ruin our lives.'

'But if you get worse—'

'WORSE?' he half shouted; half laughed. 'What the hell are you talking about, woman? How the fuck can it get any worse?'

'Please, Joe. I just want you to think about it. For me and the kids.'

He could see tears blearing in her eyes.

Crack

He tutted and pointed to the road in front of them, then crossed his arms again. Karen returned her focus to the road ahead.

The rest of the journey was conducted in complete silence.

18.

IT WAS EARLY into the nightshift when Joe looked at his watch for what felt like the seven-hundredth time; it read eleven forty-seven. *Only another seven hours to go*, he thought with his feet up on the small desk and a disinterested look at the open newspaper before him. With a heavy sigh, he picked up his torch and the keys to the work's van and left his hut to make another tour of the empty site.

The building site was huge; it was a new development, and they were laying the foundations for a new set of housing estates. He fired up the engine of the pickup truck and drove slowly around the areas. There were ten of them in total. The whole site was a series of long connecting roads between other building sites, all of them at the same foundation stages.

He was basically securing huge areas of empty or half-full concrete pits. He stopped at one of them and got out of the van to stretch his legs. He shone his torch into several of the pits and then into the foliage at the perimeter of the site before getting back in and driving back to his lodge. He logged his rounds and sat back at his little desk.

The rest of the night passed uneventfully. Six-thirty eventually rolled around, and the workmen began to drift in.

He was heralded with a chorus of 'Good night, Joe?', 'Hey, man, good to see you back.', 'How you doing, Joe?' There was even one or two 'Don't kill anyone on your way home, man.'

He knew it was just banter, and he took it in the good nature it was meant.

'Don't worry about me, Mike. I'm not going home.' He laughed as he waved his papers to one of the comedians. 'Your wife just called to let me know you'd be out for the next eight hours.'

Crack

'Hey, man, I'll go for a beer after work in that case. That way you can have her for ten,' came the quick response.

Joe was laughing as he climbed into his car. It felt good to laugh again.

The moment he got inside, a strange feeling descended over him. His palms were instantly moistened, and his heart was palpitating rapidly. As he gripped the wheel, the sweat on his palms made them slip over the smooth rubber coating. With a tremoring hand, he gripped the key in the ignition. He paused for a few moments, not wanting to but knowing that he had to turn it. Eventually he did, and as the engine gunned into life, something in his stomach dropped.

CRACK!!!

He closed his eyes.

In the darkness behind his eyelids, he saw a headless corpse strewn across the road in front of him.

With effort, he jolted his eyes back open. With a shake of his head, he slipped the car into first gear. His breathing was heavy, and laboured as he caught the biting point and slowly pulled out of the site, onto the ramp to the main road. He blinked, squinting his entire face, in a futile attempt to rid himself of that stupid vision.

Come on, Joe, you're better than this.

He dithered as he reached the junction. He'd remembered to indicate but was procrastinating making the manoeuvre. An odd panic bathed him as he watched the oncoming traffic. He felt like he'd lost the ability to judge the timing between the cars.

His thoughts were a mess.

A loud honk from a vehicle behind him made him jump. He gazed into his rear view mirror and saw an angry looking man behind the wheel of a works van; he was throwing his hands in the air at Joe's procrastination.

Joe offered him an apologetic wave in the mirror, closed his eyes, caught the biting point again, and with sweat dripping from his brow, pulled into the road.

Fifteen minutes later, he was home. He turned off the engine, got out of the car, and stood, leaning on the warm metal of the chassis.

His breathing was shallow and rapid; he felt like he'd run a marathon, in record time.

No one was home.

He muttered a silent prayer for small mercies.

On entering the house, he headed into the kitchen and opened the fridge. He stood for a few seconds, enjoying the icy cool blast on his clammy skin. He grabbed a can of beer and held it to his head, relishing the feeling of the condensation against him.

Morning is as good a time as any for a drink, he thought, cracking it open. He took a swig, emptying half of it in one gulp.

Crack

19.

DRESSED ONLY IN his pyjama bottoms, Joe closed the blackout drapes in the bedroom, killing the early morning sun streaming through the window. The only illumination now was from the small bedside lamp.

He didn't want anything disturbing his sleep.

He climbed into bed with a groan that turned into a sigh of relief as his head hit the pillow. He closed his eyes, readying himself for a full six or seven hours of total relaxation.

The moment he sunk his head into the pillow, his brain kicked into action. It woke him up, and by proxy, his whole self was now alert. He opened his eyes, considering the darkness of the room, registering each shadow and silhouette. *Fuck!* He turned over, growling irritably, trying to find the elusive comfortable position he longed for.

The illuminated display of the alarm clock shone on his face.

It read eight forty-seven.

He harrumphed, turned on his back and closed his eyes again. He tucked his arms beneath his head and attempted to clear his thoughts. Once again, the back of his eyelids rebelled on him. He watched as a motorcycle helmet rolled, bodiless, along the tarmac of a road. He was helpless to stop the vision. The gruesome helmet stopped in the centre of the road, next to the double white lines. Blood was pumping from the neck, staining the white lines. It rolled back on itself, the cracked visor pointing towards the sky.

CRACK!!!

His eyes opened, and he sat up. His heart was beating so fast, he thought he might be having a heart attack. As his head cleared and his rapid pulse began to return to a semblance of normalcy, he looked at the clock.

It read nine nineteen.

He must have drifted off, although it hadn't felt like it. Scratching his head, he got out of bed, and made his way along the landing on unsteady legs. The cool air on the stairwell caused goosebumps to raise on his skin as it contacted the still warm sweat on his body. He shivered and hugged himself. The clock on the wall read nine twenty-two. He closed his eyes, gripped the banister with his moist hand, and continued down.

His heart was set on getting another beer from the fridge, so he did exactly that. Popping the cap, he sat at the small kitchen table and chugged it down, only stopping halfway to let out a loud belch. Feeling a little better, with a light beer buzz about him, he made his way back towards the stairs. Nixon was lying on the bottom step; he wagged his tail as he looked up at his master. Joe didn't see him and stepped on his tail as he attempted to navigate the step.

The dog yelped and ran off.

'Nixon, you fucking mutt,' he shouted in a half dreamy state, before continuing up the stairs towards his bedroom.

He climbed into bed, his body rigid and his eyes wide open. *If only I'd swerved to the left a little,* he thought, the accident playing over in his head for what might have been the millionth time. *Then maybe I wouldn't have hit him. Maybe I'd have gone over his body and not his—*

CRACK!!!

He sat bolt upright again and regarded the clock.

It was eleven a.m. exactly.

His tired mind attempted to comprehend why and how time was travelling so fast when he hadn't even been asleep, or at least he didn't think he had. He lay his head down onto the pillow. 'Jesus, I'm more tired now than I was when I got home,' he mumbled, sitting up, on the edge of the bed. He hung his head in his hands and let out a long, drawn out, sigh. He made his way towards the bathroom and looked into the mirror. His eyes were bright red, and his skin looked cold, grey, like one of those zombies on that rubbish

Crack

show that Martin liked to watch. 'Come on, Joe. Get a grip,' he scolded himself. 'You look like shit.'

He did his business and went back to bed. He lay his head on the pillow and, once again, glanced at the clock.

Eleven-oh-eight

CRACK!!!

The rapid beating of his heart forced his eyes to open, and he looked at the clock.

Fourteen thirty-five.

'What the fuck is going on? That's not right.'

CRACK!!!

Sixteen twelve.

'This is fucking madness!'

Noises drifted up from downstairs that could only mean one thing, the kids home from school.

With his joints screaming, he forced himself out of bed and made his way downstairs. Annmarie was watching music videos while Martin was sitting in the corner chair playing on a handheld video console. They both looked at him as he entered the living room, their eyes giving away exactly what they were thinking.

'Jesus, Dad, you look like shit.'

'Thanks, Martin. You're a picture of health yourself, and less of the language. You're not in school now. Would there be any chance of getting a cup of coffee from either of you?'

Neither showed any interest in performing his request.

He shook his head and headed for the kitchen. 'Didn't think so,' he mumbled as he filled the kettle.

20.

'IAN, I'M HOME,' Paula shouted as she walked into the hallway of their house, closing the front door behind her.

With a wet baby smile, and a cheer that could grow a smile on even the grumpiest person, Sally toddled towards her, dressed only in t-shirt and a pair of baby knickers. 'Mummy's home,' she announced.

Paula put her handbag on the floor and bent over to pick up her child, catching the child's infectious smile in the process. 'Yeah, baby,' she gushed. 'Mummy's home.'

'Missed you, Mummy.' The little girl giggled as she grabbed Paula's face and smeared her wet lips all over it.

'Aw, baby face, I've missed you too.'

Ian walked out of the kitchen wearing jogging bottoms and a baggy t-shirt; there was a towel draped over his shoulder. 'Dinner will be ready in ten. Grab a drink, relax, and I'll bring it in.'

'Sounds good to me,' Paula said, putting Sally back on the floor, where she promptly ran off towards the TV.

Paula sat down on the couch and removed her badge, then her shoes. 'Oh my God, that feels so good,' she whispered, wiggling her toes, which were relishing their freedom from the confines of their shoe prison.

Ian popped his head back around the kitchen door. 'Did you have a good day, babe?' he asked, there was genuine interest in his voice.

'I've been on my feet interrogating that weirdo from the pawnbroker's all day. He wanted representation at one point, but we got to him in the end. He confessed everything. Turns out the pawnbroker's wife was a bit of a whore, turning tricks in the back of the shop for punters. The guy was a regular in the pawnbroker's—

selling stolen goods, by the way. He was paying the wife for her services but owed her money.'

'So, you got him? Case solved?'

'Looks that way.'

'Is Price impressed?'

'Is she ever?'

'Nope,' he laughed, exiting the kitchen holding a steaming bowl and placing it in front of Paula. 'Sally, come on honey, get your dindins from Mummy.' The little girl turned and toddled back towards her mother. 'So, what happens now?' Ian continued. 'You got anything else on?'

Paula picked Sally up and put her on her knee, then picked up the spoon from the bowl and began to feed her.

'Do you know what? For the first time, in a long time, there's nothing relevant on the board. Looks like we're going to open some cold cases.'

'Well, you can always put your uniform back on and give the real police a hand,' Ian said, carrying two large plates into the room.

She offered him a smile with raised eyebrows, and a twinkle in her eye. 'You'd like that, wouldn't you?'

Ian raised his own eyebrows and nodded as he laid the plates on a small table. 'You do look good in that uniform.'

She flashed him another wicked smile. 'Well, maybe I'll try it on a bit later, and see if it still fits.'

He sat on his chair and began twisting his spaghetti onto his fork, he was still nodding and grinning.

21.

JOE WAS BACK in his hut. His small TV was flickering away in the corner. A stupid gameshow where the contestants were knocking down giant constructions with a swinging ball was playing out on the screen, silently. The contestants were all smiles and laughs.

Joe was miserable.

His eyes were half open and stinging like he had soap in them. The stubble on his chin was rapidly turning into a beard and matching his unruly grey hair. The light from the screen washed over his disinterested face as he took another sip from the flask of coffee in his hands. 'Oh, for fuck's sake,' he shouted at the TV. 'Kill me now.' The people in the show ignored his rant and continued swinging their large ball.

The hours were passing, but for Joe they felt like three to every one, and he'd found himself doing the one thing he knew he should never do, the one unwritten rule for night security: he was watching the damned clock. Every passing second, every tick and tock, took something more from him, making him feel hours, maybe even days older.

In a disassociated blur, he watched as the shift guys began to filter in for their day's work.

He half remembered getting into his car.

He kind of remembered driving home.

He floated into the house in a thick, hazy fog, undressed, to a degree, fell into bed, and closed his eyes.

As soon as he did, a headless corpse in a blood-soaked leather outfit flashed across his vision.

CRACK!!!

Crack

He was as alert as if it were mid-day, however the clock read seven forty-five. He was confused as to if it were am or pm.

For fuck's sake, this is getting stupid. He swung his legs out of the bed and snapped on the bedside lamp, he grabbed his housecoat from the back of the door and shoved his feet into his slippers.

Karen was in the kitchen clearing up the kitchen. 'I thought I told you to get straight to bed; you look tired. Maybe you'd be better ringing in sick tonight. I'm sure they'd understand. Maybe you should go and see that doctor again, you know, Penny the psychologist.'

Joe wasn't listening. In truth, he didn't even see her in his sleep deprived haze. He walked to the fridge, opened it, grabbed a beer can. He popped it open, and took a long, deep swallow. He then turned back towards the door and let out a huge belch.

'Are you even listening to me? Beer at this time in the morning? Do you think that's a good idea?' Karen asked, putting the dish she was washing back into the sink. Her eyes followed him out of the room. She shook her head, ever so slightly.

He stopped at the kitchen door, took another swig from the can, put it on the side counter, and belched again. 'She's a psychiatrist, not a psychologist,' he snapped before shuffling out of the kitchen, and back up the stairs.

It was seven forty-nine.

He put his head on the pillow, leaned over, and flicked out the lamp.

CRACK!!!

He was wide awake again.

The clock read, ten minutes past ten.

He flicked the lamp back on. The light revealed a small brown bottle on the bedside cabinet next to the clock. There was a handwritten note next to it. He closed his eyes while rolling his eyes. When he opened them, he was hoping the bottle would be gone. It wasn't. He picked up the bottle and looked at the label. It took a moment for his eyes to focus on the small writing.

NYTRODOL

Shaking his head, feeling his pulse building in his chest, he picked up the note and read it:

Joe, apparently these are strong. Take two, they should allow you sleep. Karen xx

He put the bottle down on the table, unopened. He got up, and made his way towards the bathroom, slamming the door behind him.

CRACK!!!

He flung the door open at the noise and poked his head out, looking both ways of the landing for the source of the sound.

CRACK!!!

This time he thought it was coming from somewhere downstairs. Recalling his dreams, his heart began to pound again, and his skin was suddenly damp from his head to his feet. He could hear the TV blaring downstairs. There was some kind of forced hilarity and cheering pouring from whatever was on.
He looked at the clock on the wall.
Ten nineteen.
How is it still only twenty past ten? He looked again.
This time it read twelve ten.
Confusion was confounding him as he continued his search for the source of the ugly sound.
He watched the clock flitter between twelve ten and thirteen, ten and then back again. He shook his head in a vain attempt to clear the fuzz building up inside it, and he continued downstairs.
'Karen, is that you? Martin … Annmarie???'
The sounds on the TV stopped as he spoke.
He poked his head around the door and peered into the living room.
Three people were sat inside, around the silenced TV. They were all wearing full leather bike suits and helmets with the visors down. As one, they all turned towards him.

Crack

Abstractly, he noticed the TV was showing the same stupid game show he'd been watching at work. There were three towers, and the contestants were swinging a large ball around, trying to knock them down. Only the towers weren't towers, they were Karen, Martin, and Annmarie. The ball was a large motorcycle helmet, there was blood dripping from the bottom of it.

The contestant was a woman. She looked like the same woman from his dream, the driver of the SUV. Blood was streaming from her eyes and nose as she held the helmet in her hands, ready to swing it. When she let it go, she laughed as black, semi-coagulated blood poured from her mouth. Joe thought it was inappropriate television for the time of day.

As the helmet swung around the small arena, it eventually hit Karen, and her head fell off in an explosion of gore.

CRACK!!!

The three bikers in the room clapped and cheered as her head hit the floor, cracking open and spilling grey matter and pink jelly from it. The sounds were muffled because of their helmets.

The bloodied woman on the screen was ready to have another go. She squealed as she swung the dripping helmet again. This time it hit Annmarie, and *her* head fell off ...

CRACK!!!

Just as she was about to release the ball for the third time, Joe ran into the living room. The three motorcycle riders jumped. They tried in vain to grab him, but he slalomed between their grasping hands. He reached the TV just as the laughing, blood-soaked woman swung the helmet for a third time. He lashed out and knocked the TV to the floor with his foot.

CRACK!!!

The bikers stopped grabbing at him as their helmeted heads fell to the ground in bloody messes. Their visors cracked open, just as Karen's had. Thick, black gore poured onto the carpet.

CRACK!!!

CRACK!!!

CRACK!!!

Joe's very own features, dead eyes, streaming nose, and a mouth bubbling pink froth stared from all three helmets. Six vacant, bloodshot eyes. 'It's your own fault, Joe; you've grown used to the *CRACK,* haven't you?' all three heads asked in unison, purple lips forming the words from their dead mouths. The sound was eerie, like something from a cheap science-fiction film.

'No,' he whispered before lashing out. The heads rolled along the living room floor, leaving bloody tracks in carpet in their wake. He sat heavily on one of the chairs and before he could even register the comfort of the furniture, he was transported behind the wheel of a car.

A man in a black helmet and full leather biker outfit was laid out on the hood. He was leaning into the window. His visor was down, and blood was weeping from the seams on either side. There was a crack down the middle of the plastic glass, that too was weeping thick, viscus liquid.

'You know what you need to do, don't you, Joe?' Even though he knew the voice was the voice of the helmeted man, it was coming from the car's speakers.

Joe stabbed at the radio, attempting to turn it off, but no matter what he did, the voice continued.

'I don't know what I need to do,' he sobbed, fresh tears were rolling down his cheeks. 'Tell me what I need to do.'

'You need the *CRACK!*' the voice said with a maniacal laugh. *'YOU NEED THE CRACK, DON'T YOU, JOE?'*

The helmeted man stopped moving. There was one final:

CRACK!!!

Crack

The man's head came away from his body. As it did, a tsunami of blood hit the windshield before the helmet rolled off the car, and out of sight.

22.

KAREN WAS PUSHING the door to the bedroom, attempting to close it; it had always been stiff.

CRACK!!!

She was putting all her force onto it to try to get it closed properly, but it kept on popping back out.
All it needed was a really big slam.

CRACK!!!

Joe shot up in bed. His body covered in sweat, and his face devoid of colour. His eyes were wild, lost even. As she looked at him, her shoulders dropped. 'Oh, please, not again,' she muttered under her breath.

Crack

23.

ONCE AGAIN, JOE was like the walking dead at work. In a slow, plodding malaise, he dragged himself around the site when he had to. He falsified the logs of his rounds when he needed to and did the absolute minimum he could get away with. *Not long before I can go home and get some sleep,* he thought. This caused him to laugh. There was no humour in it, it was nothing but a cold, empty bray. *Yeah, like that's going to happen.* He hadn't had any, what anyone could call, restful sleep, in days.

A few long hours later, he pulled into his empty driveway. Using the banister, he heaved himself up the stairs and into his bedroom. There, he stepped out of his clothes, closed the curtains, and lay down in bed.

He wasn't expecting any sleep.

He wasn't disappointed.

His eyes were once again wide open as they rolled, slowly, to look at the clock.

It was seven forty-five.

The dark, stinging rat-holes he used to call eyes focused on the brown bottle of tablets. He rubbed his moist hands over his drawn face. The rasping noise of the grey stubble sounded louder than it should have in the twilight of the lamp illuminated room. He leaned over, with some considerable effort, and grasped the small bottle. He tried to focus on the label, moving the bottle a little further away from his face to stop the words from swimming right off the label. It told him that the recommended dosage was two tablets per six hours of sleep.

He closed his eyes, trying to imagine what six hours of sleep felt like. 'Bliss,' he muttered into the empty room.

With a shaking hand, he pressed down the childproof lid and turned it, relishing each click as the white plastic top unscrewed. It fell open, and he shook out four tablets onto the wet palm of his waiting hand. He sat for a short while, just looking at them. He wished he was doing something else right then, anything else, but in a jerk reaction, he grabbed the glass of water that had been left overnight at the side of the bed and slugged them all down. He flipped his head back, hoping the movement, and the water would smooth the passage of the pills.

He sat for a short while, just gripping the side of the bed, staring out into the semi-darkness. He was justifying what he'd done. The best he could come up with was that tomorrow was his day off, and he didn't think anyone would have an issue if he slept right through. He lay on the bed, rested his hands on his chest, and closed his eyes.

The instant the darkness enveloped him, a vision flashed though his head. It was a severed head wearing a cracked motorcycle helmet, bouncing off his car. 'Not tonight,' he mumbled to the severed head. The head began to dissolve before him as he drifted off into a deep, dreamless, and very welcome sleep.

Crack

24.

THE DARKNESS WAS complete and blissful.

25.

A NOISE RIPPED through the still of the night.

It was a sound that didn't belong in the peaceful delight he was currently enjoying.

It annoyed him.

CRACK!!!

This time he didn't bolt upright. The sound merely aroused him, tickling his inquisitive nature, building upon his annoyance. Eventually, his inquisitiveness got the better of him, and he had to investigate. He slipped his feet into his awaiting slippers at the foot of the bed.

CRACK!!!

He ambled out of the room, careful not to trip over anything that might wake his sleeping wife. He had no recollection of what time she'd joined him; it didn't really matter to him either way. He ventured onto the landing, wrapping his housecoat around him, tying the brown fabric belt tight against his pyjamas. His thoughts were still a little fuzzy around the edges as he wondered what the sound could be.

CRACK!!!

An idea occurred, bringing a vacant, sleepy smile to his face. *I'm dreaming again!* The thought was good because he knew anything he saw in this adventure would only be an extension of his frazzled brain and it couldn't hurt him. *I'll let it play out,* he thought. *It can't hurt me. It's a Nytrodol induced fantasy. Any minute now, I'll see men in motorcycle helmets covered in blood.* He grinned a little as he hoped it would be Penny in that yellow bikini. He closed his eyes, his heart was pounding, but he knew it was just the adrenaline rush, exactly the same as anyone would get before walking into a haunted house at a funfair or waiting for a jump-scare in a film. *I've just got to remember, they're only projections. Just leave them be.*

He wasn't surprised to find himself in the living room.

CRACK!!!

Nixon was suddenly at his feet, wagging his tail and jumping up at him. 'Hey, Nixon. There you go boy. Who's a good fella, eh?'

CRACK!!!

Each time he heard the noise, he flinched, but it was more a reflex action rather than the fear the sound usually elicited.

He looked down at Nixon and smiled. He began to tap his thighs. 'Come here, boy. Come on.' The dog padded over to him, his tail playing a drum solo on the furniture as he did. He put his hand into his housecoat pocket and pulled out two tablets. They were both white, with the word Nytrodol indented into one side. 'Here you go, boy, good dog.' Nixon sniffed his hands in anticipation of whatever treat his master was offering him.

With a sudden movement, he grabbed the dog's mouth and forced the tablets down his throat. Nixon was a big dog, and when he began to jerk to try and get out of the hold his master had on him, Joe had to battle to hold him tight. It was a battle he won, smiling dreamily as he did. 'Come on, boy. It's just a dream. You know I'd never do anything like this in real life, don't you?'

With the tablets now swallowed, he let the dog go, leaving him retching on the living room floor, attempting to regurgitate the tablets. It was sufficient to say the dog hadn't enjoyed this treat. Joe left him to his own devices and shuffled towards the cupboard where he kept his tools. He fished around, occasionally looking back at the dog. His head was low, and as he continued to gag, his eyes regarded his master with a sulky glare.

Joe emerged with a large roll of grey tape and a bag of zip ties. He held them out towards Nixon as if showing him a nice surprise. 'Here you go, boy. I got these for you.'

He was just in time to see the dog's head droop. The poor mutt's legs began to buckle beneath him, as the fast-working tablets obviously did their job. 'Good boy,' Joe purred, his words slurring. Now go on, go to sleep, big fella. Go on.'

He watched Nixon lope to one side, his big head bobbing as the animal fought the effects of the pills. Eventually, he fell. It might have been comical, it actually was to Joe, in his twilight existence, but to anyone else witnessing it, it would have been sad, tragic, a travesty to a proud, loyal animal.

He fell onto the lino of the kitchen floor, one leg still twitching as Joe, chuckling at the odd entertainment, made his way to the stricken animal. He bent down low and stroked him.

CRACK!!!

He flinched and looked around, but the source of the sound was still eluding him. He shrugged, telling himself that he no longer cared where it came from, this was just a dream anyway.

And he had dream-work to do.

Spurred on by this realisation, he took Nixon by the muzzle and began to wrap the tape around it. 'These dreams are so fucking lifelike,' he chuckled to the empty room.

He took the zip ties, and holding the stricken animal's front paws, he tied them together. He then did the same with the back ones. He picked Nixon up, staggering as the dead weight of the sleeping animal in his arms surprised him. He staggered towards the garage. 'You need to go on a doggy-diet, fella. Too many treats for you, fat boy,' he hissed as he stumbled a few times.

He lay the dog on the concrete floor and positioned him, so he was lying horizontal. He then opened the garage door and nabbed the spare car keys from an old shoe hanging on the wall.

CRACK!!!

Crack

He smiled, raising his eyebrows this time. 'This one's for you, *CRACK!*' he laughed, holding up the car keys to some unseen God in the ceiling of the garage.

He unlocked the car door and slipped in. As he turned the key, the car shook. He looked at himself in the rear view mirror. 'Joe, you're mad as fuck. You really are,' he chuckled again to himself. He adjusted the rear-view mirror so he could see Nixon lying prone on the cold floor.

CRACK!!!

With a maniacal giggle that felt wrong to him, even in this fucked up dream, he rubbed his clammy hands on the trousers of his PJs, pushed the gear into reverse, found the biting point, and eased his foot from the clutch, onto the accelerator.

He then released the handbrake.

Very slowly, the car began to reverse inside the garage. He watched as the dog's body got closer little by little. He turned the steering wheel slightly to align the driver's side wheels perfectly with Nixon's head.

Slowly, ever so slowly, he continued to reverse.

He closed his eyes as a euphoric feeling overtook his entire body. He felt the now familiar, and surprisingly comforting, bump in the car's suspension as the rear wheel edged, inch my inch, over the poor, innocent, sleeping animal's head.

CRACK!!!

This was different than the other noise.

Something about it felt… real.

There was weight behind it. It brought with it a kind of relief that Joe would have found difficult to describe to *that snooping bitch* Dr Penny.

After a few moments of peaceful reflection, he realised he had been gripping the steering wheel a little too tight and had to pry his fingers off of it. He reached down and turned off the engine before relaxing back, with a long sigh, into the worn driver's seat. The euphoric wave cleansed him, it lifted a weight from his shoulders;

the weight of negativity he'd been dragging along with him for the last few weeks.

Now, in the dawn of that last, wet crack, everything seemed to fit into place. It was like the last part of jigsaw, one that had been lost underneath the couch, or down a cushion. He'd found it, and it fit.

It was the crack after all, he thought.

After the initial wave began to ebb, he edged the car forward again, manoeuvring it back into its original position. There was an ugly, moist squelch as the tyres pulled through Nixon's remains. Joe stopped, put the car in park, and set the handbrake. He got out to survey the carnage. He'd never been in one, but he imagined a slaughterhouse would be very similar to how his garage looked right then.

Chuckling, thinking this was the strangest dream he'd ever had, he took the long hose from the side of the wall, turned on the tap, and began to wash the slabs of meat, of Nixon, from the exterior of the car and the surrounding walls.

He grabbed some thick bin liners from a cupboard, turned them inside out, and picked up what was left of the dog's headless body. He wrapped it into the bags and dumped them inside the trunk of the car. He closed it, wiping the imaginary blood from his hands as he did. He caught a reflection of himself in the rear window and noticed his pyjamas were covered in blood. He nodded at himself. 'Yup, these clothes need to go too, I think.' He shook his head and marvelled at what his imagination made him do. 'This is the craziest dream ever!'

Slowly, he removed his blood-soaked clothes, reeling as the wet cold of the material brushed against his skin. He dumped them in the trunk with the bulging bin bags, locked the car, closed the garage door, and completely naked, he walked back upstairs towards the bathroom.

Stepping into the warm shower, he whistled as the hot steaming water cascaded over him. The whole cleansing sensation was stimulating, and he toyed with the idea of masturbating.

Fuck it, he thought, as he began to stroke himself in the warm flow. After a few minutes, his knees buckled, and he released into

Crack

the gush of the shower water. He was dizzy, just for one beautiful moment, before it passed.

Towelling himself dry, he looked in the mirror, fixed his drying hair, and grinned; he looked as good as he felt.

He shook his head. 'Dreams work in mysterious ways,' he quipped.

26.

HE COULD FEEL hands on his back; they were touching him, gently, almost caressing him. He was being rocked back and forth; he was rather enjoying the sensation.

'Joe, come on, you need to get up. You've been in bed all day. It can't be good for you.'

He eased his eyes open, and the first thing they focused on was Karen's smiling face looking down at him. 'What time is it?' he asked, the sleep that was still in his voice make it sound deeper than normal, groggy like he'd been drinking.

'It's half past four. I've made you some dinner.'

He eased himself up into an upright position, and Karen fluffed the pillows behind him. The smell in the air made his stomach growl approvingly. She passed a tray over to him that was laden with hot food. It was only sausages and a bacon omelette, but to Joe's nose and his hungry stomach, it smelt like a lavish feast sent down from Heaven, just for him. His stomach voiced its impatience, and appreciation, for the food by shouting another loud growl. He put his hand on his stomach and laughed. Karen did too. It was a beautiful moment between them, in a period when the good times were few and far between.

'I think I really needed that sleep. I don't think I've felt so …'— he searched a moment or two for the right word— '…relaxed since the accident.'

'You look better for it. Maybe it's what you needed. I knew those pills would come in handy.' She picked up the bottle and shook it, then pouted in confusion. 'How many of these did you take?'

Joe took a break from stuffing his face with the delicious food. 'Of those? Erm, four, I think.'

She put the bottle down and got up off the bed, 'There must have been less in there than I thought. Well anyway, I'm glad you're feeling better.' She began to busy herself folding some clothes she picked up from the floor. 'Did you dream?' she asked, trying to look nonchalant but failing poorly.

He smiled and chuckled through his mouthful of food. 'Yeah, but I think I'm getting control over them now. It was weird. I knew I was dreaming; it was still mad stuff, but I wasn't scared this time. It was because I *knew* it wasn't real, I was in control.'

'Oh, well, let's look at that as a good thing. Maybe you're on the mend.'

'Hope so. I'm thinking that I might have turned some kind of corner or something.'

'Well, maybe you can get your fat arse out of that bed and go and help the kids.'

Joe had finished his meal in record time, discarded the tray, and started easing himself out of the bed. His feet were feeling around the floor for the slippers he always left there. He found them and slipped his feet inside. The moment he did, he retracted them and jumped, jerking back onto the bed. The slipper was freezing cold, and soaking wet. Curling his lips, he looked down at his feet. *Has Nixon pissed on them in the night?* he thought.

Ignoring his slippers, he looked up at his wife. 'Help the kids? Why? What are they up to?' An ominous feeling washed over him as he thought about his slippers and the dream. *What's happening here? Why would my slippers be wet? Nixon's no pup. He hasn't pissed in the house for years.*

Karen was still busy folding clothes and hanging them in the wardrobe. 'Well, it looks like Nixon's taken it upon himself to go missing. Can't find the damned mutt anywhere.' She turned to face him with a thoughtful look. 'It's not like him, though. I don't remember him ever doing anything like this before.' She paused, watching as his face changed. 'Joe?' Her own face falling as she cocked her head at him. 'What's wrong?'

She leaned over him and put her hand on his forehead.

He put his own hand up to remove it. 'Nothing, I'm all good,' he lied, not meeting her eyes. 'When did they last see him?' He was feeling hot now, and a greasy sweat was beading on his forehead.

Karen continued with the clothes. 'Last night, I think, before bed. Funny thing is he just wasn't here when we got up this morning.' She turned to hang more clothes in the wardrobe but shot Joe a quick glance beforehand. 'He must have found a way out that's, like, hidden or something.' She picked up more clothes without taking her eyes from him. 'That's what's worrying me. If he can get out like that, it means that things can get in.' She folded more clothes, still looking at him. 'You're going to need to fix that.'

Joe was up and out of the bed. He eased his legs into a pair of jeans that had been hanging over a chair. 'Where've they looked?'

Karen stopped what she was doing and frowned. 'Everywhere. All over the house, in the garden, and around the streets. Joe, are you OK?' With the clothes forgotten she regarded her husband, her eyes flickering all over him, as if looking for something she knew should be there but wasn't obvious.

'What about further out than the streets? Have they checked the fields?'

'I think so. Joe, calm down; it's not that important. He'll come back. Maybe you shouldn't be ...'

Ignoring her, he was out of the door and on his way downstairs before she could finish her sentence.

'Dad, you're up,' Martin said, turning away from the TV with a big smile.

'Ten out of fucking ten for observation,' he spat as he pushed past his son, who recoiled as if he'd been slapped.

Joe made it to the kitchen, looking for any sign of his dreamlike nocturnal activities. Thankfully, there was nothing obvious. He looked in the cupboard. A gush of relief exited him as he saw the electrical tape, and the zip ties, were still there.

Is this just a coincidence? Am I'm going mad? Paranoid? But what about the slippers? he thought, tapping his fingers on the cupboard door.

He centred his gaze on the door to the garage. His heart was thrashing. Annmarie walked in, smiling as she opened the fridge. 'Dad, I'm glad you're up. You haven't seen Nixon anywhere, have you? We can't find him anywhere.'

'No, baby, I haven't seen him. I've been in bed all day,' he replied absently.

Crack

'Oh yeah. Well, you look loads better today.'

'Thanks,' he replied automatically—for all he knew, she could have told him she was pregnant and didn't know who the father was out of five different candidates.

She walked out of the kitchen, and he edged closer to the garage door. He paused as he gripped the cold metal of the handle. He wondered if it was warmer than it should be, or if his imagination playing stupid games with him. He turned the key and slowly pushed the door open. He swallowed hard, attempting to quell the butterflies in his stomach, and to moisten his dry throat, as he looked in. It took a second for his eyes to adjust to the change in the light, but once they did, the first thing he noticed was the water pooled over the floor. There were puddles everywhere. They looked to have a tinge of colour to them. Once again, he hoped it was just his imagination.

His eyes made it to the car, and he frowned. The back end was a little bit cleaner than the front. Or was it?

Fuck this imagination!

He turned, checking behind him, to see if anyone was watching. Once satisfied he was unobserved, he made his way inside. Something at the back of the car caught his eye as he moved closer, through the puddles, to see what it was. A blue swathe was hanging out of the corner of the trunk. His palms were moist as he approached it.

He grabbed the latch and clicked it.

As the trunk swung open, he had to turn away and hold his nose as an unbelievable stink hit him full in the face.

It was the sickly-sweet stench of shit, death, and the onset of decay.

Leaning in on his tiptoes, one hand covering his nose, he saw the large black bin bags nestling inside the storage space. A pool of dark fluid had seeped out of them and had caked dry on the thin carpet. A canine paw protruded accusingly from one of the bags.

The blond fur confirmed, undeniably, it was Nixon's. It was stiff, unmoving, and unmistakably dead.

The blue he'd seen was a swathe of his blood-soaked, and still damp pyjamas.

Not wanting to, but knowing he had to, he reached into the trunk, and hooked the bin liner with a tentative finger. He grimaced as he took a look inside, *knowing* what he was going to find. Using only the tips of his fingers, he pulled the black plastic bin liner open.

As it peeled away, it revealed its grisly wares.

A large, semi-coagulated mess of dog.

A dog that was minus a head.

He balked and slammed the trunk shut. He turned and slid down the chassis of the car, still covering his mouth with his hands. This helped twofold; it stifled his gag, combating the urge to vomit that was welling inside him, it also stifled the scream that was building too.

Oh fuck, it wasn't a dream. It wasn't a dream. Tears welled in his eyes as he sobbed.

'Joe, are you in here?' Karen's voice carried from the kitchen.

He wiped his eyes and stood. 'I'm in the garage.'

She appeared at the door, leaned in, and smiled. 'What're you doing down there? Are you OK?'

He sniffed as he got up off the floor and walked towards her, shrugging. 'I was just, erm, looking for Nixon.'

'The kids checked in here. Come on; we're just about to order pizza.'

'Excellent,' he said with a fake smile as he passed her, heading into the kitchen. The last thing he needed was pizza.

Crack

27.

'DID YOU ORDER the cake?' Paula shouted down the stairs as Ian was making his way towards the door.

He closed his eyes and hunched his shoulders as the weight of the question fell upon him. 'Fuck,' he mumbled under his breath. 'I'm doing it today,' he lied, attempting to make it out of the house before the talented detective, who was also his fiancé, could question him anymore. 'My route takes me past Pierre's; you know, that French place.'

Paula was now making her way down the stairs. She was holding Sally in her arms. Her face was serious. 'You'd forgotten, hadn't you?'

Ian cocked his head to one side and offered a smile. 'As if I'd forget something as important as that.'

Paula shook her head and stepped down a couple of more steps. 'Unbelievable. Seven weeks to the day and no cake.'

'It's a cake Paula. How long can it take to make a cake?'

'It's not *just* a cake, Ian.'

The tone of her voice told him she wasn't joking, and he needed to be careful here. He sensed he could end up in some deep trouble.

'Do you know how long it takes to design? Do you even know how much they cost?'

Ian shrugged, wishing he'd left for work five minutes earlier. 'I don't know, ninety quid, maybe.'

She'd made it down the stairs and put Sally on the floor to toddle about. 'Yeah, Ian, ninety quid, plus the other five hundred to go on top of it.'

Ian's brow ruffled. 'What? Six hundred?'

'If you go to Pierre's, that is. If you go to McGinties, you'll get the same cake for four fifty.'

'Four hundred and fifty for a cake? Can't we just make one of our own?'

Paula stood behind him. Her hands were on her hips, and she shook her head. There was danger in that movement. 'Do you want me to be happy?' she asked, her stance indicating it wasn't a question. Ian caught a glimpse of the ruthlessness that made her so good at her job, and in that instant, he pitied the pawnbroker customer who had been the target of her last interrogation.

'Yes, baby, you know I do.'

'Then get to McGinties. Get the fucking cake ordered, and pay for it too,' she snapped, a menacing calm to her voice.

Ian backed out of the front door, holding his work bag between him and his bride-to-be. 'I told you, I'm on it.' He knew better than to mess with her when she was in this kind of mood.

He made it outside and closed the door, sighing as he rested his head against it. *Shit,* he cursed to himself. *I'll have to put in some overtime for sure*, he thought as he walked towards his motorcycle.

Crack

28.

FOR THE NEXT few nights, Joe slept the sleep of the just. He had his assigned days off work and felt like his life was getting back on track. Of course, that was *after* he'd disposed of Nixon's body. He'd gotten up in the middle of the night and driven to a nearby pond, where he'd thrown the stinking body of the beloved family pet. There had been a tear in his eye as he muttered a few nice words regarding their time together, before driving home, cleaning the stink out of the car, and going back to bed.

The kids mourned the loss of their pet, but he knew that, as teenagers tend to do, they'd very soon forget they'd ever even owned a dog.

'I'll get rid of Nixon's things tomorrow. I really don't think he's coming back.'

Karen looked at his reflection in her mirror as she applied moisturiser to her face. 'Do you think he's …'

'Dead? Yeah. Poor little bugger. It's my bet he's been run over, and his body is in a ditch or something,' he replied, slipping into a t-shirt for bed.

Karen turned and looked at him. Underneath the mask of cream, Joe could see the genuine sadness in her eyes. 'It's such a shame; he was a lovely dog.'

'Yeah.' Joe agreed as he climbed into bed. 'He was.'

~~~

Sleep came easy for him that night. A few moments after kissing his wife goodnight, he was gone.

The next day, he was up with the family as they all fussed around the house getting ready for school and work. 'Anyone want a lift?' he offered.

'Ha, yeah right, Dad,' Martin laughed as he walked out of the bathroom. 'With your track record?'

'Martin,' Karen snapped from inside their bedroom as she made the bed. 'That's not funny. You know how much your dad's suffered for that accident.'

'It's OK,' Joe soothed, shooting a joking glare at his son. 'I'll just remember that on Saturday when he wants a lift into town.' He tipped Martin a playful wink, and a smirk.

Within the hour, everyone had left the house and Joe found himself alone. He went into the kitchen and began hunting around for the various paraphernalia that went with owning a dog. Bowl, bed, food, lead. He packed it all into a large plastic bag and carried it out to the car. He opened the trunk to the stink of detergent rising to greet him. 'Jesus.' He choked before cocking his head away from the offensive chemicals. *Better than dead dog,* he thought. He put the bag into the trunk, holding his nose as he did.

He got into the car and drove to the local tip.

When he got home, it had just gone half past ten. He knew he needed to get a few hours' sleep, as he was due back in work that evening. So, he drew the blackout curtains in the bedroom and climbed into the bed.

CRACK!!!

His body jerked as if he'd been caught in a jump-scare. He was instantly covered in a sheen of cold, clammy sweat. There'd been no warning. He'd forgotten all about this noise, but now he was wide awake with the beat of his heart pulsing in his throat and ears. 'No,' he whined. 'Not again,' he croaked, swinging his feet out of the bed.

CRACK!!!

It's just your imagination. Your overactive imagination is playing games. Ignore it and it'll go away. Deep down, he knew sleep would be an unattainable destination today. He staggered to the

Crack

bathroom and looked at himself in the mirror. The dark rings that had been a constant during his dark times, were back circling his bloodshot eyes. *I've only just got rid of them; how can they be back so soon?* He made his way back to the bedroom and closed the door into the darkness beyond.

CRACK!!!

He looked at the clock; it was dead on eleven. His eyes dragged themselves towards the jar of Nytrodol on the nightstand. He took a shaky breath and closed his eyes. *Maybe I could just have one*, he thought, reaching out towards the bottle. At the last moment, he snapped it back. 'No,' he whispered. *Remember what you did under the influence of that shit last time?* he scolded himself. With an arm over his eyes, he lay back down and stared into the darkness behind his eyes, darkness that was intermittently interrupted with images of headless bikers.

Sleepless hours dragged by. At three pm, after his alarm had eventually screamed at him to get up, he dragged himself out of the bed and into the shower. With the world around him in a vile funk, dressed and trudged downstairs. He needed coffee and a sandwich. It was more to take his mind off his fatigue than to feed his hunger. He drank the cup, surprising himself when it was empty, as he didn't remember even taking a sip, and ate one of the sandwiches without even remembering what he'd put on it.

He put more coffee into his flask and another sandwich into his lunch box and left the kitchen. He entered the garage, sparing a spiteful look towards the hosepipe in the corner. With a shiver, that left his knees weak, he climbed into the car. As he fixed his rear view mirror, he caught a glimpse of his red tinged eyes.

He snapped his head around to look into the back seat as he thought he'd seen a shadow back there, as if there was someone there, with a larger head than would be normal. The back seat was empty, and he spared a small prayer of thanks.

Shook his head, slowly drove out of the garage, resigning himself to the long drive to work.

29.

'JESUS, JOE. YOU look like shit,' a large man in a high-vis vest shouted as he got out of his car. 'And you're over an hour and a half early. Is everything OK?'

'Dennis, you've told me that exact same thing almost every day since I've come into work after the accident. Can you please change the fucking record?' he snapped. 'Besides, I couldn't sleep. I just wanted to get busy, you know.'

'I get that,' Dennis replied, taking the criticism. 'Well, if you really want to do something, the guys over at east block could use some help. They're laying another set of foundations, and they could do with a leveller. Tell them I sent you.'

'Thanks, man,' Joe shouted, raising his hand in salute as he walked off in the direction Dennis indicated.

When he arrived, the mechanical tipper and three men were all hard at work directing the flow of the grey sludge into the pit. The operator waved as Joe approached. 'Hey, you here to give us a hand?' he shouted.

'Just for an hour or so. I got in early.'

'Excellent, you want to grab the plank and start levelling?' He leaned out of his window, pointing towards a long, levelling rod.

'On it,' Joe shouted, picking it up.

'Be careful, though, this slow settling stuff will suck you right in if you lose your balance,' he shouted again. Joe gave him the thumbs-up and began to work the huge area.

An hour or so later, they were done. He'd worked up a sweat and felt a whole lot better than he had when he'd arrived.

'Quitting time,' the man in the cab shouted, jumping out. 'Good work there, Joe.'

Crack

Joe was marvelling at the job he'd done with the concrete as he raised his hand absently to the crew as they began to make their way off site. He made his own way back to his lodge on foot. He couldn't help himself from looking back towards the pit of freshly laid concrete. There was something about it … something that called to him.

30.

CRACK!!!

He snapped awake like he'd fallen down a hole in his dream. Lost, he looked around, trying to remember where he was. An ugly, instant panic enveloped him; nothing seemed familiar. The darkness, the smell of the night, the silence.

Slowly it dawned on him; he sat in his security hut, in work. He lifted his head off the desk, wiping away the dribble of drool over his cheek, and looked at his digital clock. It was three fifteen am. He let out a long hiss through his nose, stood, and stretched, deciding that it would be best get some actual work done.

The night was quiet, and balmy. So much so that he decided to walk his rounds instead of driving, get himself some much-needed exercise. For some reason, maybe subconsciously, the path he chose took him to the large concrete pit on the east block where he'd been working earlier.

CRACK!!!

He flinched, reaching for his torch. He pointed it towards the surrounding undergrowth, searching for anywhere, or anything that could have caused the ugly noise. He turned the torch off and banged the top of it against his own head. *Get out of my head, stupid fucking noise!*

CRACK!!!

He walked away from the site in haste, hoping to outrun whatever was causing the noise. Although, deep down, he knew he

Crack

would never get away from it. It would follow him wherever he went; it had somehow become a part of him.

CRACK!!!

Each time the noise assaulted his ears, or his brain, goosebumps formed on his arms, and a chill blew through him. He likened he could feel it in his bones.

CRACK!!!

CRACK!!!

CRACK!!!

He covered his ears with his hands and closed his eyes, trying in vain to keep the noise at bay. He even began humming a tuneless melody, like a child ignoring his father, in another effort to block it out.

CRACK!!!

With thanks in his heart, he reached his hut and slammed the door shut behind him. His body was shaking like a leaf in a storm, and he was shouting. It was mostly just nonsense, mumbo-jumbo, anything to keep the vile sound out of his head. He sat heavily on his chair, tears running from his eyes.

'*FUCK OFF,*' he shouted into the solitude of his refuge.

He remembered his supposed dream then. The feelings he'd experienced when he'd run over Nixon's head. The relief; the euphoria. He remembered the wet noise and the exact feelings as this weight, this *shit* lifted from his shoulders, from his troubled head. *I could do with some of that right now,* he tormented himself, craving the release, the exultant waves.

CRACK!!!

Don't think about it, he scolded himself.

'Just watch it, man, this slow setting stuff will suck you right in if you lose your balance.' He heard Hank's voice again as he thought about Nixon.

NO, NO, NO, he shouted. *Don't even think about it.* He spun on his seat, his hands over his ears. He looked at the back wall.

Somewhere back there was a rifle.

He'd gotten it to entertain himself during the long, boring nights, shooting at cans and stuff.

Before he had any control over what he was doing, he was outside with the weapon in his hands. He was heading towards the bushes surrounding the site. He knew there were foxes all around the site, he'd seen them many times.

He crouched in the bushes and waited.

The night was still, almost motionless, and it was silent. At least until…

CRACK!!!

He ignored it.

CRACK!!!

He ignored it again, readjusting his fingers on the trigger of the weapon, waiting for his prey to come to him.

Eventually, he saw one, a large red fox. It poked its inquisitive head out of a bush, and he watched it emerge, slowly, cautiously. It could smell him, but the nightly hunt, and the hunger within was necessity for it to overcome any fear.

Joe wasted no time levelling the gun. He took aim and shot the beast. A direct hit, right in the back leg. Joe grinned, relishing the fact that all the practice he had gotten over the time he had been here had come to fruition. The wounded animal fell onto the ground. It began to howl, sounding more like the mewling of a new-born baby rather than the cry of a fully grown fox. He didn't let the sound bother him; he'd heard worse, and recently too. He knew there was no one around within earshot who would be bothered about a howling animal in the middle of the night.

Crack

He dragged the stricken animal by its back legs back towards his hut. He lay it down on the ground, careful not to let its struggling to get away, catch him. He hadn't worn gloves and knew that a snap from a feral animal, like this one could be dangerous. Its needle-sharp teeth were bared, but it couldn't do anything to help itself as it was in too much pain from the wound on its back leg. It was in no fit state to escape, but once back at the hut, he secured it by wrapping its body in a heavy tarpaulin from the shed. That stifled its wriggles.

He took extra special care to make sure the fox's head was free of the binding, he had designs on that. He tied thick rope around the torso so no matter how hard it tried, it could never get free. He then climbed into one of the work vans and gunned the engine. He spun the vehicle around to face the stricken animal.

The bundle was caught in the spotlights. The fox moved its head to look his way, the lights reflected eerily from its eyes.

He put the truck into first gear and crept it forward. He knew that the animal couldn't move, he'd wrapped it up expertly, so he continued onwards, very slowly, very deliberately.

Eventually, he felt the bump of the suspension beneath him. There was a small, pathetic yelp, but best of all, he heard everything he wanted, no, *needed* to.

CRACK!!!

Joe let go of the steering wheel. He pulled the handbrake and sat back. A feeling akin to his body melting into the seat washed over him, it was like an orgasm. The best orgasm he'd ever experienced; a pure, unadulterated sense of relief.

He looked down and was shocked, not to mention disgusted, to find his penis was fully erect. It was battling with the confines of his trousers, attempting to make its presence known.

After fishing around, attempting to hide his swollen appendage, he opened the door and almost fell out of the van. He grimaced at the mess over the front wing and the tyres. He looked at the road, his mouth watered with the bitter stuff, as his eyes took in the parts of the small animal's head, the parts that had exploded due to the build-up of pressure. They were scattered all over the road. As if acting on autopilot, he grabbed the rest of the tarpaulin and wrapped the lifeless carcass into it before putting it in the back of the van. He then climbed back in. He didn't need to think about what to do with the corpse, he already knew.

As he arrived at the pit he'd been working on earlier he got out of the van and breathed deep of the cool night air. Already he was feeling one hundred percent better than he had been since... He didn't want to think about Nixon, he didn't want any sadness to overshadow his euphoria.

He looked out across the smooth sea of slow setting concrete, knowing it wouldn't be anywhere near set yet. Carefully, he lifted the limp carcass from the back of the van and rolled it into the level cement. He watched, his eyes greedy, and his mouth hanging as the mixture sucked the body down, enveloping it within its grey confines, taking it, never to be seen again.

Within a few moments, there was no trace of the fox at all.

Grinning, and aroused again, he picked up the levelling pole to correct the indentation the fox had caused. He then set about cleaning the back of the van where the carcass had leaked.

Life felt good once again.

31.

'HEY, JOE, HAVE you been sleeping on the job? You look like a different person,' Dennis shouted as he turned up to relieve Joe from his duties.

'No way, not me. Just clean living and an active moisturising regime,' he shouted back with a smile.

As he drove home, he whistled, and sang along with the song on the radio. Apparently, The Rolling Stones wanted to 'Paint it Black.' He never understood why they wanted to do this—it was such a depressing change for a red door—but he liked the song anyhow, and he sang and tapped along as he drove home.

He pulled into the street just as Karen was loading up the car for her day, with the two kids in tow. 'Well, hello, family,' he chirped as he alighted his car.

'Hey,' Karen replied, giving him a once over. 'You look good. Are you feeling better?'

'Like a million bucks, young lady,' he beamed giving her a big kiss on the lips.

'Aw, Dad! Gross!' Annmarie shouted from the back of the car, sticking her fingers into her mouth and pretending to gag.

'Yeah, Dad. Get a room,' Martin shouted from the passenger side. Both kids were laughing.

Karen smiled and shook her head, the flush on her face emphasising her youthfulness. 'There's lasagne in the fridge, and your other flask is washed out and ready. So, you have a nice day. I've got to run.' She readied herself to get into her car, but before she did, she turned back to Joe and gave him a look, the kind of look he hadn't seen for a long while. Her eyes were shining, and, well ... sexy.

Joe winked and nodded in appreciation of the lady before him. 'OK, you have a nice day.' He watched and waved as Karen backed out of the drive and into the street. He exhaled a satisfied breath before entering the house. After a quick snack, he made his way to the bedroom, closed the curtains, got into bed, and was asleep almost the moment his head hit the pillow.

Crack

32.

IT WAS FOUR pm when the sound of his wife's car parking on the driveway pulled him from a deep sleep. He'd had almost a full week of rest now, since the fox, and without the aid of the nasty pills Karen had been pushing on him.

He listened, ruffling his brows as the kids were shouting at each other, making their way into the house. He lay on the bed, his eyes still closed and his breathing deep and steady. He stayed there for a further few moments, relishing the dwindling remnants of his rest and peace. He was staring vacantly towards the ceiling, the ruffle of his brow turned into a gentle smile. He sat up and stretched.

He grabbed his dressing gown and made his way downstairs ready to greet his family. 'So, how was everyone's day?' he asked.

'Did anyone call about Nixon?' Martin asked, a bored look on his face.

'No,' Joe replied, a little shocked at the question. It had been over two weeks since the dog had gone *missing*. 'I've got the phone at the edge of the bed. No calls today.'

Martin sighed and walked off towards the kitchen. His father watched him leave and shook his head; he couldn't quite believe Martin had already forgotten about being worried that the family pet was missing, presumed dead. Annmarie had her headphones in, listening to music. She flashed him a smile as she walked into the other room. He turned to look at Karen who was busy unloading her shopping into the kitchen cupboards.

'Let me give you a hand with them,' he offered.

'No, I'm fine, love. Why don't you just go and get ready for work?' she answered without looking back.

Joe winked at her as his face fell into a comical *no-one-loves-me* face. However, he took his wife's advice, and entered the house.

Half an hour later and he was ready for work. As he re-emerged into the living room the scene hadn't changed at all. No Martin, Annmarie still wearing the small white buds in her ears, mouthing along to words of songs he couldn't hear, and Karen was still in the kitchen.

'I've made you some soup,' she shouted. 'It's in your flask. I got you a new one for your coffee.' She put two flasks on the counter and turned back towards the sink.

As he walked into the kitchen something caught his eye by the door. It was something that, on the surface of it, should be normal but couldn't be. In the real world, it was an impossibility.

He turned, blinking rapidly, making sure he wasn't just seeing things.

He wasn't.

Nixon was standing by the kitchen door.

His chunky Labrador head was distorted and all out of proportion, it looked like it had been removed and reattached by a child. His two front legs were also misshapen. They were broken and at strange angles, offering impossible support to his body, that was matted with dried blood and all kinds of dirt. Somehow, Joe couldn't understand how, they were even holding him up. A black, ripped, and rotten tongue lolled from the gaping maw that was his mouth.

Behind him was a fox. It looked to be in the same condition as Nixon, impossible, unsteady, dead, but nevertheless there, in his kitchen. This small animal was covered in concrete, as if it had recently taken a bath in a pit, which of course, it had.

Joe's whole body instantly began to ache. 'Oh, sweet Jesus. Shit. Karen, get over here right now,' he ordered, his voice wavering in the middle of the sentence.

She stopped what she was doing and looked towards him, her face was asking the question if he'd gone mad. 'What?'

'Karen, put the pan down and get over here. Do it slowly.'

Still frowning, she followed his gaze across the room. Her features drooped as her eyes fell on the two dead animals, both of them baring their dangerous, if not rotten, teeth towards her. 'What the …' she whispered, putting the pan softly onto the counter. The water inside it sloshed and spilled.

Crack

Martin appeared at the door to the kitchen. 'Nixon,' he shouted, his face braking into a boyish grin. A grin that changed into something else, something not jovial, as he saw the condition the family pet was. in. 'Nixon?' he stuttered. 'What happened to you?' He knelt on one knee and called to the dog.

Nixon's attention shifted, as the once faithful dog showed his bleeding snarl to Martin. Some of his teeth were missing, exposing gums that were dark and dripping something black, that Joe thought might be blood. Pink drips from his ravaged muzzle fell onto the kitchen linoleum.

The animal, contrary to his condition, looked sharp and dangerous.

The fox mimicked Nixon. Its teeth were shorter, more needle-like, but nonetheless, they looked in condition to rip and tear effectively.

Slowly, Joe raised an arm towards his son. Without taking his eyes from either animal, he whispered slowly. 'Martin, stand up, right now, son. Do it slowly, no sudden movements. That's not Nixon, or not *our* Nixon anyway. Get away from them.' His whisper sounded calm and calculated, but the undercurrent of fear and panic was just underneath the surface, like a dangerous current in a river. The fox, detecting the rise in fear levels, turned its calloused, dead eyes from the boy and looked at him.

'But, Dad, look, it *is* Nixon.'

Joe tried to swallow the last of the spit in his bone-dry mouth. 'No Martin, it's not. Now get up and move away from it. Do it now, son, nice and slowly. No questions.'

At that exact moment, Annmarie popped her head around the door. Her face was confused but in a happy way. 'What's going on here?' she asked.

As if on cue, both animals decided there were far too many humans in the room for their liking and launched an attack in unison. Two sets of jaws, wide open, baring bloody, dangerous teeth, flew across the kitchen.

They landed their short flight on a surprised Annmarie.

The weight of Nixon hit her in the chest and knocked her off balance. She wheeled to the floor, banging her head solidly on the linoleum, with the concrete floor beneath it.

Joe felt as if his feet were glued to the ground as he watched the violence happen in slow motion, right before his eyes. He was helpless, frozen, as the two zombie-esque dogs ripped and tore at his daughter's face. A muffled scream that sounded like it could have been in another room, or maybe in another house, was followed by a short spray of blood signalling the puncturing of the carotid artery in her neck. A thick, maroon spray arched over the room, decorating the white wall and the refrigerator door.

Joe blinked. He couldn't take it all in. He didn't know if the spray had come from the animals or from his daughter.

'GET THE FUCK OFF HER.'

The shout that came from Joe's left, made him jump. Karen, with her own teeth bared in a savage snarl, pushed him out of the way, and set about attacking both dogs with the pan she'd been holding. Joe didn't know who was more dangerous, Karen or the feral animals. With grim determination, she took a devastating swipe at the fox. The pan connected to its small head with a comical dong, that was followed by a pitiful yelp, as the smaller, ginger animal flew across the kitchen.

But no CRACK, Joe thought.

The fox's neck bent at an impossible angle as it crashed against the cupboard door, coming to rest heavily on the floor. As it lay there, its legs and head were twitching. It was an ugly scene to witness.

Martin, gaining courage from his mother's assault, grabbed a knife from the block on the counter. He, too, screamed, and with a mighty thrust, buried the blade deep into Nixon's back.

Joe watched this happening, and even through his horror at the situation, one that *he* had caused, his admiration for his son's bravery almost shamed his own inability to do anything, or indeed, move.

A sickening yelp and another thick stream of blood filled the kitchen. It assaulted his ears and decorated the floor and cupboards at the same time. Joe could tell the spray was coming from the dog this time, as Nixon's back legs buckled from underneath him. As he ripped his foaming mouth away from chewing Annmarie's face, there was a sickening tear as a large portion of the teenage girl's cheek came away in its teeth. Joe watched with morbid fascination as a chunk of flesh fell to the floor with a wet slap. Then, the dog-from-hell turned to face his attacker, baring his gore ridden teeth.

Martin kicked out at the decrepit, but dangerous beast. His foot connected with the knife that was currently protruding from its back. There was another yelp, and Nixon twisted his head into what looked like an impossible angle. He was attempting to bite at the knife in its back with its bloody jaws.

Joe was still frozen to the spot. His body was letting him down as he stared helplessly at his daughter lying on the floor, wallowing in a shallow pool of dark liquid. The lights from the ceiling were reflecting in it. Her beautiful face was ruined. It no longer looked like her, she'd been replaced by a ragdoll, one that had been well chewed by a family pet. A mess of torn skin, exposing the white of the cartilage where her nose used to be, and a hole in her cheek where he could see the side of her tongue and her teeth, had replaced her.

To him, she looked dead.

Karen was still screaming, still beating the small fox to death, or to something like re-death, with the pan. The handle was almost broken now, and there were chunks of gristle hanging from it. *No more pasta from that pan,* he thought, he berated himself for that thought. How could he think about pasta when Annmarie was dead, killed by the very animals that had given him his blessed relief from... *from what, Joe?*

He turned to witness his son kicking his pet to death while stabbing it again and again with a large kitchen knife. The rictus of hate, and pink spit dripping from his blood-spattered mouth, turned Joe's stomach.

He looked on helplessly, pathetically. Back and forth his eyes flicked, between the animal beatings and Annmarie's ruined face. One of her eyes was bleeding, bubbles of red were growing from the corner of her eye. He couldn't, or maybe didn't want to, take his own eyes from the spectacle before him. He took a single step backwards. He was blinking back tears as he continued staring at her dead, staring eyes.

Suddenly, she turned towards him.

What she could manage of a smile appeared on her ruined, flapping, frayed face. 'CRACK, Daddy?' she whispered. It was a dead voice, one that bubbled, and gargled, as if she were choking on blood, saliva, or maybe even vomit.

One of her ruined eyes winked at him, the bubbling blood continued to pour from her socket as she did.

She then closed her eyes again, this time he knew they would stay closed, forever.

Crack

33.

AGAIN, JOE SPRUNG upright.

Disorientation was squeezing him in a death grip. It caused his head to swim, taking his stomach with it, as his eyes darted around the darkened room. He was searching for something, anything to help him recognise where he was. His body was drenched in a cold sweat, from what felt like every pore in his skin, soaking whatever it was he was wearing.

'Annmarie?' he whispered into the silence.

Saying her name broke his dream, and a relief washed over him as his eyes began to adjust to the darkness, and he knew where he was. He was safe in his bed, in his bedroom. After the initial relief abated, the realisation dawned upon him that the bad dreams were back. The dreams he'd hoped he'd left behind.

His heart felt like it had imploded.

Since the fox incident, he'd had four days of undisturbed sleep, and uneventful nights at work. Was all of that over now?

He looked at his clock; it read eighteen thirty-three.

Ignoring the goosebumps on his cold skin, he picked the moist duvet off him and ran a shaking hand through his wet hair. As he pulled himself out of the bed, the joints in his knees screamed at him, and his back joined in the chorus. Dealing with the aches and pains, he reached out in the darkness to where he knew his housecoat would be, and wrapped it around himself, protecting his soiled pyjamas from the cool air. With a stuttered breath, he headed downstairs. He *had* to know if his family were all right; he needed to see Annmarie.

They were all there in the living room, all of them safe and sound, and very much alive. Annmarie's face was, thankfully, still intact.

'Joe, are you OK?' Karen asked looking up at him from her chair.

He was lurking in the doorway of the living room, standing in the shadows. His skin was stinging where the sweat was drying, and the thought of how weak, how pathetic he must have looked to his family, made his stomach squirm, to add to his woes. 'I just … I had another dream, that's all.'

Karen got up and put her hand on his forehead. 'Another one? Have you been taking those tablets?'

He shook his head. 'I can't be dealing with that shitty chemical sleep,' he whispered. 'I need real sleep without these stupid, fucking dreams.' He exhaled slowly through his gritted teeth, then turned to leave the doorway. 'I've got to go and get ready, otherwise I'll be late.'

Karen reached into her pocket and removed the small brown bottle of pills that she seemed to carry with her everywhere these days. 'Take these with you. Give them about thirty minutes to kick in. Take two, or even three just before you leave work, so you should be nice and drowsy by the time you get home. They're herbal, so you shouldn't have any chemical induced side effects.' She slipped the bottle into the pocket of his jacket, which was hanging on the stair post, and returned to the living room.

Joe nodded as he yawned. He knew it was useless to fight her on this. 'All right. I'll take them when I'm nearly home, but it's your fault if I get stuck in traffic and fall asleep at the wheel.'

As he turned to go back upstairs, he spared a glance at his family. His eyes lingered on Annmarie a little longer than the others. The relief of looking at her untorn, normal, beautiful face was almost too much for him.

He smiled.

She smiled back, squinting her eyes. 'Are you all right, Dad?'

Joe nodded. 'I am, baby. I'm just tired. I'll see you all later.'

'Yeah, Dad, have a good night,' Annmarie said, returning her eyes to the TV screen.

Martin lifted his hand in the air to offer him a lazy high five. Joe responded to the offered hand, slapping it hard with his own. He bent down over the back of the chair and kissed the top of Karen's head before heading upstairs to get ready for work.

Crack

Half an hour, a shower, and a change of clothing, later, as he got into the car, he thought he saw something in the corner of his eye. Something large, brown, and Nixon-shaped lurking in the alleyway next to the house. He rubbed his tired eyes and saw it was only a bin liner that had fallen out of the garbage cans.

'You put Nixon in a bin bag,' a disassociated voice in his head said.

Joe rubbed his tired eyes, trying his best to ignore the rasping voice as he pulled out of the garage, and drove to work.

34.

IT WAS THREE am, and Joe was sitting at his desk; physically shaking.

He gripped his flask with aching fingers, attempting to pour some of the hot soup into the plastic cup. He ended up with more soup on the desk than in the cup. There was also dark orange stain spreading down his crisp white shirt. 'Fuck,' he spat as he slammed the flask down onto the tabletop.

He moaned as he delved a hand into one of the pockets of the coat hanging on the chair behind him. The ache in his shoulders, and his arms was almost too much for him to bear, and he almost gave up his search for the handkerchief he knew was in the pocket. As he searched, his frantic fingers wrapped themselves around a small bottle that rattled as he disturbed it. He removed it. Even though he knew what it was, he couldn't help but stare at it. He squinted as his sore eyes strained to focus on the label.

Nytrodol.

'Should I?' he whispered to no one. 'Just one to get rid of this fucking fatigue.'

CRACK!!!

The sound caused him to swallow, involuntarily. It seemed distant somehow, like a thunderstorm happening miles away, but not too far away to not know what it was.

CRACK!!!

It *was* an encroaching storm.

Crack

As the bottle rattled in his grasp, he stared at it. He knew he couldn't sleep on the job, that it was a sackable offence, but he also knew he didn't have the tenacity to deal with that noise. Not tonight, not after that dream this afternoon.

CRACK!!!

He put his hands over his ears and rested his elbows on the desk. He wanted to cry, but he knew it wouldn't get him anywhere, it wouldn't make any difference to his situation. *It might make my eyes feel less itchy,* he thought. The sound was *in* his head, it wasn't anywhere else. This he knew, but he needed something, anything to drown it out.

CRACK!!!

'You know what you have to do, Joe!'
Joe jumped.
The voice came from nowhere. There was no one else in the hut, and as far as he knew, there was no one else on the whole site. His body stiffened, his chest the only part of him still moving. He shuddered then, as freezing fingers caressed him. It made his nipples stand out and rub awkwardly against the fabric of his shirt, against the cool damp of the spilled soup. He flicked his eyes around the hut, hoping to catch a glimpse, but at the same time hoping *not* wanting to catch that glimpse, of whoever had spoken.
'Hello?' he whispered. Anxiety swelled inside him like an inflating balloon. It caused his voice to croak. 'Who's there?'
He grabbed the torch at his side and waved it around, shining its beam out of the window.
'You *know* where my voice is coming from. You *know* I'm in your head. You're not stupid, Joe. You know exactly how to get rid of ... this!'
Then, as if right on cue ...

CRACK!!!

The sound was louder now, as if the full extent of the storm it was bringing was travelling on a collision course with the very cabin he was sitting in.

'Wh-What?' Joe stuttered, not sure who it was he was talking to. 'What do I need to do? I can't stand that fucking noise.'

'That's not entirely true, now, is it?' The voice spoke down to him as if it were the teacher and he was an unruly, unresponsive student. 'You hate the noise because of what it means to you, and because of that, you hate the fact that you're craving it.'

Joe put his hands to his ears again and spun his seat around. 'I don't know what you're talking about. I don't crave it. It's ... it's horrible.'

'Is it?'

CRACK!!!

The sound rang in his ears. It was close now.

CRACK!!!

'Is it horrible, Joe? Are you sure you don't want it, need it? The last time you heard it, the real, wet, heavy version of it anyway, you slept like a baby for four days solid.' The voice paused; Joe could feel the drama in the silence. It then continued with a question, one that Joe didn't want to answer. 'Are you sleeping now, Joe?'

Joe began to sob. 'No, I'm not. You know I'm not,' he whispered.

'Then you know what you have to do.'

Joe sat forward in his seat, his hands covered his face, they muffled his voice. 'What? What do I need to do? Tell me, you bastard. WHAT THE FUCK DO I NEED TO DO?'

CRACK!!!

Joe felt like he was spinning. He was out of control. The room, the windows, the table, the small TV, they were all dancing around him. Each shadow was a carnival of madness, filled with every horror imaginable. He felt sick, his stomach flipping over, again and again. His head was whirling and the very ground beneath him felt unreal, as if it were water.

'BRING ON THE REAL CRACK, JOE!'

The shout reverberated in his ears, it was coming from the walls, the trees, the sky above him. But he knew where it was really coming from, he had no doubts about that. It was coming from deep inside his mind. It made his temples throb and sent pins and needles up and down his legs and arms.

He tried to stand, but there was no strength in his limbs, and the floor didn't feel as if would support him. He did it anyway, steadying himself on his desk.

'BRING ON THE REAL CRACK!'

He pulled at his hair. More nausea rose within his stomach, so much so he could taste the bitterness of the bile in the back of his throat.

'BRING ON THE REAL CRACK!'

His legs finally gave in, and he fell, heavily. As his head bashed onto the floor of the porta cabin, the room stopped spinning and the voice inside his head became suspiciously silent. A small noise—like one of the cracks, only softer—came from the floor, somewhere next to him. He flinched, closing his eyes, and curling up into a ball. He didn't want to know what would come next.

It was just a small sound, but it was getting nearer. He opened one eye and watched as the brown bottle of Nytrodol rattled along the floor towards him.

The voice was closer when it returned, like the speaker, or whisperer, was leaning into his ear. 'Bring on ... the real ... crack,' it teased. 'It will give you all the respite you require, Joe. Even if it is only for the short term.' The voice soothing, lulling, but to Joe it felt like it was blaring through a megaphone. 'Bring on the real crack, Joe. Make it come back ... if only for the short term.'

It whispered this mantra over and over again.

The same words, in the same order, at the same pitch. He could feel the world beginning to swim again.

He had to take stock of where he was. He knew he was on the floor; his squashed forehead and nose told him as much. His breathing was deep and laborious; it was also hot, and it smelt of garlic and staleness as it bounced back into his face. He turned his head.

The bottle was lying next to him.

The small white, plastic lid was almost touching his face.

'Urgh,' he uttered, and dragged himself up, into a sitting position, resting his back against the leg of the desk. Despite the thumping agony in his head now that the dizziness had abated, he never once took his eyes from the hateful brown bottle. His hands were damp, so he rubbed them on the leg of his now dusty trousers. Turning his head so he didn't have to watch, he reached a shaking hand and grasped the bottle. In a flash, the childproof lid was off, and he was shaking three small tablets onto the floor.

He slammed the bottle down and wrapped his arms around himself. His eyes, although sore, never wavered from the small, yellowish pills. He didn't want them, not after what happened last time, but he knew he couldn't live in constant fear of *that* noise coming back to haunt him. He had to do something.

An idea occurred to him then.

In his fevered state, he couldn't tell if it was his own thought or if it had been planted there by a certain disembodied voice, but the thought was a good one.

He pulled himself off the floor, picking up the three pills as he did so. He searched the hut for a saucer, or a plate. He ended up scraping the crumbs from the one he'd recently used for his sandwiches and dropped the pills onto it. They made pretty little *plinking* sounds as they hit the porcelain. He then took the spoon he used for cereal, or soup, squashed the tablets into the plate, crushing them into a fine powder.

'That's right,' the voice purred at him. 'Make them as fine a powder as you can.'

Joe did as he was bidden. He then searched through the cupboards where he kept his emergency tinned food, for those long nights when he couldn't make it through without a snack. There was a tin of thick beef stew with potatoes, he didn't know how old it was, nor did he care; it would suit his needs perfectly.

'You know what to do. Use what you have. Bring on the real crack!'

Crack

The voice was everything to him now. In his susceptible state, he would have followed its instructions even if it had told him to burn the hut down, with him inside.

With a vacant grin slashed across his face, he opened the tin and poured some of the cold, greasy contents onto the plate. He mixed it up with the crushed tablets. He looked at the mixture and grinned again.

He then hurried out of the cabin carrying the blend, being careful not to spill any. He marvelled at the fact that the shakes that had been racking through him only moments ago were gone.

About ten yards out, he placed the plate on the ground and retreated back inside the hut. From inside, he kept a watch.

About five minutes later a fox peeped its head from the nearby bushes. With caution, it made its way shyly towards the saucer, where it stopped and looked around.

Joe held his breath.

The fox sniffed at the plate. It looked around again, wary of the free food. Once it was happy it was alone, it began to eat.

'Good boy,' Joe whispered. 'Go on, eat it all up.'

The animal lapped up all the offering, going so far as to lick the plate clean. When it was done, it nudged around the dish, looking for more.

Joe watched, the smile on his face almost as big as the erection in his trousers.

His eyes were wide, and he was surprised to find his fists were clenching and unclenching, rhythmically.

Realising there were no more free treats forthcoming, the fox looked once more before making its way off, back towards the undergrowth.

For an uneasy moment, Joe thought it was going to make it. He knew that if it got back in the bushes, he'd never be able to find it again. To his luck, not to mention his relief, the wretched creature only made it a few yards before its back legs buckled beneath it. As he watched what was happening, Joe's heart began to beat a little faster, and he began to lick his dry lips.

Teetering on four, unsteady legs the animal continued its attempts to get to the bushes, but it failed miserably. After a few more unsteady moments, it gave up its brave fight and it fell flat onto the ground. Its body was twitching, and Joe watched as it began to relax, falling into a deep, drug-induced sleep.

With mixed emotions, some elation and a lot of revulsion, Joe left the cabin and picked the fox up. He carried the limp, almost lifeless body to the road where the company van was parked.

CRACK!!!

An impish grin spread across his features. *Yes, CRACK. I'll get you soon,* he thought. A giddy euphoria was spreading through him, and suddenly he felt an affinity to that pathetic, wretched figure from The Lord of the Rings, when he had *his precious* in his grasp.

He lay the sleeping body on the road, moving it into the correct position for what he had in mind. Stepping back from the scene, he breathed deeply as he admired his handiwork. Grinning, he climbed into the cab of the waiting van. He fished around in his pockets for the keys, shifted it into reverse, checked his mirrors, and then slowly released the brake.

The van edged backwards towards the sleeping animal. He could see it, illuminated by the high-level reverse lights on the bumper of the slow-moving van. As it drew closer, he could hear the wheels crunching the asphalt that the sleeping canine was lay on. He was close enough to his target that he could no longer see its reflection in the mirror.

His chest began to heave.

Each beat of his hollow heart sent another hot surge of blood through the capillaries of his already rigid penis, making it throb, and ache.

The anticipation of what he was about to receive was almost too much for him.

Then he felt it.

The small resistance on the path of the van's wheels.

It was only there for a moment or two; a light stab onto the accelerator put paid to it, bringing the familiar bump of the shock absorbers shivering through the van. It was exactly what he'd been waiting for. He pressed down a little further on the pedal, and the van continued its lethal—for the poor sleeping beast—journey. Cold beads of sweat were dripping down his forehead. In his semi-

Crack

delirium, he imagined his stiff penis resembling the alien, as it attempted to burst from Kane's chest on the table of the spaceship in that horror film, he'd watched so many years ago.

Acting on autopilot, he reached his free hand down between his legs and caressed his cock.

CRACK!!!

He had brought on the real crack.

The sound was thick and deliciously wet. It had weight, feeling, meaning. A numbing sensation flowed over him as he sat back in the driver's seat. A deep sigh hissed from him, the air escaping via his mouth and nostrils simultaneously. His eyes were closed, and he still had a tight grip on both the steering wheel and his penis.

He waited, expectantly for a sweet release. He could feel the tingles, the rush of his enjoyment.

It was about to spill, and he held his breath.

But nothing happened.

He'd expected something more. Something akin to what happened last time, maybe even better than last time, due to his build up. He expected the oppressive weight, the burden of the headless biker, to lift from his shoulders, to release him from his own personal Hell, exactly like it had last time.

But it was all for nothing. Something was missing, something big. He got out of the van. His erection was still throbbing as he examined the carcass of the fox. Its head was gone, shattered, and popped, by the weight of the van's wheels. Its small skull had exploded, and its brains were currently dripping from the foliage around the road.

CRACK!!!

Even with the carnage he'd created, and the wetness of the sound, it wasn't enough.

CRACK!!!

With one hand still clinging to his erection, he dropped to his knees. His other hand pinched at the throb at the other end of his body, the one in his temples.

CRACK!!!

Something, or someone, tutted behind him. Joe knew exactly who it was even before it spoke. 'You're going to need more than that pathetic little thing,' the voice explained. It was either coming from inside the van, or from inside his head; either way, it disturbed him, as he knew he was alone.
'You're going to need something … BIGGER!'
'Bigger?' he sobbed. 'How do I get something bigger?'
'That's the easy part,' the voice replied.

Crack

35.

THE VAN'S TYRES scraped along the concrete curb of the dark, seedy street. They slowed and eventually stopped. Fumes belched from the exhaust pipe at the back of it, stinking the night as the heat from the engine slowly cooked the fox blood, and the bits of gore clinging to the metal. The driver wound down his window and adjusted the cap on his head at the same time. Most of his face was hidden between the dim glow of the yellow streetlamp and the deep shadow of the van's interior.

Even though he'd never been to this part of the city before, Joe didn't want to chance anyone recognising him.

A young girl, she looked like she was still in her teens but trying her best, maybe too hard, to look older, looked over to his vehicle. She dropped her cigarette and stamped on it, extinguishing it with the sole of her cheap high-heeled shoe. Fixing her short shorts, she shimmied towards his open window.

Joe noticed painfully she was trying to look sexy as she walked towards him but was missing the target by a country mile. As she leaned into the van, there was a flirtatious smile on her lips, one that hid her desperation, and her addiction, as well as if they were hiding behind a wall made of clear glass.

He hated himself as he regarded her. She looked terrible. Her eyes were pink and the black rims around them told of too little sleep, and too much stress for a girl her age. *I'm one to talk about too little sleep,* he thought, stifling a humourless chuckle. Her face was heavily made up, a thick coating of concealer barely covering acne-ridden skin. She looked like she'd been made up by an eight-year-old girl, practicing on a plastic doll.

The sores at the corner of her mouth were weeping a clear liquid, and her greasy hair was tied back in an attempt to look sultry.

As she smiled, her mouth opened, releasing a multitude of aromas languishing on her breath. It was an ugly mixture of substances she'd obviously been taking to ease her through the night. Cigarettes, cheap wine, and some kind of mint mouth wash.

'Hello love. Are you looking for some … company?' She spoke the last word as it was obviously meant to sound, dirty, cheap, and seedy.

Joe's fingers flexed on the steering wheel. His proximity to this girl was making his hands sweat and his throat tighten. The familiar twinge in his trousers, as his penis began to spring to life, was back, maybe stronger than ever.

His eyes investigated the girl's head. Her slicked back, greasy hair clung to her scabbed cranium. It emphasised her beautiful round skull.

Joe licked his lips.

CRACK!!!

The sound took him by surprise. He blinked, shaking his head, doing everything he could to ignore it. His brow ruffled as he looked up at her from the window.

She hadn't heard the noise, and if she'd noticed his flinch, she was ignoring it. *She's probably seen too many weirdos in her time that one little flinch isn't going to scare her off,* he thought.

'Are you deaf?' she asked, sounding bored by the lack of transaction. 'I asked if you wanted company, or not?'

He pondered her from the safety of the shadows. The sickly throbbing in his head was in complete synchronisation with the bittersweet aching in his trousers. He adjusted his hands on the wheel again, still refusing to make eye contact with the underage girl. He could feel the greasy stink of his sweat, and the guilt of the vile thing he was here to do. It oozed from his hands as his grip tightened.

'Are we doing this or what?' she asked, sounding nervous now, and more than a little hesitant.

This time he did look at her.

He wished he hadn't.

Crack

She was too young, and her eyes were beyond scared, she had the look of a calf going to slaughter. Again, he had to stifle a nasty chuckle. Just glancing into her pink, tired eyes, he could see her life, filled with tragedy, sadness, and despair. She'd been brought to this junction, not by her own poor decisions, but ones made *for* her, probably when she was far too young to have any say in them. Underneath everything, underneath the pain, the rejection, underneath the cheap makeup covering spots and sores on her face, underneath all of that, he saw how much she reminded him of Annmarie. In a sudden panic, he pushed her face away from his window and pressed the button to wind it back up. He threw the car into gear and hit the accelerator. The wheels of the van screeched as they pulled away from the curb and out of the dank street, at pace.

The girl was left alone, stranded as the van's lights winked out into the distance.

'Yeah well, you can fuck off,' she shouted, flipping her middle finger in the direction of the van before walking slowly back towards her spot by the streetlight.

~~~~

Back at the construction site, the van's engine was dead, the lights were off, but Joe was still inside. His hands were still gripping the steering wheel, his face was ashen, and his mouth was chattering as if he were cold. Shame, fear, hate, all of these emotions, plus more that he didn't think he would be able to name, were coursing through his veins. The shame was for going there in the first instance, the fear was for what he had been contemplating, and the hate was for himself, for *not* doing what was necessary to rid himself of the infernal noise.

He rested his head on the centre of the wheel and sobbed. As the despair passed, he was surprised to notice that it was getting light, and cars were beginning to arrive for the day shift.

He must have fallen asleep behind the wheel.

Quickly, he got out of the van and made his way towards the cabin. 'Hey, Joe, what the fuck happened here?' Dennis shouted from somewhere behind him. The site foreman was inspecting the back of the vehicle.

'What do you mean?' Joe answered with a frown as he surreptitiously wiped the tears from his eyes.

'Did you hit something? It's a fucking mess back here.'

Joe closed his eyes, scolding himself for not cleaning the remains of the fox from the chassis. 'Oh, fuck. I think I got a fox or something up by east block,' he shouted back. 'Sorry, man, I meant to clean it up.'

'Jesus, you did hit a fox. There're bits of the poor bastard all over the wheels and the underside. Shit man, is that its body over here on the road? Fuck, Joe. You squashed its head.' The foreman was kicking stiff bits of the fox's head from under the van, grimacing as he did.

'I'll get a shovel and sort it out,' Joe replied with a tired sigh.

Dennis looked at Joe. His eyes were bright red, and his hair was sticking up at odd angles. He shook his head. 'No, it's all right. You get off home and get some sleep. I'll get someone else to sort this.'

The stiffness fell from Joe's shoulders, but only a little. 'Thanks, buddy,' he said with an overly long blink.

He climbed into his car, took a quick look at his reflection in the rear view mirror, and drove off as quickly as he was able.

Crack

36.

'WOW, WHAT'S UP with you, Dad?' Martin asked as his father lumbered out of his car. 'You look like a zombie.'

'Thanks, son,' Joe mumbled, tipping his head a little.

Karen looked at him. He could see something akin to sympathy, and maybe a little fear clouding her expression. This made him angry.

'You're dreaming again, aren't you Joe?' she whispered. He knew she already knew the answer, and he also knew that deep down she really didn't want him to answer. The joys of long-term relationships.

'No, nothing like that. Just a bad night in work; that's all. I'll get my head down, and I'll be as right as rain. Besides, I'm off now for a few days now. I'll be all good by the time you're home.'

'OK. There's pie in the fridge, just heat it up, and if you get a chance, we need some milk,' she said, getting into her car.

Annmarie walked past him. She was on her phone, ignoring him completely.

'I'm all over it. Have a great day,' he said, waving his family off before turning and stumbling into the house.

As he got into the bedroom, his head was reeling and throbbing. The headache was messing up his thinking. *What the fuck was I doing on that street? What did I do to that fox? What is going on in my life?*

With these questions clinging to his brain, he climbed into bed, in the darkened room, ready to embrace a full dreamless day.

CRACK!!!

If he had to be honest with himself, he knew this was going to happen. He had resigned himself to it, but when it happened, it was still unpleasant. He pulled the covers tight over his head and screamed at the top of his voice, using the blankets to muffle the sound. 'OH FUCK, JUST GO AWAY … PLEASE!'

CRACK!!!

He flung the covers off him and sat up. Something was different about the room now. There was something cold and sinister looming in the shadows, he could feel it but didn't know what it could be.

He didn't think he wanted to know.

Everything felt weird, like there was another presence in the room with him, watching him, stalking him. With a shaking hand, he reached out in the darkness, groping for the lamp at the side of the bed. Eventually, he found it. His fingers rested over the little switch halfway up the cord. He had a mental argument with himself about switching it on. *If there is something in the room, do I really want to see what it is? Do I?*

His pragmatic side won, and he clicked the small switch.

The instant illumination, even though it was dim, caused him to blink and shield his eyes.

When his vision focused, he could see a man wearing a motorcycle helmet and full body leather suit. He was standing motionless, as still as a statue, next to his bed. The helmet's visor was cracked, and although Joe couldn't see his face—as he assumed it was a man—he knew he was looking at him; the helmet was facing his way.

He should have been scared, petrified at the intrusion, but in some dark recess of his mind, some subconscious corner of his brain, he'd been expecting him.

The words of Penny the psychiatrist ran through his mind. *'I want you to try to develop this motorcycle helmet persona. I want you to talk to him, find out what he wants, befriend him even. Then, when you no longer need him, you can send him off on his way.'* This scared him in a deeper way than he expected. It wasn't a horror-film kind of scare but more a how-is-this-ever-going-to-end kind of thing.

Crack

'What do you want? Why won't you leave me alone?'
The man pointed towards the crack in his visor.

CRACK!!!

Without any warning, there was a gush of pink, red, and grey as the helmet exploded. The gore spattered the walls, the bed, and Joe with foul smelling froth.

He opened his eyes, and a relief descended over him, it was a physical weight, when he realised he was still in his bed.

He was sweating, and his head was pounding. He pulled the covers from his wet body, relishing the cool breeze on his clammy skin. His eyes were still struggling with the darkness, searching for the horrible vision in the shadows.

The room was empty; he could feel it, empty, dark, and desolate. He planted his fists into his eyes and rubbed them until a veritable firework display of colours and patterns lit up behind his eye lids. He wasn't aware he had already begun to cry.

In an instant, everything changed. The feeling of not being alone returned, even though he knew he was no longer dreaming. He couldn't see anything in the blacked-out room. 'Who *are* you? What do you want?' he sobbed into the darkness.

'You know who I am!'

The light flicked on. Joe wasn't entirely sure if he'd done it or if the owner of the disassociated voice had, but either way, it happened, and the light revealed the same man he'd just been dreaming about.

As before, he was stood next to his bed.

'You also know why I'm here, Joe,' the man said, but Joe could feel the words coming from inside his own head.

'Are you the man I killed on the road? Are you haunting me?'

The figure shook its head. 'No.'

'Then who are you?' he asked, not really wanting an answer but craving it all the same. 'It's not fucking Christmas, so you can't be here to show me all my mistakes.'

Not getting Joe's joke, the ghost spoke. 'I'm you, Joe!'

All he could do was stare at the tall, looming, leather-clad vision. He could see his own distorted reflection in the cracked visor of the helmet. His face was a distortion, one full mask of confusion. 'You're me?'

'Yes. I'm you.'

A terrified curiosity made his features screw, as he looked harder at the spectral visitor. 'How? Why would I haunt myself?'

CRACK!!!

At the sound, Joe pulled the bed covers tighter. 'What is that noise? Why do I keep hearing it?'

'It's your conscience,' the figure replied.

'My what?'

'Your conscience. Your brain is struggling to comprehend what's happened to you. It replays the noise because you can't deal with the horror it signifies.'

'Can't I just have a talking grasshopper and be done with it?' Joe asked.

The man didn't answer.

'So why did I feel relief when I killed Nixon, and the fox?' he continued. He wanted to be the dominant character in this ape-shit relationship, but he knew he'd already lost that privilege.

'Because you crave the sound, Joe. It's sending endorphins through your body. Your brain, and nervous system, you now rely on that noise to function normally.'

'I can't keep on killing foxes or dogs. I just can't.'

The man in the motorcycle helmet sat on the edge of the bed and leaned in towards him. Joe noticed that the mattress didn't move, it didn't register the weight of the man, it was as if there was no one there sitting with him.

He was still staring at his distorted reflection in the dark visor.

'No, you can't.'

With that, the vision flickered out. As he did, a bottle of Nytrodol tipped over of its own accord. He turned to look at it. Hate, and longing merged in his brain.

'You know what to do, Joe,' the disembodied voice whispered from all around him. 'So do it.'

Crack

37.

HE MUST HAVE fallen into a deep sleep, as the ever-joyful sounds of his loving family, returning from their day, gently roused him from his slumber.

Martin was shouting and stomping through the house. He concentrated on what was being said. 'Annmarie, you're a complete bitch. Why would you do that?'

~~~

'I don't know what you're talking about,' she replied, her tone indicative of the fact that she knew exactly what he was talking about and had done whatever he was accusing her of doing, either out of spite or malevolence. 'You've been mooning over her for ages. Everyone knows it. We all think it's pathetic, and people were laughing at you behind your back. At least now you know she doesn't want anything to do with you.'

'The whole fucking school knows.'

'MARTIN! Language,' Karen shouted in an authoritative, but ultimately bored, voice. Joe guessed she'd been hearing this argument all the way back from school.

'Mum, I can't go back to that school now. She's made a show of me in front of everyone. You're going to have to find me another school, Mum, a million miles away from this one … and from her.'

'CAN YOU ALL JUST SHUT THE FUCK UP DOWN THERE? I'M TRYING TO SLEEP,' Joe shouted as he walked down the stairs, tying his dressing gown around his waist. His face was flushed, his eyes were wild, his anger was building.

Karen looked up at him, her face was shocked. The kids, who had now continued their argument in the living room, were suddenly silent. 'Hi, honey, did you get any sl—'

'Martin, you whining little bastard. You're not moving school, don't be so fucking dramatic. And you, Annmarie, you heartless bitch. Why the fuck would you want to embarrass your little shit of a brother any more than he does himself? You make me sick to my stomach, the fucking pair of you.'

Both kids stopped fighting, their differences forgotten in the aftermath of their father's vile diatribe. Annmarie's face changed. She dropped her sardonic smile to favour a confused frown before finally bursting into tears. She ran off, up the stairs, pushing past Joe as she did.

Martin glared at him as he walked towards the front door.

'Joe, what's gotten into you? What was all that language about? In front of the kids too.'

Joe regarded her as if she were a piece of filth that had somehow grown arms and legs and walked into his house. 'You can fuck off too, you fat cunt. Maybe lose a few pounds, eh? No wonder we don't have sex anymore; it'd be like sticking my dick into a tub of butter.'

As she looked at him; horror, devastation, and, ultimately, humiliation passed over her features.

Joe glared at her, his eyes were red and rheumy, his skin ashen with scarlet blotches.

'Joe?' she whimpered in disbelief, her voice was soft and weak, barely audible.

'Oh, fuck off. I'm going back to bed,' he spat, his lips were nothing but white slashes at the bottom of his pale face. He stomped back up the stairs, leaving Karen standing in the living room holding two plastic bags filled with shopping.

She was staring up at him.

Real tears were spilling down her cheeks.

38.

IAN ENTERED THE wedding dress boutique to a chorus of bells from the front door. He turned to see where the cacophony was coming from, as it really was that loud. A sudden anxiety washed over him as he found himself in unfamiliar, and if the truth be known to him, terrifying surroundings. There were hundreds, his mind told him thousands, of white, lacy dresses hanging on rails. They were all hanging, waiting, mournfully for expectant women to come and allow them to make their day that much special.

He swallowed and ruffled his brow. He shrugged, attempting to shake off the shiver that was crawling up and down his spine, and entered into the shop.

He was on his lunch break and still wearing his full motorcycle police uniform, minus the helmet. The lady behind the counter looked up from what she was doing, and her face fell. 'Oh, good afternoon, officer. What can I do for you today?' she stammered, obviously intimidated by the uniform.

Ian cocked his head. 'What?' He checked himself and remembered the uniform, it did tend to have an effect on some people. 'Oh, no, this isn't police business. I'm Ian Locke. I'm here to pay for the wedding dress for Paula Ashton.'

The woman behind the counter visibly relaxed; she put her hand to her chest and smiled. 'Oh, right. Well, I am a little relieved that I'm not about to get arrested for anything,' she laughed.

Ian smiled a forced smile. He heard jokes like that a hundred times every single day on the job. 'Not unless you have something you need to tell me about?' he replied, knowing he'd crack that same reply again before his shift was over.

She leafed through a large book that was on the counter before her. After a few moments, she looked up, her face beaming. 'Oh yes,

Miss Ashton's dress. One of my most beautiful creations, even if I do say so myself.'

'Excellent. So, what do I owe?' he asked, reaching into an inside pocket of his biker jacket to retrieve his debit card. 'You do take card payments, don't you?'

'Yes, it's all anyone takes these days. Let me see now.' She picked up an order book and flicked through the pages. 'Right, Miss Ashton. That's seven hundred and eighty-five left to pay.'

Ian's eyes widened. 'What?' he spluttered, blinking back tears.

The woman looked up at him from the book. It was her turn to respond to the reaction she received more than once a day from future husbands paying for dresses. 'Seven hundred and eighty-five. The fifteen percent deposit has already been paid.'

Ian regarded the woman blankly, before shaking his head just a little. 'Seriously?' he asked, fighting to find the words. 'Nearly eight hundred pounds for a dress, she'll only ever wear once?'

'But remember all her life, Officer.' The woman smiled curtly, and professionally.

Ian swallowed and reached into his jacket for his wallet. He slid his debit card back inside and removed the credit card. He presented it to her with a faux smile. 'Do I get to see this eight-hundred-pound investment?' he asked, the genuine smile making a comeback.

The woman looked at him as if he had two heads. 'Of course not,' she snapped. 'Didn't you know it's bad luck for the groom to see the dress before the big day?'

'I know, but—'

As if on cue, a young girl pushed a mannequin from behind the large red curtain at the back of the shop. 'Here you go, Angela; I finished the Paula Ashton amendments. What do you think?'

At hearing Paula's name, Ian looked up, right at the mannequin. It was wearing the most beautiful gown he'd ever seen. It was low fronted, with diamanté and sequins covering the bodice. 'Wow,' he said, 'Is that Paula's?' His mouth hung open as he stared, agog. 'She's going to look fantastic in that.'

'Kirsty,' the woman hissed at the younger girl. 'Get that out of here right now. This is Mr Locke, Miss Ashton's groom.'

Kirsty turned her gaze from the owner to Ian; the genial smile on her face disappeared, as if it had never been there, replaced in an

Crack

instant with a look of terror. She pushed the mannequin back through the curtain as quickly as she could.

'I am so sorry, Mr Locke; you shouldn't have—'

'No, I shouldn't have, but I'm glad I did. At least now I know my money is going on something beautiful.' He finished paying, tapping his PIN into the machine on the counter, before putting the card back into his inside pocket. As he walked out, he turned and flashed her a smile. 'Anyway, it can be our little secret, OK?'

Angela looked at him and smiled back—although, to Ian, it looked more than a little forced. 'Our little secret,' she repeated as he walked out of the door, to another cacophony of jingles.

～～～

As soon as the door was closed, she slammed the large book in front of her and threw back the red curtain, rushing into the room behind it. 'Kirsty,' she snapped. 'What were you thinking wheeling that into the shop when I had a customer?'

The poor young assistant was almost in tears.

～～～

'Eight hundred quid for a dress? You're joking, right?'

He feel the tension on the other end of the line. 'Nope. But believe me, I'll blow you away when you see me in it.'

Ian believed her. 'For that amount of money, something else will be getting blown, that's for sure,' he laughed. 'Well, I'm going back on shift. Will you be home normal time tonight?'

'Not much happening around here today. I'll see if I can cut early and pick Sally up, then I'll make some dinner. Sound good?'

'You know it does.'

'Good, then I'll see you later. Stay safe, baby. I love you.'

'Love you too,' he said before hanging up and getting onto his bike. He was smiling as he fixed the straps under his chin.

39.

FEELING AS IF he'd aged at least one hundred years, Joe eased himself out of the bed. The room was pitch black, and his arms and legs felt like they were made from lead. His back screamed, and stabbed at him as he changed position, and a small, miserable moan escaped him. In the darkness, he shuffled over to the curtains, miraculously without stumbling into any potential obstacles and pulled them open. He was more than a little surprised when he saw it was as dark outside as it was inside. He stretched, easing his lower back muscles from their sleep memory, before finally putting both hands to his temples, attempting to ease the throb coming from inside. In the gloom, he looked at the bottle of pills on the side of the empty bed, and then at the clock.

Four minutes past eleven.

Where's Karen? he thought. *She's usually well in bed by now.*

He opened the bedroom door and popped his head out. The house was still and dark. He checked the kids' rooms; usually, there was some proximity of life coming from inside, no matter what the hour. Tonight, there was nothing. He shrugged and began to creep down the stairs. A note caught his eye that had been prominently placed on the small dining table in the kitchen, obviously to get his full attention.

'Pasta bake in fridge' was all it read.

He opened the refrigerator, closing his eyes, defending them from the bright light inside. The bowl had aluminium foil over it. He removed it and threw it into the microwave. He sat at the table, releasing a heavy sigh as he did. *Shit, that was some dream,* he thought. *Those tablets bring on the heavy shit; that's for sure.* The microwave beeped, and he removed the steaming meal.

Crack

As he began tucking into his late-night dinner, a noise like, someone moving about above him, caught his attention. Martin made his way down the stairs. He was wearing pyjama bottoms and an old t-shirt; he looked tired, but worse than that, he looked angry.

'Hey,' Joe greeted him with a smile. 'You want to share some pasta bake with your old man?' he asked, trying to sound chirpier than he felt.

Martin ignored him as opened the refrigerator, pulled out a bottle of lemonade, mumbled something that Joe didn't quite catch, and walked out again.

'Martin? Are you OK?' he asked, putting his fork down and looking at his son.

Martin turned and looked at him. 'I said go fuck yourself, Dad.' Then he turned away and continued back upstairs towards his bedroom.

This deflated Joe. *What did I do to deserve that?* he thought. Then he remembered the dream. He cringed. *No way. Please tell me I never called Karen a fat cunt.* He put his head in his hands. *And Annmarie a bitch? No, I didn't. It was one of the stupid dreams I've been having. It was. It has to have been. I'd never ...*

He pushed his, now unwanted, meal away from him and got up from the table, making his way into the living room. He turned the little lamp on. The illumination revealed Karen tucked up with a blanket and pillow on the couch. 'Karen? Karen, are you OK? Are you ... crying?' he whispered, not really believing what he was seeing.

'Go away,' she sobbed from beneath the blankets. 'Leave me alone.'

'Karen, it wasn't me; it was the pills. I thought I was dr—'

'Dreaming?' she asked, suddenly angry. She wriggled herself up into a sitting position on the couch. 'Dreaming, Joe? Don't you think I've had enough of your fucking dreaming lately? Don't you think it's hard enough bringing up two teenagers without the complication of a fifty-one-year-old baby in the mix?'

Joe felt as if he'd been slapped.

CRACK!!!

Oh, fuck no, not now ... please not now.

CRACK!!!

His eyes searched the room. They were looking in the shadows for the man in the motorcycle helmet. He shivered when he saw there was no one there.

CRACK!!!

'You're not even listening to me, are you?' Karen shouted, snapping Joe back into the room, and the argument. 'I've had it up to here, Joe,' she continued, indicating the top of her head. 'I can't live this way. I'm walking on fucking eggshells with you.'

CRACK!!!

He looked around again. This time, he saw it. The silhouette of the helmeted man was standing in the doorway. Despair ripped through him. He looked at Karen; she was still talking to him, or at him. She couldn't see the malicious silhouette in the doorway. *That's because he's not real*, Joe thought. *But if he's not here, then how is he beckoning me over?*

'Follow me, Joe. Let's go and get what you need.'

'You give me so little respect. I cook; I clean. I made you a fucking pasta bake even though you called me a fat cunt. Do you know how humiliating …? Are you even listening to me? Joe, Joe, where're you going?'

He'd turned away from her rant and made his way towards the front door. Acting on autopilot, he reached out and picked up his keys from the key-hang by the window. Karen went after him as the front door closed. She made her way onto the path just in time to watch his car reverse onto the road, and out of their street.

Crack

40.

HELMET MAN, AS Joe had now come to think of him, was in the passenger seat. His visor was pointing towards the windshield. He was completely motionless; so much so, he could have been a mannequin. Joe was in the driver's seat, still wearing his housecoat and pyjamas. Trying to negotiate the car's pedals in his slippers was not something he was accustomed to doing. 'Where're we going?' he asked. He felt silly talking to the man next to him, as he was obviously not there, yet he was, in his obvious delirium. He wasn't expecting an answer, and when the man spoke in a booming, bass-heavy voice, it made him jump.

'To your work site. There are things we need there.'

'I can't go on site. Rufus is working tonight.'

'You know his schedule. We can work around it.'

Joe gripped the steering wheel a little tighter. He had a burning question, but he didn't know if he wanted the answer to it. He asked it anyway. 'What do I need? What am I going to do?'

'You're going to do what you failed to do the other night.' Helmet man's head turned to face him. Joe saw his distorted reflection in the cracked plastic. He looked awful, horrific, like something from a creature feature horror film, twisted and hideous. 'If you do this, I *guarantee* you'll sleep like a baby. You're going to bring on the real crack.'

He looked at Helmet Man as if he were a child requiring reassurances from a responsible adult. The only movement was his head turning back towards the empty road ahead.

'You do?' Joe asked, the child now asking for sweets. 'You'll guarantee that I'll sleep?'

'Yes. You'll need overalls, gloves, boots, a cap, and one of the work vehicles.'

Joe turned and looked out towards the dark trees rushing past his car. 'I can get all that stuff from the stores; I've got the keys. But if Rufus sees one of the vehicles missing, he'll raise hell.'

'Are there not two vehicles in the garage for service?'

Joe nodded his head slowly. 'Yeah.'

'Then we'll take one of them. Rufus won't be checking in the garage. You never do.'

With a newly found enthusiasm, Joe continued towards work, a strange smile filled the entirety of his tired face.

~~~~

As they approached the site, Joe parked his car a little way down from the main gate, behind a copse of trees, where it wouldn't be noticed. He waited patiently, watching as his colleague, Rufus, drove past in one of the site vans. He knew he would be on his way to the other side of site and would be gone for the best part of an hour, giving him plenty of time to do what was needed, and to get what he required from the stores. When Rufus's lights disappeared into the darkness, he let himself in the gates with his keys. He headed straight to the stores and let himself in there too. He removed his night clothes and slipped on the overalls and other garb; he wasn't at all surprised to see Helmet Man in the room with him.

'How did you get in here?' he whispered.

The man didn't move; he just spoke. 'I didn't. I'm not here. I'm you, remember. I'm the projection Penny wanted you to develop, to help you deal with your situation. And here I am, helping.'

'Oh yeah,' he replied with a smile. 'That's right.'

CRACK!!!

'Will this help me get rid of that noise?'

'Yes.'

'Good, it's driving me fucking crazy.'

'More than you think.'

Joe looked at the man. He wasn't entirely sure if he that had been a joke, but as there was no humour in the current situation, he let it pass. 'What is that sound?' he asked as he buttoned up the overalls.

He turned, but Helmet Man was gone.

He slipped out of the stores, wearing the overalls, boots, and a cap, his night clothes in a plastic bag. There were gloves hanging out of his back pocket. He strolled over to the workshop and let himself in. Rooting around, he found the keys to one of the vans awaiting servicing. He opened the garage door and drove it out. Even though he knew Rufus would be over the other side of the site by now, well out of range, he still drove the van, with the headlights off, out of the main gate.

He noticed Helmet Man was back in the passenger seat, sitting in his customary position, facing out of the windshield.

'So, where to now?' he asked.

'You know where. You've been there before.'

Almost instantly he was freezing cold, despite the heater being on in the van. He thought he could feel the blood draining from his face. He wasn't naïve; he'd had an inkling about what he was going to have to do. But it wasn't until right now he realised he would actually be doing it.

'Tomorrow is Sunday,' Helmet Man spoke again. 'The site will be closed. The young kid, Michael will be working the day shift. You know he leaves the site unattended while he goes to fuck his girlfriend, don't you?'

'Yes,' Joe answered obediently.

'That's when we'll dispose of it. But first, we must go and do the deed. Take a left up here.'

Joe's world was wavering, he felt sick to his stomach, and he knew he shouldn't be driving in this state, but he found himself unable to disobey this passenger.

CRACK!!!

He cowered, and shuddered at the sound pierced his head. He could feel the pasta bake sloshing around in his stomach. It was heavy and greasy. He could even taste it as saliva began to well in his mouth.

The van pulled into the same street he'd visited the night before. The lighting was dim, and the silhouettes of the street girls were eerie in the low yellow light.

'That's her, over there by the lamp post. The same one from the other night. She'll think you got cold feet and drove home. She's the one.'

Joe felt every bone in his body stiffen. He was still cold, but he was also hot and sweaty.

CRACK!!!

He winced.

CRACK!!!

He swallowed hard. A bitter taste of bile and pasta settled in his mouth, rising from his churning stomach. He stifled the urge to gag, he thought if he threw up now, not only would it spoil his chances of that sleep, but he might never get it again. He would have given anything to be anywhere else but here right now.

CRACK!!!

CRACK!!!

CRACK!!!

'Do it, Joe. You know you have to. Bring on the real crack. Feed the fever you have. It's real, you know it is, and this is the only way you can get through it. Get her into the van, take her back to site. It'll come naturally. You'll *know* what to do.'

The desperation within him was devouring his soul, he could feel his damnation every time he looked to the streetlamp. He dragged his eyes away from his corruption and looked at the passenger seat. Once again wasn't surprised to see it was empty. His persuasive passenger was gone, nowhere to be seen.

With his pulse pounding in his ears and sweet adrenaline rushing through his body with every thump, he pulled the van over and

Crack

parked it beneath the same streetlight he was at the night before. It took a few moments for the young girl to notice him. She grinned, took a final drag at her cigarette before dropping it onto the floor, and making her way towards him. There was a knowing smile on her lips, and the little shimmy in her walk, spoke of a little more confidence than the last time they met. His window was already down by the time she got there, and brazenly, she leaned into it. Joe could once again smell the cacophony of odours from her—mint from her chewing gum, sweat from her clothes, all covered up by cheap perfume, and, of course, alcohol and cigarettes.

Somehow it didn't seem as bad as last time.

He could also smell shame, but he didn't know if was coming from him or her.

'Hey, Mr Chicken. Not going to run tonight? You must have liked what you saw, eh?' Her voice was young *and* ancient at the same time. It was a sad sound. She was still young, just old before her time.

'Take her, Joe,' Helmet Man said in his head. 'She won't be missed any time soon.'

Joe looked her up and down, trying his best to stop the terror that was consuming him from registering on his face. He knew he wasn't doing a good job. She saw his fear, it made her smile.

With more than a little bravado, almost as if she had control of the situation, she continued. 'Hey, cutie, you don't have to look so scared, you know. I won't bite, unless you pay extra for it of course.' She laughed at her own, old joke.

'D-do you ... want to get in?' he stammered. All the saliva in his mouth had dried up, and he felt like he was speaking through a mouthful of glue.

The girl shrugged. 'Why not? By the looks of things, you're more scared of me than I am of you.' She looked back towards the streetlamp, Joe thought she was searching for someone who wasn't there. She gave up trying to find them after a few moments, before struggling on her ridiculous high heels, around to the passenger seat, and climbed in.

Joe tried to smile at her—he wanted to put her at ease—but if anything, the failed smile looked like an evil grin, and he watched her brow ruffle. Before she could change her mind about getting in, he put the van into gear and drove off slowly. He fought every impulse in his body that wanted to screech the wheels and get away from this seedy street as soon as he could. He knew that would just attract attention to himself and to his presence here.

Once clear of the street, he put his foot down, and the van sped up.

'Whoa, slow down, mister. You don't want to get pulled over for speeding, do you? Not with me in the passenger seat, doing this ...'

Joe looked into her lap as she lifted up her short skirt, revealing a pair of purple panties that complimented her bruised and pale thighs. He swallowed hard with a gulp, wiped at the sweat that was building beneath his cap, and turned back towards the road ahead.

She was laughing as she pulled her skirt back down. 'I know a place, it's just a little further up here on the right. We'll have total privacy. So, what will it be? A blow job is thirty-five; full sex is seventy-five. I don't do anal, and I'll only do you, none of your friends, OK? I'm expected back within the hour. If I'm not, people will know. You OK with all of that?'

He looked at her. She was blurring in and out of focus as his eyes were attacked with stinging sweat dripping into them. He wiped his face again. 'Erm, yeah. That's all good. I mean, it'll do. Just the blow job for now,' he stuttered, not really knowing how this worked.

He looked into the rear-view mirror. Helmet Man there. His oversized head nodding, slowly. He turned away, catching another glimpse of his own face in the curved reflection of the cracked visor. He didn't like what he saw.

The fucking hunchback of Notre Dame, he thought.

It wasn't a funny thought.

The girl turned with him, looking into the back seat. 'There best not be anyone hiding back there,' she warned. 'I've heard stories of girls being raped by two, sometimes three men who'd been hiding in the back of the cars.'

'There's no one there,' he assured her, wishing it was true, as Helmet Man continued to sit stoically back there.

She looked again into the darkness of the back seat. Joe could have sworn she looked right at his helmeted friend. 'OK then,' she said, looking out of the window as if she was searching again. This time she saw what she was looking for and pointed to it. 'Pull over here, will you? It's just this little turn off on your right.'

Joe saw the small side road that led off into the woods. 'No, not here, I know a better place. It's only a little bit further on.'

The girl looked at him, the fear in her eyes was back, as she realised the power paradigm was shifting. 'No, pull in here or I bail. You don't need to worry, no one's gonna see us. It's Saturday night and everyone's in town. No one's going to pay for it if they don't have to. It won't get busy till gone two. Till then, it'll be just you and me.'

'OK. Whatever you say, let's go.'

Without indicating, as there was no other traffic on the road, he pulled into a small lane he'd never noticed before. There were trees on one side of the road, and a large dark wall on the other.

'If you pull in just about … here. There's a little outlet you can get the van into. We can go in there and be totally alone, in our own little world.'

As Joe turned, he felt a hand on his crotch. 'Oh, an eager little beaver, aren't we?' She giggled as her hand caressed him.

He looked down at what she was doing and was surprised to see a large bulge in the front of his overalls.

'Money first, though,' she said with a little smile.

'Oh, yeah. Right. My wallet's in the back.' He stopped the van in a small layby that looked like it had been made by vehicles either doing what he was doing, or something very similar.

He clicked the brake in place and leaned over into the back of the cab to give the illusion of getting his wallet. His eyes were closed as he did so. So much self-doubt overcame him, and he questioned himself, if he could really do this.

She was just too young.

'You *can* do this,' came the instant reply, and then, as if on cue … 'and you *will.*'

CRACK!!!

'Do it. Hit her with the crow bar. One strike on the bridge of the nose will knock her out. She won't suffer. She is a nothing but a whore, no one will miss her. She fellates strangers for money, Joe.

She'd have no problem sharing all that disease she has on her face with you. Then you'd pass that on to Karen, who would then pass it on to the children as she kisses them off to school. Is that what you want? Disease-ridden children? If she could, this wretch would slit your throat and run off with your wallet without a second thought. Do it, Joe … HIT HER NOW!'

'OK, I'll fucking do it,' he shouted angrily, his voice filling the cab of the van.

'Do what?' the girl asked, as she removed her chewing gum and flicked it out of her wound down window.

'Do what, asshole?' she asked.

Joe flicked the switch on the dash that locked all the doors.

'Hey,' she shouted grabbing at her handle. 'What the fuck are you doing?'

'This,' he said, and produced the heavy crowbar bar from the darkness.

CRACK!!!

Her eyes widened as they fell upon the weapon. Suddenly she looked every inch the child she truly was. He swung the thick, curved bar of heavy metal, utilizing the limited space inside the vehicle. It struck her on the temple as she was turning, pulling on the handles of her door.

She tried to scream, to lean her head out of her window, but the dull thud of the rod hitting her skull put paid to all her shouts. It stole her voice, and her breath at the same time. The crack was louder than he thought it might have been. It wasn't the right sound to satisfy his lust, or his need, and he found himself hitting her again.

Her head flopped to the side and banged against the window. Her body slid down towards the footwell she flopped, her arms and legs helpless, unable to move of their own accord.

With a stoic chuff, Helmet Man's voice was back in his head. 'Good, now do what you have to do, Joe. You've done it before; you can do it again.'

CRACK!!!

Crack

'But this is a human. A living, breathing person. She's not a fucking fox,' he hissed.

'That doesn't matter. One head is as good as another. They all go...'

CRACK!!!

A deep panic blossomed within him as he stared at the unconscious body crumpled in the passenger seat; it was accompanied by a deep revulsion. He couldn't believe what he'd just done, what he was considering doing, what he was becoming. 'Can't I just, I don't know, dump her somewhere and go find a dog?' He smiled as if it might appease someone, or something, perhaps a certain person who wears a motorcycle helmet. 'Yeah, that'll do it. A large dog, larger than Nixon—'

CRACK!!!

CRACK!!!

He gagged both times. Shivers flashed up and down his arms, and his skin tightened all over his body. As he looked at the unconscious girl, he could taste the pasta bake again, he could feel it shifting around his stomach. 'Yeah, a massive dog with a huge head. A St. Bernard, or a Rottweiler. That'll get me through a few days, won't it?' He corrected his position in the van, nodding rapidly, readying himself to drive off. 'I'll do that. I'll just put money in her pocket ... here.' He opened the glove compartment and fished around for his wallet.

CRACK!!!

'That won't do, and you know it won't. The dog and the foxes were merely snacks. You need to feed this Joe. It needs a meal. She is your main course.'

He looked at her, his eyes hating what he was seeing. The pasta bake shifted again, and he suddenly had the urge to use the toilet.

'Besides, she's seen you now. She's seen the van. She'll tell everyone. You'll lose everything. Your job, your family, your reputation. Most of all, Joe, you'll lose your freedom. They'll call you a sex pest. A dirty, curb crawling pervert. Your children will disown you, they will be bullied, beaten. Their life will be ruined, even before it starts. Just do it. You have to. Sooner or later, you need to feed it Joe. Do it now and get it over with …'

CRACK!!!

He opened the door and threw himself out of the van and bent, almost double, for a few moments. His mouth open and his stomach tensing. The urge to vomit was strong, but nothing was forthcoming as he dry-retched. After a few moments, it passed, he wiped his mouth, and made his way to the passenger side and hefted the unconscious girl onto the dirt of the layby.

'Good, good …' Helmet Man soothed. He sounded like an evil Emperor chiding a subordinate into doing something unspeakable, a long time ago in a galaxy far, far away. 'You're doing great here.'

Joe looked into the backseat and glared at Helmet Man, wishing he would just fuck off.

CRACK!!!

He dragged her small, battered body to the front of the van, marvelling at just how heavy she was. She was a skinny little thing but must have weighed double what Nixon did. As he lay her in the dirt at the side of the road, he stepped back to catch his breath. He watched her chest rise and fall in slow motion. The only thought in his head was him wondering what the fuck he was going to do now.

'Finish it, Joe. Tonight, you'll sleep like a baby.'

CRACK!!!

'Will that fucking sound go away?' he spat. He didn't know if he spoke that out loud or if he thought it. Either way, he was past caring now.

'If you want it to, it will.'

'I do want it to.'

'Then it will, but you complete this task first.'

Joe rubbed the tips of this thumbs over his fingers as he looked at the girl. He then bent down, he slid his gloved hands beneath her armpits and heaved her into the layby at the side of the road. Once she was there, he stood away and rubbed his back.

'Her head needs to be on the road,' Helmet Man instructed from inside the van.

Joe glared at him. 'Do you want to get out here and give me a hand?' he snapped.

Helmet Man didn't move, that was his response.

'Yeah, I thought so. I'm not stupid, you know.' He repositioned her head, so it rested on the packed dirt of the track while the rest of her body lay in the ditch at the side.

CRACK!!!

He snapped his head back when the sound ricocheted around his skull, half expecting to see someone lurking in the bushes, watching what he was doing. With his heart thumping in his throat, he scanned his surroundings, but of course there was no one there. He returned his attentions back towards the girl. He knew she wasn't dead, but he wished deeply she was. He wished he'd killed her with the two blows to her head. It might have made what he now knew needed to be done easier somehow. Maybe it would have made him feel better about it, making the task just a little bit simpler.

CRACK!!!

Fat tears began to plunge from his eyes. They were for himself, for what he now amounted to, but they were also for this pathetic little thing lying, beaten, moaning on the road. They were for the dreams and the aspirations he was about to remove from her for the sake of his own sanity and—yes, he had to admit—his own gratification.

'You'll be erasing one more piece of filth from the world, Joe. Just think about the depravity she's had to put up with in her short life. You'll be doing this wretch a favour. Her *and* yourself. Think of the benefits of what you are about to do. She won't have to suck fat, dirty old married men's cocks anymore. There'll be no more wiping twelve different people's cum from between her legs when she gets home at night. Just think of that. Then think about all the peaceful sleep you'll be getting too. You've got a wife, and kids, who love you, rely on you. They need the best *you* that you can offer them. You can't function correctly with this—'

CRACK!!!

Joe glanced into the cab, his gaze falling on the silhouette of Helmet Man in the passenger seat. He took in a deep breath, filling his lungs with the cold, fresh night air before making his way to the front of the van. He paused for a moment, looking back at the girl lying unconscious in the damp soil, just once, then shaking his head, he climbed into the warm cabin. He paused one more time before gunning the engine and flicking on the headlights. There was another moment of self-doubt, another moment of hesitation as he realised what he was doing. The girl was lying on the road, illuminated and stark in the whites of the van's headlights. Her head was resting on the compacted earth, not too far away from the front wheels. She was facing him, her eyes were closed, but he had a strange idea she could see him, that she knew, somewhere deep down inside her, what he was about to do.

He didn't *have* to do this, did he?

CRACK!!!

He knew the answer before the thought was even fully formed. It was yes; *yes*, he did have to do this. There was no turning back now.

He looked at Helmet Man, and an uncomfortable smile broke on his face. He nodded. A calm descended over him, it began in his head, and floated down, through his entire body. He was ready. 'Let's do this,' he half whispered into the empty cab. Helmet Man was gone. Joe didn't mind; he didn't need him now.

He slipped the stick into first gear, caught the bite on the clutch, and gently touched the accelerator. He released the brake ever so

Crack

slowly. He didn't want to lurch forward; he knew whatever was about to happen, it needed to happen slowly.

The van edged forward, inching closer to the girl's head. The headlights were picking up reflections from the bushes on either side of the dirt road. An audience of dogs and foxes maybe? A part of him hoped so; he liked the irony of it.

Suddenly, he couldn't see it anymore. He laughed, just a little. *I can't see it anymore.* When had *she* turned into an *it*? It was as though the girl had ceased to be human and had morphed into something for him to use for his own twisted devices.

The van inched forwards again, just a little faster when he put a little more pressure on the pedal. The wheels met their expected resistance, just that little bit quicker. He knew exactly what it was, he knew exactly what he was doing. *nothing will ever be the same, Joe.* He didn't know if it was him thinking that, or Helmet Man talking to him. He no longer cared, as he couldn't tell the difference anyway. Closing his eyes and holding his breath, he pushed his foot and the engine revved. The revs built up, but only for a moment. The van caught the bite of the gears again, he muttered a little prayer to … someone—he didn't know who— then he let it go. A few breathless moments later and he felt the familiar bump of the shock absorbers.

It was bigger than the recent ones. It was more akin to—

'To your first time, Joe? Out there, on the main road?'

Again, he didn't know who was in his head; he didn't care. In the darkness, behind his closed eyes, he saw the thick rubber of the van's tyres tearing into her flesh, ripping it, pulling her nose off her face. Then, the wheel hitching on top of her skull, the weight of the chassis causing the cranium to swell with pressure. He saw her eyes popping from their sockets, the pressure mounting until it all got too great and—

And then he heard it.

CRACK!!!

It was louder, it was fresher, wetter than the other times. It was dense, thick, and it was disgusting. There was a real weight behind it, as if the other three had all been poor imitations of it. The sound was everything he'd dreamed it to be, everything he needed. He could see the pop of the contents of the head splashing underneath his van. The visualisation of the spray of gore washing over the watching trees, was real to him. The fresh, warm, matter steaming as it cooled in the cold air. Grey mixing with the red, and the whites. A tsunami of euphoria picked him up, enveloped him, carried him down a river of blessed *nothingness*. The weight from his shoulders, from his neck, from his back, from every single bone in his body was gone, washed away with the thick, wet surge.

The only pressure he was feeling now was inside his trousers, but it wasn't long before that was released too. His orgasm was in perfect synchronisation with the demise of the young girl.

He yelled in delight, in horror, in relief. Every feeling he could ever express gushed at once, in equal measures.

After a few glorious, breathless moments, the numbness began to recede, leaving a heavy sensation of pins and needles up and down, through his entire body.

When he could, when his head had stopped reeling, when his vision was back to a semblance of normal, he engaged the gears, and drove out of the dark lane and back along the road.

Still floating in the most intense out-of-body-experience he could have ever imagined; he was extra careful to keep to the speed limits. The chances of being pulled over at this time of night were practically none, but the last thing he wanted now was to be caught with gore all over the front, and the underneath of the van.

With the headless body of the poor girl left behind on the dirt road almost forgotten in his euphoric state, he continued until he was back, safe within the confines of the construction site. He waited, patiently scanning for any sign of Rufus. He had a whole new outlook on life now, and he didn't think *anything* could change his mood at that precise moment.

His headlights were off and noticed the first signs of rain falling onto his windshield. Absently, he flicked on his wipers and smiled as the dirty smudges streaked over the glass.

Eventually, he saw lights in the distance. They were travelling in the opposite direction. He grinned. Rufus was on the move, and he had his window of opportunity. With the buzz still bouncing through his head, and all around his body, he opened the gates, and drove the van back into the garage. He parked it over the inspection pit, locked the door, and removed a hose.

The front, and the underneath, was a bloody, pulpy mess. The thicker gore and gristle came away with ease as he pointed the high-pressure hose and sprayed. After he swilled it all down into the industrial drain, he locked up the shop and made his way off site, remembering to watch for Rufus on his rounds. He returned to his own car and drove home.

He looked at the clock on the dash. He chuffed a little when he saw that it wasn't even three o'clock yet. He turned his radio on and smiled at the song. A band called D-Ream were letting him know that things could only get better!

He thought it could be the universe talking to him, letting him know he was on an upward trajectory.

He began to whistle and beat his fingers on the steering wheel along with the beat.

When he arrived home, the house was in complete darkness. He went into the living room to check on Karen, who was fast asleep on the couch. He kissed her lightly on the head before climbing the stairs. He slipped into his empty bed and was sound asleep almost as soon as his head touched the pillow.

41.

HE OPENED HIS eyes. He waited for the aches and the pains of the morning to kick in. He waited for the black cloud, the black dog to fog his mind, and ruin his very existence, but they were not forthcoming. He sat up and swung his legs out of the bed. He stretched, filling his lungs with the fresh air of the new day.

He felt fantastic.

He caught his reflection in the mirror in the bathroom. He noticed, with a smile, there were no black rings around his eyes. They looked fresh, alive, more than they'd done in weeks—hell, maybe even years. His skin wasn't blotchy, but there looked to be a healthy glow to it.

A waft of morning smells tickled his nose—bacon and eggs. A traditional Sunday morning breakfast when he wasn't working. It made his mouth water, and his stomach rumble.

As he walked into the kitchen, tying the belt on his housecoat, everyone turned, as one, to look at him. Once he knew he had their undivided attention, he smiled, it was a small sheepish smile.

'Please, listen everyone, I've got something I need to say. I'm so sorry for what happened yesterday. You know I haven't been myself, and I don't blame any of you for being angry with me. In my defence, I'd taken quite a few of those sleeping pills, and they kind of knock me loopy. I actually thought I was in the middle of a dream or a horrible nightmare, or something. There's no way I feel like that towards any of you. You're my family, for Christ's sake, and I love you.'

'You did say some horrible things, Dad,' Annmarie said, a small, sad smile on her lips.

The sadness he'd caused almost broke his heart. 'I know, baby, but you have to know I love you. If I'd have been myself, I would never have thought those things, never mind said them. You have to know that.'

Everyone looked at everyone else.

Joe put his arms out towards them. 'Come here, will you? I'm so sorry.'

The whole family fell into his arms, and he hugged them all as one. 'I'm so sorry. I love you all so much.'

With him now forgiven, they all settled down into normality, enjoying their breakfast together before the kids went out and Joe and Karen enjoyed a nice day in each other's company.

~~~

The rotting, decapitated body of the young prostitute lay in the mud on a seedy dirt road. While Joe tucked into his sausages, insects, and other more ravenous wildlife were tucking into what was left of her.

The thought of her never even crossed his mind.

42.

LATE THAT NIGHT, Joe woke up as he'd planned. He checked on Karen. She was snoring lightly on her side of the bed. He got up and made his way down to the garage. Once inside, he flicked on the light and opened the trunk of his car. The overalls and gloves he'd used the night before were still inside, in black plastic bags.

He bit the inside of his cheek as he looked at them. Knowing what was inside them, and what he'd done, aroused a dichotomy within him. His mouth watered as a small shiver ran down his spine as he recalled his actions, the cold callousness of what he'd done, and how he'd done it sickened him, but then a smile broke on his lips as he remembered the sound and the pure euphoria when the deed was done.

He reached in and grabbed the bag. Holding it out in front of him as if was a dirty nappy and carried it to the garden. He opened the small incinerator bin he used for burning leaves, wood, and sensitive papers, and scooped out half of the moist contents and placed the bag inside. He then replaced what he'd taken out, dumping it on the top of his stash.

He made a mental note to have a small garden fire sometime later that day.

His eyes scanned the darkness of the garden, paying extra attention to the shadows, of which there were many. He half-expected to see the silhouette of Helmet Man lurking somewhere in the bushes, maybe with a female friend, and a dog and two foxes in tow.

The shadows were devoid of the dead.

He took in a lungful of the moist air, held it for a second, or two, before letting it all go, watching his breath steam up as it left his mouth. He hoped he'd just exhumed the remains of the last few awful weeks, not to mention the terrible deed he'd had to do to rid himself of the noise.

He turned the lights off in the garage and made his way back to bed, where, with his arm wrapped around Karen, he slept the sleep of the just.

43.

THE WHOLE OF the next day was like floating through a fluffy dream. It was Monday, and the kids were out early to school. It was his day off, and on that rarest of occasions, Karen's day off coincided with it. They spent a full lazy day together. The only reason they bothered to get out of their pyjamas was to make love.

And to both of their surprise, it happened twice. They hadn't done that since they had been in Lanzarote before Annmarie was born.

They ate, laughed, snoozed, and watched TV together. The kids came home from school, and then went their separate ways. Joe helped Karen to make dinner, which they ate as a family.

Joe was of the opinion that life couldn't get much better than this.

Crack

44.

'IT LOOKS LIKE we've picked up a murder,' a uniformed policeman quipped as Paula made her way through the mud of the dirt track they were on.

'No shit, Officer. Do you think that might be why they called us?' She rolled her eyes but continued her smile towards the rookie. 'Is this your first one?'

The younger man stood up straight, looking proud of himself. 'Yes, ma'am.'

'You nervous?'

The man's shoulders fell a little at the question, as if involving himself in a conspiracy. 'Yeah, a little,' he admitted.

'You want some advice?'

'Yes, please.'

'Don't fuck up. If you can remember that you'll do OK. Now, can you tell me how many people have been through here since the discovery?'

'There's the guy who called it in, with his dog. Me, I was first responder, and Officer Harvey, as my superior. Detective Ambrose is here, and he allowed the forensic guys to set up, but no one else has been through.'

'Good work. No one else except me, Ambrose, and the CSI guys are allowed into the scene. You got that? You're doing a good job, just don't be too eager, OK?'

The rookie policeman smiled another nervous smile. 'Sure, Detective.'

Wishing that she had worn her older shoes—because she was just about to ruin these new ones in the mud—she made her way over to the CSI tent in the cordoned off area; her partner, Detective Ambrose, was already there.

'So, what have we got?'

'A guy walking his dog this morning got concerned when the dog picked something up off the road and began eating it. He noticed chewing gum in the dog's fur and went over to try to get it out. That's when he saw what the dog was eating. It was this …' He pulled open a flap, allowing her into the small tent. 'I know you've got a good stomach, Paula, but steel yourself for this one, OK?'

She pulled a face. 'Really, on a Monday morning?'

He nodded, there was little humour in his face, or indeed in anything about him today. 'Really!'

As she squeezed through the flap into the gloom of the tent, she noticed the sheet on the floor covering what she presumed was the body. She took note of its location to the road, noticing it was in an odd position. Most of the torso was in the layby rather than on the road itself. Kneeling on the tarpaulin, she pulled the cover away slowly. She took an involuntary intake breath. The body was still intact, but the head was gone. It hadn't been removed; it had been ripped, or torn from the body and, by the looks of the mess all around her, completely shattered.

Paula stood up and dusted off her trousers. She noticed the drying blood that was covering a lot of the foliage within the tent. Small tags were next to as many as they could put markings on.

'Only a small amount of the ground seems to have been disturbed, meaning she mustn't have put up much of a struggle. She might have been unconscious or already dead prior to being placed here. Maybe it was some sort of kinky game she'd been playing.'

'Why is everything some sort of kinky game to you?' she asked, her small grin out of place in the grim tent.

'Because my whole life is a kinky game, Detective. You want to take me in?' He offered his hands out to her so she could put handcuffs on them.

Paula turned away, laughing but still investigating the ground around the body. A small amount of disturbed earth grabbed her attention. 'I'd say she's been dragged from over here.'

Alan Ambrose turned to look towards the track of dirt she was pointing to.

'Are there any footprints?' she asked, looking all around.

Crack

'Nope, it rained pretty heavy last night, and it's swilled the whole area. We've filtered out the dog walker's prints, the officers, and the SOTC guys too. We have a partial tyre print, but I'm not sure it's much to go on.'

'Well ...' she said, wiping her muddy, gloved hands together. 'It looks like we've picked ourselves up a murder,' she quipped, mimicking the officer who let her into the tent. 'Looking at her clothing, I'd say she's a prostitute. If that's the case, we're not going to get a lot of cooperation from that direction.'

'There's no identification on the body either, so we don't know who she is. We'll have to take fingerprints as it's not like we can do dental, is it?' he laughed. 'It'll be tough finding out what patch she works. There's quite a few around this area.' Ambrose looked out of the tent, at the greenery and trees that were abound. 'There's not even anywhere to canvas. I think she's going to be a Jane Doe for a while.'

'Unless we get lucky and the killer strikes again,' Paula added, absent-mindedly.

Ambrose looked at her and laughed. 'Detective Ashton, you're one cold bitch. You do know that don't you?'

She smiled at her partner as she walked away, removing her soiled rubber gloves. 'Why do you think I'm so good at my job?' She tipped him a sassy wink before exiting the tent.

45.

JOE WAS WIDE awake, just as he should have been, given he was sat in his porta cabin in work. He was awake but not mentally aware. He'd had a strange feeling all day, and he had been finding it difficult to concentrate. It was worse now he was alone at work, in the dead of night. Sometimes, between the hours of two and four, he would feel like he was the only person alive in the whole world, just him and the wildlife.

He also thought that the wildlife hated him.

The small TV was on, and its flickering picture was illuminating the darkened room with a rerun of the same stupid game show that seemed to be on constantly these days. He was beginning to think the show was haunting him. That thought sent freezing fingers down his spine. He shook his head attempting to rid himself of the nasty feeling. His glassy, empty gaze slid over the boring TV show and focused—if you could call it focusing—on the wall behind the small screen. A roar of laughter interrupted his reverie, and he shifted his attention back to the screen, just for the merest of seconds, before shifting again. This time he focused on the small window, on the fitting, oppressive darkness beyond.

A small quip he'd heard once—but had obviously meant something to him because he'd stored it, in his subconscious, for times like these—ran through his head. He'd thought it was funny at the time, but now it seemed like something else that had come back to haunt him. 'I'm only paranoid because everyone hates me,' he mumbled into the dark abyss beyond the mirror.

A dour smile spread across his face.

It had been a week since he'd done what he did.

Within that week, he'd slept like a king. He'd made love to his wife; he'd built bridges with his children—after the drug induced faux pas. It had been a fantastic week, probably one of the best he could remember in recent history, or at least since the- what did the therapist call it- the incident?

Life had been peachy.

Until yesterday.

Yesterday when he'd gotten home from his remarkably uneventful shift, he'd been tired but that was nothing new from a gruelling shift. The instant he entered his empty refuge, an ugly, dark fog had descended over him.

His stomach instantly began to churn, and a familiar feeling reared its ugly head. It was an unwelcome sensation, and he feared what it meant.

There was someone, or something, watching him.

Whatever it was, it was wrong. It persisted when he climbed into bed in the darkened room.

It nagged like a parody of a mother-in-law in his mind. The constant murk continued, impeding him from reaching anything remotely like relaxation.

All he could do was lie on his bed, his eyes wide and his body shaking.

Just like old times. The thought was not welcome.

Then the tendrils of guilt snuck into him.

Guilt for the girl.

She may have only been a prostitute to him, someone to use and dispose of for money, but she'd been the whole world to someone else, even if only for a short time. She'd been someone's daughter, and that someone could be worrying about her right now, hoping she was OK, and that she would come home soon. The fact that she would never go home, ever again, and that it was all *his* doing, ate at him. People could be worrying about the kind of life she was leading, worrying about the people she was associating with. Worrying if she was alive or if she was dead. Not knowing she was lying, discarded and headless, on a filthy, isolated layby, exposed to the elements and everything else.

How could they know?

These thoughts forced their way into his brain. They were forcing anything that resembled nice, or restful deliberations from getting in, keeping them at more than arm's length from him.

How could he have done such a - despicable was the only word he could think of even though it fell short by at least a million miles, thing to another human being? How could he have had the courage to pick up a prostitute, never mind doing it with the sole intent of killing her in such a hideous way?

These thoughts had blocked his sleep.

Anytime there was a noise in the house, a car pulled past, or even a siren from the main road blaring its way through town, he was up, convinced it was the police coming to kick down his door and drag him off to who-knows-where for the murders of a dog, two foxes, and a prostitute.

Even now, as he sat at his desk in the desolate porta cabin, these thoughts vexed him. He was tired, paranoid, pissed off, and more than half crazy. His eyes drifted back to the TV, and the bland images flashed over his worried face, hypnotising him.

CRACK!!!

He couldn't believe what he was hearing. He felt his bowels shift uncomfortably, and suddenly he needed to urinate, so bad that he thought it might be seeping out. His head began to pound, inviting in the mother of all headaches who'd been lurking in his peripheral all day.

He was instantly wet from head to toe.

He knew exactly what the noise was.

Oh, please no, he pleaded as he stood, to make his way towards the small bathroom at the back of the cabin. He tried to go, but despite his eagerness, not a drop would drip from his penis. His head dropped onto his chest as he gave up any hope of peeing.

He'd hoped his dirty deed of a few days ago had cured him of this *fucking noise*; it had barely been a week.

CRACK!!!

He washed his hands and, not really wanting to, but he made his way to the window in the main cabin. His reflection made him look like he was wearing a Halloween mask, one that looked like the one worn in the film about the murderer on Halloween all those years

Crack

ago. The name of the movie eluded him right now. He had to turn the lights off for the dark mirror to offer him what he wanted, or didn't want, in truth he had no idea why he was even looking out of this window. After a few moments, his eyesight adjusted, and he looked out onto the empty, lonely building site. There was no one around for miles, and the night was still and quiet.

CRACK!!!

He spun, sweeping his gaze across the dark room. Thankfully, it was still empty. With his breath short and his breathing shallow, he flicked the light back. The darkness was beginning to eat into his sanity. *Or what's left of it,* he thought. As his eyes adjusted to the artificial light from the halogen strip bulbs, he felt the presence of someone else in the room. Someone he had come to hate, to loathe with every last remaining fibre of whatever good was still left within him.

Standing next to him in his reflection was his old friend.
Helmet Man!

CRACK!!!

The dark figure's cracked visor faced him. It cocked its head to one side slightly, then it spoke. 'You know what you have to do, don't you, Joe? You know it's the only way you're going to get any respite.'

Joe backed away from the window. Even though he knew this persona was just a product of his imagination, and therefore there was nowhere he could run to get away from it, he had to try. 'I can't,' he hissed. 'I just can't. I'm not a killer.'

Joe could sense a smile beneath the dark visor.

'It's too late for regrets, Joe. You've set yourself off on this path, and now you need to see it through. It's got nothing to do with killing. It's simply a way for you to exorcise this particular demon stuck in your head,' Helmet Man spoke directly into his head.

Joe covered his ears and flopped down onto a chair by the wall. The silver illumination from the TV was casting crazy shadows over his grief-stricken face.

'I can't.'
'But you will.'
'I won't. I can't.'

There was a brief pause before Helmet Man spoke again. 'OK, but when the sound comes again, and it will, I might not be here to guide you through it.'

Then, as if on cue …

CRACK!!!

'Can't you just leave me alone?' he sobbed as clear mucus poured from his nostrils, mixing with the sweat beading on his upper lip. 'Please … just go … fuck off and take that god-awful noise with you.'

Helmet Man nodded slowly. 'Oh, I can go, that's not a problem, but the noise isn't going anywhere. It will remain, and it will be as loud, as grating, and as horrific as it has always been.'

'But why? Haven't I suffered enough?'

'It's not about why, Joe, and it's definitely not about suffering. It just *is*. That's the be all, and end all of it.'

'I'm a good man.' Joe's voice broke halfway through this cry, it rose to as high a pitch he thought he had ever gone. It was pathetic. 'Or at least I was,' he whispered, mostly to himself.

Helmet Man shook his head slowly. 'No one is refuting that. It's not about being good or bad. Think of yourself as a good man if it helps. A good man with needs.'

CRACK!!!

Joe sniffed. His tears were openely falling down his cheeks as Helmet Man leaned in close. The man had no smell he could discern. *Of course, he hasn't, he's not there, he doesn't exist,* Joe thought, his brain scrambling to make sense of this nightmare. He caught his reflection in the cracked visor and wished he hadn't.

'You know what you need to do.' The ghost was speaking to him as if he were a naughty child. 'There'll be no rest until it's done.' The last part was spoken softly, as if soothing a child.

Crack

Joe's sobbing was out of his control as he fell from the chair onto his knees, the porta cabin rocking slightly as he did. He put his head in his hands as his shoulders and chest heaved in perfect rhythm with his sobs.

'I don't want to kill. Not again.'

'Don't think of it as killing. Think of it as putting yourself out of your misery and doing their wretched lives a justice in the meantime. Think about that. Look at the horrible, desperate way they live. What they do, how they debase themselves for the shit they put into their bodies.' Helmet Man's voice was little more than an angry hiss, the buzz of a disturbed wasp. 'They're more like animals than humans. You're doing them a favour. They're scum, Joe. No longer human.'

So am I, he thought.

'Animals, Joe. Nothing more than rats, scurrying and scratching over each other to grasp their next fix. Uncaring about anything, or anyone else other than themselves.'

So am I!

This thought was abhorrent to him. It was so vile that, in his own good conscience, he couldn't bring himself to vocalise it. 'I can't,' was all he was able to stutter between his sobs. 'I won't.'

'You can, and you will.' Helmet Man leaned in closer. His voice was now akin to a growl.

Without any prompting, the keys to one of the vans fell from the hook they had been hanging on. The noise they made hitting the floor was minimal, yet it captured Joe's full attention.

He stared at them, seeing three sets through his wet eyes.

CRACK!!!

More tears poured down his haggard face.

CRACK!!!

A shaking claw began to edge towards the fallen keys. It took him a moment to realise it was his own hand. It had a life of its own, like a spider with five legs crawling towards its goal.

CRACK!!!

Reaching into his pocket with his other hand, he found a Nytrodol bottle resting inside. Helmet Man's voice filled his head. 'Get into the van and drive, Joe. Do it … NOW!'

CRACK!!!

'DO IT NOW!'
He did it!

Crack

46.

JOE PULLED THE van over to the curb. The air in the cab was close, and he was struggling to breath normally. He could smell his own stink, a heady mixture of sweat, adrenaline, and desperation.

He wound his window down and gulped at the cold wind that blasted in like a drowning man gasping for air. He felt the hairs on his body stand on end as they attempting to trap the cooling air to combat his overheating flesh.

Normally, he would enjoy this sensation, but not tonight.

Tonight was not a night for enjoying things.

He sat in the idling van and waited for a minute or two. He licked at his dry lips as he observed his surroundings, catching his breath. It was dark. The only light came from a tired-looking streetlamp that cast a dim, yellow glow onto the unpleasant street below it. It was suited to its surroundings. His mind flashed back to the last time he was here, with the young girl leaning into his window. He thought he could smell her rancid stink, even now. He swallowed, tasting her on the wind. She tasted like the worst, most rancid meal he had ever eaten, but he enjoyed it, savoured it even. *Jesus, was that less than a week ago?* He marvelled at how time had caught up on him.

A woman—maybe in her late thirties, or even her late fifties, it was difficult to tell in the weaken light, and with the amount of makeup that was currently plastered over her face—approached the van with something resembling a smile.

'What you doin', Joe?' she asked in a singsong, out-of-town accent.

The words hit him like a slap, full in the face. His head jerked back, and his eyes widened. 'What did you call me?' he spat, not quite believing what he'd heard.

'Hey, calm down, Joe. That's what I call all my punters,' she laughed. The noise was akin to a honk, almost like a donkey's bray, and the familiar waft of cheap wine and breath mints floated into his vehicle. It turned his stomach, yet he felt his dick growing hard in his pants. 'But now, it seems, I know your name, eh?'

Helmet Man's voice, spoke inside his head. 'You'll be doing this one a favour, Joe. She's a fucking mess. Nothing but a blight on society. Do it, Joe. Plus, you can't let her go anyway, not now that she knows your name.'

CRACK!!!

Joe twitched, trying his best to ignore the sickly noise that he knew was languishing somewhere deep in his head, like a cancer that couldn't be cut out.

'Do you ... fancy a drink?' he asked, his voice shaky, his words fighting to escape the porridge that he thought he could feel in his mouth.

The woman looked around the empty street before tipping her head to one side and nodding. 'Don't see why not. I don't tend to get invited out to many formal occasions these days.' As she laughed her the donkey bray again, she sprayed Joe with her sickly, stinking spit.

Her face changed then, her laughter was gone, replaced by something serious and business-like. 'I know a place.'

'I know a better one,' Joe replied.

'Do you now?' She brayed again as she made her way, wobbling in her high-heeled shoes, around to the passenger side of the vehicle and climbed in. She laughed as she closed the door, making Joe grimace. That sound was almost as bad as the *CRACK*.

'So, Joe, now I know your name, where *is* this better place?'

He looked at her. His head was thumping so hard it was affecting his vision. Her face jumped with every pulse. His cock was uncomfortably hard in the restricted room of his trousers. That too was throbbing in time with his head. 'It's not that far. Do you want a drink?' he asked, indicating the plastic bottle of soda in the cup holder.

Crack

'I would, but I'd want you to drink from it first. Can't be too careful these days; one of our girls wound up squashed the other night.'

Joe smiled outwardly while, inside, he thought he felt what little humanity he had left, seeping out of him. He picked up the bottle and put it to his lips. He faked taking a gulp, allowing his tongue to block the bottleneck enough to make it fizz. He let some froth trickle down his chin. 'Sorry,' he said, wiping the liquid from his stubble. 'I just think I'm a little nervous.'

The woman looked at him and brayed her laugh. She took the bottle from him and raised her eyebrows. 'Well, maybe you've got something to be nervous about, eh?' she said, taking a long, deep, thirsty gulp from the bottle.

CRACK!!!

Maybe I have, he thought as she buckled herself into the seat. He put the van into drive and pulled away from the kerb.

~~~

She was no longer laughing; the donkey bray had ceased about ten minutes after pulling out of the street. Even if there was anything funny about her current situation, she wouldn't have been able to laugh. It would have been tough to do while face down on a wet tarpaulin in the middle of a construction site. Her hands and legs were bound together with plastic zip ties, and there was a rag pushed deep into her mouth.

Her eyes were open, but there was a foggy distance to them, as if she were in a state of awareness to her situation, but also unaware at the same time. It was a strange look, and Joe marvelled at it as he regarded her in the intense beam of the van's headlights.

He was in the driver's seat; his own eyes were wide, and the knuckles of the hand he was gripping the steering wheel with were almost sheer white. His other hand was gripping something else, something that had grown hard again between his legs. Helmet Man was next to him, staring emotionless out of the windshield, towards the direction of the stricken woman.

Joe's foot pressed lightly on the accelerator, and he felt the satisfying thrum of the engine reverberate through his body. As he removed his hand from his cock to engage the gear stick, another hand gripped him, almost as tight, and as gentle, as he had just been. He looked at Helmet Man. The mysterious ghost was reaching over and stroking him with a leather gloved hand, while he continued looking out of the window, towards the bound victim.

'Don't think of her as a victim, Joe,' Helmet Man said, his voice not wavering, and his grip not releasing his cock. 'Think of her as a means to an end. And you are nothing but a good Samaritan to her. Helping in her hour of need.'

He imagined he saw the woman's eyes light up. He didn't know if this was because she was rousing from her drug-induced slumber, or if it was all in his head, but for a moment the van's headlights reflected upon her irises.

She was less than twenty yards away from the front of the vehicle, and he could see her face clearly in the headlights. Her body began to wriggle, as if she were a worm on a hook. He liked that. *Worm on a hook!*

A grin settled over his features, settling his eyes.

She *was* now awake. His heart begun to beat faster, heavier, he felt short of breath, as Helmet Man began stroking his cock faster, with a tighter grip.

She had a look on what little of her face he could see, because of the gag over her mouth. There was a dream-like quality about her movement, as if she were a ballet dancer and this was her swan song, like she had awoken from a deep sleep to find herself in the middle of a nightmarish world, a hellish reality.

Which, of course, was what had just happened.

Realisation must have dawned on her, of her immediate peril, or predicament, and she began to thrash wildly, all the time her eyes never left the bright lights spotlighting her. Joe smiled as he thought that her eyes must have been hurting, looking into the lights like that. He watched as she tried, frantically to free herself of her bonds. She had a look of a fish trying to get back into the safety of the water after being caught on a fisherman's hook.

A worm on a hook, he laughed again at the thought.

Crack

Still smiling and still enjoying Helmet Man's grip on his cock, he caught the bite of the clutch, and released the handbrake. As the vehicle edged forward, he readjusted his sweaty grip on the wheel, closed his eyes, and took in a deep breath. His head swam with the excess oxygen, but he never wavered in his conviction that he was doing the right thing. He swallowed an uncomfortable gulp and allowed the van to continue on its deadly tract.

He kept his eyes closed as death inched towards the woman on the road. He didn't even know if she *was* a woman anymore or if he should think of her as a victim. Or maybe just a *thing*? His brain refused to allow him to think of her as human.

'She is a means to an end, Joe,' Helmet Man spoke, his stroking of his cock stopping, momentarily.

He wanted to witness this deed. He wanted to see the terror in her eyes as the fucking van drew closer. Tonight, there would be no hesitation, there would be no second guessing. He'd come too far for that. All he needed was to keep the wheels turning.

CRACK!!!

The noise was almost alive; alive, fresh, and wet. It was everything he been expecting it to be. He imagined the rush an addict got from the first push of liquid heroin piercing their veins, and the opioid blasting into his veins. This must have felt like that. Everything was just carried away on a velvet cloud. All his cares, all his woes, everything flittering away in that a single moment of ecstatic elation. He felt the tingle of the orgasm run up his legs as Helmet Man rushed to finish him off. It wasn't long before he lost control of its release. The hot spray of semen inside his trousers was in complete tandem with the explosion of the woman's skull beneath his van.

After a few moments of basking in the afterglow, he turned to smile at his helmeted partner in crime. As he did, he caught another look at himself in the cracked visor. A stupid grin was spread over his face, and his hair was wild. *Is this how Karen sees me after sex?* he thought absently, his goofy smile reflecting back at him from the visor.

'You need to go and sort the mess out,' Helmet Man instructed as he looked at him.

Joe didn't know what mess he was referring to. The gruesome one outside the van? The easily fixed one inside his trousers? Or the complete and total one inside his head?

He let out a whistling sigh while pulling at the front of his trousers. The warm ejaculate was now cooling and, with the cool came the itch. He opened the van door and climbed out.

The scene was one of carnage, a total and utter bloodbath. There was red everywhere. Blood, bone, brains, and other unidentifiable chunks of what he could only describe as meat had decorated the tarpaulin and quite a bit of the plant life around the road. None of this bothered him; he was basking in the sweet relief of the moment, and the victory over the noticeably absent crack noise. He walked to the back of the van and regarded the ruined remains back there. Her torso was still bound but it was now motionless. Her head had popped like a watermelon, and there was not much left of it attached to her body. Just a few scraggles here and there, the majority of it had sprayed over the road and the vehicle.

He smiled, not really comprehending, or even contemplating the enormity of what he had just done. The guilt paled into insignificance next to the release from his self-imposed mental prison. He tugged absently at the front of his trousers, grimacing as the cold and clammy wetness caressed his leg. Walking as if he'd just dismounted a horse, he entered the shed next to the road. He exited again a few moments later holding a large pressure hose and a spade. He put the hose on the floor before dragging the body, by the tarpaulin he'd laid her on, over towards the cement pit behind the shed.

Looking back towards the van, he was neither surprised, nor particularly bothered to see it was empty. He shrugged; he didn't need Helmet Man now anyway. With a grunt, he dragged the tarpaulin with the remains of the poor woman towards the pit. He rolled the incomplete cadaver into the waiting cement and watched it sink. The grey surface greedily sucked her down into its hidden depths. The irony of her getting the sucking at the end of her life was not lost on him.

Crack

Smiling, he dragged the now empty tarpaulin over to the vehicle and turned on the high-pressure hose. He began to whistle a tune, one from a cartoon he used to watch as a child, about a family of cavemen living as if it was 1960's America. He turned the hose to the van, then the road and the flora surrounding it, then finally the tarpaulin. He cleaned off all the evidence of the dead woman, and all of his servitude to the stupid noise at the same time. When he was done, he climbed back inside the vehicle and continued his rounds of the site.

When the first workers turned up at six am to begin their shift, they found Joe in good form as he waved them all goodbye and left the site with a new spring in his step.

47.

'WELL, LOOK AT you,' Karen beamed as his car pulled onto the path. 'What's with all those big smiles?'

'Oh, I don't know,' Joe shrugged, blushing slightly. 'Maybe it's just the sunny day.'

'Well, I'm off today; do you fancy doing something after I've dropped the kids off?'

He looked at his wife with a twinkle in his eye. 'Do I?' he replied saucily, tipping her a wink. It was Karen's turn to blush before flashing him a pretty smile. He mused that he hadn't notice her smile like that for quite some time.

'Hey, Dad,' Martin greeted him as he climbed into the car.

Then Annmarie leaned in from behind; she kissed him on his cheek as she got in. 'Morning, Dad,' she sang, the little white buds still in her ears.

'Have a good day,' he shouted, waving Karen's car out of the driveway. Once they were gone, he turned and skipped inside the house.

48.

'WELL, I DON'T know what's come over you,' Karen sighed, out of breath as she flopped onto her side of the bed.

Joe lay with his arm raised above him on the pillow, an impish smirk caressed his face. 'Well, you know how it's been.'

'Shhh,' Karen's finger touched his mouth, quietening him instantly. 'I don't mind. Listen, if you're getting your libido back, then that's not a bad thing. Let's not push it, or over think it, eh? We're both getting older, and I know everything you've been going through. Sex has been the last thing on your mind of late.' She started to laugh. 'So, twice in a couple of days! I'm not going to complain.'

She removed her finger and kissed him on the mouth before flopping back on the bed again.

'Well, maybe all those problems I've had are behind us then. Listen, maybe we should go on holiday,' she said, still trying to catch her breath.

'Huh?'

'A holiday. We haven't been on one for years.' She shifted position onto her elbow and leaned over him. 'It would do us the world of good. I mean, with everything you've been through, my job, the kids in school. It'll give us something to look forward to.'

Joe sat up and looked at his wife's expectant face. The joy of being relieved of the sound and the bliss of ejaculating for the second time that day had put him in a good mood. 'Well, why not? I've always fancied Canada in the autumn.'

Karen's face changed instantly. She had gone from the dream of a swimming pool in the sun to the wonder and amazement of a holiday of a lifetime in Canada. 'Seriously? Joe, that'd be fantastic. A little cabin in the mountains. Could we afford it?'

Joe looked at her and raised his eyebrows. 'Maybe we could forget to take the kids,' he laughed as he leaned over, pulling the covers over both their heads.

'Oh, Joe …' Karen squealed.

Crack

49.

PAULA AND IAN were lying in bed. The TV screen was flickering ignored images of colourful beings that seemed to live in a hill underground with little TV screens on their chests. Sally was in between them, purring like a cat in her sleep. Ian was absently stroking the little girl's hair while leaning in and looking at the brochure Paula was showing him.

'So, the cabin holds up to six, it has its own private beach, and there's a hot tub in the bedroom.' The brochure was for honeymoons and exotic wedding locations. She was currently studying a spacious six-berth private villa in the Bahamas. Her face was flushed as her eyes devoured the pages. 'There's a free mini bar topped up daily, and you get free access and treatments in the on-site spa. 'Ian, this one sounds fabulous,' she gushed.

Ian wasn't as enthusiastic. He took the brochure from her and inspected it a little more closely. His brow rumpled, and he developed a pout the more he read. 'Have you seen the price of it?' he asked. 'Come on, in all seriousness, why do we need a six berth villa? Unless you're planning on asking your mum to come and look after Sally for us.'

Paula laughed as she tried to grab the brochure back from him. 'Don't be stupid.'

'The beach thing I get, but the hot tub in the room sounds a little, I don't know, dangerous, maybe. What if Sally wanted to get up in the middle of the night and she fell in? Shit, what if I wanted to get up in the middle of the night and fell in?'

'Then I'd jump in with you. It's our honeymoon, after all.'

He couldn't fault her on that answer.

Paula looked at him with big baby eyes, the ones he could never resist. This time, however, he was going to be resilient. 'Ian, I've

175

always wanted to go to the Bahamas, and I want to go with you. This is our chance to make this whole thing … special.'

'Where are we going to find five thousand pounds on top of what we're paying for the wedding already? Also, there doesn't seem to be a lot for Sally to do there.'

She flashed him the puppy dog eyes again. She sniffed and began to stroke their still purring child. 'Well, I was thinking of only going for a week, and I've already asked my Mum, and she said she'd look after Sally.'

Ian couldn't believe what he was hearing. 'Without Sally?'

'Just for one week. You know, a little me and you time,' she whispered, nuzzling into his neck. 'It could be just exactly what we need. Get the wedding over, get away from it all for a week, then look at a big family holiday later in the year, somewhere we can afford, somewhere where Sally can have a ball with us.'

Ian leaned back in the bed, there were obvious signs he was enjoying the nuzzling, but now his interest was piqued as the holiday was just for the two of them. Tucking himself away, as he didn't like to be aroused around Sally, he focused on the brochure. 'Do *you* think we could go a week without seeing this little one?'

Grinning, Paula moved away from his neck and gestured towards his crotch. 'I don't know, I think we'd be seeing quite a lot of the little one,' she whispered, laughing.

Ian's hand hid his arousal from her too and laughed.

Still grinning, Paula kissed Sally on the head; as she did, the little girl turned, trying to find that elusive comfortable position children have difficulty locating. She looked up at Ian and sighed. She cocked her head and clicked her mouth. 'I know what you mean. It'll kill me not seeing her, but I also think that we need to connect after the wedding. I don't think it'd be too much of a problem. I mean, she'd be with my mum, and it's not like we can't video call her every day, is it?'

Ian put the brochure down and looked first at his wife-to-be, then at their daughter. As he exhaled, his body shrank a little. 'I know what you mean. We've worked hard for this.' He picked up the brochure again and looked at the villa one more time. 'I'm sure she'd survive a week without us. We can always put her into abandonment counselling afterwards.'

Crack

Paula's smile beamed as she kissed him before kissing the top of Sally's head again. 'Thank you,' she mouthed.

Ian looked over the top of the brochure. 'It looks like we're both going to have to kill the overtime for this, especially if there'll be two holidays.' He put the brochure down again. 'Have you got anything new coming in that you can drag the hours on?'

Paula was fussing around Sally, trying to pick up the four-year-old up, to carry her into her own room. 'Nothing much.' She strained. 'We're still considering the cold cases. Now that's *boring* work.' She stopped what she was doing and looked at Ian. Her mouth twisted to one side. 'Although, we're still working the case of the prostitute found off the A41. You know, the one in the woods with no head.'

'I remember you mentioning it.'

'Well, something else flagged up the other day. It might be nothing, but …' She trailed off into thought. 'Another prostitute went missing about three days ago, from the same area. Now, I'm not saying it's another murder or anything, there's not been any body found in the first instance, but something about it screams at me. I think there's a connection. The hard thing about it, is that the women who work the streets by nature are so transient that you never know if they've just upped and left for somewhere else.'

Ian was nodding his eyes focused on her. 'We've had nothing but trouble in that area.' He grinned at her then. 'You've got one of your hunches, haven't you?'

She stopped fussing with Sally and looked at him. 'I think I do. But the brass has still got us on the cold cases until something meaty comes up on the headless case. No pun intended. But I think these cases could be connected.'

Ian took Sally from his wife's arms. As he carried his ragdoll of a daughter out of the room, he turned and looked back towards Paula, who was now sat on the edge of the bed, fiddling with the remote control, trying to turn the TV off. 'Well, start getting them dots connected. We've got a wedding and two holidays to pay for.'

Paula smiled as she turned the TV off, removed her t-shirt, and slipped out of her pyjamas. 'Hurry up,' she shouted. 'It's freezing in here. I think I need warming up.'

Ian didn't need to be told twice.

50.

CRACK!!!

Joe pulled the covers away from his head. Although his eyes were wide open, they still needed to get used to the darkness of the room as they scoured the shadows for the source of the sound. There was nothing there, but he knew that already. He checked Karen's side of the bed and saw she wasn't there either. With blurry eyes, he regarded the clock.

A quarter to eleven pm.

'Shit!' He was instantly full awake. He fumbled his way out of the bed and switched on the light. A low-level panic was building within him.

He was late for work.

He was never late for work.

'Karen,' he half whispered, half shouted; there was no answer. He dived into the wardrobe and dragged out one of his uniforms. He stumbled on one leg a couple of times, steadying himself on the chest of drawers, as he struggled into his trousers.

'Karen,' he shouted again.

There was still no answer.

He opened the bedroom door could see the flickering lights of the TV downstairs casting shadows on the walls. He leaned over the landing banister and looked down. He couldn't hear any sounds so assumed the TV must either be on mute or the volume was turned right down. But he could hear movement. Someone was down there. 'Karen,' he shouted again, but, annoyingly, there was still no reply.

He made his way down the stairs, following the lights from the TV streaming from the living room door. As he got closer, he could hear muted sounds from the TV after all. It sounded like that same

Crack

stupid game show he'd been noticing so often these days. *Jesus, is there a time through the day when that show ISN'T on?* He had an assumption of what he'd see when he entered the living room— Karen curled up on the couch, eating a bowl of crisps, maybe drinking hot chocolate, wrapped up in her housecoat watching the garbage that spewed from the TV screen at this time of night.

'Karen ... are you there?' he shouted, gripping the knob at the bottom of the banister tight. His mood was turning into thunder; not only was he late, but he was growing pissed off too.

'Karen, why didn't you get me up? I'm l—' He stopped short, not able to finish his rant. His mouth fell open. He had never, in one million years, expected to see what he was seeing now in his living room, or anywhere else for that matter.

Karen was naked. She was bending over the back of the couch, looking at him. In between pulling theatrical facial exertions, the very same exertions she reserved only for him, she was laughing.

A fat, black man was gyrating behind her. He was also naked.

CRACK!!!

'WHAT THE FUCK IS GOING ON HERE?'

The sweating man looked at him, his face changed from pure concentration in what he was doing, to a friendly smile. He raised a hand in a greeting. 'Hey, Joe,' he gasped, out of breath from his physical exertions. 'How's it going, man? Hope you don't mind me fucking Karen.' His voice was deep, and breathless.

Karen's face was contorting, and her eyes were fluttering in ecstasy each time he entered into her. 'Oh ... don't mind ... him ... ohhhh fuck! Rufus ... you ... holy shit, holy shit ... you ... just keep ... sticking it ... deep ... deeper inside me,' Karen replied, equally breathlessly.

Joe's breath was gone. His words were gone with it. His eyes were wide and lost. He couldn't tell if he was angry, upset, it was probably both. He was just totally unable to process what he was witnessing. 'Rufus,' he spat. 'What the fuck?' was all he managed when he finally had the wherewithal to speak again.

'Karen told me you were having, you know'— he made a gesture with his fist— 'problems getting it up and what not, you know, since the accident. She said she needed a man inside her, and she wanted him to be a man of colour.'

His eyes began to roll to the back of his head, as his mind reeled. The room was spinning. For some reason, he wasn't surprised to see Helmet Man standing in the corner. Although Joe couldn't see his face through the cracked visor, it looked like he was watching what was happening. He was touching himself as he did. Joe watched the helmet turned to look at him and tip a nod before returning his attention back to the action on the couch.

'He's next, Joe—Oh, FUCK! Once I'm done with Rufus's beautiful big black cock, then the guy in the helmet's next,' she gasped, panting, pointing towards him. 'After all, Joe—Oh fuck, Rufus, that's deep—After all, Joe, he's you anyway.'

Joe's anger snapped. His wide eyes blazed, and his lips pulled back like a dangerous dog, exposing his grinding teeth. An involuntary roar escaped him as he sprang towards his wife and his work colleague. He grabbed her around the throat and squeezed, tight. Rufus jumped away from the attack. Joe watched as his wet erection slid out of his wife as he moved back.

'What about me, you whore? You're no better than them, the others. You're just a slut like all the others,' he screamed.

Karen laughed in his face. 'Yeah, *what* about them others, Joe? You limp dicked little fuck. You didn't fuck them, did you? No, you just killed them because you couldn't get it up. You're too interested in the—'

CRACK!!!

The noise came from Karen' mouth. Maybe, finally, he'd gotten to the source of it. His hands tightened around her throat, and her face began to flush red. The whites of her eyes were turning pink and were bulge from their sockets. Her lips were blue as if she were cold, but the smug, horrible smile on them was still there. He removed one hand from around her neck and balled it into a fist. He pulled it back, ready to hit her.

'Oh, yeah, go on, Joe, hit me …' Karen's voice sounded plummy, and thick, as the air that was leaving her throat was constricted by the hand still wrapped tight around it. 'I like it like

Crack

that. When I've rode Rufus's dick dry, I'm going to get him to hit me. I fucking love it rough.'

'Shut up, bitch,' Joe shouted. The hand holding her gripped tighter, while the other was poised to hit her.

Rufus was on the couch, his penis still erect. He was masturbating as the drama unfolded before him.

'Go on, you coward, hit me; FUCKING HIT ME,' she baited, her dark red face now turning purple. 'Hit me and then run over my head; maybe that'll make your cock hard.'

The room began to spin. The walls moved. The ceiling felt like it should be the floor. Bright, vivid colours flashed before his eyes, turning his wife's face into a hideous, monstrous mask. With a flash, her head was adorning a large motorcycle helmet with a crack in the visor. He tightened his fist so tight that he heard the cartilage in his knuckles crack and snap. Then he felt it connect with the helmet. The visor shattered beneath his fist. He pulled his hand back and lashed out at the face inside. He felt, rather than heard, the crunch as his fist obliterated her nose.

CRACK!!!

Blood gushed from the ruined face below him, splattering over his white t-shirt. It stood out, stark against the clean fabric. It acted like a red rag to a bull. The sight of it spurred him on.

'Go on, Joe,' she baited him, her voice muffled as blood poured from her ruined nose and swollen, bruised lips.

51.

'JOE, PLEATH!' He could hardly understand what she was shouting, her voice was puffy. The nasty look she'd had in her eyes was gone, replaced with something that was half destroyed. The glint in her eye was now a look of fear and submissiveness as the last punch crunched her nose beneath his knuckles.

'Pleath, let me go.'

She was crying, or at least trying to. The tears falling from her swollen eyes were mingling with the blood that was pouring from her nose and her fat, split lips. 'Pleath, Joe, thtop hitting me,' she fluffed. 'Let me go …'

He looked around him, the living room was gone, replaced by their bedroom. Rufus and Helmet Man were gone too. His eyes fell on his raised fist, it was almost white, the exact same colour as when he gripped the steering wheel before driving over those women's heads.

He let go of Karen's neck, and jumped back away from her, as if she were something dangerous that might bite him at any given moment. As if she were Nixon, or maybe a fox.

She fell onto the bed, moaning and sobbing.

He was stood over her, wearing his pyjama bottoms and a white t-shirt. His hand, the one he'd had her throat in, was covered in a thin sheen of blood.

Karen's blood.

She was face down on the bed. Her bloated, bleeding, pleading face was turned towards him, attempting to look at him while hanging over the edge of the bed. One of her hands was in front of her face in a pathetic attempt to stop him hitting her. It was more of a natural reaction than any real attempt to protect herself. 'Joe, thtop. I'll… I'll do anything. Pleath don't hit me again,' she sobbed.

Crack

Confusion made his head whirl. He staggered back from her, banging into the wardrobe behind him. He looked again at his white fist and then at the blood stains on his t-shirt. Finally, he looked at his hand that had been around her throat. There was a swathe of her hair intertwined through his fingers. He flicked it, hoping to get it off him, thinking that if it was no longer in his fingers, then it wouldn't exist, and this shit situation would reveal itself to be one of his vivid dreams. *Like the one you were just having?* his own consciousness swiped at him.

'What the fuck?' he uttered as she turned away from him, leaving a bloody imprint of her face on the white cotton sheets.

Her very own Shroud of Turin.

He staggered away, along the wardrobe, looking all around him, hoping, pleading with himself to wake up from the nightmare he'd become trapped in. This was a whole lot worse than the nightmare he'd just snapped out of.

'I …' That was all he managed to stutter before something hit him from behind, and his world went black.

52.

IAN AND PAULA were lying in their bed. Once again, Sally lay between them, snoring softly. Ian was looking at her and was shaking his head. 'We really need to stop her doing this.'

'Doing what?' Paula asked, not taking much interest, as her head was deep inside a book.

'Allowing her to fall asleep in our bed. She needs structure in her life.'

'She's four,' Paula said, snapping her book closed. 'She'll get all the structure she needs when she goes to proper school.'

Ian pouted, nodded, and continued stroking the sleeping girl's head.

Paula looked at them. She would have signed an affidavit right there and then, confirming her heart had just melted in her chest. 'So,' she said, changing the subject. 'The dress is all paid for, the cake is ordered, and the band is booked, correct?'

Ian pulled a face. 'Shit, I forgot about the band.'

'Ian, we have to have the Boogie Beatles; they're the best wedding band in the country. If you don't get them, we'll just end up with a stupid DJ cracking crap jokes all night,' she moaned.

Ian's smile widened.

'You bastard,' she gushed, hitting out at him with a playful slap. 'Don't do that. You know I've got a load on my plate at the moment. The wedding is in four short weeks, and we've just picked up another case.'

'What one?' he asked, welcoming the break of talking about the wedding, the same topic for what seemed like forever.

'Remember I told you about the prostitute found with her head squashed down Brook Creek Lane, off the A41?'

Ian nodded; his interest piqued.

'Well, it looks like the head had been run over by the wheels of a car or a van. The body was mostly unmarked, no sign of a struggle.'

'Run over?'

She nodded. 'Completely squashed, not much left of it at all.'

'Jesus, like that RTA I got to a few weeks back?'

'Shit, I'd forgotten all about that. Yeah, how weird us both picking up cases like that.'

He chuffed. 'Ghoulish, if you ask me. So, it's a murder then? What happened to the other one? You said there was another one, another prostitute gone missing.'

'Yeah, well, we haven't had anything on that one yet. She's filed as a missing person, but no body has turned up as yet.'

'You got anything to go on, on the murder?'

'A few partial treads, and maybe a footprint, but that's about it. No witnesses, or at least none willing to come forward. We don't even know if the evidence we have is related. It's a forensics mess on that little patch of track. The rain didn't help either.'

Ian puffed out a breath. 'Sounds like that's going to be a tough one.' Slowly he climbed off the bed and walked to the door, careful not to wake Sally.

'Where're you going?' Paula asked.

'To get a drink.'

'Get me one too. We haven't even nearly finished making these wedding lists yet.'

Rolling his eyes, Ian groaned and walked out of the bedroom.

53.

THE ACHE IN his head slowly brought him back to consciousness. His mouth was bone dry, and his whole body was throbbing, badly. With one eye still closed, he looked around the room. It was a little while before he recognised it as the bedroom, and he was alone. Absently, he rubbed at the side of his head but had to pull his hand away quickly, wincing. There was blood on his hand as he looked at it. On closer inspection, he realised that it was dry.

It all came back to him then, in glorious Technicolor.

'Fuck,' he whispered into his blood-soaked hand.

He closed his eyes, mostly to stop the room from swinging, drunkenly around him, but also to make sure this wasn't one of his dreams. He put his hands to his sides, palms flat on the floor, grounding himself. He attempted to get onto his feet. The manoeuvre was unsteady, and the dizziness and painful throbbing in his head made him feel like he had the mother of all hangovers. Once the waves of nausea from his brain had ebbed, he made his way, unsteadily, towards the door. He put all his weight on the handle as he gripped and turned it. It didn't budge. He tried again; it still wouldn't open. He grabbed it with both his hands and pulled on it. It rattled somewhat in the frame, but otherwise, it didn't move an inch.

'Hey,' he shouted. 'Is there anyone there? Anyone? Let me out.' He moved away from the door after shouting holding a blood-stained hand to his eyes. The room was spinning again, and the build-up of saliva in his mouth made him almost certain he was going to vomit.

After a short while, it passed without incident.

'No, Dad. You're not coming out of there.' It was only a small voice, but there was a lot of courage in it.

Crack

'Martin!' He brought his voice down to a comfortable level, to calm the boy down and lull him into his confidence. 'Come on, son, let me out of here. I need to make sure your mother's all right.'

'She's all right now, you prick. What did you think you were doing?'

'That's it, son, I don't know. I was asleep, I think.'

Martin's voice went up a pitch. 'You think? Seriously, Dad, you really did a number on her. You should see her face.'

'You're right, son, I need to see her face. Does she need to go to the hospital? If so, I can take her.'

'If she needs to go, we'll get a taxi. You're not going anywhere near her.'

'Son, is she there?'

'She's downstairs with Annmarie. Her face is fucked, Dad. You've gone too far this time.'

'This time? What are you talking about, Martin? I've never hit her before. I've never hit any of you. I'd never…'

'You fucking did.' Martin's voice sounded grown up, maybe *too* grown up. It hurt Joe's heart, his head too.

'What do you mean by that?'

There was no answer.

'Martin, tell me what you mean by that.'

There was still no answer.

Noises drifted in from beyond the door, banging, scrapes, and hushed whispers. He put his ear to the wood. 'What's happening out there?' he shouted, before banging his fist on the door. It rattled in its frame again. 'Open this fucking door,' he shouted, pulling at the handle. 'I'm not messing around here. Open it NOW!' As he screamed the last word, his vision went white, and he staggard away from the door.

After a short while, when his anger and the dizziness had abated somewhat, he turned from the door and slid his body down it. He put his head in his hands and began to sob. 'What the fuck's going on?'

After almost an hour of the continuing bangs and scrapes, he heard the door to his enforced prison unlock. He pushed himself away from it, wincing from his screaming limbs and cracking knees. The door opened; Martin and Annmarie were outside the room. Martin's arm was wrapped tightly around his sister. Her head was bowed, but he could see she'd been crying. They were both wearing coats.

'Martin, Annmarie ... thank you. Your mum? Is she—'

'Leaving,' Martin cut in before he could finish.

'What?'

'We're going, Dad. You... you need h... help or something,' Annmarie stuttered, shaking her head.

'Where are you going? Karen?' He leaned out of the room and shouted. His heart broke again as both children flinched.

Martin stood his ground better than his sister and attempted to bar his way. In a twisted way, Joe admired him for his bravery. 'She won't see you, Dad. You really messed her up. She needs the hospital, but she won't go. She says there'll be too many questions, questions she doesn't want to answer.'

Joe leaned out of the room again; his fourteen-year-old son was standing between him and his wife. 'Karen, I ... I love you; I'm sorry.'

Annmarie glanced back at him as she and Martin turned away. 'I'm sorry,' she said. 'We'll ring you and let you know we're OK. Please get help, Dad. You really need it.'

And with that, they were gone.

He thought about going after them, grabbing them, shaking them, telling them he loved them. Screaming it until they got it into their stupid heads. He knew it wouldn't do any good as the last thing they needed now was to witness more physical violence.

The front door opened, and his heart sank deeper inside his chest. He looked out of the bedroom window, pulling the curtain back and watched them leave.

Martin was dragging a large suitcase to the back of Karen's small car, where two others were waiting for him. Annmarie climbed into the passenger's seat as Martin rushed back into the house. Seconds later, he emerged, supporting an old woman in his arms. She looked frail, wearing a winter coat with the hood up. It took him another moment before he realised it was Karen. Her hood was up to hide her face from the world, and it worked, at least until she stopped and looked back at the house, then up towards their window.

His breath caught in his throat as he witnessed the extent of the damage he'd caused; damage he'd inflicted on the face of the

Crack

woman he'd vowed to love and protect. Her nose and eyes were black and swollen, there was a large plaster over her eye, and she was holding a paper towel to her mouth. When she removed it, even from his distance and elevated position, he could see deep, and dark red stains on it from her swollen lips.

Martin got her into the driver's seat. He was fussing about, making sure she didn't hurt herself any more than she already was. Once they were all in, they drove off, Joe noticed that it was without any hesitation at all.

He was amazed she could drive in the state that she was in.

The silence of the house was deafening.

The realisation dawned on him that he was now all alone in the house. His narrowed eyes searched the corners of the room, taking in every shadow, every nook, every cranny.

There was nothing there.

He tried to trick himself into not knowing what it was he was looking for, not wanting to admit it, not even to himself.

'Karen,' he whimpered like a child, left alone in the dark. 'Don't do this. Don't leave me alone here, please. Not on my own,' he sobbed into the empty room, the empty house … his empty life.

He flopped down heavily in the corner, his back supported by the two walls. He raised his bruised and swollen hands, wincing as he flexed his fingers, in and out of a fist. Then he closed his eyes and used his sore hands to cover his face.

54.

IT WAS LATE. Joe was in his porta cabin, with the TV switched off, but the lights were on. He was not inclined to watch that dreaded, awful game show anymore. The bang, bang, bang inside his head was turning his stomach, making him nauseous and anxious. Two, long days had passed since Karen and the kids had left. They hadn't even called or sent him any kind of message letting him know they were safe, or where they were. He felt like someone had taken a huge bite out of his life and swallowed it whole.

He had an idea who it had been.

The bruises on his hand had begun to heal, but they were still a constant reminder of what he'd done, and the ordeal he'd put his two beautiful kids through.

He'd spent the last two nights wide awake and anxious. Every noise from the house had been amplified, and turned into foxes, hounds, prostitutes, all from the grave, all returning to return the service he had given them. If they weren't returning ghosts, they were the precursor of that dreaded noise, the one that, as of yet, had not made a resurgence. There was a niggling feeling in the back of his head, relentless, like a mouse gnawing on wire, that he would be hearing it again.

And soon.

As he paced the cabin, his eyes flicking towards the bottle of Nytrodol sitting on his desk. He eyed as it might suddenly grow fangs and try to bite him. He didn't remember bringing it into work with him, and that worried him more than anything.

Eventually, he snatched at the keys to one of the vehicles parked outside and left the cabin, slamming the door behind him.

CRACK!!!

Crack

There it was.

He knew it would be back.

His hunched shoulders, closed eyes, and grimaced mouth were back too, his body assuming it's position. He had a small hope it had only been the porta cabin door slamming and not the *dreaded* noise that had been haunting him.

But he knew better.

A semi-relief washed over him as he turned to look at the cabin's door. It was closed, maybe it *had* been the sound of the slam. Shivering, he shook his head as the biting wind found every tiny bit of the cold sweat that had sprung up over his body. He rushed to the vehicle, this time slowly, and deliberately, closing the door behind him, making sure not to slam it.

The instant he turned the ignition, he grimaced again.

CRACK!!!

A shudder ripped through him as he grasped the steering wheel with his bruised hands. It took a moment to realise that the sound might have been the radio coming on. Whoever had been in the van last had detuned it. White noise hissed from the speakers. His grip tightened, and every muscle in his body was taut, stiff, and flexed as he thumbed the button to turn the painful noise off.

He closed his eyes, trying to calm himself down, to get a grip of his life and indeed, his sanity. He took in a deep breath. After a few more, he felt his heart returning to a more acceptable rhythm, and he dared to open his eyes. Checking the rear-view mirror, he was once again happy there was no one there. No one wearing a leather biker suit and large black helmet with a cracked visor. He pulled the van away with every intention of beginning his normal rounds of the building site.

With his subconscious in control, and acting entirely on autopilot, he drove to the main gate, opened it, and drove straight out without a second thought. His eyes were glazed, and his mind vacant. He was acting completely on impulse as he drove into the dark and cold night.

55.

'DO YOU WANT a drink?' Joe asked as the pretty young girl leaned into his window.

'What do I need to do to get one?' she asked with a wink.

Joe's stomach flipped. The girl was hardly older than Annmarie. He felt like a dirty old man, flirting with a girl who was probably not even a quarter of his age. But he knew the ends here would at least justify his means. 'Oh, I don't know,' he replied grinning. 'Maybe get in and come for a drive with me?'

'Now that sounds good. Anything to get out of this cold. Where would we go?'

'I know a place. It's quiet; we'd have all the time in the world.'

The girl twisted her mouth and looked up to the sky. In that moment, saw she was a real beauty. He wondered why and how a girl like her could have fallen so low to end up here. 'Hmmm,' she put her finger to her mouth and grinned. 'I think I could do that. But I might need to borrow fifty bucks from you. That bottle of cola sure does look nice, though.'

Joe smiled and flashed his wallet; it was fat with notes. 'I think I could go that far. Get in, maybe you'll get some of both.'

The girl made her way around the front and climbed in. As she did, she flashed Joe a nervous smile. He guessed then that maybe she hadn't even seen her twenty-first birthday yet.

'I'm sorry to ask, but would it be possible to get that fifty upfront? Things have been a bit strange around here lately. Two of the regulars have disappeared. There's a rumour that one was found with no head and all the blood drained from her body.'

Joe laughed. 'No head? That's a bit ironic,' he said, handing the girl three folded notes.

Crack

She frowned at him as she took the money. 'What? Was that a joke?'

'No head,' he explained. 'I hope the guy got his fifty quid back.'

'Oh yeah,' she replied, looking out of the window, into the darkness beyond.

He knew the joke was ghoulish, and probably out of order, as this girl might have known the women he'd...

He didn't finish that thought.

However, it didn't really matter, as in an hour or so, this young lady would be in pretty much the same state as the last two.

He pulled out of the seedy street, heading in the direction of his work's site. His vacant, spaced-out look had made a reprise, and he was driving on autopilot again. The only difference was the small, creepy grin on his lips.

Every now and then, she looked at him between taking long swigs from the cola. 'So, where are we going?' she asked, her nervousness evident in her wavering voice.

Joe looked at her, the creepy grin still evident on his face. 'Not far, just a little further up this road,' he replied in a monotone voice.

She regarded the two twenties and one ten in her hand, like she was of two minds, as if she wanted to give them back and get out of the car.

Joe laughed inwardly at her nervousness.

'It's easier when they're scared,' Helmet Man said, either from inside his head, or from the back seat; Joe didn't know, and he didn't care. He was just glad his friend was back.

He spared a sideways glance at the girl. Her head was drooping a little, and she kept jerking it back, trying to look alert. She set the soda bottle against her face as if the cold would keep her awake by touching her skin. Then, she took another greedy swig of the dark drink inside it.

As they pulled up to the gates of the work site, she was eyeing her surroundings through her droopy eyes. Her face was creased in confusion. 'We can't go in there,' she half giggled. 'What if someone sees us?'

Joe's eyes brightened briefly. 'Don't you worry your pretty little self. I'm security on this place. It's deserted at this time of night. It'll just be me and you. I've got the keys, look.'

He pulled out a set of keys from his pockets and jangled them in her face. As she looked at them, she blinked heavily and slowly, as she tried to focus on them. It was exactly what he wanted to see.

'It's … just …' she mumbled, handing the three crumpled notes back out to him.

He looked at her, tilting his head. Her eyes were already rolling back in their sockets. With a feeble effort, she began to scratch at the door, flapping in her drugged state for the handles that would give her the freedom she wanted from this man.

CRACK!!!

Joe was ready for it this time. He welcomed it. Leaning forward, he looked up at the sky through the windshield. Grinning, he turned, and there, exactly where he expected him to be, was Helmet Man, in his cracked visor and leather suit. Sitting as still as a statue. With the smile lingering, he climbed out of the van and opened the gates.

Crack

56.

'WAKE UP, BITCH! Wake the fuck up.' As the man was shouting, white plumes of breath unfurled from his mouth, disappearing up into the night sky. Steam was also rising from his forehead.

There was a sharp sting followed by an intense, and sustained pain on her face. It woke her from the funk she was feeling, and the nasty dream of being tied up in a car. She fluttered her eyelashes before opening her eyes, wide.

She *was* tied up, bound, but she wasn't in a car.

Instant panic rose within her, and with her face still smarting from the slap, she began to thrash, trying to break free of her shackles.

Something was in her mouth stopping her from breathing or screaming. It was leaving an oily taste in the back of her throat, where it had been pushed in deep. There was also something on her cheeks, pulling at her skin, keeping whatever was in her mouth in place. The panic welling inside her blossomed like a tulip in spring. She'd heard of situations like this, but it was usually consensual; this was something different, something too sinister for her to contemplate.

She continued to wriggle, or that was too nice a word for what she was doing. She bucked and squirmed, trying to free her hands and feet, but there was no movement in either of them. A muffled scream began in her chest, but the thing in her mouth—she guessed it might be a rag of some sort—caught it killing it instantly. The scream got no further. Her wide, pleading eyes looked up towards the man leering above her. He was upside down vision, but he was looking right at her. Behind him was a bright light.

The cold beneath her told her she was lying on the ground. The uncomfortable feeling beneath her was a rough kind of material.

Once again, she attempted to wriggle and scream.

What's he doing? she thought. *Holy fuck, what is he doing?*

The man was looking all around him. He was wincing, hunching, and laughing. He reminded her of the Hunchback of Notre Dame from the old Disney movie she'd seen as a girl. If this hadn't had been such a grave situation, she might have laughed. The dance he was doing was hammy, in an overacted kind of way. Her wide, petrified eyes watched as he danced off towards the light source behind him. The glare was so bright that he turned into a sick parody of a silhouette puppet show. He was twitching and dancing in such an erratic, creepy way, she was reminded of old stop motion kids programmes she's loved when she was younger, in a more innocent, safer time. The dawning horror that this man was unhinged, psychopathic, enhanced the swelling panic inside her.

With a sinking feeling in her already twisting, knotting stomach, she realised what the light source must have been …

Headlights.

Car headlights.

She surmised she was on a road, and she took the opportunity to turn her head towards the cold, wet material beneath her. She was not comforted by the close-up view of the stained tarpaulin she was laid upon.

Through her silent panic, she heard the door to whatever vehicle it was that had its lights on—she suspected it was the same van she'd been picked up in—slam closed and the engine roar into life. Still thrashing, she looked towards the headlights, squinting as she attempted to filter out the glare flowing into her recently awakened eyes. She was expecting the lights to move backwards as the sick bastard left her out here, on whatever road she was on, exposed to the elements, but very much alive. However, they didn't. Instead, she saw them heading *towards* her.

They were edging closer and closer.

The snap and crack of small stones beneath the tyres rang in her ears as lights advanced on her position. She was beyond panic now. The stink of the dirty tarpaulin, and the rubber of the van's tyres,

Crack

filled her world as the lights continued to advance. *Surely not.* This thought was almost rational as they continued to close in on her.

A scream was coming from somewhere. At first, she thought it from herself, screaming and shouting. She imagined hearing herself from some detached location, like an out of body experience; but then the sound changed. It was a man's scream. It sounded muffled, like it was coming from inside the oncoming vehicle. That thought didn't comfort her one bit. The screaming, even over the noise of the engine and the crunch of the tyres, sounded as panicked and as frenzied as she was.

The lights kept getting closer.

Suddenly, the van was so close that headlights disappeared, all she could see was its underneath, rusted and dirty. Adrenaline, and terror rose within her, making it difficult for her to breathe through her nose.

She had never been religious. She hadn't set foot into a church since she was a small girl, and her mother, the drunken slut that she was, had left her home alone most Saturdays and Sundays, forgoing the spiritual upbringing of her little girl for a life of cheap drink, drugs, and a parade of men, every single one of them a loser, and more than a few of them with a preference for underaged daughters. None of that mattered now as she prayed. She prayed like she'd never prayed before in her short, sad existence. She was pleading to God, or Jesus, or even Allah, anyone who would listen, anyone who could make the vehicle stop. When she resigned that it wasn't going to, she prayed for a miracle, something that might stop, or halt, what she couldn't quite believe was happening.

Not really expecting one to happen, she'd learned from an early age that miracles didn't happen to the likes of her, she closed her eyes and waited for what was now inevitable.

Even as the grip of the tyre began to pull at the skin of her face, she still couldn't comprehend that the madman driving this vehicle would actually drive it over her head.

Until he did.

~~~

Joe was shaking as he regarded the girl, tied, and bound, on the floor. It was a cold night, but the shake was more about the adrenaline coursing through his body than it was about the temperature.

CRACK!!!

'You might want this one awake when it happens, Joe,' Helmet Man, said as he stood next to him, also looking at the girl.
'Why?'
'It'll enhance the experience,' he replied. 'Wake her up.'
Joe bent down and slapped her face, hard. 'Wake up, bitch,' he spat. 'Wake the fuck up!'

CRACK!!!

The girl roused, opening her eyes, looking confused and disorientated, but he was far too distracted by the noise that had returned, to even notice.

CRACK!!!

He winced and turned, a crazed smile forming on his lips.

CRACK!!!

Once again, he spun, searching the shadows for the source, knowing he was never going to find one.

CRACK!!!

He spared another glance towards the wriggling girl. He noticed she was now trying to scream.
'Good,' Helmet Man purred. 'Go and do it, Joe. Now!'

CRACK!!!

Crack

He hunched his shoulders, spinning around in a crazy jig. He was looking for Helmet Man, laughing to himself as he did. He saw him through the windshield of the van and danced his way over to the driver's side.

CRACK!!!

He slammed the door and started the engine.

'Not too fast,' Helmet Man advised him. 'You're going to want to savour this. Do it nice and slowly.'

Heeding Helmet Man's words, Joe released the brake, caught the bite, and the van began to move forwards, slowly.

'Slower, Joe, slower. Don't rush this. Just go nice and easy.'

'I KNOW HOW TO DRIVE A FUCKING CAR,' Joe screamed at his passenger. 'I'LL DRIVE THIS VAN OVER THAT BITCH'S HEAD IN MY OWN TIME. THEN YOU CAN FUCK OFF AND LEAVE ME ALONE LIKE YOU ALWAYS DO. DEAL?'

As he shouted, cold sweat dripped from his ashen face.

Helmet Man disappeared almost as quickly as he'd appeared. The emptiness of the van was just fine by him, as he inched towards his prey, his victim … his fix!

It didn't take him long to miss his helmeted companion, and he hoped he'd be back. He wanted someone to share this drug with, or rather he needed someone, but that person—*or the figment of who I think that person is,* —was nowhere to be seen. He wondered briefly if he could do this, if he could take this fix without Helmet Man holding his hand, or his cock.

In a moment of clarity, he remembered where he was and what he was doing. He took his foot off the accelerator and touched the brakes.

But he was too late.

The van had momentum.

Joe sat aghast. He was gripping the steering wheel, holding it tighter than he'd held any of his children, tighter than he'd held his wife on his wedding night. He felt if he let go, he would fall, tumbling into a deep abyss, where he would cartwheel and spin in a sick, velvety obsidian of his own twisted depravity, for all eternity.

The monster he'd become, and the actions he'd committed would dance before him until the end of days.

Then the familiar feeling of the van's wheels stroking the girl's head, crushing it beneath its weight, presented itself. The van buffeted as the suspension compensated for the human obstacle.

CRACK!!!

The delicious, moist, and warm noise enveloped him. It folded over him like a thick foam, or fog. It comforted him as it seeped into him via his ears, his nose, his mouth. Its texture flushed all the horror away in one smooth motion. All the despair, and the anguish he'd been feeling floated away on a red cloud of bloody euphoria once again. He sat back in the driver's seat and exhaled. A warm and satisfied smile was sitting on his face.

He opened the door and climbed out, once again to a landscape of carnage.

Methodically, once again on autopilot, he began to deal with the ramifications of his fix, of his sweet salvation, in much the same way as he had the last one. He rolled her warm, decapitated torso into one of the large cement pits and watched as the grey liquid swallowed the evidence of his addiction into a deep, uncelebrated grave.

A resting place that would never be found.

A chill ran through him; it was odd, delicious, yet terrifying all at the same time. He looked towards the idling van. Ignoring the horror show that was the girl's remains all over the front of it, he looked through the window.

In the passenger seat sat Helmet Man.

He's back!

Smiling, Joe shot him a wave.

The imaginary man in the cracked motorcycle helmet waved back.

57.

THE VERY NEXT night, Joe was back in the van. He was parked in the same street, beneath the same streetlamp. The vile noise was gone, as was his helmeted passenger. He was feeling fresh, having showered, and shaved, and changed his clothes earlier in the day. He was feeling good about himself. There was just a little *something,* that was niggling at him. Something he thought he wanted, but in the back of his mind, it was evident it was something he needed.

I don't have to be here tonight, he thought. *I could just drive away and spend the rest of the night at work, at peace with my thoughts. I will; I'll just get this over with. Just one more, and I'm done. This WILL be the last. It has to be! If I feed it forward, then maybe, just maybe, I can rid of it and that helmeted bastard once and for all.*

He sat for a few moments listening to the music spilling from the van's speakers. John Cougar Mellencamp was singing a little ditty about Jack and Diane, and Joe was trying to help by humming along to it, trying desperately to convince himself he was enjoying his new-found freedom. He loved that no one knew where he was, that he didn't have to explain himself to anyone regarding his whereabouts. He wasn't answerable to anyone right now. The world is my oyster. He was a lone wolf, waiting for his prey to come to him. He was proud, knowing that he could just leave if he wanted to. He'd convinced himself about that, but it was just that tonight, he didn't want to leave.

Tonight was for him.

A few rough-looking types had walked past him, expressing interest in what he might have to offer, but they all seemed wary somehow. None of them had wanted to approach.

Maybe tonight's just not my night.

With a disappointed click of his tongue, he reached underneath the dash to turn the ignition key. *There's other places I can go,* he thought, when a knock on his window surprised him.

She was another young girl. This one couldn't have been more than fifteen years of age, even that was at a push. She peered through the window and offered him a timid smile. Her thick, poorly applied makeup had the opposite effect to what she was attempting to achieve; it made her look younger rather than older, and a whole lot more desperate.

'Hey, mister, are you after a good time?' she shouted through the closed window, her voice breaking halfway through the sentence.

Inside, he cringed.

'How many bad movies has this piece of filth watched?' asked the familiar voice of Helmet Man, from inside the van. Joe was genuinely surprised to see him there in the back seat. He smiled at his guest.

'What's so funny?' she asked with a sass she didn't possess.

He turned back to her and smiled again before shaking his head. 'Oh, nothing. It's a private joke. Yeah, I *am* after a good time, actually. Can I tempt you to a drink?'

58.

'THAT'S FOUR WOMEN now, all from the same area, all reported missing over the past few weeks. Two of them in the last couple of days.' Paula was at her desk, staring into a computer screen. Her partner, Alan Ambrose, was hovering over her with an open file in his hands.

'That's a bit of a jump, Paula. Two are missing, one there's concern about, and we have one confirmed murder of someone who may or may not have frequented that area.' He offered her a tilt of his head. 'It's a leap, don't you think?'

Paula shook her head. 'I don't know. You know when something just jumps out at you, and won't let go?'

'Yeah.'

'Well, I've got that right now. How long has it been since the murder?'

Ambrose looked in the files. 'Eleven days.'

'And the last disappearance?'

'Well, there was an anonymous call yesterday morning around about a quarter to eleven. Whoever it was stated that one of the girls, a newbie known affectionately as Cherry, if you can believe that, didn't make it back after catching a punter the night before. She was last seen about half-twelve. The tipster stated the other girls are now wary about taking on unknown tricks.'

He put the files on the table and shook his head again. 'I'm sorry, but I just can't feel the sympathy I probably should for these women.'

Paula made her way to the coffee machine. It was her turn to shake her head. 'Jesus, Al. Look at the files. These are desperate people. Some of them are forced into this life, others graduate into it. Can you really see anyone wanting to sell themselves willingly? Can you think of it as ever being a career choice? No, these are the victims of physical and sexual abuse, drug and alcohol abuse. They're in bad situations, Al, and that horrible situation has just gotten a whole lot worse.'

'You're jumping again, Ashton,' Ambrose replied, taking the admonishment on the chin.

Paula sat back at her desk and looked at the file Ambrose had just handed to her. 'I don't think so. I think there's something going on here. I've got a feeling there's more to it, Al. A lot more.'

Without looking at her partner, she stood and walked towards the Sergeant's office at the far end of the office. She knocked on the door, and a small voice shouted invited her in.

Paula hovered in the doorway of the neat room; feeling like she was waiting to be seen by the headmistress in school. A small, unassuming woman was sitting behind a desk that looked far too large for her.

'Ma'am, can I have a moment?'

The diminutive Sergeant Price looked up from her computer and beckoned her in. She offered Paula a pleasant smile. 'What can I do for you, Detective?'

'Ma'am, I've got an interest in something I think may warrant further attention.'

'Can you elaborate?' offered Price.

'It's this. I think it's a lot bigger than it looks on first glance.'

The Sergeant leaned over the desk and accepted the offered file from Paula. She sat back in her large seat and opened it. 'I'm listening, Detective.'

Paula swallowed before proceeding. 'You're familiar with the murder we picked up on Brook Creek Lane?'

'I am.'

'Well, not far from there is a notorious red-light district. A lot of ladies plying their trade. Well, the assumption is that the victim might be one of them, a prostitute.'

'This is just a theory,' Price stated.

'At this moment, yes. We can't confirm either way yet, but all evidence is kind of pointing towards it.'

'Go on,' the Sergeant said, leafing through the file as she nodded.

Crack

'Well, there've been two more disappearances and one suspected disappearance since. All of them from the same area.'

'Working girls do tend to be migratory. Do you think they might have just moved on to a different patch?' the small sergeant asked, looking up at Paula from the open file.

'That was my first thought too, but then I thought that they must all be scared, or concerned at the very least, if they're reaching out to contact the very people who try to stop them from making their living. That's us. They must be pretty desperate.' Paula took a moment to catch her breath and to gauge Price's opinion on her theory. Noticing her positive, albeit negligible, reaction, Paula was spurred on. 'There's obviously some kind of bond between these girls. That made me think that something deeply nefarious is happening here.'

The sergeant raised her eyebrows. 'Well, Detective, I think there may well be something to this.' She sat back and regarded Paula and the silent Al, stood on the opposite side of her desk. 'So, how do you want to proceed with this, detective?'

Paula opened her mouth but hesitated. A horrible twisting feeling overwhelmed her. She'd stormed into Price's office without a real plan for going forward with this, and was going to have to back track on this. 'Well, erm, I'm … going to take tonight, give it some serious consideration. I think that a case as potentially important as this one requires scrutiny. I don't want to rush into anything.'

'You have my approval then,' the sergeant said, standing up and handing the file back to her.

A smile spread across Paula's face as she gathered up her files. 'Thank you, ma'am. I'll have a plan of action for you in the morning.'

Price smiled at her; it was her cue to leave.

59.

'NO WAY. ABSOLUTELY no way, Paula. Why would you even want to do this? It's four weeks till the wedding.' Ian shouted, his face a glowing deep pink. He was bouncing around the living room of their home, trying his very best not to look at his wife-to-be.

She was sitting cross-legged on the couch, surrounded by pillows. There was a physical, and psychological barrier between them. 'It's an opportunity. You said we need all the overtime we can get our hands on, what with the wedding and the honeymoon to pay for. So, there's that, plus the added factor that there just might be a serial killer running free through Birkenhead, who needs bringing down before he can strike again.'

Ian flapped his arms; not believing what he was hearing. 'This isn't a box set crime caper, Paula. There has to be others who can do this. Why does it have to be you?'

'Because I'm the one who's seen the link, Ian. I've seen the pattern. No-one else has. Just me.'

Ian stopped bouncing and faced her for the first time since she'd brought up the subject. 'Paula, we get married in four weeks. I don't want, sorry, *we* don't want you to be tied up in a case and too engrossed to even think about the big day, never mind enjoy all the build-up. You know what you're like, you know how you get.'

'I won't this time.'

He turned away from her again, directing his rant towards the wall. 'You will. You always do. You get too emotionally involved.'

'Ian, innocent women are disappearing. They need someone to look out for them.'

'See,' he shouted, pointing his finger. 'You're already involved. Emotionally attached. You're not a fucking superhero, Paula; you don't wear a cape, and bullets don't bounce off you. You're my fiancée, and you're Sally's mother.'

Paula took the hit on that one; she recoiled as if she'd been slapped in the face. But like the true, tough detective she was, she bounced straight back at her attacker. 'These women are daughters too.' She left that shot hanging in the air between them, for a moment or two. 'They've hit some hard times, but they're still people. Someone needs to do something for them, to look out for them.'

'But why you?' He threw his arms in the air. 'Oh, for fuck's sake, I don't even have it in me to fight with you about this anymore. Let's forget it. I've said my piece. You do what you need to do.'

Paula got up from the couch, making sure not to wake Sally, who was sleeping on the other end.

'Where're you going?' Ian asked, his face still brooding, his eyes like thunder.

'I'm going to make a cup of tea. Do you want one?'

He scoffed and shook his head. 'Yeah, go on then.'

Without looking at him, she walked out of the living room, towards the kitchen.

His eyes followed her. He adjusted the still sleeping Sally on the couch, so she wasn't in danger of falling off, and then sat down with a loud sigh. He glared towards the door where Paula had exited, then looked at the TV remote control. He grabbed it and prodded the button to change the channel, almost breaking the fragile plastic in the process. His eyes glanced over what was on the screen for a few moments before throwing the remote onto the chair on the other side of the room. It bounced, hitting the floor hard.

He closed his eyes, crossed his arms, and sighed again.

60.

SIMILARLY TO IAN, Joe was nervous too. Only he was trouncing around his bedroom alone. His bed was unmade; his clothes were strewn about the floor and furniture. Dirty dishes were piling up in every room. The curtains were half open, and the blinds behind them were crooked. His face was pained, and he was biting at his nails as if there was some kind of delicacy behind them that he was eager to get at.

His hair was greasy and unkempt, and his grubby pyjama bottoms and t-shirt looked long out of the washing basket, far too long. This was how he was coping on his own, trying to get used to the fact he was now single, and the reality of his newfound addiction.

He perched himself on the edge of the bed and eyed the telephone on the bedside table as if it was a dangerous animal, something not to be trusted. Three times he'd picked it up, and twice he'd failed to make the call, dropping the receiver as if it were hot or was going to jump up and bite him. Eventually, he'd built up the courage and grabbed it again, handling it as if it were a dangerous snake or something slimy and disgusting that he would rather not be touching. He was looking at the dial pad, his breath was shallow, and his pulse was pounding in his temples. He pressed a couple of buttons and waited. There was a loud *BEEP*, and then the message began.

'Joe, Joe, if you're there, please pick up …' It was an electronic version of Karen. 'I don't think he's there,' her voice spoke, obviously talking to someone else in the room with her. 'OK, OK. Joe, I need to tell you something. We're staying with my cousin in Newcastle. Her place is big enough, and she hasn't seen the kids for years. She said we can stay as long as we want. Now, I need you to

Crack

know a few things. I don't blame you for what happened, I don't. But I do think you need more help. You've got a deep psychological issue, Joe. It's been there ever since the accident.'

CRACK!!!

It was as if the mere mention of the word *accident* brought the noise with it. He winced, hunching his shoulders; his eyes began to dart around the room. He expected to see Helmet Man standing motionless somewhere deep within the shadows.

A sense of relief settled over him when he saw there was no one there.

'You've been cranky and out of sync,' Karen continued. 'You've been having nightmares, and you even told me sometimes you don't know if you're awake or if you're still dreaming. That's not right, Joe. You need to go back and see that Dr Saunders. She's the only one who can help you now. I *had* to leave; you have to understand that. I needed to get away for my safety, and for the safety of the kids.'

There was a long pause.

CRACK!!!

'Anyway, I'm going to have to go now; this call is upsetting me as much as I think it'll upset you when you hear it. The kids are fine. I think they're kind of missing you, but what happened has left a lasting effect on them. It really has. Listen, I'll ring again in a day or so. You look after yourself, and please ... get in touch with Dr Saunders. You need more help. Goodbye, Joe.'

There was another *BEEP,* and the line went dead.

He picked up the phone and pressed R. An automated voice came through the receiver. 'The number you have dialled has not been recognised. Please replace the handset and try again.' His vision doubled, and his face creased as he stood up. He was all set to throw the phone against the wall. He longed to watch the hateful thing smash into a hundred thousand little unfixable pieces. *Maybe I'll get off on the fucking crack it makes,* he thought.

He stopped himself from doing it. The rage ebbed from in him almost as fast as it had flown. Deflated, his shoulders sagged, his head followed suit. There was just no use in smashing it; he'd only regret it later. He sat back down on the edge of the bed and put his head in his hands.

His body shuddered with each sob.

CRACK!!!

'You knew she wouldn't come back, didn't you?'

The sound of the emotionless, monotone voice made his blood boil again. Adrenaline surged through his body. The bitter taste of bile filled his mouth. With his heart banging in his throat, he opened his fingers and peered through them. He wasn't expecting to see Helmet Man sat on the bed next to him, but he wasn't overly surprised he was.

'No! No, not you again. Why can't you just leave me the fuck alone?' His shout became a rant. His voice broke midsentence. 'Why you, you bastard? Why you and not Karen?'

'Karen's not coming back any time soon, Joe. But you knew I was. She can't give you what you need, not like I can.'

Joe threw himself back against the headboard where he curled himself into a ball, hiding his head from his unwanted friend. Tears poured freely down his cheeks. 'You can't. You've ruined my life. I'm going back to therapy. I'm going to ring that Penny Saunders. She can help me. She can help me fuck you off, once and for all.'

Helmet Man loomed over his pathetic figure nestled at the head of the bed. The muffled laughter that escaped the cracked visor was strange to Joe's ears. 'She created me. Do you not see the irony there? She's the one who told you to give me a form, and a name so that you can communicate your grief, and anxiety, before waving me goodbye. How did that turn out for you, Joe? It wasn't me who ruined your life. You do realise that now, don't you? Dr Saunders, or *Penny,* can't help you now. Not with the kind of help you need. I'm the only one who can do that for you. I'm the only one who can make your existence … tolerable.'

Crack

'AT WHAT COST? AT WHAT FUCKING COST? MY SOUL? MY ... MY FUCKING INNOCENCE?' he screamed, suddenly angry again.

'Maybe,' Helmet Man answered calmly. 'But at least you'll be able to sleep at night. And you have to admit,'— he began to undo the straps of the helmet, beneath his chin— 'you kind of like it, don't you?'

He watched with a dawning sense of horror and a wave of revulsion, and depression overwhelmed him. He watched as Helmet Man slowly lifted his helmet off his head.

His face lengthened and the breath from his lungs was stolen, snatched away in a smash and grab. His eyes were wild and unfocused as he cowered further into the bed, putting as much space between himself and the ghoulish monstrosity that was revealing itself, as he could.

Helmet Man finished removing his cracked helmet and turned slowly towards him.

It was difficult to look at, and his eyes felt as if they were not working, or just refused too.

The faces of the four dead women morphed slowly over each other, like a bad movie special effect.

It merged between them again and again, and again. He wanted to scream as they all smiled at him. He could imagine them all wanting a drink of cola.

The morphing slowed, before ultimately stopping on one face. It was the worst of them all.

Joe's own laughing, but ultimately ruined face was left on Helmet Man's shoulders.

Joe knew if he screamed now, he might fall into a chasm of madness and might never stop screaming again.

Suddenly his breath came back, and with it came the screams.

61.

IT WAS DARK, cold, and wet at three in the morning. Joe might have mused that it was a great euphemism for his life, if he knew what a euphemism was. He was in the driving seat of the work van, parked underneath the same dim, yellow streetlamp.

It wasn't really a surprise for him to find himself here.

His mouth was nothing more than a white slash on his face, as the street was deserted.

He opened the glove compartment, and the mostly empty bottle of Nytrodol rolled out. 'Shit,' he cursed, picking it up from the footwell. When he raised his head, he reeled, as the figure of an older woman was peering into the driver's window.

When she saw him, she backed up a little, but stopped herself, and offered him a rather forced smile.

That's right, baby, don't run away, he thought. There was a moment where he wondered if it had been him who'd made that comment. He looked around the cab for Helmet Man, but he was alone. *Of course, it was me. It's always been me!* This thought didn't exactly fill him with feelings of butterflies and fairies.

The woman made as if to re-approach the van. She hesitated, looked the other way, down the street. Smiling, Joe wound his window down and beckoned her over.

'Listen,' she addressed him in a hiss that he guessed was supposed to be a whisper. 'I'm only out here because I need the money. All the other bitches, they went home, or they just never came out at all. I'll blow you right here for thirty, but I'm not getting into the van or going anywhere else with you.'

Joe smiled at the woman's resolve. Although he wondered how anyone, no matter how desperate they were, would be able to get an erection with this woman on her knees before them. She was truly hideous. Her hair was obviously a wig, and the fleshy jowls of her face gave her a look of a put-upon bulldog. Her makeup had been hurried, and her eyes had such an ingrained sadness within them. This woman had seen too much; she'd had too much harm inflicted upon her. There was understanding somewhere in there too, the realisation that her advanced age and the ravages of her body would soon force an end to everything she did to make money, everything she did to survive; everything she knew.

Joe read all of this in her heavily made-up dark eyes.

'A blow job here is just as good any anywhere else, right?' he said, offering her his very best politician's smile.

She looked at him. There was no humour in her ugly face, only desperation. Joe surmised by her stink that she had a serious drinking problem, or maybe something a little deeper, heavier than drink; but then, he didn't think he should be judging people on their addictions, not in his state.

'Show me the money first,' she demanded.

He put on a show of sighing and rummaging around his pockets. Eventually, he pulled out his wallet and flashed two twenty pound notes at her.

She regarded them with greedy eyes. 'I haven't got any change,' she said, not taking her eyes from the money.

Joe could see by her greedy, expectant face that she needed this money. The worm on the end of his hook had done its job.

'I don't want any,' he replied. 'Just get in, get me off, and get out. Quick as that.'

'I'm not driving anywhere with you,' she reiterated defensively, wrapping her long, cheap coat around her poorly dressed, thick torso.

Joe envisioned her headless torso sinking slowly into one of the cement pits back at the site. It brought on a, not entirely unpleasant, tingling sensation in his trousers. 'I'm not asking you to.' His politician's smile made a comeback.

She gave the area another scan, as if looking for someone, anyone, but there was not another soul in the area. She tightened her lips and exhaled. The stink of her breath repulsed him.

She climbed into the passenger seat, all the time searching the street for an elusive witness of her getting into this vehicle. 'You need to pay me before anything happens,' she demanded again.

'Why don't you have a drink of this first?' he asked.

'I don't want a drink. I want my money or no business,' she snapped.

Joe smiled at her. *I wonder how this one ever gets any business at all,* he thought, leaning into the back seat. 'Just let me get my wallet,' he said.

She eyed him suspiciously. 'You had it in your hand a moment ago,' she snapped again. 'I really need to get my money and get home.' She hugged herself, looking out of the window. She wasn't too nervous to refuse the forty that was on offer.

She turned back towards him.

There was an angry glint in her eyes, but he knew the anger was only masking how scared she was right now. 'Are you hard? I don't want to be fucking around down there trying to get you hard. I need to suck you and then get away.' She was fidgeting now, unsure what to do with herself as he fumbled about in the foot well of the back seat. 'What are you still rooting around back there for? You need to be getting yourself hard. I'm not messing about here, fella.' The waver in her voice was making what she was saying almost indecipherable.

Joe smiled at her again. The woman's flabby face dropped as she looked at him. 'Oh, don't you worry.' It was his turn to hiss, although this time it was with an edge of manic to it. 'I've got something really hard for you right … here.'

He whipped out the tyre iron that had fallen from the back seat into the foot-well and whacked the woman across the temple with it. It tore open a nasty gash across her forehead. The resulting blood spatter drew a Rorschach pattern across the passenger side window as her head swung with the force of the blow. *I'll have to remember to clean that up,* he thought, looking at it.

Her face swung back to look at him. The blood from the gash on her temple was already flowing, ruining her thickly applied makeup. It dripped down her head, collecting a fair amount of bronze foundation with it. It turned her already hideous face into an oozing, dripping Halloween mask.

Crack

Her sad green eyes looked at him.

Yes, there was fear and anger in them, but they were not the forefront emotions he could see. He didn't see it straight away, but when he did, what was left of his black heart broke for the poor beast before him. The look he saw was resignation. Maybe there was even a thanks in there somewhere. It was as if she had been expecting something like this to happen, like she'd known her ending would come this way, that it had been somehow predesigned.

He couldn't stand the look. It was too accusatory for his liking. So, he hit her again in the same area, hoping to wipe it from her, to stop her from being grateful for what he was about to do to her.

He hit her one more time, spit drooled from his mouth as his did. He wiped absently at it as the dark, sad light in her eyes blinked out.

His relief then was almost as great as it would be later, when he brought on the real crack.

Her lifeless body sank into the passenger seat.

He leaned over and felt her neck for a pulse. He didn't want her dead; he didn't want *any* of them dead.

His fingers fumbled before finding an active pulse; it was faint, but it was there.

He'd done his job.

He offered a cursory glance around the street. He knew he'd taken a chance doing what he had just done actually on the street, but he also knew that his needs were orchestrating this situation. Satisfied that no one had seen him conduct his business, he continued about his grisly trade. Taking an old rag from his pocket, he laid it across the bloody gash on the woman's head. He didn't want to have to explain excess blood inside the van in the morning, and he really didn't relish the idea of shampooing the upholstery tonight; there was far too much fun to be had. Satisfied he'd stemmed the bleeding; he clicked his seatbelt and drove out of the dingy street.

~~~

When he got back to site, he parked the van by the newest cement pit that had been laid today. He exited and stretched, taking his time, breathing deep of the clear early morning air. He let out a shout into the air, he'd read about primal scream therapy on the internet, and he did think it worked. He opened the passenger side door and allowed the woman's body to fall out onto the road.

This woke her up, and a few moans escaped her. Even though she was still unconscious, she wasn't too far away from waking up.

He had to get her secured, and soon.

He opened the rear passenger door and removed the bag he'd stashed there. Inside were plastic zip wires and duct tape that he needed for a job of this size. He'd gotten good at this. He strapped the woman's hands together, then her feet, with the plastic ties. He removed the rag from her bleeding head, marvelling at the amount of blood a small laceration on the forehead could produce, before stuffing it into her mouth and securing it with the tape

Once her airway was blocked and her only avenue to breathe was her nose, she began to rouse. Her eyes flickered open. It took her eyes a few moments to focus and understand what was happening to her. The sad green eyes opened wide, and her nostrils flared as she overcompensated her panicked breathing through the small holes. She tried to wriggle free of her bounds, but they were too powerful, and she was, by now, severely restricted in her movements. He dragged her unceremoniously across the little road and opened the door to the small cabin at the side of the pit. She was a bigger woman than he was used to, and he struggled dragging her inside.

~~~~

Her old eyes slowly adjusted to the gloom inside the shed. She had absolutely no idea where she was, but she knew it probably wouldn't end well for her. Once the whirl of thoughts slowed, and her eyes began to see in the gloom, she realised she was not alone. As it dawned on her, what she shared this small, musty space with, she began to wriggle and thrash harder, trying hard to scream, but no sound other than the odd muffled, 'ugg' made it past the filthy tasting thing in her mouth.

Inside the cabin were three other women, all of them dressed in the same style she was. She guessed they were the same as her: working girls. They were all in the same predicament, tied up with tape covering their mouths. Three pairs of eyes looked to her. They were all filled with the same horror she was feeling.

'Now, why don't you ladies get yourselves acquainted, and I'll be back in a few moments to commence the show,' the man she'd been talking to on the street said, as a psychotic smile spread over his face.

He left the little cabin, slamming the door behind him, causing all the women inside, including her, to jump.

The latest addition to this odd harem looked around the gloom. All the eyes were on her. She could see the hope in them, as they all looked to her as maybe the one who could save them from whatever the maniac wanted from them. She could feel the expectation these women had for her.

Nausea sloshed in her stomach as the taste of the bloody rag and the cheap wine in her reacted badly. She was in no position to help any of them, she was old, tired, ready to lie down and accept everything that was coming her way. Maybe she deserved all of this anyway.

She had enough about her to know that if she vomited now, it would be all over, she would choke. The hot liquid would have nowhere else to go but back down. The ache in her head wasn't helping, as it beat like a marching drum, stemming from the open wound on her temple. The sting of the blood tricking into her eyes wasn't helping her situation either. She saw that none of the other women had head wounds, all they had were wide, scared eyes. She might have recognised one or two of them from the street, but as they weren't exactly a community down there, she couldn't be sure.

The door burst open, and all the eyes in the room released her from their capture. They were all on the figure re-entering with such a bluster.

The man's eyes were wild and even in the darkness, she could tell there was something wrong with them. From her low point of view, he loomed over them all like a spectre, a portent of doom, or maybe the Grim Reaper himself.

The way he entered, and the way he was glancing out the door, he was spooked, as if he didn't want to be here, doing this; like something, or someone, was coercing him into it.

Without a word, he leaned in and grabbed the nearest woman to the door, dragging her outside. She struggled and kicked, but her bonds were too tight for her to get any purchase on the floor and stop him from his course of action.

The gag across her mouth muffled her screams.

'Come on you, it's time.' He spoke as if she were nothing but an animal going off to slaughter.

Which in effect, was exactly what she was.

Crack

62.

'GET THEM ALL in a row,' Helmet Man barked. There was an air of expectation in his voice, as if he were excited by what they were doing.

CRACK!!!

Joe recoiled, shying away from the horrible, yet excitable noise as he dragged the first woman unceremoniously across the tarmacked road.

'They need to be at least fifty feet apart.'

Joe dumped the woman on the side of the road and stood back, he was rubbing his back as he cocked his head.

She looked at him, her petrified eyes were pleading with him. He ignored her pathetic looks as he reached down to reposition her head.

'That's about right. Now go and get the next one. She needs to be about …' Helmet Man disappeared, before reappearing roughly fifty yards further down the road. 'Here,' he directed.

Joe came back from the cabin, dragging another wriggling woman behind him.

'Just lay her down about here,' Helmet Man shouted. Something in his voice gave away his enjoyment in this activity.

Joe was sweating, despite the chill in the night air, as he dragged the writhing woman towards where Helmet Man was pointing. He laid her on the edge of the road, positioning her head in place exactly as he did with the first.

He stepped back once again and pouted, mentally measuring the distance between his two fixes. He nodded his own approval and made his way back to the cabin.

CRACK!!!
CRACK!!!
CRACK!!!
CRACK!!!

He did his best to ignore the noises; he had more work to do before he could have his fun. He was damned if he'd let the stupid phantom sound ruin it. With his face dripping with sweat, he pulled another woman out of the cabin, hauling her towards where Helmet Man was standing roughly another fifty feet further down. He positioned her exactly as he'd done with the previous two.

'Only one more left. This is going to be the best of them all,' Helmet Man shouted.

Joe emerged from the cabin with the last woman and roughly yanked her all the way along the road to where Helmet Man was indicating. As he pulled his haul the full two hundred feet, the exposed flesh on her arms and legs ripped where it contacted the rough road. Blood poured from her open wounds, the ones opened by the cruel tarmac, and the one on her forehead. None of this meant anything to him. These women had ceased to be human a long time ago; they were now merely a means to an end, instruments he needed to feed his addiction, to get him to where he wanted to be … or was it where he needed to be?

If he was honest with himself, he wasn't quite sure anymore.

~~~

She was the last one out of the cabin. He reached into the darkness that had enveloped her and birthed her into the cold, dark night. He dragged her along the road, past the other stricken women laying on their sides, bound and gagged, watching her as she passed them. Six terrified eyes, accusing her of allowing this to happen to them. Asking why she wasn't the one who could have saved them. They were all cold eyes, expecting her to do something she just couldn't do. She felt like she had been their last hope, the one slim chance of them getting out of the terrible situation they'd found themselves in, and maybe able to live at least another day of their awful, miserable, existence. But it wasn't to be. She was as doomed as they were. She felt sorry for them. They were younger than her, it was possible for them to get out of the downward spiral of their lives, break free of whatever it was binding them to a life of addiction, and selling themselves to low paying punters, who thought they were just there to punish for their own failings in life.

She was old now. Past her prime. This was as good a swan song as she could have hoped for.

She felt like she deserved this.

They didn't.

The scrapes and lacerations from the road didn't hurt her. The throb in her head no longer registered. She was a convicted prisoner, being punished for living a bad life.

I'm being dragged towards my very own guillotine, she thought, heralding back to her minimal education. She closed her eyes and thought about her children. A son and a daughter, both living away in a warmer climate, with their father and the slut he'd taken off with. She laughed at this; the irony was too much for her. The fact she thought of that woman as a slut, and here she was, being dragged down a deserted road, bound and gagged, all because she needed to suck someone's dick to fuel her fix.

She thought about the children's beautiful faces, back when they were all together, a loving family, before the hard times, before the external influences brought forth this deserved demise.

~~~~

Oblivious to the internal drama unfolding in his fix's head, Joe had his eyes fixed on Helmet Man, thinking about how long it would take to do what was needed to do.

Once the last part of the jigsaw was in place, a hand landed on Joe's shoulder. It made him jump. He turned to see Helmet Man beside him.

'Good work. Now you know what you have to do.'

Joe's demented look changed in an instant. As he stared into Helmet Man's visor, he watched his smile slip from maniacal to warm and vibrant. He was pouting and nodding as he almost staggered towards the cabin. Inside, he grabbed the keys to the van, then climbed into the driver's seat.

He paused for a moment, admiring the view.

For at least two hundred yards in front of him lay pure salvation. A salvation that came in the form of four fixes. The throb in his trousers had become almost too much for him to bear, and he grabbed at himself through the overalls he was wearing. A delightful shiver coursed through him. It felt wonderful, but he knew it could, and would, feel even better when Helmet Man appeared next to him, and grabbed it for him.

That was exactly what happened next. He turned to his friend, staring into his own reflection, as a leather gloved hand stroked his cock, teasing it gently.

He closed his eyes, wanting to savour the moment, to enjoy the anticipation of what was to come. He felt like a child on Christmas Eve; the magic was in the anticipation.

When he was ready, he could feel a slight tingle in his feet, always a precursor to a sweet, sweet orgasmic release, he twisted the keys, kicking the van's engine into life. It roared like a lion. The headlights came on, fully illuminating his two-hundred-yard journey of fun. Four pairs of wide eyes stared towards him, each reflecting the lights in much the same way as a cat's eyes did in the middle of the road.

A grin washed over his face as he gripped the steering wheel and instantly began to sweat again. He took four deep, relaxing breaths, one for each of his fixes, and released them in stuttering exhales. Helmet Man matched each breath with a squeeze of his erection. More teasing.

Countless butterflies were beating up a riot in his stomach, and along the shaft of his cock.

CRACK!!!
CRACK!!!
CRACK!!!
CRACK!!!

Crack

The noise was incessant, relentless. He embraced it, understanding what he was about to receive. 'Yes, crack,' he muttered beneath his breath and turned to smile at his passenger.

CRACK!!!
CRACK!!!
CRACK!!!
CRACK!!!

Helmet Man was breathing hard beneath his visor. Joe could hear him; it sounded like an impression of the bad guy from one of those science fiction films he liked when he was a kid. As he looked at him, he could see a resemblance to the character. All dressed in black and wearing a helmet. *What was that guy's name?* he thought absently. *Dark something?* He pushed the thought to the back of his mind, listening to the excitement in his voice. 'Take it, Joe. Enjoy it, embrace it. Replace that fake noise with the real thing. This will take it all away, give you relief, even if it's only for the short term.'

He reached out to Helmet Man; he suddenly wanted to hold his hand. He wanted to hold the hand that was gripping his throbbing cock, but he couldn't.

He knew he was on his own here.

'Go on, you can do this. You've wanted this all along. You *know* you need it. Release yourself from the hell you're trapped in. BRING ON THE REAL CRACK!'

Joe turned away from the helmeted demon, or seductress, in the passenger seat and looked towards his short journey ahead.

Licking his lips, he could taste the salt laced sweaty build up in the scruffy grey stubble above his upper lip. He slipped the van into first and pressed lightly on the accelerator. The vehicle edged forward, ever so slightly. He was on his way. He was ready to grasp his destiny. His slick, sweaty palm slipped from the ball at the top of the gear shift, and he absently wiped it on his overall leg. Then he did grip Helmet Man's hand, the one holding his erection. He enjoyed the feeling of being close, on the edge, but not allowing himself to go just yet.

Will power, he thought. *The enjoyment is in the build-up.*

He tapped the accelerator, and the van gained momentum.

CRACK!!!

The sound was deliciously real again.
It was wet and rich and … yes, it was wonderful.
'Keep going, Joe. You've only just begun.'
He pressed the accelerator again, and the van continued forward on its terrible journey.

CRACK!!!

The familiar resistance and the familiar bump of the suspension happened again as the wheels stroked the second woman's head. He loved it, desired it, craved it. It was the only thing he wanted in the whole of the world. *Fuck Karen,* he thought. *Fuck those ungrateful bastard kids of mine. This is all I love; this is all I need.* His legs were shaking as pure, undiluted adrenaline coursed through them.

The van kept moving. His heart was beating faster than he'd ever felt it do before, and his erection was equalling the throb. He was the hardest he had ever been, even when he was a teenager. He laughed as he thought about the erection he would always get just before his stop on the bus, and the embarrassment of having to tuck it in while pushing past people to get to the doors.

CRACK!!!

Moist, dense, thick, and fabulous.
It was an ugly sound, he knew that, but it sent him a shiver of pure euphoria. It lifted all his negative feelings, allowing them to flitter off into the ether. It was a kaleidoscope of butterflies taking off, as one, within his stomach and his loins.

'OOOOOH FUCK,' he moaned as he closed his eyes. The waves of endorphins surging through every fibre of his being, were almost too much for him.

'There's still one more to do,' Helmet Man whispered in his ear, as he squeezed his cock eve tighter. 'How good are feeling right now? It will be nothing compared to how you'll feel after that last hit.'

Crack

He turned towards his passenger. He was having trouble focusing on anything solid. He knew he should be feeling uncomfortable doing what he was doing with another man, but he was beyond caring. *He's me anyway,* he thought. *I've been doing it with him around all my life!* He almost giggled at this thought as he turned back to the job at hand. The last woman was wriggling and kicking, her eyes were how he envisioned a demon's might be as they reflected the radiance of his headlights. He pressed on the pedal again, continuing his deadly path forwards.

The bump came; the noise came—

CRACK!!!

—and then Joe came!

The release of tension within his body synchronised with the release of ejaculate within his trousers. It was almost too much for him to bear. It was sensory overload. This feeling would be too intense for anyone to bear. For just a moment, his whole world turned white. He felt as if he were on a different plane of existence. Nothing moved, but there was a warm breeze. He was in a car, he was on a highway, it was sunny, there was a beautiful, semi-naked lady in the seat next to him, she was gripping his cock, tight…

The next moment he was leaning forward in the driver's seat of his van. He was still in spasm, shouting, screaming with an ecstasy that he had never experienced before, not even once, in the whole of his life. This was the ultimate primal scream therapy.

The van came to a halt, idling on the tarmac, but it was some time before his multi-orgasm followed suit.

Eventually, the ecstasy in his stomach, groin, and head subsided, and he threw himself back into the van's seat. His eyes were closed as an overwhelming fatigue filtered through every single muscle, tiring, and elating him in equal measures. A wave of sleepiness enveloped him, and he closed his eyes, relaxing into the comfort of his seat.

A goofy smile spread across his face.

With a jolt, he opened his eyes. His heart, his head, and his cock were all still thudding as he looked out of the window.

The last thing that he could do now was to succumb to this fatigue and fall asleep. He licked his dry lips as he regarded the clock, relieved to see that less than ten minutes had elapsed since his, *what was it, a journey of enlightenment?* He liked that description.

He opened the door, relishing the blast of cold air on his hot and clammy face. It woke him, revived him. Oblivious to the thick, wet patch at the front of his trousers, he exited the van and bent down to study its wheels. The vehicle was a confusion of blood, hair, bone, and brains. It was quite literally a bloody mess. Sporting a smile from the joke he'd just made, he dared to look back down the road he had just travelled.

It was a two-hundred-feet trail of gore.

He scratched his head, smiling vacantly. 'It's going to be a long night,' he muttered. He re-entered the cabin and grabbed the tools he now thought of as his cleaning up kit and made his way down the blood-drenched road. It was tough going dodging the pools of human remains that had gathered on the tarmac.

63.

'OH, MY GOD!'

Alan Ambrose poked his head over the computer monitor that separated him and his partner. He knew from experience, when she blurted out random things, it meant she was on to something. That was what made her an excellent detective, and an even better partner. He was eager to hear whatever it was she had to say now. 'What is it?'

'I put a shout out to the vice departments around the city and the surrounding areas. Just a speculative email to see if there was anything unusual reported by the street-girls and the beat cops.'

Ambrose stood up, a steaming cup in his hand. He made his way around to Paula's side and bent over her shoulder to look at her screen. 'And?'

She flashed him a smile, the kind of smile that tells you everything you need to know before the person says it. 'And … another girl went missing from our favourite spot the night before last.'

Ambrose nodded. 'So that's four in total now. I think we need to get this out there.'

Paula shook her head. 'It's bigger than that, Al. On the same night, the night before last, two girls went missing from Springfield, and one from a street in Manton, by the docks.'

Ambrose put his cup down and leaned in closer. The screen was showing a map of the surrounding areas, at twenty mile radius, with three red dots on it.

'I think we need to see the sergeant again,' she said. 'I want to do a stakeout on this street.' She was pointing to their favourite part of town, the one where the majority of the girls had disappeared from.

Ambrose tucked his shirt in. 'Let's go,' he replied. She was already up and halfway across the office before he had a chance to follow her.

Price's door was open, but Paula knocked anyway.

'Come in, Paula. You don't need to knock.' The small woman behind the big desk stood as they entered.

'Ma'am, we've got something. I think it's solid. I've just forwarded you a little something via email.'

The Sergeant sat down and began clicking at her computer. After a moment, she settled and began reading something on her screen, her brow ruffling the further she read. Paula and Ambrose were standing on the other side of the desk, neither of their eyes leaving the smaller woman's.

After almost a minute, she looked up at the two detectives. She was nodding. 'This is excellent, detectives.'

'I didn't have much to do with it, ma'am. This is all Ashton's work. I'm just here to make the coffee.'

The sergeant fixed her gaze on Paula. 'So, now that we've got our link, what do you propose next?'

'I was thinking we should stake the street out, get someone undercover, see what the vibe is like out there. Get a handle on the mood.'

Sergeant Price pulled a face that said that she wasn't very happy with this plan. 'That's a lot of commitment, overtime, and resources. Who would you propose went undercover?'

'Well, me, ma'am,' Ashton said. 'I've got the experience in the field, and I recommend I'll be armed.'

'And I'll be her back up. She'd be wearing a wire on her at all times, and I'd be no further than fifty yards away in the car,' Ambrose added.

Paula looked at him and smiled.

The sergeant looked from one detective to the other; she gritted her teeth. 'The fire-arm permissions may be an issue, but I think the idea is a good one. I'll have to see if they'll go for it upstairs. I'll give it my seal of approval and see what they say. Just don't start counting your chickens just yet.'

Paula's jaw was hanging open.

Crack

Price looked at her. 'Yes, Detective,' she said, emphasising the file in her hand. 'This is excellent work.' And with that, they were dismissed.

Paula and Ambrose made it back to their desks in silence. Paula put her hands behind her head and exhaled.

Ambrose was nodding. 'You know, if this comes off, it's going to put you in line for promotion.'

She nodded slowly. 'I know, and if I get it, you're coming with me. I'm going to need someone to carry my handbag.'

'If there's a pay rise in it, I'll even shine your shoes.'

'Hold that thought, Detective Shoeshine,' Paula laughed.

64.

'NO, ABSOLUTELY NO way on God's green Earth. I'm going to allow you to go out there dressed like that.' Ian's glowing flush was spreading from his face, down his neck, and onto his chest.

Paula was in the bedroom, standing before a full-length mirror. She was twisting and turning, trying to get a look at her outfit from all sides.

Her outfit consisted of a purple glittering mini skirt and a sequined boob-tube top that showed off most of what God had given her. Her hair had been gelled back and pulled into a rattail style ponytail. Her normally, minimally made-up face was caked in cheap cosmetics, making her look at least ten years older. There were bruises on her arms and legs where she'd blended mascara and eye shadow, in the hope they looked authentic.

They did.

'I won't be out there alone. Ambrose will be covering me,' she replied, face him. 'Anyway, it's not your call to tell me what I can and can't do, is it?' she snapped, looking back into the mirror.

'For Christ's sake, Paula, see sense, will you, please. We're getting married in a few weeks.'

She turned from the mirror to look at him again; the anger merging with the thickly applied makeup made her pretty face look vicious in the stark lights above the mirror. 'What's that got to do with any of this? Nothing, that's what. Listen, three nights ago, four girls went missing from our streets, making that a total of seven, that includes the murdered girl. Remember her? She was the one minus a head.' She stepped towards him still standing on the landing. 'If there's a serial killer out there, then I'm going to bring him in.'

Crack

Ian's fists were clenching and unclenching as he tried to control his shallow breathing. He also knew he was fighting a losing battle. He flapped his arms and turned away. He couldn't abide seeing her wearing that makeup. 'Why does it *have* to be you?' He knew he needed a different tract for this argument, and the correct ammunition was stored in his arsenal. 'Sally wouldn't want her mummy going out looking like that.'

The mention of Sally's name seemed to tip Paula over an edge. The thick foundation plastered on her face darkened. 'Don't you fucking *DARE* bring her into this, Ian. That's not fair, and it's wrong,' she hissed, her face flushing a deep scarlet as the tirade spilled from her mouth.

Ian didn't want to back down, but knew he had to, for all their sakes. 'OK, that was out of order, I'll give you that, but why can't we just get Sally to stay with your mum and I'll be your lookout too? Two set of eyes and all that.'

'The office won't authorise extra overtime.' She dismissed him by turning around and fixing a small handgun inside her mini skirt.

Ian looked at the gun and shook his head. 'What's that?'

She ignored the question.

He rolled his eyes.

'Listen, Price doesn't need to know. I wouldn't be claiming overtime. I'd just be looking out for my wife.'

She turned back towards him as she fixed the gun, so it was fully concealed inside her skirt. Her nostrils were flaring, and her face was still flushed beneath the circus-like makeup.

'I'm not your wife yet,' she spat.

'You know what I mean.'

'No, Ian, I don't know what you mean. Why don't you tell me?' she asked, crossing her arms.

'I just …'

'Look,' she said, the harshness in her voice softening just a little. 'I'm a detective. I have to put myself on the line for the job. No one knows that more than you.'

As he looked at her, his mouth pouted, and he folded his arms, mimicking her stance. 'But I don't go out dressed like a whore to do it,' he mumbled, like a child being scolded for taking the last biscuits from the tin.

'Well, we're just unlucky this killer isn't targeting respectable female business types then, aren't we?'

'You're fucking impossible.'

'No, Ian, I'm just good at my job.'

Her anger died as she watched him sit on the edge of the bed lowering his head. She wasn't cold hearted, or a hard woman; in fact, she was quite the opposite. Her empathy made her the fantastic detective she was today. She knew he was only looking out for her with genuine concern, due to the love he had for her. She exhaled and closed her eyes. 'I'm armed, I'm trained, and I'll have proper backup if anything goes awry. I'm only going out there on surveillance. I'll be back about two, and we'll have a good laugh about it, about the people I meet.'

Ian reached up and held her hand. 'I'm just worried. I've got a bad feeling about this, that's all.'

'You've got bad feelings about everything.'

'Only when it comes to your safety, and the safety of my family.'

Paula checked herself in the mirror once more, making sure the gun was still concealed. Once she was happy, she turned towards her husband–to-be, sulking on the bed. 'Ambrose will be waiting for me. I've got to go,' she whispered, tightening her lips into a thin, emotionless smile. 'I'll see you tonight?' she asked, raising her eyebrows towards him. 'You'll be waiting up for me, right?'

Ian nodded solemnly. 'I won't be getting any sleep anyway.'

She leaned in and kissed him on the top of his head; he never reacted. She left the room and made her way downstairs to the front door, picking up the cheap faux fur coat she'd bought earlier that day from a charity shop. Sparing one last glance upstairs, she grabbed her keys and opened the door. Ian's shadow on the landing wall was slowly making its way towards Sally's room. 'I love you,' she whispered. 'Both of you.'

She exited the house, closing the door gently behind her.

~~~~

Ambrose's eyebrows raised, and he whistled as Paula got in the waiting car. His eyes roamed up and down her outfit. 'Whit whoo, Detective Ashton.' He patted around his jacket and trouser pockets, all the time looking at her, shaking his head. 'Let me see if I've got a twenty-pound note with your name written on it.'

She looked at her partner, the humour of the situation cracked her stony exterior. 'Three things you need to know, Alan. One, fuck you. Two, I've got a gun. And three, its gonna cost you *a lot* more than twenty to get a slice of this,' she laughed, buttoning her coat up.

'Hmm, I like my hookers with attitude.'

'Just drive, dickhead.'

As the car pulled away, she gave the semi-lit windows one last mournful look before steeling herself for the long night ahead.

65.

JOE WAS FEELING good. He was relaxed, getting enough sleep; maybe a little too much. The only area of his life that was lacking was his inability to communicate all this to Karen and the kids.

His mood faltered a little when he thought about Annmarie and Martin, about what he'd put them through. It made him sad, and a small, humourless smile cracked on his lips as if to emphasise this point.

As he got into his car to go to work, he mused on the fact that it had been four days since … Well, since he did what he liked to refer to, in his own company of course, to 'the event.' He'd had eight hours sleep every night since, and he kept telling himself that nothing like it would ever happen again, ever. He wouldn't need to

He was determined to put it all behind him. That included what he'd done to his family, the noise, and, most importantly, what he'd been doing to quell the noise. He was determined not to lose the euphoria he had been enjoying over the last few days. The last thing he wanted was, *the noise to come back.* His eyes darted around the interior of his car, more to distract himself from his negative thoughts than to find *that helmeted bastard.* He turned the radio on and drove out of his street. He started to sing along with the tune that came on; an old rock song by a band he'd followed since the seventies. He loved the fact they had a ridiculous name, Rainbow. To him it sounded more like a kid's TV show than a fantastic group of musicians. This was one of their more famous songs where the singer was bragging that he could go all night long.

When he was a mile or so from work, his mobile phone began to vibrate in his pocket. It made him jump as the damned thing hadn't rung in a few days. He fumbled in his trouser pocket,

Crack

eventually retrieving it, hoping he wouldn't be too late and whoever it was would ring off. Eventually, he fished it out, steadying himself on the road as he did, inwardly cursing that he should know better than to do something like that on the motorway, especially after everything he'd been through; but he didn't want to miss this call.

He looked at the screen. The display read MARTIN.

With his heart thudding, he pressed the answer button and put it on speaker. 'Martin! Oh, mate, I'm so glad you rang.'

The voice on the other end didn't share his enthusiasm for the call. 'Dad, I'm not ringing for any niceties. I'm ringing because Mum asked me to.'

It was Martin's voice, he knew that, but the electronic version of him sounded older, sharper, more grown up than the slip of a boy who not that long ago was crying because his sister had made fun of him in school.

The chirpiness he'd felt earlier began to ebb in response to that opening statement. He swallowed hard and replied. 'That's OK, son. Is everything OK?'

'Yeah, it is.' There was a long pause. Joe was about to ask if he was still there, but his son's voice came back again. 'Mum's been to see a solicitor.'

Joe's world collapsed in on him, and he swerved a little, narrowly missing a vehicle in the middle lane. An angry horn blurred out at him as the car eventually past. 'She's what?' he asked.

'She's been to see a solicitor, Dad. The injuries you caused aren't healing anytime soon. You broke her jaw and shattered an eye socket. She was lucky not to lose the eye.'

'Son, I—'

'Save it, Dad. I'm not interested. She has me and Annmarie as character witnesses to say you've been a bit'— he paused dramatically— 'unhinged since the accident.'

'I can explain all of that, son. I think I've exorcised those demons. I really have.' He could hear himself pleading to his fifteen-year-old son; it wasn't his proudest moment.

'It's too little too late, Dad.' There was another long pause, neither man, on either end of the phone, knowing what to say.

'Martin …'

235

'Dad, look …' He paused again, and Joe fancied he heard his son swallow, hard, on the other end of the line. He wanted to say something, but whatever it was proved difficult to say. 'I do still love you, so does Annmarie. I even think, deep down, Mum does too.'

No wonder he paused, Joe thought, *that must have been a tough thing to admit.* A surge of pride for the man his son had become overwhelmed him.

'You need help. Unfortunately, it's too late for Mum. You and her are done, but I think me and Annmarie might come around. We just need a bit of time and space, even if it's only for the short term.'

Tears were streaming down his face, and he had to sniff to stop mucus from doing the same from his nostrils. The phrase, *even if it's only for the short term,* rang true to him. It was something Helmet Man had said.

'Look, I'm so sorry, Martin,' he sobbed. 'I really am. Please tell your sister I am too. Let her know that her daddy loves and misses her. Will you? Will you do that, Martin? Can you do it for me?'

There was more silence for a small while. All he could hear was the traffic passing him on the road, and more than a few horns blaring at him, due to him slowing down. 'Yeah, Dad, I will. I think she knows, but this is all a shock to her, to all of us.'

'Tell your Mum as well, tell her I'm sorry. Tell her I've been in touch with Dr Saunders, the psychiatrist, she'll remember her. Tell her I'm talking to her today. Will you tell for me?'

'Yeah, Dad, I'll tell her. It'll hurt her, but I'll tell her anyway.' Martin paused once again, and another few seconds of silence passed between them. 'Listen, Dad, I have to go now.' He sounded rushed, in a hurry to get off the phone.

'OK, son, ring me soon, like maybe tomorrow. Yeah? I'll give you an update of what Dr Saunders says. I think she'll put me under some kind of therapy and maybe I can get past all this, all this shit that's keeping us apart.' He winced a little at the use of the word 'shit.' Although he'd never kept his mouth clean around the kids, using it now just felt wrong somehow.

Crack

'Yeah, OK, Dad. Look, I've got to go. I'll speak to you soon. Goodbye.' The line went dead, leaving Joe in the car alone, crying as he gripped the mobile phone a little too tight.

'OK, Martin. Speak soon, son, speak soon,' he sobbed into the silent device.

As he pushed it into the cradle on his dashboard, a loud rumble of thunder, and a streak of lightning exploded in the sky. Joe's watery eyes drifted towards it. Then they turned to look at the passenger seat.

Helmet Man was sitting next to him.

CRACK!!!

66.

PAULA REGRETED HER decision to wear the thinner, more revealing clothes, as the cold of the night drew into her, nipping at her exposed skin. It was a vile night, windy with a threat of rain, and all she had to keep her warm was small, faux fur coat and black nylon tights.

The street was dark, seedy, and mostly empty. There were a few ladies dotted about here and there, and she thought that if she was going to spend the rest of the evening in their company, then the least she could do was introduce herself. As she approached a group of three women huddled together against the cold of the night, all of them smoking, she put on a friendly smile. 'Hi, I'm new around here,' she offered. 'I was just wondering if …'

One of the women turned on her, looking her up and down, her eyes were far from friendly. 'We were wondering if … you were about to fuck off any time soon,' the woman spat at her, there was real venom in the words.

'What?' Paula gasped.

'Don't be coming around here and taking our spot with your little hard gym body, you fucking whore,' one of the others interjected, also looking her up and down with contempt.

'I was just—'

'We don't care what you were *just*. Fuck off and get your own spot, bitch. We don't want your kind around here.'

Strangely, the words hurt her, as she did walk away, it was with the thought that *her kind* was exactly the kind they wanted around here, especially these days.

The three women huddled together again, watching as she slunk off to the darker part of the street where one solitary streetlamp illuminated no other workers. 'Jesus. Alan are you still there?' she said to no one.

'Yeah, I'm enjoying the entertainment. They were nice and pleasant, were they not?' he asked sarcastically. 'Do you think you'll be invited to their Christmas night out?'

Paula huffed. 'It's not a bit like you see in the films, is it?'

Ambrose laughed down her ear through the small device hidden inside. 'What did you expect, Ashton? Julia Roberts?'

'I did, actually,' she laughed. 'The hooker with the heart of gold. Where are you? Do you have line of sight?'

'I can see you walking down the other end of the street. I'll lose sight of you down there, but I can't move right now in case it gives the cover away. That'll blow this sting fast.'

'OK. Just don't leave me here alone.'

'You got that, Detective.'

As she reached the solitary lamp, she scanned her immediate area. It was almost half past nine. She was wet, cold, and the night was fully dark. She watched as some headlights turned into the street. 'Right, sit tight, Al. I can see a pickup truck turning in.'

'Be careful, Paula. Don't forget to get the registration.'

'I will ...'

The truck slowed as it approached her streetlamp, and the driver's window rolled slowly down. A young man of maybe eighteen leaned out; Paula could see another three of them inside. 'Ford pickup, licence plate Romeo, Kilo, Eight, Zero, Tango, Zebra, Tango.'

'Got it,' came the reply.

'Hey, boys ...' she said in her sexiest voice, wincing internally at how it came out. It was too natural.

'Shake that ass over here, you whore,' came the shout from inside the truck.

She sauntered over with disgust. 'Boys getting their kicks,' she whispered into the hidden microphone. 'What can I do for you ... fella?' she asked, smiling as she looked at the boy in the driver's seat.

'How much to suck me off and let these losers here feel your tits at the same time?'

'Fuck you, Lee. I at least want a wank,' came a disgusted but obviously young voice from inside.

'I'm sorry, Lee.' Paula smiled, raising her eyebrows. She was trying to look salacious, but it was difficult facing these loathsome youths in *Daddy's car*. 'But I only do one at a time. It's a kind of ... a policy. Now, if *you* want to go for a little drive, then it's you and you alone.' *And then I'll bust you and your shitty little attitude,* she continued in her head.

Lee looked disappointed, and he curled his lip. 'Fuck you, whore,' he shouted before hocking up something nasty and thick in his throat. He spat at her as he drove on.

Luckily, her reactions were good, and the spit missed her. She watched, shaking her head as the van moved further up the road towards the other girls around the streetlamp, where she saw the red brake lights engage. A humourless smile took over her face as she shook her head. 'Jesus Christ. There goes the future of Great Britain,' she said, her small microphone picking it up.

'He could be a member of the Tory party with charm like that,' Alan added with a laugh.

'No wonder society is so fucked up. I've got a feeling this is going to be a long night.'

Crack

67.

JOE WAS IN his porta cabin. The TV was flashing hated images of a hated game show over his hate-filled face. The lights were off, and he was cast in flickering shadows as he leaned back in his chair, his feet up on the desk. He was turning a small business card, opposite points of the rectangles, between his fingers, all the time staring out into nothing.

The last two days had been hell. Ever since that phone call with his son, sleep had been hard to come by and he'd been jumping at every little noise. Thankfully, the sound hadn't come back since that last thunderclap, but he had a nasty feeling it was never really too far away.

His eyes were red, rheumy, itchy, and tired. There were tracks down his face left by tears that had been falling for almost three days. His mobile phone was on the desk next to his shoeless feet. The battery was mostly dead, as he'd been trying to ring his son, his daughter, or his soon-to-be-ex-wife all day.

The card he was turning over in his hands was Dr Saunders's office and mobile numbers. She'd given him it on his first, and only, session with her. Since then, there had been numerous attempts by her office to get back in touch with him. All of them had been ignored, but he was thinking that maybe tonight, he might need her.

CRACK!!!

There it was. He knew it would be back.

His eyes closed involuntarily, and his body began to shake. The sound resonated around his head, and he fancied he could feel it physically bouncing off the walls insides of his skull, passing through his brain, creating holes in it like Swiss cheese. With it came dark thoughts regarding his life and his life choices. About how, since the accident, all he'd done was spiral ever downwards into despair, depression, and yes, depravity. How, since the accident, he'd become a wife beater, an animal abuser ... *Shit, say it, Joe,* he taunted himself, swallowing hard before continuing the thought. *You've become a fucking murderer too.*

That last thought hit him the hardest.

It brought everything home about how far he'd sunk, and asked the question about just how much further it was possible for him to descend. The tips of his fingers scratched away at the skin on his forehead as thoughts of the women, and what he'd done to them, disgusted him.

He looked at the card in his hand again. There was an office number; all he needed to do was ring and book an appointment. It really was that simple. He could tell Penny all about what he'd done, but he'd tell her they were fantasies, things he thought he *might* do if he continued to be left unchecked. *Once I tell her, then she'll fix me. I'll be better, and Karen will come home, bringing the kids back with her, just in time for Christmas ...*

His mouth turned into a grimace, and he shook his head as a horrible thought entered his brain. *No, that wouldn't do me any good. She'd lock me away in a mental facility before I even knew what was happening. I'd never see the kids again ... ever!*

CRACK!!!

He jolted upright in his chair. Every time the noise hit him, another piece of him died, inside. He picked up his mobile phone and flicked it on. He took a couple of deep breaths, just to steady his nerves, and looked at the card again. He held the last breath in his mouth for a few seconds and dialled. He knew this was a folly; he knew the office would be closed — it was half past nine at night.

The number rang twice, and Joe was shocked to find himself talking to a real, live person.

'Good evening, Dr Saunders' office. How can I help?' The voice was bright and young; he could see the rather attractive girl on the reception in his mind's eye.

Crack

He wondered how her head would sound underneath his wheels.

He found himself breathless and unable to speak.

'Hello? Hello, is there anybody there?'

With sweating hands, he pressed the CANCEL button, killing his connection.

CRACK!!!

He looked around the cabin for Helmet Man, knowing the noise usually heralded his appearance sooner or later, but he was nowhere to be seen. He looked at the keys hanging on the wall. He saw them as the keys to his salvation, but also the keys to his demise, to his damnation. Without thinking, he grabbed them; he also grabbed the bottle of Nytrodol that was standing proudly next to the silent TV. He opened the fridge in the corner of the room and removed a bottle of cola, before leaving the cabin.

68.

PAULA DIDN'T THINK she'd ever been as cold in her entire life as she was right now. She was fed up, and her head was throbbing. She'd been out on this street three nights on the run; equating to at least three arguments with Ian and a good few *deaf and dumb* meals between them.

There had been minimal contact with the few girls frequenting the street. Not one of them had wanted to trust her at all. She couldn't blame them; with the way they lead their lives, it had to be hard to trust anyone, even the ones they'd known for a while. There was precious little evidence they even liked each other, but they cracked on, playing the hand they'd been dealt.

'Al, I think I'm going to call it a night,' she said into her microphone. 'My head's banging, and I've seen enough low life scum the last few nights to last me a lifetime.'

'I can't fault you with that. Do you want me to drive around and get you? Make me look like a punter again; at least then the girls will see you getting into a car.'

'If you don't mind. I'm getting a bit of a complex here. I go to the fucking gym and work out, keep myself fit, and all the punters go for the scraggy-ends down the other end of the street.'

Al laughed. 'Listen to you, almost wishing you'd gotten a punter.'

'A girl likes to know she's wanted, even if it is by creeps looking for cheap thrills.'

'I wouldn't say fifty was cheap,' Al responded. 'But, then … erm, I wouldn't know what the going rate is,' he stuttered, laughing as he did.

'Al, you make me laugh, but I really do worry about you. I honestly don't know whether to believe you, or not.' She paused

Crack

then as something caught her eye. 'Ambrose, are you on your way around?'

Al's voice became serious, professional once again. 'Yeah, why?'

'Double back a minute; a van has just pulled up. I want to check it out.'

'OK, you're the boss. Be careful, Paula.'

'I will.'

She stood on the corner of the road, out of sight of the other girls down the brighter end of the street. She was facing the other side, where a van was idling.

Wrapping her coat, a little tighter around her as if to stave off the cold but using it as a stalling tactic enable Ambrose to get the registration report. 'Delta, Victor, One, Nine, Mike, Hotel, Alpha. Copy?' she said into her concealed microphone.

'Copy that, Detective. I'll run the plate now and see who it's registered to. Be careful.'

As she was rummaging in her handbag, making sure the handgun inside was within easy reach, the van flashed its headlights. Paula took in a deep breath. She pulled out a packet of chewing gum, making out that was what she was rummaging for, and popped two of them in her mouth.

There was something about this van she didn't like, something she couldn't put her finger on. Wearing a brave face, she smiled a sultry smile, and made her way over the road.

~~~

Joe beat his thumbs in a rhythm on the steering wheel. He knew he shouldn't have left the site tonight, but it wasn't as if this was the first time. He'd parked the van underneath a lonely streetlamp and left the engine idling; he wanted to keep the cabin nice and warm, making it an attractive prospect against the cold of the night outside.

The street was deserted, but he was a patient man. He knew what he was looking for, would be along soon enough.

CRACK!!!

He'd been expecting it, and when it came, it no longer fazed him. He was here tonight to do something about it. *Even if it's only for the short term,* he told himself.

CRACK!!!

'I know you're here somewhere,' he whispered into the empty cab. 'I'm ready for you tonight.'

Helmet Man was yet to make his appearance.

He looked at his bottle of cola and the Nytrodol pills he'd brought with him. He had a gut feeling they were not going to do him any good tonight.

Then he saw her. She seemed to appear from nowhere, from the opposite side of the street. The light from the streetlamp cast a dim yellow glow on the scene as she wrapped her inadequate coat around her, staving off the cold. Then she began to rummage in her handbag.

Joe leaned down towards the compartment where the cola and Nytrodol was. He needed to give the bottle a small shake. He liked the way it felt in his hands, and the sound of the pills rattling around soothed him somewhat. As he did this, he accidently knocked the lever for the headlights, inadvertently flashing them.

When he sat back up, he saw she was making her way over towards his van.

~~~

As Paula approached, she could see there was only one man inside. His silhouette was moving about, twitching and fidgeting. He looked like he was having a conversation with someone, someone who Paula couldn't see. Maybe he was talking on a hands-free system. She was mentally and physically ready for this, even though her heart was pounding, and despite the cold, her palms were sweating too.

She knocked on the window as she approached. Her brightest, friendliest smile beamed at the man inside.

The window wound down, slowly.

Crack

CRACK!!!

Joe watched her acknowledge his flashing lights. His heart was thudding in his throat as she crossed towards him, smiling as she approached. Helmet Man appeared next to him. Even though he was expecting it, his sudden appearance made him jump. 'Jesus!' he exclaimed 'You scared the life out of me.'

Helmet Man ignored him, and just continued staring out of the window. He began to shake his head slowly. 'Cola and Nytrodol won't do for this one, Joe. Something tells me she won't go for that. There's something different about this one.'

Joe looked at him, his eyebrows almost meeting above his nose. 'What do you mean, something different?' he asked.

'This one isn't like the others, Joe. Be wary!'

The woman had nearly made it all the way over towards him. She was still smiling.

She was beautiful.

'Well, hello there,' she greeted him from the street.

Joe wound his window down.

The man inside the van took one look at Paula and his face lost all its colour, he looked like a rabbit in the headlights of some advancing vehicle, intent on squashing the unfortunate animal. He blew air from his mouth, emitting a white vapour as he did. He was about thirty-five years old, with short ginger hair, and unmitigated fear written across his face.

He was fiddling with something in his lap. Her detective instincts kicked in, and she almost reached for her gun before she looked down at what he was doing.

He was trying to remove his wedding ring.

'Having trouble down there, handsome?' she asked, indicating towards his crotch.

'I, erm ... No, I'm just trying to ...'

'Forget the fact that you have a wife and possibly kids back home?' she asked finished for him, raising her eyebrows as she looked him in the eyes.

His eyes darted from side to side, looking anywhere other than at her. 'I'm ... well, my wife is ... you know. I have these, erm ... needs.'

The man was obviously scared to death of her and not at all used to being in a position like this. She knew he wasn't her serial killer. 'Listen, Joe'— she didn't know why she called him that, it just kind of fitted— 'why don't you go home and talk to your wife. I'm sure you can work it all out. You don't need to be out here doing this. What do you say, eh?'

The man's head bowed. The heat of his embarrassment was almost inviting to her, she really did long for a bit of warmth.

'Could... could I just get a quick blow job first?' he whispered; deep shame permeating every single word.

Paula would have laughed if it hadn't been so sad. Instead, she shook her head. 'No, I'm sorry, no can do. Go home before you fuck your entire life up and the lives of those you love.'

The man looked up at her, his baby eyes were welling up. He bit his lower lip.

'Don't ask me for a hand job either. I'm not going to get you off any way tonight.'

The man deflated again. 'OK then ... thanks.'

He wound up his window and drove off without looking back at her, not even once.

Paula watched him go. *I hope he doesn't get a complex from getting knocked back by a prostitute,* she thought with a grin. 'Alan, I'm ready to go home now. Can you come and get me, please?'

'Only if I can have a quick blow job first,' he laughed through her earpiece.

She laughed herself as she removed the piece and wrapped her coat around her again, already looking forward to how warm it would be in the car.

~~~~

Crack

'I know this is a little, erm, unorthodox. But I really need to see you,' Joe said, leaning out of the window.

Dr Saunders looked at him and smiled even though she looked taken aback. 'Mr O'Hara, sorry, Joe, yes, this is indeed unorthodox. You need to book an appointment. Speak to my—'

'I did ring tonight, but I don't know, I couldn't bring myself to book the appointment.'

'Why ever not?' she replied, looking at him with a hint of uncertainty in her gaze.

He shrugged. 'I'm having …' He took in a deep breath and then let it out slowly, shakily. 'A bad time of it lately. Karen's left me and taken the kids, and I'm having difficulties dealing with… that, and other stuff.'

'Listen, I can't see you tonight; it would be unprofessional of me, and I have a prior appointment. Please ring me in the morning. We can talk these things through. As it happens, I have a light schedule tomorrow, and I can move some things around. How does that sound to you?'

CRACK!!!

Joe did his best to ignore the sound.

CRACK!!!

Again, he ignored it. He just stared at the doctor.

She cocked her head slightly towards him. 'Are you OK, Joe?' The concern on her face was genuine.

'Take her. Hit that condescending bitch with the tyre iron, right now. There's no one about. No one's going to miss her until the day after tomorrow at least. Do it, Joe.'

Joe rolled his eyes and bit his cheeks. Helmet Man's voice was ranting in his head, but he knew he couldn't let Penny know this. 'Yeah, that sounds great. I'm just not coping very well.'

CRACK!!!

'Hit her, Joe. Smack this cunt. Feel the crack of her skull beneath the tyre iron. That can be your starter course, a prelude to what you'll hear, to what you'll feel when the van drives over her pretty little head. Think about it.'

Penny looked at him, her eyes had narrowed. 'I can see that,' she said, backing away from the van as Joe twitched. 'Listen, ring the office first thing in the morning, we can discuss it all then. I'll shift my sessions to accommodate you. How does that sound?'

CRACK!!!

'You're letting her go, you fucking loser. Hit her, Joe. DO IT NOW!' Helmet Man screamed.

CRACK!!!

Joe's ghostly passenger continued to rant in the seat next to him. Joe was trying his utmost to swallow him, to absorb his vile creation, but it wasn't as easy as he thought it might be. His eyes were skittering as he tried to distance himself from the fevered madness of his imaginary self.

'OK, Penny, sorry, Doctor. I'll ring in the morning.'

Joe hurriedly wound up the window, and sped off along the street, away from her, and her office.

Penny watched him go. Her whole body was shaking from the encounter. She was already dreading what tomorrow might bring.

Crack

69.

'FOR FUCKS SAKE, Paula. Do you know what I've been going through every single night you're out? Do you? Every moment is an eternity of anguish. I know that sounds dramatic, but fuck it, it's the truth. Every single moment, I'm thinking I'm about to get a phone call from Al telling me something's gone wrong.' Ian was stomping around the living room again; not bringing himself to look at his fiancé.

'I'm getting the overtime in, Ian. We need it for the wedding. We talked about this.'

Ian turned to face her; his features were confused, as if he hadn't quite heard her properly. 'What?' he snapped.

'I said we need—'

'I heard what you said. I'm just pretty fucking dumfounded that you said it.'

'You know, this is becoming an old argument now. Listen, there was a vibe out there tonight; the other girls—'

'The OTHER girls? Fucking hell, Paula, are you in a fucking union now? Are you all meeting up after work for cocktails and swapping stories about sucking cock?'

Paula's face tightened. 'The other girls…' she continued determinedly, '…are scared. Something happening out there. You know what that street's like; you've been called there enough times yourself. It's usually full of women plying their trade. It's not like that anymore. It's like they know someone's stalking them, hunting them. I've got to go back.'

Ian shook his head. 'I can't do it, Paula. Sally—'

'Don't …' she snapped, her hands shooting to her forehead as if she was suddenly suffering a headache. '…bring Sally into this.'

She finished the sentence in a normal voice but there was more than an edge of tension in it.

Ian sat down with a heavy sigh. He hadn't stopped shaking his head since she came home.

'Look, tomorrow's Saturday. It'll be busy, but it won't get busy until late. It'll be the last night I'll go. I'll get someone else to do the street walking. Then I'll be in the warmth and safety of the car.' She sat next to him putting her hand on his knee.

He still refused to look at her.

'I promise,' she added.

Ian continued to look the other way.

Paula looked around the room. She knew Sally was in bed, but wanted to be sure before starting what she was about to do.

'I'll make it up to you,' she whispered.

Ian still didn't react, so she slid her hand around to the crotch of his jeans. 'In a way that I know you'll like.' She felt him beginning to harden, and she knew she had him. She buried her head into his neck and began to bite his ear lobe—he could never resist that. 'What do you think about that?' she whispered.

A ghost of a smile appeared on his lips.

Crack

70.

JOE'S KING-SIZED bed was empty without Karen beside him, keeping him company, keeping him warm. His eyes were wide open. They were crawling the darkness. His skin felt like it was crawling too, like he was covered in a million insects, scurrying, biting, burrowing. He was desperate to find the source of the itch, but the insects shifted, evading him every time he reached out. All he got for his efforts were deep red scratches over his face and arms. Tiny beads of sweat were clinging to his flesh as he shivered uncontrollably. Shivering, and scratching, he pulled the covers tight up to his chin.

CRACK!!!

Lots of different emotions flashed across his face, but the most prevalent was anger. His mouth pulled back in a sneer, as a growl escaped him, he made a claw with his fingers. 'That fucking noise,' he hissed.

CRACK!!!

'You wouldn't be hearing now if you'd done what I told you to do with that doctor.'
Joe closed his eyes. It made no difference in the dark room. He tried to control his breathing, but it was impossible with an imaginary version of himself, dressed in full motorcycle leathers and helmet, was suddenly lying next to him.
His stomach flipped, and he slid slowly away from the newcomer. He couldn't tell if he wanted to vomit or if the feeling needed to expel itself from the other end. He might even have been

hungry. His head was just everywhere. In this fevered state, he didn't know anything, only that he needed *something*, a fix to dull his pain. 'I'm not a bad person. I can't just … just kill people on a whim.'

'You can. You know you can. You've done it before. You did four in one night not so long ago.'

Joe shuddered at the memory and swallowed the spit building in his mouth. The thought sickened him. The absolute horror, and revulsion of what he did, the taking of four innocent lives just to relieve him of his needs. The guilt he associated with the delight, and the delicious moist sound of their heads cracking open and spraying their contents over the road, ate into him. He knew it was consuming him. It was killing Joe O'Hara and giving birth to something, or someone, else.

Yet still, the memory of the feelings, the delightful simplicity of what he'd done stirred something deep inside him. He felt a twitch in his pyjama bottoms as something else began to stir. This turned his stomach. He'd liked to think it was only a small part of him that shuddered with delight, but in reality, he knew he was craving the noise. He wanted it now. *Shit, maybe I even like it,* he thought with revulsion.

CRACK!!!

He turned around to face Helmet Man. He was equally disturbed and thrilled at his twisted reflection in the cracked visor. He looked like a troll, or some kind of golem, something ugly and bad. But he thought it also made him something else; something that was better than human. His erection was complete now. The dichotomy of his reflection brought conflicting emotions.

'I do remember,' he whispered. 'And I remember how glorious the sounds were. But I just knew I couldn't take the doctor. She has a family, friends, a life, personal and professional. I couldn't remove that from her. I'm not a fucking monster.'

The only movement Helmet Man did was to reach out and grab Joe's erection. 'What about the prostitutes, Joe?' he asked, squeezing tightly.

'You said I was doing them a favour.'

Crack

'You were, but don't you think they had family, friends, lives? You should have taken the doctor. You wouldn't be in the state you're in now if you had.'

CRACK!!!

Joe turned and lay on his back. The feeling of Helmet Man masturbating him continued, even though the vision hadn't moved. Joe wasn't stupid, he knew it was himself, pleasuring himself. He was thinking of broken skulls and brains, and thick, moist noises. He was close, but he wasn't quite there yet. When he brought himself to fruition; he wanted to be thinking about Karen and how things had been thirty, twenty years ago ... *hell, even two months ago.* He looked at the clock on the bedside table. It read four fifteen a.m. It was too late to go out hunting for prey now.

He *did* wish he'd taken Penny back to his work site. Not even thinking of what he would have done about Rufus, about the logistics of the routine. All he knew now was that he needed to do something.

He was bringing himself to the edge, stopping, and starting when the feeling in his feet started to climb.

CRACK!!!

Helmet Man tugged him at the noise. He looked at the clock; he wasn't interested in the time, but he was interested in the bottle next to it. The small, brown bottle that read Nytrodol on the label.

CRACK!!!

Tomorrow was Saturday. He wasn't in work until six p.m. He wouldn't need to be up until at least four in the afternoon; that would give him almost twelve hours of much needed sleep. He reached out a shaking, clammy hand and grasped the bottle. He sat up slowly and shook out three tablets. It was a harder job than he'd envisioned. As he looked at them, a melancholy blossomed inside him. He didn't want to even think about what would happen after he swallowed them. After all, it was taking these things that got him in this shit in the first place.

After swallowing the tablets with a swig of water from the plastic bottle next to him, he lay back on the bed. The first thing he noticed was Helmet Man had gone, disappeared without a trace, he smiled at the small mercy he had been gifted. He then closed his eyes.

As his mind and body finally relaxed, just a little, he decided he would finish himself off, after all.

~~~~~

Dr Penny Saunders was lying on a lounger next to a deep blue swimming pool. The hot sun in the cloudless, azure sky was glistening, bouncing off her oiled, bronzed, and exposed skin. She was holding up a large cocktail glass towards him. All kinds of exotic fruits and stirrers were sticking out of the multi-coloured drink. Her yellow bikini was small, and it fitted perfectly wherever it touched her hard body.

Now, if I can just get through this dream without killing her, I might actually be able to enjoy myself, he thought, accepting the offered drink, and leaning over the lounger next to her before kissing her passionately on the lips.

It's always nice to be kissed back, he thought.

Crack

71.

BREAKFAST WAS A strained affair. Ian was up early with Sally and had her washed, dressed, and fed before Paula dragged herself out of bed. She walked into the kitchen to find Ian pretending strips of toast were aeroplanes that needed to fly into Sally's mouth to land safely. They were both giggling. To her, it was the most beautiful sound in the whole wide world. She smiled as she watched them from outside the room.

Her hair was sticking up at every angle it could find, a by-product of all the spray and gel she'd had on it over the last few nights. Her skin looked, and felt she had to admit to herself, grey. The long, cold nights on the street, followed by the argument and then finished off with the forced, tired sex, had taken its toll on her. Her head was throbbing, and she was grateful to Ian for not waking her when Sally got up, for allowing her that extra couple of hours in bed to sort herself out.

'Mummy,' Sally shouted making her way over to her.

'Hey, baby, how's my little chicken wing this morning?'

'Great. Daddy's landing aeroplanes in my mouth.'

'Well, I can see that. Good for him.' She flashed a smile to Ian, who only gave her a cursory nod before standing up.

'You want eggs?' he asked, still not looking at her.

'Oh, yes, please, she sighed. 'I'm starving.'

She sat down next to Sally and gave the little girl a big hug. 'So, how many aeroplanes did Daddy land?' she asked.

She smiled a big, beaming little girl smile back at her. 'All of them,' she replied proudly.

'Well then, your daddy must be a fantastic pilot.'

'He's the best pilot in the whole world,' she shouted in the over excited way only four-year-olds can achieve.

257

Paula got up from her seat and wrapped her arms around Ian's waist as he stood next to the stove. 'That he is,' she replied resting her head on his back as part of the hug.

Ian shrugged this embrace off and moved away, back towards his immediate job at hand, eggs.

Paula sighed and watched him walk away. 'Are we still playing this game?' she asked, with more than a hint of frustration in her voice.

'We're playing a game?' Sally shouted, looking up from her plate, her eyes wide and filled with the joys that playing games with adults can bring.

Paula looked down at her daughter and smiled. 'Not right now, baby. We've got to eat breakfast first.'

Sally's face fell as she turned back towards the table, continuing her morning meal.

'I thought we'd worked this out, you know, last night.' Paula was attempting to wrap her arms around her husband-to-be again, but all she got was a second shrug off as he moved from the stove to the kettle. 'Well, obviously not,' she observed, putting her hands on her hips as he shifted positions again, for no other reason than to move away from her.

'We did. I just ... I still don't like the idea. It's dangerous, and its unnecessary too.' He was busying himself with coffee cups and milk, doing anything to avoid her.

Paula sat next to Sally, helping her with her breakfast, but all of her attention was on Ian. 'Yes, it's dangerous, but it's not unnecessary. If it stops one more woman from ...' She looked at Sally, who was eating her meal and playing with a small toy elephant. Paula knew she was listening to their conversation. 'From going missing, then it's all worthwhile. Without sounding cliché, it's what we signed up for.'

Ian came over to the table and put a plate of eggs and bacon in front of her, before fetching her coffee. He sat opposite Sally and began fussing with her. 'I know, but it doesn't stop me from worrying. I love you, Paula, and I want you safe. Jesus, we get married in three weeks.'

She leaned over and kissed him on the lips. Sally watched and laughed. 'Ooh, you two need to get a room,' she quipped.

Crack

Both Ian and Paula burst out laughing and turned to look at the little girl. She went bright red and looked at them both, fear grew on her little features. 'Did I say a bad thing?' she asked.

Ian calmed down and took his little girl's head, pulling her in for a kiss. 'No, baby, you didn't. But where did you hear that?'

'The TV,' she replied sheepishly.

'Well, that's not something you're going to be watching again,' Paula concluded, grabbing at Ian's hand, and mouthing a silent thank you when he grabbed hers back.

72.

PENNY SAUNDERS BLUSTERED into her office. She was in a strange mood. She normally started late on a Saturday, as it was usually her busiest day, but towards the end of September, for some reason, it always quietened down for a small while.

The meeting with Joe O'Hara in the street last night had put her hackles up. There was something about that man that intrigued her and scared her in equal measures.

'Good morning, Maureen. How are you?'

'Fat and miserable.'

Maureen was the Saturday receptionist and was heavily pregnant. She looked ready to drop at any moment. Her stomach was huge, but she still had almost two months to go to full term.

Penny laughed. 'Have there been any calls this morning?' She asked this in two minds. First, she was hoping Joe O'Hara would keep his promise and call to book an appointment, but second, there had been something about the look in his eyes; it had been something wild, something … very wrong, that she hoped he might have called to cancel.

'Nope, no cancellations, no new appointments, just every day, run-of-the-mill kind of things.'

She was relieved, but also a little disappointed. Joe O'Hara would make a great case. She might even get a paper published about him. 'OK, well, I'm kind of waiting on a call from a Mr O'Hara. If he calls, can you tell him I'll call him right back and then come and get me? Even if I'm in a session. I really need to speak to this one.'

Maureen was writing all of this down on the pad of paper she had in between the bag of doughnuts and the telephone. 'Got it. I think your ten-thirty appointment has turned up,' she said, pointing towards the glass doors behind Penny.

She turned to see if it was Joe and was more than a little relieved when she saw it wasn't.

'OK, give me five minutes and then send them in, would you?'

Maureen gave her a sugary thumbs-up before putting it into her mouth to suck the sweetness off it.

Penny smiled and entered her office.

73.

IT WAS LATE; or was it early? Paula was too tired to even contemplate that question. The night had been long and arduous. She was freezing, tired, and hungry, but above all else, she was missing Sally.

She knew it wasn't a fight they'd had today; it was more a simmering argument, but whatever it had been, it had continued through the afternoon and well into the evening. Ian had kept digging and digging and then snapping right back into his sulky mood. Even Sally had gotten onto his negative vibe and given up her attempts to play with him. She took herself off into her bedroom to play on her own with her dolls.

Because she'd known it was going to be a late one, she'd gone to bed for a few hours. She knew she'd need all the energy she could get. As it was around the time Sally usually took her nap, she'd been half expecting Ian to come in and join her for a little bit of afternoon delight, or maybe just a cuddle. But no, all she'd heard was the front door slamming and then opening again maybe half an hour later.

He hadn't even given her a proper kiss before she left. All she'd gotten was a grunt and an offer of his forehead. She knew she was putting him through all kinds of hell, but this was important to her. It was something she felt she had to do, for her own sanity, and for the safety of the women on the street, not to mention that it wouldn't look too bad on her application for promotion. Right now, though, it was beginning to feel like it was all for nothing. The night, and possibly the case, was becoming a bit of a bust. There'd been a few people pass through, cruising mostly, but nothing that was even remotely resembling the profile of the suspect.

Crack

The other women were still giving her a wide berth, wary of everything she did. Some of them even drove past her with their punters, giving her dirty looks, as well as flipping her a finger, as they passed. Acting as if they'd gotten one over on the younger, prettier new girl. She'd been a little jealous of them, though, but only because of the warmth of the cars they were in, not where they were going, or what they would have to do once they got there. They could keep that part for themselves.

She'd relayed to Alan the licence plates of every punter's car who had come into the street. Alan had in turn used the laptop to run background checks on each and every one of them.

Once or twice, she'd had to fend off the advances or the unwanted intentions of several punters herself, but she had always been helped by Al pulling into the street and 'picking her up' himself as one of her regulars. This had the desired effect of seeing off the attentions and allowing the other girls not to get too suspicious of her not taking any custom for the night.

But now she was ready to throw in the towel. The fight with Ian and the absolute wash out of the night had drained every tiny bit of spirit within her. She was beginning to think that the perp, whoever he might be, had finished with this area and had moved on to pastures new. This thought depressed her even more than the fight because it meant she might have to widen her search, and her promise to Ian that this would be her last night on this job might also be a bust.

All she wanted now was warmth, her little girl, and her nice comfortable bed. *If there was a coffee somewhere in the middle of all that, or even a brandy, that would be excellent.*

'Alan, what do you say to half an hour more, then we give it up as a bad job? The walkers at the top of the street are looking like they want to kill me, and I haven't seen anything that even remotely fits my hunch. Plus, my feet feel like they have swollen to seven times their normal size.'

'Don't people pay extra for feet stuff?' he laughed. 'Yeah, I'm all for that. I'm starving.'

'OK, I'm just going to walk up to the top, make one more pass at these women, then I'll come back around to the car.'

'Do you fancy a coffee and a hot roll? There's a place just over the next road. It's just a little van that hooks up there on the weekends, but it looked at least a little bit clean when we passed earlier.'

'Oh, Ambrose, if I wasn't getting married in three weeks, I think I'd give everything up and run off with you, just for the offer of coffee.'

'Still time. You want sugar?'

'Is that a proposition?'

Alan laughed. 'You wish, bitch. You couldn't handle the Latino maestro.'

'Alan, you're Scottish; the nearest you have to Latino is wanking off to J-Lo videos. Two sugars and extra bacon, with brown sauce on my roll.'

'Brown sauce? You dirty bitch. Coming right up. Oh, and by the way, leave J-Lo out of this. We have a complicated relationship.'

Paula was trying not to laugh as she hobbled, feeling like John Wayne after a three-day trail on his horse, back up the street towards the other women huddled up there. They regarded her with the usual distain. She'd seen them getting business all night, and she'd made notes of every registration plate, just in case they never came back. She'd had their backs; they just didn't know it or appreciate it. Luckily, the girls *all* made it back, and all of them were still living and breathing. She skirted around them, feeling their icy glares burrowing into her, before making her way back to the spot by the streetlamp.

'Yeah, keep walking, bitch,' was just one of a number of insults that was thrown her way. She was so tempted to flash them her badge and tell them what she'd been doing for their ungrateful, drug addled arses, but she knew it would only be in anger, and in doing so could blow the whole investigation.

A sarcastic smile and wave would suffice. If any of them fronted her, she could handle herself in a fight.

Once around the group, she swaggered back towards her spot and the hopefully glorious, luxurious warmth of Alan Ambrose's car.

Crack

It was then she saw the van parked opposite her spot. Its engine was running, but she couldn't see inside the window. Something about it bothered her. 'Alan, there's another punter,' she whispered into her hidden mic.

There was no answer.

'Alan, are you there?'

There was still no answer.

Shit, she thought biting her lip as she watched the driver's side window roll down and an arm drape out. The hand at the end of it beckoned her over. She watched as the arm relaxed on the sill of the window. She was of two minds whether to go over or not; something about this screamed out to her. *That's your man,* it shouted in her head.

'Alan, where the fuck are you?' she whispered into her microphone with a sharp rasp.

Despite her better instincts, she made her way over anyway, smiling and swaying her hips.

'Excuse me,' a male voice from the gloomy interior of the van beckoned to her.

She made to pass by the vehicle, trying her best to get a look at the driver. She smiled and waved, offering him an apologetic smile. 'Not me, baby. I'm off shift,' she shouted back, still trying to get a look at who was inside. His face was hidden in the shadows of a cap, and he'd parked almost directly underneath the streetlamp, offering him maximum shadows to hide in.

A handful of cash appeared out of the window. 'I can make it worth your while,' he replied.

OK, you prick. I've got you right now on soliciting, she thought.

'Oh, now you're speaking my language. What do you want me to do for this money?' she asked. *Ask me for sex, please ask me for sex*, she thought.

'Whatever you want,' he replied.

That'll do, she thought, walking over.

She turned away from the van, as if she was looking for someone, and relayed the licence plate to her absent partner. 'Alan, if you're getting this, licence plate Lima, Romeo, Seven, Two, Alpha, Delta, Hotel.'

There was still no answer.

A rising unease grew in her stomach, but she hid it so well. She was cool and unabashed. *Fuck*, she thought, reaching under her flimsy top for the little wallet that had her police warrant card inside, and feeling under the welt of her dress for the small handgun, hidden back there.

Here goes!

As she approached, she offered him a false smile and continued her sexy swagger. She leaned into the window, taking a long look at the driver. He was white, late forties to early fifties, average build, blue eyes that looked a little bit too wild for her liking. She profiled him in just the few seconds. *Just your average fucking serial killer,* she thought.

'Well, I'm certainly up for earning a little extra. But just to let you know, anything wild ...' She paused and raised her eyebrows. 'And it'll cost you more.'

The man winked at her. The cold, alligator smile alone was enough to send another shiver through her.

'I'm not the wild type,' he replied. There was danger in that voice, Paula knew it, but now she was stuck in a bad situation, and she was on her own until Alan got back on the radio. 'Get in, I know a nice quiet place.'

If I get in, will Alan be able to trace my signal? she thought. 'Well, you're the boss,' she said. As she pulled back to lean out of the window, the man's hands, quick as lightening, grabbed her and something hit her, hard.

Her whole world went black.

Crack

74.

HE GRABBED THE whore and hit her with the tyre iron. The heavy bar struck her right across her temple. He knocked her back, with such force that something small and black fell out of her ear and bounced across the wet tarmac of the road.

In his fevered frenzy, he didn't notice it.

Her body flopped, her arms and legs suddenly lifeless, made her fall forwards, and he grabbed the ragdoll through his window.

He secured her, and scrambled out via the passenger door, and was around the other side of the van, grabbing her from behind, in a flash. He never figured that the sudden dead weight of the woman would be so heavy. It was a stupid mistake when he thought that over the last few weeks, he'd been dealing with more dead bodies than he could wave a stick at. *Or a tyre iron,* he laughed to himself. She fell back onto him, and he struggled to keep his balance. Using all his strength, he pushed her back against the vehicle, keeping her in an upright position.

He looked both ways up the street. Fortunately for him this section of the street was deserted. He opened the back door and pushed her into the rear seats.

She flopped inside.

Once inside, he shifted her body to accommodate her legs. As he turned her, something else fell away from her, once again it went unnoticed by him.

The heavy, metal object slipped from the welt of her skirt, and thudded as it hit the carpeted beneath the front seat.

He stood upright and massaged his lower back. He looked around again, hoping nobody had gotten nosey to what was happening and decided to investigate. Luckily for him, he was the beneficiary of his own notoriety; due to the women going missing from this area over the last few weeks, very few people had been making it out around this area. He stretched again, cracking his back and sighing, before climbing into the driver's seat. Shifting the van into first gear, he pulled out of the street, slowly so not to attract any attention to himself.

He was grinning.

He'd done this before.

The whole transaction had taken less than two minutes. The moment he was clear of the street, he relaxed behind and released the deep breath he had been holding entirely too long. Within another two minutes, he was driving along a deserted road, heading towards his building site. Within a further five minutes, he was safely inside the locked railings and making his way towards one of the huge cement pits on the far side.

Crack

75.

AMBROSE STRUGGLED BACK into his car, laden as he was with goodies from the fast-food van—two cups of steaming coffee and a large white bag filled with hot, greasy food. As he'd put the cups down on the roof of the car, to fish out his keys, one of them slipped a little, spilling hot coffee down his shirt. 'Fuck,' he snapped and reached into his pocket for one of the napkins he had in there. He cleaned himself up as good as he could. He sat into in his seat and fixed the bags so he could reach inside for easy access to the hot, delicious smelling food inside.

Eventually, he reached over to the passenger seat and picked up the headset he'd left while he went for the coffee. 'Fast food my arse,' he mumbled, fixing the earpiece back into his ear. He reached over and turned the radio on.

'I'm back,' he announced. 'I got cinnamon rolls too,' he said absently into the mouthpiece as he rummaged around in the bag. It was a few seconds later before he realised Paula hadn't answered.

He tapped the earpiece. 'Paula, Paula, are you there?' he asked again, biting into his warm bacon roll.

'Paula, come in,' he continued between chewing. 'Detective Ashton, come in.' He swallowed a lump of greasy bread before dropping the rest of his sandwich onto the white bag on the passenger seat. He tapped the headphones. 'Come on, Paula. Don't fuck around here. Are you receiving me?'

There was still no answer.

'Fuck!'

He wiped his mouth on the wet napkin he'd wiped his shirt with and got out of the car. With a hand to his eyes shielding the lights from the street below, he surveyed the area, praying for a glimpse of a soaked, pissed off detective stomping towards him.

She was nowhere to be seen. He slammed the car door and burst through the thin line of trees and down the small embankment, onto the street where she'd been working.

It was empty.

The drizzling rain had stopped, and he spun on his heels to look up the other end. He could just about make out three women a little further up, the same women who had been giving Paula a hard time. If anyone knew where she was, it would be them. He just hoped they'd know who he was talking about when he asked them. With the world going a little hazy all around him, he ran down the street.

'Hey, hey, you,' he shouted, getting the attention of all three of them at once.

Their demeanour changed in an instant as all three of them put their hands on their hips and looked at him, brimming with sass. 'Why, hello mister.' One of them stepped forward, away from the others. 'What can a lady do for you tonight?'

Catching his breath, Alan pulled out his badge.

'Police,' he panted.

The other two girls ran, leaving the lead girl looking around her, wondering where her friends had gotten to so fast. 'What the fuck?' she spat, anger and annoyance replacing her confidence, almost as fast as it had appeared.

'I need to speak to you,' he gasped. 'It's urgent.'

The woman was turning away, looking for an escape route. 'I'm not speaking to no po,' she said angrily. 'I haven't done nothin' wrong; you've got fuck all on me.'

Ignoring her bad grammar, and the double negative, Ambrose bared his teeth. 'I'm not interested in what you did or didn't do. All I'm interested in is if you saw another woman hanging around here tonight.'

She looked at him with a grimace that didn't do anything to hide her disdain towards him, and what he represented. He sensed a little of the sass coming back when she realised she wasn't in any trouble. 'Well, there was a little skinny bitch hanging around earlier, but she didn't get much bidness. Fucking whore. Thought she was too good to be round here.'

'Did you see where she went?'

Crack

'I don't know; maybe she got bored and went home. She wasn't getting a lot of attention, if you know what I mean. The fellas around here want a real woman, not just skin and fucking bone, like that one.'

Ambrose had stopped listening to her. This whole thing was far too important to be wasting valuable seconds on a dead-end lead. 'It's not likely she went off with a punter. She was a police officer too. It's imperative I know where she went.'

She looked at him with a face that said, *What the fuck does imperative mean?* Then her face changed, turning mean. 'I fucking knew there was something wrong with that one. You fucking pigs coming around here and stopping a girl from making a living. It's not right. I have to eat, you know.' She turned away from Al and began to make her way off.

He grabbed her by the back of her dress and swung her around. Her face changed again. She was instantly a child, a small child who may have taken any number of beatings, along with other things, as a course of life. He didn't have time to play psychotherapist. 'Listen, I couldn't give a rats arse how you make your living,' he shouted in her face. 'I just need to know where my friend, where Paula, went.'

The woman's face changed again. He thought by giving out her name, her real name, he'd given her a persona. It changed her attitude towards him. She pointed to the bottom of the street, pulling a face that looked like she'd just bitten into an apple to find half a worm in it. 'She was down there, by that light. She either got lucky or went home. There was a van up there earlier.'

Alan turned towards the light the woman was pointing at. His eyes were wide as he ground his teeth together. 'What?'

The woman was laughing again now; the humanitarian in her was gone, and the hard-faced prostitute was back. 'Looks like your bitch be moonlighting. Maybe she realised she loved the game more than the police, eh?'

'Or maybe she was picked up by a fucking serial killer,' he replied absently, cursing himself for blurting it out loud.

The woman snarled her lip in a poor imitation of Elvis before taking advantage of Ambrose's lapse in concentration, and hobbled off in the opposite direction, her gait uneasy in the ridiculous high heels she was wearing. Uninterested in anything else she had to offer, he let her go. He made his way back down the street towards the streetlight he'd seen Paula working by. He spun again, trying to look everywhere at once, but he couldn't grasp anything that might have been out of the ordinary.

A high-pitched whining noise pierced his brain. He winced and put his hand to his ear. Pulling out the small black bud, he looked at it as it continued to whistle at him.

He took a step back and felt something under his shoe. Pulling out his mobile phone, he turned on the torch function and searched the road. He picked a small black plastic item up from near the kerb. He rolled it about in his fingers as it too screamed at him. 'Oh, sweet Jesus, no,' he mumbled as he cradled Paula's earpiece in his hands.

Crack

76.

JOE WAS IN the van's driver's seat. He was soaking wet, and his t-shirt was sticking to him. He had to keep peeling it off, and itch where it had been touching.

He couldn't keep still either. A twitch, or spasm in his shoulder was making him look, and act like a madman.

CRACK!!!

His description of himself was altogether accurate. He gritted his teeth, attempting to stop the involuntary spasms, and turned to look at the rear seat. Thankfully, she was still there. the girl, *whore,* was lolled over the upholstery. She looked asleep, but he knew better. She was twitching, just like he was, but hers were more alarming to him. They were accompanied by a small, pathetic little moan.

She was coming around.

'Things are getting desperate,' he mumbled. 'I'm taking stupid chances. Too many chances,' he spat knowing Helmet Man would be sat next to him if he looked.

He didn't look.

'You're only making it difficult for yourself,' Helmet Man answered in his annoying, calm, monotone voice.

'What do you mean? I just fucking bludgeoned a woman in the street and dragged her into my van.'

Helmet Man didn't even turn; he just looked straight ahead. 'That was your own fault. You should have offered her the drink, as per usual.'

'Usual? There's nothing fucking *usual* about this. In fact, this whole situation is unusual.'

CRACK!!!

'You captured four women just last week. You ran over four heads. I think this is becoming your new normal.'

'A new normal,' Joe shouted. 'Just what the fuck is a *new normal*?'

'It's what you've brought into your life, Joe. This is it; this is you now.'

He chuffed a humourless sound. 'What do you mean, it's me now? I can't be doing this for the rest of my li...ife.' He sobbed the last word as he gripped the steering wheel tighter. 'Please, please, whoever you are, whatever you are, tell me I don't have to do this, this shit, forever.'

He could hear how pathetic he sounded, like Ebenezer Scrooge pleading with the Ghost of Christmas Yet To Come, telling them he'd be good, he could change. He just needed a chance. *I do need a chance,* he thought. *I can change, I can be a better man.*

Helmet Man shrugged. 'You can't change unless you can kick the habit. The only way to do that is to go cold turkey.'

The cracked, shiny helmet turned towards him only slightly. Joe averted his eyes back to the road; he didn't want to see his reflection, never again.

'Are you man enough for that?' Helmet Man asked.

Joe gripped the steering wheel tighter and casting his mind back to the sleepless nights, the cold sweats, and the shakes, all due to his *new fucking norm*. He took in a long, shaky breath and held it for a moment before exhaling slowly, as he did Helmet Man's hand grabbed the shaft of an erection he hadn't realised he even had.

Thick tears were falling from his eyes.

Crack

77.

PAULA BECAME AWARE of her surroundings, through a gradual awakening of her bodily functions. Blurred eyes and a shrill ringing in her ears where the first indicators that something was wrong. Then there was the sick feeling in her stomach, followed by an almost vomit inducing throbbing in her head. It wasn't pain, exactly, but it was some kind of slow release of toxins into her psyche.

Slowly, she was able to piece together where she was. The realisation that she was prone, in the back seat of some sort of vehicle, did not fill her with confidence.

The man was sat in the driver's seat seemed to be in the middle of a heated conversation with someone she couldn't see, but just because she couldn't see him didn't mean there wasn't anyone there. Her view from her position was limited, at best. She mustered all her strength and tried to move. As she did, the throb in her head overwhelmed her, it dizzied her and her sickening stomach. This was like a frighteningly bad hangover, but infinitely more deadly.

Come on, Paula, you're in a situation here; get your shit together, she thought, even the act of thinking made her feel ill.

She began to move her feet, just wiggling her toes, and found she could do it with little effort. Next, she moved her legs, again with no real strain. As she stretched her foot, she touched something solid underneath the driver's seat. Something metal and heavy. Fighting nausea, she slowly moved her hands to feel around the back of her clothing where the handgun should have been. It wasn't there. She moved her head slightly, and after a few moments of swallowing excess saliva, she shifted position to see what she'd kicked.

She prayed it was her gun.

Whoever was listening, answered. It was dark in the back seat, but by the dim lights of the passing streetlights, she could just about make out the silhouette of the gun by her feet.

An enormous sense of relief washed over her.

'Kick this habit?' the man shouted towards whoever he was arguing with. 'Do you think running people's heads over is a fucking HABIT? Do you think I enjoy this? That ... that it gives me some sort of a fucking rush?'

Paula was stunned. She didn't know if she had heard him correctly, but if she had, it was all she needed for the arrest. *I've got you, you sick fuck,* she thought as she fought to hook the gun with her foot.

'No, it's not an addiction; you're wrong. I've lost everything because I listened to you. Yes, I know you're me, or some fucking stupid extension of me, but it's gone too far now. This one HAS to be the last; she *has* to be.'

A panic like she'd never felt before began to swell inside her. Her breath was shallow, and she was fighting to keep the fact she was awake from whoever it was driving the vehicle. If she didn't grasp that gun, and soon, she would suffer the same fate as the other women.

Whatever that fate might be.

Did he mention running people's heads over? she thought. *That would certainly fit with the MO of the first murder.*

'Seven girls. My wife and kids, my fucking dog! You've taken them all from me, you bastard.'

Oh my God. He killed his wife and kids too; you're one sick puppy, she thought, resuming, and redoubling, her struggle to retrieve the gun but also to do it as quiet as she could. As she moved her head to get a better view of whoever the driver was talking to, an involuntary moan emitted from her.

The man stopped arguing and turned his head to look at her. 'Look, she's awake now. We'll have to finish this later,' he snapped at his unseen colleague.

Christ, she thought, and lay as still as she could on the seat. As she closed her eyes, the blackness of the world around her began to swim, and she went dizzy again. She could feel the sloshing of her

Crack

stomach, like waves crashing on a rocky shore, and vomit was rising in her throat.

The car stopped and the man got out; the whole vehicle rocked as he slammed the door shut behind him. She took the opportunity to fight her nausea and wriggle towards the gun. She tried to hook it with her foot again. This time she succeeded. With herculean effort, she leaned forward and grasped it, relishing the feel of the cold, deadly metal between her fingers. She adjusted her body and nestled the gun back under her clothing just in time as the driver wrenched open the door and leered in at her. From what she could see, and remember from the street, he was just a normal, everyday person. Someone who might not jump out at you from a police line-up.

This was why her work here was so important; not all villains looked like they did in the movies. Usually, they were like the guy who served you coffee, or the one who delivered your parcels.

Mr Normal leaned into the van. His face was filled with concern that looked genuine. 'Come on now, this way,' he said, putting his arms around her. Then he uttered the most chilling short sentence she had ever heard in her life. It was only three words, but they scared the living hell out of her.

'Not long now.'

She allowed her body to relax into a flop, knowing this would make it harder for him to pick her up and hopefully give her enough time to reach for her gun when she needed it. As she was moved, the throb of her headache built; wave after wave of sickening, vertigo crashed into her. Disorientation took hold as his strong arms lifted her out of the back seat. Her head was resting on his shoulder, her arms drooped lifelessly by her sides. The intent was to grab the gun and pistol whip him around the back of his head, thus ensuring her escape. It was fantastic in its simplicity but ultimately was ruined when her nausea finally broke. Her mouth filled with water, and she tasted the warm, bitter bile on the back of her throat. She knew now she wouldn't be able to keep it in. Opening her mouth, she retched over her captor.

'Urgh! You filthy bitch,' he shouted, dropping her to the floor, trying to avoid the stream of stinking vomit that was pouring from her open mouth. She hit the floor hard, far too hard. It knocked all the wind out of her. As her head bounced against the freshly laid tarmac, stars began to flash before her eyes, stars that rapidly turned into multiple colours and patterns. Although dazed, she had the wherewithal to understand what was happening, and her training, and survival instincts, kicked in.

As she lay on the floor, she grabbed for the gun from the elasticated waist of her skirt, ready to aim it at—and possibly shoot dead—this sick bastard. Unfortunately, her stomach selected that exact moment to churn again, and she turned her head towards the road. Her mouth filled with the same warm saliva that was already drooling from her lips as she opened her mouth to expel it. A shudder of retching gripped her, cramping her stomach and weakening her limbs. In her delirium, all she managed to do was fumble the gun from its makeshift holster, dropping it on the tarmac. The clatter of metal bouncing its way along the road made her wince. It came to rest inches from her grasp. The reach of her outstretched hand gained a little purpose on its hilt, but it was tantalisingly too far away to be any use. She looked up at her captor. His full attention was on the stain of vomit down the front of his shirt, trying in vain to rub it off without having to touch it. He was unaware of the weapon lying just a few feet away from him.

Paula exerted a spurt of strength and launched herself at the gun. Her eyes closed for a moment as a short prayer of thanks left her lips, making its way to whatever God had listened to her before, and now. She relished the feel of the grip. She flicked the safety off and tried her best to get her body to sit up. It resisted violently. The world blurred, swimming back and forth. With one hand steadying herself from falling, she pointed the weapon towards the man currently phasing in and out of focus.

Closing one eye, all three visions of the bastard merged into one target before they split again. She pointed her gun at the one in the middle, steadied her aim, and put pressure on the trigger before a devastating blow turned everything black.

Crack

78.

'SHE'S GOT A gun,' Helmet Man said in his strange monotone.

Joe was busy trying to wipe the bitch's vomit off his shirt when he looked up to see what Helmet Man was talking about. He was right. His latest fix was sitting upright.

She's got a fucking gun!

As she faulted, wavering the arm that was holding the obviously heavy firearm, he took his chance. As anger flared like lightning through him, he kicked out at her head. His steel toed boot connected with her jaw, and his fix, who already looked fragile, flopped onto the tarmac in a crumpled heap.

'Whoa, this is a feisty one, Joe. I think you'd better get this one done as soon as you can.'

CRACK!!!

Reluctantly, Joe embraced the sound. *I don't need this,* he thought. *Since when do whores go around carrying guns?* He stepped back and regarded her sprawled on the road. She was unconscious, he could see that, but he'd seen too many films with jump scares at the end, to trust in his instinct.

CRACK!!!

He shook his head. The world, his carefully crafted bubble, was breaking down into a kaleidoscope of confusion. It was then he became aware that the whole of his body was shaking. He looked at his hand, it was almost a blur to him, before he delved it into his pocket, just to get it out of his sight. *I can't live with this noise anymore. I've got to have my ...* his face ruffled, and he pouted. 'Fix?' he said out loud, surprising himself. He imagined Helmet Man smiling; it made him hate him even more than he already did, if that was even possible.

'That's right, Joe. She's your fix, your drug. Welcome to your new norm, your new existence. Just think how good you'll feel once you hear that wet, silky noise. It's so much more *luxurious* than that dry, crisp, empty sound you hear in your head all day, every day, isn't it? This'll give you what you need; it'll quash your craving. It's the rush you need to eliminate that shit for a day, or maybe two, or perhaps even a week. It's only for the short term, either way.'

Helmet Man was leaning in towards Joe as he examined the woman on the floor; he imagined a sick smile cracking on his face—*my face,* he thought.

'You'll have to hurry with this one. There may have been witnesses to the haphazard way you bagged her.'

Licking his lips, Joe reached into the pocket of his coat and fished out a bag of zip wires. He made a loop out of a couple of them and wrapped them around her wrists and then her feet. He then left her lying on the road and went into the cabin to get a rag and some tape for her mouth. When he returned, he noticed the woman was rousing again. Her eyes were flickering, although it looked like she was still having trouble trying to wake herself fully. He reckoned he still had a few moments grace.

'Get a move on. I smell danger on this one.'

Joe regarded Helmet Man, giving him a look while shaking his head. 'You're not helping, as per fucking usual.'

'Who's ... not ... helping?' the woman croaked. Her voice had a lisp as it escaped from her swollen jaw.

Joe stepped back and regarded the incapacitated woman. 'What the f ...' he muttered.

He watched, his pounding heart calming, just a little, as she began to wriggle in her bindings. Learning early that she wasn't going anywhere, fast, she slowed her fight.

'What's ... happen ... ing?' she croaked again, her eyes opening.

Crack

Joe saw they were looking a little sharper now. 'Let me ... go.' She paused to swallow a large gulp. 'You ... you're in... big trouble here. I'm a po—'

Not listening to what she was saying, he leaned in and shoved a large oily rag into her mouth.

'Mummmmf wum fwuuum,' she concluded as the rag did its job.

'Shut up, lady. Just you shut the fuck right up,' he demanded.

Her eyes widened as they looked up at him.

He produced large roll of silver tape from behind his back, tore a piece off with his teeth, and covered her mouth with it, securing the rag in her mouth. As he stood back to admire the scene, a smile spread across his face.

He watched her eyes follow him as he stepped further away. His grin grew wider as the bulge at the front of his trousers grew thicker.

CRACK!!!

It was showtime.

79.

'THIS IS DETECTIVE Alan Ambrose. I need back up, immediately. There's a detective missing.'

Alan was gripping the hand piece of the radio as if his life depended on it. Sweat was pouring from what felt like every pore of his body.

'Can you confirm your location, Detective Ambrose?'

'I'm on Lime Grove Road. Detective Ashton was last seen on this road about ten minutes ago.'

'Can you give me more information? I've dispatched cars and will direct foot patrols to your location.'

Alan was hardly listening to what dispatch was saying as he frantically scanned the area, hoping, beyond all hope, Paula would walk out of the bushes with a stupid grin on her face. 'Erm, we were working the street, investigating a series of disappearances from this location. Detective Ashton was UC. I... she's—she's ... disappeared!'

He cursed himself for stuttering, he was better than that, but he understood that this was probably the biggest call of his career.

'Was there any other activity in the vicinity, Detective? Any hostiles?'

Alan was becoming irritated now. 'No, if I'd seen any hostiles, I'd be beating up a fucking bad guy right about now, instead of being on the radio to you,' he snapped.

'OK, Detective. Have you begun to canvass the area? The first responders are three minutes away.'

Alan calmed down now that he knew backup were on the way. He knew the woman on the other end was only doing her job, trying to be as thorough as possible. 'OK, dispatch, I'm sorry for being curt. My partner...' he began but ended up swallowing his words. 'Thank you,' he offered, calming down. 'I want this area flooded.

Crack

Whoever this bastard is, he can't have gotten far. I'll start looking around now. There's a large building site about a mile or so from here. I'll start there. There might be a watchman or something. Someone's going to need to inform her fiancé of her disappearance. He's Officer Ian Locke, a motorcycle patrol officer, out of Bromborough station.'

'We'll get on that right away. Be careful, Detective. Out.'

'I will,' he said into the handpiece, before clicking it off.

He sat back in the car seat and closed his eyes, exhaling a long, shaky breath. His frustration didn't recede with the steamed breath he plumed into the cold night air. He looked at the bags of greasy food next to him on the seat and banged his hands onto the steering wheel of the car. The horn blared, momentarily startling him in the quiet night. 'Fuck,' he screamed while grabbing for the keys to start the engine.

As he did, he heard the sirens approaching as the first responders arrived at the scene. He flashed his lights towards them, letting them know where he was.

80.

JOE DRAGGED HIS fix to the side of the road. He was amazed at how physically fit all his recent activities had made him. He remembered when he'd first begun this adventure, how heavy the bodies had been and how he'd struggled to move them. Now, he could move a body anywhere he wanted with only the minimum of effort. *Maybe I should release a Christmas DVD. The Joe O'Hara Workout: Motivation by Murder,* he thought, smiling.

The girl's eyes were open wide; he could see the panic in them as she thrashed around, attempting to free herself. He knew her efforts were futile, as he'd made sure she was secure. He wasn't taking any chances with this one, she was feisty. He'd seen it before with most of the girls, the ones that were still conscious, anyway, but none of them had as much fight in them as this one. He dumped her, and repositioned her body so her torso was lying off the road and only her head and neck were resting on the tarmac.

For some reason, unknown to him, he leaned in and stroked her hair. He liked that this one was so awake. There was something special about her, something he couldn't quite put his finger on. He turned her head, so she was facing his vehicle, parked only a few feet away. He manoeuvred her into a position that she couldn't move from, and after taking another step away to admire his kill scene, he walked back towards the van. He turned, just once, to again take stock of the scene.

He was happy with what he saw, very happy indeed.

A twinge of disappointment clouded his thoughts, just for a moment, as he reminisced on his opus, his triumph of the week before. The Four in a Row, he'd taken to calling it; it sounded so much better than The Event. He hadn't ventured too far down the line of madness to understand that he'd taken far too much of a risk

Crack

that night. The next time he was going to do something like that, or maybe even bigger, he'd have to plan it a lot better.

This single fix would do for tonight's purpose.

She was more than enough.

~~~~

Paula's eyes widened and her nostrils flared as she heard the engine start. Then she closed them again as bright lights dazzled her. She could see the silhouette of the man leaning out of the driver's window. He looked to be aligning the wheels with—

My head? Fuck, no, he can't be. She refused to give into that panicked thought. Steadfastly refusing to believe this could be happening to her. *In this day and age, people don't just drive over other people's heads.*

Regardless of her rationale, the vehicle began to move forwards. She could still see the man leaning out of the window. She could imagine the shit-eating grin on his face.

From somewhere in the distance, faint over the roar of the approaching vehicle, there came a banging, and a voice calling out from the darkness.

She closed her eyes. *Saved,* she thought.

The man with his head out the window could hear it too. She swallowed hard, which was difficult to do with the vile tasting rag in her mouth. The vehicle stopped. The engine died. The driver's head and neck were stretched as he strained to hear what was being shouted.

The silence from the vehicle allowed the disembodied voice to travel over the night air.

'Hey... Hey! This is the police. Is there anyone in here?'

It was coming from somewhere in the distance.

'I just need to ask a few questions.'

Paula's eyes darted back and forth between the direction of the voice and the van. She closed her eyes. *Is that Alan? Oh, please let that be Alan. Oh, God, please, please.*

~~~~

Joe turned off his engine, as he thought he could hear a voice. He looked off toward the direction of the sound. In all the time he'd worked on sites, he'd never once heard anyone shouting in the middle of the night. *Only myself*, he thought with irony. His face was like thunder as he turned back inside the van. Helmet Man was in the passenger seat, looking out the window towards the girl ahead of them.

'You'll need to go and see who that is, Joe.' The monotone voice rattled in Joe's head. 'Take the tyre iron with you. You might need it.'

'Hello… My name is Detective Ambrose,' the voice continued. 'I just need some questions answered. It won't take long.'

Joe looked at Helmet Man again. A million questions of his own ran through his head. The most pressing one was: how the hell had this policeman gotten here? Did it have something to do with the girl currently lying on the road in front of his van? It couldn't be, she'd only been missing thirty minutes, tops. He got out of the vehicle, sparing a look at his fix, then turned back towards the direction of the voice.

Through tear-filled, relieved eyes, Paula watched the man get out of his van. He spared a single look her way, before walking off in the direction of Alan's voice. She tried to wriggle free, to spit the rag out of her mouth, but it was all to no avail. She needed a different tack. There was something in the man's hands, something long and potentially dangerous; maybe it was the same something that the bastard had used on her. As she watched him walk off, she began to wriggle again, working on loosening the plastic zip ties that were binding her.

Joe was brimming with anger as he stormed off towards the gate. 'What the fuck could this guy want?' he mumbled repeatedly to himself. Helmet Man had chosen not to accompany him on this excursion.

CRACK!!!

Joe's eyes rolled at the commencement of the noise. *Always when I don't need,* he grumbled.

As he approached the gates, he could make out a man standing in the shadows beyond them. He was waving something in his hands. An ominous feeling overcame him, so he slid the tyre iron into the long leg pocket of his overalls.

As he got closer, he recognised the thing the man was waving as a police warrant card.

'Hey …' the man shouted as he saw Joe approaching. 'Hey. My name's Detective Ambrose. I need to ask you a few questions.'

Joe could hear the man was out of breath, and he could also detect a hint of panic in his voice. His wariness of the newcomer built, tenfold.

'Be careful, Joe. There's something going on here, something we haven't foreseen.' Even though Helmet Man was not with him, he was speaking directly into his head.

'Can I help you, Detective? It's nearly four in the morning.'

The Detective's face was frantic, his hair was mussed, and his eyes were red; it looked like he'd been crying.

'Sir, I need your help. I … w-we've …' The man was stuttering, trying to catch his breath, hindering him getting across what he needed to say. 'There's a situation occurring about a mile from here …' He swallowed hard, as if relieved that he'd gotten all his words out. 'I just need to know if you've seen any suspicious behaviour out here, anything at all.'

Joe shook his head. 'No, Detective. I haven't seen or heard anything out here. But then I've been working over at the carpool most of the night. I do maintenance during down time, and believe me, you get quite a bit of that on this job.'

Ambrose smiled and nodded. 'Is there anyone else on site with you tonight?'

'Nope, just me. You know, cutbacks and all that. They got rid of the double shifts just over a year ago. Can I ask what's going on? What's the situation?'

'Have you been off site at all tonight?'

Joe scoffed at the question. 'What? Leave the site unattended? And lose my job? Detective, for a man with my level of education, jobs that pay like this aren't that easy to come by. I got on site at six pm, and I leave at six am. I haven't been anywhere else all night.'

Ambrose was shaking his head; he looked drained. 'So, you haven't seen anything or anyone suspicious about at all?'

Joe pulled his mouth down into a grimace and shook his head. 'I did my rounds about twenty minutes ago. Nothing unusual to report. I've got my log in the cabin if you want to come in and see it.'

Joe twitched his leg, enjoying the feel of the heavy tyre iron in the long pocket, relieved to know it was there if the detective decided to call him on his bluff.

The detective was gripping the bars of the gate, looking pained. Joe didn't like the way his eyes kept darting backwards and forwards from him towards the site behind him.

The detective reached into the inside pocket of his jacket and took out a small white card. He looked at it for a moment before passing it to Joe. 'This is so important. If you see anything, or if you remember anything, anything at all, give me a call on that number. It's of the utmost urgency. Have you got that? Anything.'

Joe accepted the card and looked at it before nodding. Right now, he would have agreed to anything to get rid of this nosey detective so he could get back to his job at hand. 'I sure will, Detective. Now if you'll excuse me, I've got an alternator to strip.'

'Just one more thing; I need your name for my records.'

Joe continued to nod. 'It's Joe. Joe O'Hara,' he said as he walked away.

'Well, thanks, Mr O'Hara. You have a good night. Don't forget to call me if you see or remember anything.'

CRACK!!!

Helmet Man was suddenly next to him. 'You did well.'

'I know, but what do you think he was talking about?'

'I don't know, but I've got a feeling you should hurry this one along. Get back to business. My bad feeling has just gotten worse.'

Helmet Man disappeared then as fast as he'd appeared.

Crack

CRACK!!!

With a glance towards the gate, making sure the detective had gone, Joe made his way back to the van and his latest *fix*.

81.

THE BEDROOM WAS quiet and dark, but it was the gloom that hung the heaviest. The only illumination was the sliver of light creeping in from underneath the door. The landing light had been left on. Ian was wide awake. He hadn't slept a wink since Paula left for the night, except for a small lapse when he lay down with Sally. To be truthful, he hadn't had much sleep all week, ever since she'd started this foolish business. The nap had done nothing for him, except enhance his anxiety through terrible dreams. The most memorable one had been where he was being chased by zombie-like prostitutes with decapitated heads. It had given him an unwanted flashback to the day, a few months back now, when he'd arrived at the scene of the accident. In the dream, headless corpses had gotten up off the same busy road, fixed their heads back on to their bodies, and ran after him, laughing maniacally from their ill-fitting craniums.

He turned for about the fiftieth time, to look at Paula's side of the bed. There was no chance of the sandman coming for him tonight, not until she made it home, cold, pissed off, wet, but, safe. The argument tonight had gotten out of hand again, but hopefully he'd gotten through to her. He just couldn't allow her to put him, or Sally, through this again.

A light flickered from the bedside table alerted him. The buzzing that came with it was extra loud in the ominous silence of the room. He sat up in a flash and grabbed the mobile phone. He didn't want Sally to be awakened, even though he knew she would never be able to hear this from her room.

His tired eyes just stared at the screen for a few seconds. The fuzz in his head made it difficult for him to comprehend what the text on the bright screen was telling him. His heart sank as the letters eventually came together, forming words, words he didn't want to see. He took another glance over to Paula's side of the bed. Her absence was even more pronounced now than it had been seconds earlier. He looked back at the vibrating screen in his hand, hoping he'd read it wrong, hoping it read PAULA like it was supposed to. He wanted it to be her, ringing to tell him she was on her way home, that they'd caught the killer, and her undercover work was done, so all they had to do now was concentrate on planning the most perfect wedding anyone had ever managed.

But no. The mobile phone display was a bastard traitor. It wasn't on the same page as him. It had an agenda all of its own. There were two words on the screen, two of the worst words he could possibly read at this time of night, at this junction of Paula's assignment.

The screen read: DISPATCH, in black, capital letters.

Something inside screamed at him not to answer. It told him to press the red button, not the green one; to go back to bed, put his head on the pillow and sleep, then when he woke in the morning Paula would be next to him, snoring. He knew deep down that was all just a nice fiction. He knew this call was far too important to ignore.

Something had happened, something bad.

'Hello.' The phone was to his ear.

'Hello, may I speak to Officer Locke, Officer Ian Locke?' the professional sounding female voice on the other end asked.

'Speaking. What's happened? What's going on?'

'Sir, I'm sorry to have to be the one to break this to you.'

Oh shit, he thought. *She said sorry, this is it.*

Right then, he wanted nothing more than to drop the phone. He wanted to stop the person on the other end from talking. He wanted to go into Sally's room, wake her, dress her, and run away, far away. Away from mobile phones, from motorcycles, prostitutes, potential serial killers, and undercover night shifts.

He wanted to take Sally, wake Paula up from her slumber, and disappear, but that boat had already sailed.

'Sir, Detective Ashton is missing.'

One word stuck in his head. It revolved around and around and around until he was dizzy. It felt like an eternal ricochet from a random bullet bouncing off every surface of his skull. He didn't even realise he still had hold of the phone as that single word—*missing*—engulfed him.

He swallowed before allowing himself to breathe, let alone speak. Eventually, his voice came out in a whisper. 'Missing? What do you mean? Missing?'

'We don't have the details right now, sir. All we know is Detective Ambrose called in to say Detective Ashton was missing from the undercover operation they were undertaking.'

The information he was being fed felt like it was sucking him into a dark vortex, dragging him down to another level he didn't know existed, one where bad only things happened.

The female voice on the other end of the line began to whisper to him, conspiratorially. 'Listen, we've dispatched an inordinate amount of squad cars, and foot officers to the location, and we've begun a search. We've pulled some in from the surrounding areas to help too. We'll find her, Officer Locke.'

'What ... what do I need to do? Should I get to the station? I'm on my way. I just, I just have to, erm ...'

'Officer Locke'— the woman's voice switched back to a professional tone— 'we're aware you have a child with you. We're conducting the search right now. Your time will be better spent at home, keeping your child safe. We will, of course, keep you updated on any development the search may produce. Do you have anyone you can call to keep you company?'

Ian told her he did, thanked the woman, and hung up. He took a lingering look at the screen. It was a shot of the three of them smiling into the camera. It was too much for him right then, and he flung the phone clear across the room, where it hit the wall, smashing into pieces. He didn't care if it was broken; in fact, he hoped the loathsome thing was. He saw it as a just and rightful punishment for bringing him such shitty news. A small part of him knew he was going to regret that action in an hour or so, but right then, it felt right. He got himself out of the bed and went straight into Sally's room.

She was lit by the gentle light. A light snore rose from her. He knelt, stroking her head, as the first of his many tears began to fall.

Crack

82.

PAULA WAS ON her side, on the cold, damp, and rough tarpaulin. She was taking full advantage of the small window of opportunity Ambrose had unwittingly provided her. She couldn't see the madman who had captured her and couldn't hear Al shouting from the fence. She prayed this was a good omen, that Al had seen right through him and arrested the sick fuck, or killed him. Right now, she had no preference either way.

She was hedging her bets, just in case he hadn't done either, by continuing to wriggle, trying desperately to get her hands free of the thin plastic ties currently cutting into her skin. The tough white strips were hurting rather badly, due to how tight they held her, but she was relentless. Blood was flowing from deep cuts where the thin plastic had sliced into her flesh, but it was slickening the plastic, giving her room to manoeuvre. Her fingers had gained enough room to attempt to get underneath the small plastic flap of the crude mechanism that was keeping her bound.

Jesus Christ, I'm going to need a fantastic manicure after this is over, she thought with a laugh.

Her probing fingertips located the plastic toggle that kept the zip ties closed, and with effort, she was able to manoeuvre her fingernail beneath it. She very nearly caught purchase on it before it snapped back, taking the remains of her fingernail with it. She took a sharp intake of breath through her nose, as her nail tore away from her finger. The rush of air, mixing with the pain made her dizzy. She cried a muffled moan into the vile tasting rag filling her mouth. When the pain subsided to a dull throb, she began to use another finger to make the same attempt. This one worked better. It caught, allowing the zip tie to loosen just a couple of clicks.

Fucking hell, come on, Paula, she scolded herself. Once again, she tried another fingernail underneath the snap. *Come on, come on, come on,* she urged. *Just fucking ... come on*! The fingernail gained more purchase, and she managed to loosen the thin plastic strip even more—again, only by another couple of clicks, but it was progress.

The night sky was beginning to brighten. She hazarded a guess that it must have been five, maybe a quarter past. *Got to get it this time,* she thought, *snap that bastard right off.*

She collected her thoughts and concentrated on the job at hand. Once more, ignoring the searing pain in her fingers and the dull aches of her hands where the plastic zip tie was cutting in, not to mention her throbbing wound where she guessed he'd hit her. Once again, she managed to get her fingernail beneath the small plastic flap, and once again, she managed to pull the zip loose. This time it slipped three or four clicks. She tried to slip her hand out of the bind, but even with the thick slickness of her fresh blood, it was *just* too tight. All she ended up doing was stripping another thick layer of skin away.

One more try; oh, Lord, please, just one more try, she pleaded through her tears.

She hadn't even realised that her eyes were shut until she heard the noise of the van's door slamming closed and the horrific roar of the diesel engine turning over. The bright lights of the vehicle's headlights blinked back on, dazzling her and forcing her to close them again.

Her heart was hammering, and even though she knew she couldn't, her body attempted to force her to take deep breaths.

Panic was spreading its terrible wings within her, and she worried about it taking a full grip of her, especially with a rag stuck in her mouth; but most of all, she worried that she didn't have enough time to free herself of the bindings, *before that maniac runs my fucking head over.* She tried to force herself to relax, attempting to slow her racing heart, but everything was all too real for her to focus.

As she opened her eyes again, all she could see was a stark, bright light. Everything else in the world had paled to be replaced by two new suns, twin suns that were edging closer and closer. A thought occurred to her, and it came with more than a little clarity: *This is how he killed the girl in the woods, the first one.* With dawning horror, she realised the bright lights were not slowing. The madman really was driving the van towards her.

Towards her head.

The smell of the fresh tarmac merged with the stink of a diesel exhaust, and the fresh, early morning smell. It was a total contradiction, and it was making her sick. She felt woozy, like she did earlier when he whacked her on the head did. All her attempts to calm were failing miserably as she continued, frantically on the snap of the plastic tie. She was so close to getting it off. All she needed was just one, or maybe two, more clicks and her blood-slicked hand would be able to wriggle free, then she could lever herself out of the path of encroaching death.

She braved a peek and was horrified to see that the headlights had closed in on her a good distance.

Come on, Paula. It's only a fucking plastic tie.

The rag in her mouth was absorbing all her spit, making her throat dry, therefore hampering all attempts to swallow. The thick, black stink of the rubber, mixed with the exhaust fumes were killing her. They overpowered the tarmac, and the fresh morning smell completely. As she could only breathe through her nose, it was even worse. It was making her brain dance. Her head was spinning as she continued to work on the zip tie as fast as she could, wriggling her hand at every opportunity to test how free she was, ignoring the blistering agony as the inflexible plastic cut deeper into her wet flesh.

A sense of relief washed over her as the tie eventually slipped from her bloodied hand. She flexed her fingers, involuntary attempting to stem the numbness that had taken residence there. As she did, it slowly dawned on her that the world around her had turned dark.

She opened her eyes, looking up from her prone position. The beautiful brightening sky had been replaced. The dark, black dirt of the underside of the van and the thick dark tread of the front passenger side tyre had replaced the purples of the gorgeous, dawning morning.

A peaceful feeling descended upon her, like her body had been wrapped in cotton wool and she could finally relax. The absence of the stresses of life, as they ebbed from her was wonderful. She likened it to the feeling of finally flopping into bed after a long, arduous day.

An acceptance of what was about to happen washed over her as the black wheels of death continued towards her.

In the last moments of her life, she had only one thought.

Sally!

Crack

83.

JOE DROVE THE van slowly, and deliberately towards the woman lying on the road. She was wriggling quite a bit, but the way he'd tied her, he knew from much experience she wouldn't be able to move her head, and that was fine by him. *Let her wriggle all she wants.* He looked towards Helmet Man sitting next to him and caught another glimpse of himself in his cracked visor. He was surprised to see he was wearing a huge, sickening smile on his fevered face.

He was shaking from the fight with this victim, and the run-in with the policeman—that had unnerved him more than he'd realised, and he had to concentrate on keeping his driving straight. The anticipation was becoming too much. He was tempted, more than once, to expedite his short journey just to get to the destination, and the relief faster. He needed to get his fix. He knew it would be a mistake though; he knew he had to get this right. The way this one had fought, she was indeed different than the others, Helmet Man was right. The way this one was struggling too, if he missed, even by a short distance, it would be a disaster, and he would need to find another one. He knew by the presence of the detective at the gates, that would not be happening tonight.

He needed his noise.

As it turned out, he didn't have to wait too long. The familiar throbbing in his cock, helped along my Helmet Man's experienced hand, coupled with the familiar bucking of the van's wheels meeting a delicate obstruction were both a welcome relief. At last, he could press down a little heavier on the accelerator, giving the van the momentum it needed to compensate for the obstruction. His face flushed and Helmet Man's grip tightened as the blood his thrashing heart was pumping, coursed around his body.

There was a brief pause as everything in his own personal bubble, including the pulsing and throbbing in his ears, went silent. At that precise moment, he felt as if he could be the only sentient lifeform in the whole of the planet, maybe even the universe. He was floating, nothing could touch him, he was an elevated being.

Then he heard it ...

CRACK!!!

It was beautiful yet sickening. It was the sound of another skull *cracking* beneath the wheels of his van. Another head opening and distributing its contents for his pleasure. His tyres, and the weight of the van forcing pressure on another cranium until it became too much, and—

CRACK!!!

He closed his eyes and allowed Helmet Man to get him off before once again relaxing into his seat. There were pins and there were needles. They were in the tips of his fingers and his toes. They ran down the shaft of his rigid cock. They frolicked down his legs, through his stomach, up his neck, before fizzing through his brain. His heart peaked, and his vision blurred, the whole world turned white, and for another sweet moment, Joe O'Hara was formless, he ceased to exist.

His heart kicked back in, later he would doubt it had stopped, otherwise he would have been in some serious trouble, but accepted it was his brain dealing with the situation.

He was soothed, eased, and, once again, Joseph O'Hara, security guard, husband, father, the nice guy, was back, and was at peace with the world.

Crack

84.

SALLY'S EYES FLICKERED open. She had been awakened by an odd dream, that she didn't know if it had scared her, or not. As they adjusted to darkness of her room, she noticed Daddy was sleeping while leaning on her bed, his head resting on her blanket. A small, muffled snore came from his turned away face.

A smile spread across her pretty face.

'Silly Daddy,' she whispered, reaching out to stroke his hair. 'Did you fall asleep on my bed?'

Ian's eyes flicked open.

The instant he heard his daughter's voice, the troubled and fractured sleep he had been in broke. He lifted his head and looked at his daughter.

'Hey, baby,' he whispered, attempting to smile.

She sat up and stretched, yawning as she did.

~~~~

As her little arms raised into the air, he noticed her pink fluffy pyjamas, and his heart broke again. He experienced a flashback of Paula picking them, last time they were shopping.

Was that only last week? He thought. *It couldn't be.*

'Where's Mummy?' Sally asked, snapping him out of the daydream of happier times.

He didn't answer her, not straight away. He didn't think he had the words. He just took hold of her and held her tight.

~~~~

She was shocked by how tight Daddy held her, and the funny sounds that were coming from him. *I didn't think daddies could cry,* she thought. She was glad he was there, that he was holding her, but she knew something was wrong.

Crack

85.

THE SUN WAS well into its rise, pushing its intrusive pink light through the edges of the wispy clouds. As Joe got out of the van, he looked upwards, appreciating the morning for the beauty it was brought into a dark, dangerous world. He had everything he needed for the clean-up operation he'd gotten used to ready and at easy reach, that gave him time to just stand there, for a few more precious seconds, marvelling at the sky above him, breathing deep of the brand-new day, and enjoying his escape from the horrors of the dreaded sound.

Eventually, he broke his gaze away from the natural beauty and brought it down to regard, what he had come to think of as, a different kind of natural beauty. He looked at the headless body of his latest fix, lying motionless on the tarmac. He mused on the way this one had fought and wriggled. *Well, you're not wriggling anymore, are you?* He laughed at this thought.

Something about this one had been different, but whatever that had been, it had passed. He'd gotten his fix and banished the dreaded noise from his head for—he hoped—at least another week or so.

As he looked at the body again and something caught his eye. There was something different about her hands.

Still basking in the afterglow of his deed, he made his way over to the carnage and looked closer. He shook his head as he marvelled at the fact that she had managed to free herself from the ties. There were deep lacerations where the plastic had ripped into her skin, and they were covered in blood from where she'd struggled, but the thing that disturbed him was the fact she'd managed to get free of them.

First a gun, and then getting free of the binds, he thought absently. *Plus, a detective at the gates. I'll need to be more careful next time.*

Shrugging it off, he began to drag the body, by the tarpaulin she was lying on, off the road, towards the large concrete pit just behind the small cabin. He dumped the headless mess at the side of the pit and proceeded to unravel the power hose from inside the cabin. His first duty was to clean himself up in the cab, then he had to clean the van and the roadway before he could enjoy the slow sucking and swallowing of the body into the cement. This had become almost ceremonial to him. He'd come to think of it as the ritual sinking of his addiction.

Once he finished cleaning up, he could relax and enjoy the disposal of the body, the cathartic properties of watching his mess, his problems sinking away into an abyss, never to be seen again. Nursing his back, he dragged the hose back to the cabin, grabbed the corpse's lifeless legs again, and pulled it closer to the pit.

As he shifted it, something fell from her top, it was small and black. At first, he thought nothing of it; some of the others had hidden keys and things within their bras, and they had all gone into the cement pits, lost for all time. But there was something different about this small, black wallet. Something about it warranted his attention. Curious, he put her legs down and retrieved whatever it was. He held it out before him, allowing it to drip. Slimy morsels of grey and pink meat fell from the leather binding, splatting on the headless body beneath him. *We can't leave anything lying ...*

He never finished his thought.

He opened the wallet using just the tips of his fingers. What he saw caused him to stagger. His eyes were wide, and the world around him began to spin. Down was up, the sky was the ground, and once again he was floating in a cushion of confusion.

He was holding a bright, polished police shield.

Reality hit him with what could have been a physical crash, as the enormity of what he'd done, what he'd been doing, came home. The horrors of the past month, or so, dawned on him as he looked at the ruined, leaking corpse on the verge of the cement pit. Other than a few cuts and bruises to her arms and legs, the rest of her was relatively unscathed. It was only when his gaze reached the location

Crack

of where her head should have been that the evidence of how much of a monster he had become was revealed.

The shoulders had been torn and pulled, and the torso ended in a ripped, bloody mess of bone and gristle.

The sick feeling he had been fighting for the last few minutes, came to the fore, and he lost the fight to it. He bent double, opened his mouth, and let everything in his stomach that was fighting to escape, out.

When he had finished dry retching, he wiped his mouth and looked back towards the gate where he'd confronted the detective not even hour earlier. He wiped the gristle from the plastic cover of the ID card and read the name. He looked at the photograph of the woman on the opposite side of the badge. Minus the cheap, tarty makeup she'd been wearing, the face was the same woman he'd solicited, and had just killed.

She was Detective Paula Ashton.

His head whirled as he looked back up at the sky. It was nowhere near as beautiful as it had been minutes earlier. 'FUCK!' he shouted to whatever God was hiding in the bright blue above, looking down on wretches like him.

'She's the fucking police,' he whispered.

He spun around, wanting to see everything, all of what was in his immediate vicinity. The greasy fingers of paranoia were prodding him, worming their way inside his head.

He was convinced someone was watching him.

That's when he heard the police sirens in the distance.

He didn't know if they'd been there earlier and he just hadn't noticed them in his elevated state, or if they had only just started, but they were coming from the direction he'd travelled many times, most of them with a fix in the back of the van.

It'll be what the detective was asking about before.

He slumped to his knees next to the body. He was still holding the cursed wallet. He looked at the oozing, headless corpse next to him and shook his head.

This wasn't a *fix*, this wasn't a thing to be played with, used to appease his own addictions and cravings. She wasn't a tool to facilitate the removal of the wretched noise that was plaguing him.

This was a woman, a victim—*his* victim. *She* had been a person, a person with a name, an identity … a life! Her world would have been filled with people who worried and cared about her. Her life would have been a rich tapestry of family and friends.

Joe was lost.

All he could do was gaze around him. His face was vacant, his mind was vacant. He gripped the wallet tight enough to crease the leather binding, grasping it as if it were an anchor, a last straw to clutch to, to keep him sane, in the normal everyday world with all the other human beings who'd found themselves in similar circumstances in the hope it might save him, drag him back to sanity.

Similar circumstances? He might have laughed at that, if he wasn't so lost in his own quagmire of conscience. He knew there was no one with similar circumstances as this. He was out there, on his own, with no one he could talk to about these issues. Not without being thrust into a white coat with his arms secured around himself, for his own safety, and the safety of others.

He did laugh when he realised, he'd never see sanity again.

Helmet Man reappeared at his side; his black, bulbous head facing him. Joe knew he was there, but he didn't acknowledge him, at least not straight away. Instead, he held the wallet out towards him with a shaking hand.

'You wanted me to take the doctor, and I couldn't. I tried to keep it to the unfortunates one off the streets. I even went further afield to seek out …' He paused thinking what he should call them, now he couldn't think of them as fixes anymore. Finally, he looked up at his ghostly companion. It didn't help. All that happened was he came face-to-face with a reflection of a murderer, a serial killer, a madman, all of them hiding within the cracked visor, and all of them looking exactly like him. 'Victims,' he concluded.

Helmet Man pointed at the wallet. Joe's eyes followed. There was a small compartment inside that he hadn't noticed. As he investigated it, his shaking, blood-covered fingers disturbed something, causing it to slip out and fall into the gore that had amassed next to the body—*Paula's body,* he thought.

Crack

The small plastic square of paper landed in a streak of blood. He looked down, and for a second or two, his mind couldn't, or wouldn't, register what he was looking at.

His logical brain took control, and the item swam into focus. As he looked on it, the last remnants of his rational life crashed around him. He wanted to cover his ears to mask the noise of the crash, but he knew it would be as impossible as masking the cursed CRACK.

The small square was stuck in thickening blood. He bent over and picked up the photograph. He wiped it and looked at it.

Instantly, he wished he hadn't.

It was a picture of a family.

The woman was young and beautiful as she smiled into the camera. Joe recognised the smile from the woman he'd picked up from the street earlier, the one who was currently laid out at his feet, dead, by his own hand, *or van,* he thought with no humour attached to the words. She was not the scraggy prostitute anymore; she wasn't a police detective either. She was a vibrant woman, a mother. Her long, slightly curling, blond hair was hanging down to her shoulders, and she was smiling. The smile lit up her whole face. The same face that had been plastered with cheap makeup to attract—the likes of him.

She was—

No, Joe, he no longer knew if it was him thinking this, or if Helmet Man was speaking in his head.

S*he HAD been*—beautiful.

She was holding a young girl of maybe three or four years of age, in her arms. The girl was the double of her mother. She had the same eyes and the same bright smile. Next to them was a tall, handsome man. He had his arm wrapped around them both, holding them, protecting them.

They looked happy, they looked like they had a whole future before them, one filled with magic, romance, mystery, and each other. He'd take all of them away from them, and he'd done it on a selfish whim.

As he stared into the photograph, a memory of what felt like other life, took him by surprise.

He was a younger man, a much younger man. He was walking into a photographer's shop on a high street with a much younger Karen. Four-year-old Annmarie was toddling alongside him; she was holding his hand. He was her daddy, her rock, her protector from everything bad that was out there in the world, whether it be monsters under her bed, or boys teasing her. Karen was pushing a pram, inside it was eighteen-month-old Martin.

In a flash, they were before a camera, laughing and giggling as several bright flashes exploded before them.

His memory searched for that picture now. It found it framed, hanging proudly over the fireplace at home. In the shot, he was holding Karen tightly. He was actually squeezing her on the orders of the photographer so that she was caught in the moment with a natural laugh. She was holding Martin's hands as he was sitting up. Annmarie was sat on Joe's shoulders, her whole face one huge, wet, grin. The picture was all about the laughter. It was a moment of happiness, caught forever in sepia, and framed. His eyes welled with tears as he looked up to the sky for the third time that morning.

'What the fuck have I done?' he shouted. 'Who am I? What am I? I've ruined ...' He stuttered as a sob hit him, then taking a shaky breath, he concluded, 'Everything.'

He looked at the body next to him. Nausea bulged in his stomach, and he had to turn away. More vomit spewed forth, hot and thick, onto the roadside. On his hands and knees, his body continued to heave for minutes rather than seconds. He thought he was dying, and he welcomed it; he felt as if he deserved it.

When he was sure he was empty inside, in more ways that one, he wiped his mouth. Looked around, he expecting to see Helmet Man.

Once again, in his hour of need, the bastard was nowhere to be seen. 'Where the fuck are you now, eh? Where are you now, *Helmet Man*? Where the fuck are you?'

There was no answer; his helmeted friend did not grace him with his presence.

He returned his teary eyes towards Detective Paula Ashton's body and wiped his running nose with his sleeve. Helmet Man or not, he still had work to do. There was no point sitting around crying about it.

Crack

He stood and brushed himself down before. Looking at the body made his stomach churn again. The very fact that he, Joseph Brian O'Hara, father, husband, son, could do something like this to another human being killed him inside.

As he didn't relish the reality of spending the rest of his day holed up in a psychiatric facility, being analysed and prodded every single day by the likes of Dr Penny Saunders, he needed to get rid of Paula. He leaned over the corpse and rolled her towards the cement pit. The touch of her cooling, response-less body on his hands made him recoil. She felt like wet clay, he'd never noticed the feeling of the dead flesh on any of the... *others*, and he was once again reminded of what he now was:

A murderer!

When he had gotten her to the verge of the pit, he stood and rubbed his aching lower back. He took another deep breath, groaned, and finished his work. He closed his eyes tightly and rolled her lifeless corpse into the hungry grey pit with his foot.

Even after his realisation of was happening in his head, and in his life, he still enjoyed watching the cement gratefully accept his offering. It pulled the body down, folding itself over her, receiving its sacrifice with welcome folds, and taking her to a place where she would never to be seen again.

It took a few moments for her to submerge. Seconds before she was gone forever, he remembered to throw in her wallet, complete with the badge and the photographs.

He sat at the edge of the pit. He watched as the grey skin found its level. He felt his lower lip begin to quiver, right before the tears came. He had a mad compulsion to say a prayer or maybe just a few words, to mark Detective Paula Ashton's passing, but he thought maybe it would have been a step too far, maybe a little hypocritical.

So, he just cried instead.

He cried for Paula and her family, just like he cried for his own family—for Karen, Annmarie, and Martin. But most of all, he cried for himself, for what he'd become, and for what he'd lost along the way.

86.

THE DAYS PASSED in a blur for Sally. Every hour merged into one long, confusing day. Her Daddy spent a lot of the time on his mobile phone, the one with the cracked screen. If he wasn't on that, then he was hugging her, telling her that everything was going to be OK. She didn't understand what was happening, but she did know she didn't want to let him out of her sight just in case he disappeared like Mummy had.

She didn't understand what had happened to mummy. Nanny Ashton had been around almost constantly, both day and night, which had been good for hugs, and general playing, but she wasn't nowhere near as good at it as mummy was. There had been lots of people coming and going through their house, but none of them had been the one she'd needed the most. It frustrated her that her mummy hadn't been home because she had all sorts of secrets, she wanted to tell her. She wanted to tell her that she missed her, she needed her, and, most of all, she loved her.

There were moments, when she was sat on her own, thinking that mummy hadn't come home because of something naughty, or bad, that she'd said or done. If this was true, then she intended to tell God at every opportunity that she was sorry and that he could let her mummy come back to her, to them, now.

All the time she was talking to God, her daddy was on his phone. He was either swearing, shouting, or, worst of all, crying. Each time he cried, he tried to hide it from her, but she knew what he was doing.

This made her cry then; daddies weren't supposed to cry.

And all along, there was no mummy.

When the police had come, Daddy went through the same changes as he did on the phone. He would hug some of them, he'd shout and swear again, Sally hated that part, then he'd cry again. But in the end, they always went back to the hugging parts.

Then they would hug her too.

Some people brought food, most of it was delicious, and she enjoyed that part, and the bit where she got to stay up late. She also got to sleep with daddy in the big bed, which was nice because she could smell mummy on the pillows, and that gave her dreams of Mummy being with her in the bed, hugging her, and kissing her.

These dreams were nice, but when they ended, mummy still wasn't there. Sometimes there were nightmares too, where bad things crept into the house and stole mummy away; it stole her toys too, but it wasn't them she cried for.

She cried for her mummy.

87.

THE DAYS WERE one long blur for Joe too.

He rang work and told them he was sick. They were not surprised at all by his call, and he had to repeat his name to the person he spoke to, twice before they realised who he was. He heard them call him *the head guy* in the background before they then knew who he was.

That gave him the only laugh he'd remembered having since this whole sorry affair had begun.

He'd lost his appetite completely and had noticed his clothes hung from him where once they were tight. He'd become ignorant to the stink coming from his body, and the clothes he's worn for days and days on end, but he hadn't gotten blind to the sweat, the grime, and the scum that was building up in the creases of his unwashed body.

He didn't see the point in washing if he wasn't going anywhere.

He sat in his filthy living room, in his grubby house, wearing soiled pyjamas and a housecoat. His hair was grease bound, and his skin was blotchy, itchy, and flaky.

He'd caused a dent in his armchair from sitting day after day, night after night, staring into a blank TV screen.

If the saying was true, and the eyes really were the window to the soul, then he knew that his soul would be truly black and withered, like a dried-out husk that had been buried for hundreds of years, lost for all eternity in an ocean of darkness.

CRACK!!!

'Fuck off,' he shouted, his voice hoarse and cracked.

Crack

CRACK!!!

'Fuck off.'

CRACK!!!

This torment continued for nearly a week. The noises were coming thick and fast.
Helmet Man had made a reappearance. Joe didn't care if he was there or not, but at least he was someone to talk to.
'I wondered when you'd come back,' he growled. It was the first time in over a week he had spoken anything, other than to curse the noises in his head.

CRACK!!!

'Don't you think it's time, Joe?'
'Fuck off.'
'What have you brought to this world, Joe?'
'I told you to fuck off.'
'Nothing, that's what. Your legacy is one of pain, misery, and fear. How do you think that young family are doing right now, Joe?'
'Fuck. Off.'
'I'll tell you how they're doing. The husband is trying to explain to that little girl why mummy isn't coming home ever again. The little girl is crying, thinking that she's done something bad and that's why her mummy left. The husband is telling her that it's not her fault. He's telling her that her mummy loved her very, very much, and she wanted to come back, she just couldn't. The poor man isn't even aware that he's already talking about her mother, his wife, in the past tense.'
Joe's hands were over his ears; his face twisted.

CRACK!!!

'Leave me alone.'

'I can't, Joe. You've brought this on yourself. It's my bet the husband has thought of killing himself too, by now. I bet he's held a sharp blade to his wrist once or twice. Maybe he's even cut into his skin a couple of times, muttering the old saying *horizontal for attention, vertical if you're serious*. It bet he was going for the vertical option, Joe. He'll have wanted to end the pain, the unknowing. The only thing stopping him is the little girl. The same one who has just lost her mother. He can't bring himself to do it because he can't bring any more hurt into her young life. Any more pain that *you* have brought on them.'

'Leave me alone. Please, just leave me alone.' Joe was sobbing into a cushion that he was holding over his face.

'I'll go, but just for today. It's been more than a week since your last fix. You're going to need me again soon, unless you do what you think needs to be done.'

Joe stood and threw a cup at Helmet Man. The vessel sailed harmlessly through the cracked helmet before hitting the wall behind him and spilling cold tea all the way down the wallpaper.

Flopping onto the chair, Joe hid his head in his hands and wailed.

CRACK!!!

Crack

88.

THE ROOM SOOTHED him, and it was cathartic, exactly as it had been designed to do. The lights had been lowered to a level that induced relaxation, whether the person wanted it, or not. The couch he was currently enjoying was thick and comfortable, and his head was propped with a luxurious cushion that he guessed might have cost more than a month of his wages. Joe O'Hara's eyes were blinking heavy, and he was in serious danger of falling asleep, exactly how she wanted it to be.

Dr Penny Saunders had no idea how lucky she was to still be alive, and she knew nothing of her being in the presence of one of the most prolific serial killers the UK had not caught yet.

She'd been glad when he'd reached back out to her, especially after the strange encounter in the street. There had been an affinity with this man, and she had thought about him often. She knew she wasn't supposed to gain opinions, or feelings for her patients, or prospective patients, but she thought he was a sad, but interesting, case.

'I have these, these, impulses,' he confessed. His eyes were closing, and a genuine, benign smile was nestled across his face. 'Well, I'm not sure if you'd call them impulses. It may be more of an addiction.'

'I'm listening,' she replied, her large pad and pencil poised to begin taking notes.

'It starts with a noise, a loud, crunching noise, more like a crack, but I don't think it's real. I think it's only in my head. When I hear it, it makes me want to … do things.'

'What things?'

He paused; his brow ruffled for a moment as if a troubled thought had just passed over it. 'Bad things. My dreams become intense, and I can't seem to separate them from reality. It's as if I become a separate person.'

'Do you have these feelings of detachment regularly?'

'Just lately, yes. I—I see things. I see me as another personality.'

'You mean there is another voice in your head?'

Joe paused at the question. 'Not exactly. Well, I mean, yes, probably, but it's more than that. I *see* myself. I see myself as a person in a motorcycle outfit, wearing a huge black helmet with a cracked visor. I only ever appear when I hear the noise.'

Penny was enjoying this and was busy writing notes onto her pad. 'Do you interact with this persona?' she asked after a few seconds of scribbling.

'Yes.'

'How does that work?'

Joe's face became troubled again; his eyebrows ruffled again, and his lips tightened. He began to squirm on the couch.

SUBJECT BECAME UNCOMFORTABLE WHEN ASKED ABOUT INTERACTION WITH OWN EXTENDED PERSONA. CLASSIC PTSD SYMPTOMS, she wrote before looking at him again with professional deadpan expression.

~~~~

'He, I mean I, tell myself to do things. Things that I, or he, or whatever, claim will get rid of the noise.'

'What things does he tell you to do, Joe? And more importantly, do you listen to him, act upon them?'

His hands tightened together. They became white with the effort he was exerting on them. He began to his wriggle his feet.

He didn't answer.

'What things Joe? Do you act upon them?' she repeated.

'FUCKING BAD THINGS!' he shouted.

With a spurt of energy and life, he didn't even know he had, he leaped from the couch, and grabbed her.

She dropped her notepad and pencil as she recoiled from the unexpected attack.

Crack

He was on her in a flash. His hand clawed at the blouse she was wearing. He tore it open, causing her buttons to fly across the room. His other hand gripped her solidly in a choke hold, one he knew would leave bruises, but he didn't care. He pushed her back, into the chair she was sitting in.

His wild eyes looked her up and down. Her short, tight skirt had ridden up her legs, and he could see the tops of her sheer, black stockings, and some yellow fabric between her legs. His sneer was deep as he allowed his eyes to roam up her body. If his eyes had tongues, he would have licked her, tasted her. His breathing was fast, shallow, and he could feel the familiar twinge in his trousers, the one he'd had to work so hard to achieve when he was with Karen, but came naturally when he had a *bitch,* under his wheels. He licked his lips as her ripped blouse revealed something that was the same shade of yellow as what was between her legs.

It was the stringed top of a bikini; the same one she'd been wearing in his previous fantasy.

He grinned into her face, exhaling slowly from his nose. It was less of a sigh, more of a grunt.

As he opened his mouth, thick, white saliva strands bridged the gulf between his jaws.

Her face had lost its fear now, and as she was staring back into his wild, animalistic eyes. A smile spread across her face. It was alluring, and salacious. She looked at him as if he were feral. 'Do it, Joe,' she whispered. 'Take me like the fucking animal we both know you are.'

He looked at her; his face twitched, his eyes grew wider, and his cheeks puffed with every breath.

'Do it,' she whispered again. 'Hit me, you cunt. Beat me like you did Karen, then fuck me.'

He widened his mouth, reeling in the sting of his gums as his teeth grew, narrowing to long, dangerous points. His face contorted, elongated. He was now a dog, maybe he was a Labrador called Nixon, or even a fox, whatever he was now, he was less than human. His elongated face descended on hers with ferocity, so much that his human forehead contacted with the bridge of her nose.

The blow made a satisfying *crack.*

I've heard better, he thought as he brought his head back to look at what he had done.

Her beautiful face was ruined.

Her nose was swollen and disjointed. Blood was pouring from it, coating her face and torn blouse. It hadn't quite made it to her bikini top. Still, she was grinning. 'Finish it, Joe. You know you want to.' She smiled through the gore and attempted to wink a swollen eye. Her face was grotesque, ugly, ruined, but alluring all at the same time. 'You know what I mean. Finish me, do what you have to do.'

As he looked at her, the blood stemmed from her nose, going from a waterfall to a trickle that dripped down her features.

'I know what to do,' he replied, blinking as sweat ran into his eyes.

'Then what are you waiting for?' she asked through swelling lips.

He opened his mouth, stretching his animal lips back from his teeth, baring them as if he was a rabid mutt, and she was his prey.

She tried to smile through her broken face.

He shushed her, lowered his head, and bit through her soft, salty flesh …

~~~~~

'Bad things,' he replied as he lay on the couch. His eyes were closed tightly, attempting to banishing the daydream that just woke him up.

The doctor's non-ruined face regarded him for a moment. She tapped the eraser end of her pencil against her teeth. 'Hmm,' was all she said before looking up at the clock.

'It seems our time is up, Joe. But I'd really like to see you again in a few days. I think we need to discuss this alternative personality of yours and the *bad things* he's asking you to do. Should we say Wednesday? Two days from now, at eleven thirty?'

Joe was in the process of slipping his shoes back on and looking up at her. 'That sounds excellent to me, Penny,' he replied, with a genuine smile.

Crack

'OK, I'll put you in the diary. If you speak to Sandra on reception, she'll give you an appointment card.'

'I don't think I'll need one, Doc. I'll remember. Wednesday, eleven thirty.'

He left Penny's office with a clear view of what his next move was to be.

89.

IT WAS WEDNESDAY morning and Joe was in the shower. He was singing along to a song on the radio, one that he loved but hadn't heard in a long time. Thin Lizzy were urging him to Don't Believe a Word. The lyrics seemed kind of apt to him. They were along the lines of a woman's heart being something like a promise, there to be broken. *Wise words, Phil,* he thought as warm water cascaded over his body.

His thoughts heralded towards Karen and the kids, and a smile washed over his face as he scrubbed himself clean.

He got out, towelled himself dry, and faced himself in the mirror to shave. The song changed, and Credence Clearwater Revival were doing their very own take on the most fantastic I Heard It Through the Grapevine.

He was looking good.

'I bet you're wondering how I knew …' he whispered as he inspected his skin for missed stubble. The blotchiness of his bad skin had gone, and his hair had some of its old lustre back. Even his eyes, for once in his life, didn't look tired and puffy. They looked rested, and their natural colour shone through. He half mumbled about plans to make him blue, but he's forgotten the majority of the lyrics.

He shaved the remaining fuzz from his face and took another look at himself. He looked a few years younger and was nodding while he posed. He'd lost a lot of weight, and could now see the dimples in his cheeks, for the first time in maybe twenty years.

He chuckled at the irony that today, of all days, he looked the best he had in years.

He made his way downstairs and gazed about the house.

It was a mess.

Crack

He took a bit of time and straightened it up, vacuuming every room, washing the dishes, and wiping all the surfaces. Next, he took out the ironing board and fished out one of his best shirts and the trousers that he only wore for special occasions.

After dousing himself in aftershave, he rechecked his appearance in the mirror. He was looking good and feeling as good as he looked.

It was very fitting for his appointment today.

He then let himself out of his house, locking the door behind him.

He didn't want to be late, not today.

90.

'YOU WILL BE coming home today, won't you, daddy?' Sally's big eyes and ruffled eyebrows almost broke Ian's heart for the millionth time in a week. He was dressed in his motorcycle policeman's uniform and was ready to leave for his first day back at work. As he knelt to embrace the trembling little girl, and hug her tight, she jumped on him, clinging to him.

'Of course I will, sweet pea. You know daddy has to go to work to pay the bills. We talked about that.'

She nodded, trying to smile, but her eyes were already full of tears. She cleared her throat, obviously wanting to get something off her chest but not knowing how to go about it. After a short pause, she decided, as children often do, that the direct approach was best. 'Mummy went to work and never came back again,' she whispered, unsuccessfully trying to hold back a sob.

He looked in her teary eyes, hoping he could convey his sincerity to her. 'I'll be coming home again, Sally.' He paused for a moment, wondering if he should say the next part, but she not only deserved it, but she needed it too. 'I promise.'

Sally nodded; a glint of sunshine broke through the gloom of her tears.

'Now, you go spend the day with Nanny Joan. She's going to tell you loads of lovely stories all about mummy and how she'll always be with you, with both of us, right here. OK?' Ian said, pointing to his heart.

Sally looked sad, but he could see her attempts to be brave.

As he stood, he realised his own eyes were heavy with tears.

Joan took his arm. 'She'll be OK. She'll adjust.' A sincere nod and a smile told him everything he needed to know. Sally would be OK.

Crack

He nodded. 'I know, but will I? Will we ever get to know what happened to her?'

Joan looked away; there was a lot of tear fighting happening this morning.

'I'm sorry, Joan. I've got to go. This is the only way I think I can deal with what's happening.'

'Just be careful. Don't do anything rash. Remember Sally will be looking out the window, waiting for you to come home.'

He wiped his eyes and took in a shaky breath. 'I know, and thanks, Joan. I know how this is affecting you too.'

Joan took Sally and cuddled her. 'Well, I've got this little monster here to keep me happy.' She gave Sally a little tickle.

Ian smiled when he heard her giggle.

'You two have fun, OK. Remember, I love you guys.'

'I love you too, Daddy,' Sally replied in a sad sing-song voice before he walked out the door towards his motorcycle.

91.

IAN'S VISOR WAS UP, as he rode along the motorway, enjoying the breeze on his face. He was allowing all his bad thoughts and all the negative emotions of the last couple of weeks, to ebb away. Even though he knew it was only a temporary fix, he was enjoying getting lost in the simple pleasure of riding.

He pulled in at a petrol station and removed his helmet. The relief as the cool air hit his sweating head made him sigh. He hung the helmet over the handlebars, stretched, and opened the little compartment behind him. He took out a package of sandwiches and a small coffee flask and proceeded to eat lunch.

A static burst from the radio interrupted his break. 'All units,' the disembodied voice called from the small speakers on the side of the bike. Ian's training wouldn't allow him to ignore the shout. 'We have a code 10-56A on the Gateway Bridge, East Side.'

10-56A, potential suicide, he thought. He grabbed the receiver and spoke into it. 'Officer 776 reporting. I'm right on that, about five minutes away. Officer responding.'

'10-4, Officer Locke. Backup will be there ASAP.'

'Copy that. I'll take it from here.'

He put his lunch away and slipped his helmet back on, then drove out of the rest stop. The bridge was half a mile from his current location and was already visible on his horizon. As he rode towards it, the traffic had already begun to slow. This wasn't an unusual event around the bridge, and he had to use his sirens to get past the many angry, and bored drivers stuck in the aftermath of what was happening.

An odd sensation caused him to shiver as he realised this scene was eerily reminiscent of the accident he'd attended a few months back, the one where the motorcyclist had his head removed by the

Crack

car. *Jesus, that seems like a lifetime ago,* he thought. He didn't want to give voice to the ugly thought running through his head that told it *had* been a lifetime ago... Paula's.

As he got closer and made his way onto the actual bridge, there was a man standing on the lip, just beyond the rail, at the bridge's highest point. He was looking down at a one-hundred-and-fifty-foot drop into the rapidly flowing river below.

Ian alighted his motorcycle. He was in a hurry and hadn't taken the time to remove his helmet as he made his way to where the man was precariously perched.

'I wondered how long it would take you to get here,' the man said, still with his back towards him.

'What?' Ian asked, a little confused.

The man turned and looked at him, nodding as he realised who it was. 'Oh sorry,' he shouted over the brisk wind. 'I thought you might have been someone else.' There was a chuckle in his voice, as if he'd made a small joke.

'Nope, it's just me. So, what's the story here, my friend?' Ian asked, his limited suicide negotiation training kicking in. The priority was to form a relationship with the potential suicide, gain their trust, get them on your side, then reel them in, off the ledge.

'Isn't it obvious?'

'The only thing obvious to me is you out there on a ledge. You want to talk about it?'

The man turned away and looked out towards the mouth of the river, a few miles out. The strong breeze rippled through his hair as he shook his head slowly. 'Nothing to talk about, Officer.'

Ian made his way towards the railing, slowly, making sure he kept a safe distance. The last thing he wanted was to startle him into doing anything rash. 'Sure, there is. If there wasn't, you'd have already jumped by now.'

The man chuckled again. 'Maybe I'm waiting for the right wind.' He lifted his head into the air again, allowing it to blow through his hair. 'An ill wind.'

'Or maybe you're waiting for someone to talk to you? Someone to listen,' Ian offered, sidling a little closer. 'What could be so drastic that this way seems the only option?'

The man shook his head, still not looking at him, but smiling. 'I know what you're up to. You're trying to get me on to your side, to make me think we're friends so I don't do it.'

He turned towards Ian. For some reason, he looked familiar, but then with everything that had been happening over the last few weeks, everyone's faces were beginning to blur.

'Do me a favour; if we have to talk for a bit, can you remove your helmet? It's a little'— the man's eyebrows came together in a wrinkle— 'distracting.'

Ian removed his helmet and placed it on the floor, then stepped a little closer. 'I'm not trying to be your friend, or even pretending to. I just don't want to have to fill in all kinds of suicide paperwork on my first day back on the job.' He was smiling as he spoke, trying to calm this man, but to Ian, he already looked calm, and rather placid.

'You been on holiday or something?' he asked distractedly.

'Nothing as nice as that. I've been on compassionate leave,' Ian replied stoically, turning his head, looking out towards the same direction the man was looking. It was his turn to let the cold wind run through his sweaty hair. His was shorter than the man's and the effect was nowhere near as dramatic.

This got the man's attention. He looked at Ian before turning away again, as if something fantastical was happening down the estuary that he needed to see. 'Someone die?'

Ian shrugged. 'We don't know yet.'

The man looked down towards the river flowing beneath them, and the mud flats out in the distance. He was nodding as he tapped on the metal bar behind him, but Ian could see he'd struck a raw nerve with that one.

'I feel like someone died,' the man said eventually. 'Maybe I died. Or part of me, anyway.'

'That bad, eh?'

Quick to anger, as he snapped his head around in a flash towards Ian. 'Yeah, it's that bad. I had an accident, and it changed me. It turned me into someone else, *something* else.'

Ian was happy with the way this exchange was going. He'd kept him talking long enough, knowing the backup and the ambulances would arrive soon. He just needed to keep this rapport

Crack

going for a little while longer, giving time to allow the professionals to set up, and do what they were trained for.

He was also aware of the build-up of spectators behind him, all of them vying to get a peep at the man on the edge, both physically and mentally. 'But you're still you, aren't you? You got a wife? Kids?'

The man offered another chuckle. There was a raw sarcasm in the humourless sound. 'Oh yeah, I got all those things, although none of them want to know me anymore. I told you, I'm something else now.'

'Are they still alive?' Ian asked, edging a little closer.

The man turned to look at him. His eyes had a distant look to them. He nodded slowly, as the ghost of a smile broke on his lips. 'Well, I haven't killed them if that's what you're thinking. Yeah, they're still alive; they're just ...' He paused as if thinking of where they could be. 'Somewhere else.'

'Can I get hold of them for you? I'm sure no matter how far your relationship has stretched, they're not going to want to see you like this. What's your name?'

The man looked at him. The smile that spread across his face, although it lacked any humour at all, was genuine, as it brimmed with sadness and regret. 'Joe, Joe O'Hara,' he replied, shaking his head again. 'I don't think they'd give a shit about me right now, not after knowing what I've become. I've done things, you know, terrible things.' Tears began to fall from his eyes, and Ian guessed they weren't there because of the stiff wind blowing in his face.

'Joe, I'll let you into a little secret. I've been like you too. I've been thinking of ending it all. You see, my fiancé is missing. She's missing, Joe. Do you understand that implication? We don't know if she's dead, so we can't mourn; she's not left me for another man, so I can't get angry; she's not moved away somewhere where I know she's safe. None of those things, Joe. She's *missing*, and no one knows where the fuck she is.'

He stared at Joe, biting his lower lip as his eyes began to sparkle with the moisture building within them.

'I feel like Joe's gone missing,' Joe said, in leu of a reply. 'Can you understand that? He's disappeared too, gone. My life is just one big pile of shit right now.'

Ian nodded. 'Mine too, but you've got one thing in your favour; your family is alive and safe. Look at me. I'm out here on the job, hoping to find the man Paula was looking for, to find him and hope beyond hope that he resists arrest. To just hope he gives me that one excuse to kill him.' Ian paused; he needed to reel himself back in. He was here to help this man off the bridge, not for a psychotherapy session. 'But I can't live like that, Joe. I've got a three-year-old girl, and now, I've got to live for her.'

'You said your fiancé was missing. Was she murdered?'

Ian noted that Joe's face became animated as the question fell from his mouth. He was gripping the barrier behind him tightly as he looked at the bigger man.

Ian looked down at the water rushing past them hundreds of feet below as he answered. 'That's the thing. I don't know; no one knows. One minute she was there, and then the next she wasn't.' He closed his eyes tight as he relived the disturbing dreams, the nightmares where he'd been dwelling, and had resigned himself to the fact he would probably continue to dwell for a long time to come. Finally, he looked back at Joe and smiled. 'So, you see, whatever it is that you think you need to run from, there's always someone out there dealing with a Hell that's just as bad, or maybe even worse than yours. Shit, I've had to leave my Sally at home with Paula's mum because I have to work this job.'

He slumped on the side of the bridge putting his head in his hands, his mouth pulling down in a rictus of sorrow, with little diversions of anger built in. His nose was tingling as a precursor for tears to flow. As he looked back at Joe, the whites of his eyes were pink. 'Don't jump, Joe. Whatever it is, I'm sure you can fix it. Get help, get therapy, shit, get drunk. Just don't jump.'

~~~~

Joe didn't want to look at him, but he had an urge to. *Paula,* he thought. *Policewoman, undercover, little girl.*

It all began to knit together in his head. He couldn't help but smile, it wasn't amusement, but a dark sense of irony. After the accident, he'd hit an all-time low for self-esteem and he didn't think he could have stooped any lower, at any point in his life, but now, at

Crack

this juncture, this must have been an all-time record. The only difference was that this time, the low wasn't for him. It was directed towards the policeman sitting next to him. It was all too much for him to bear. Here he was, being talked down from the precipice by a victim of what he needed to stop.

He felt the need to confess. To get what he'd done off his chest. To take, maybe even welcome the punishment he so richly deserved. Even if it meant putting himself at the mercy, or quite possibly the fury, of the unstable man next to him.

'I've got ... compulsions,' Joe confessed. The vista of the river's estuary behind him, give a picturesque backdrop to the gruesome confession he was about to give. 'It's an addiction. I don't know how to stop,' he whispered.

Ian looked at him, wiping his face. The wind was blowing directly onto him, exposing his pink, tear-stained face. 'There's always help, for any addiction.' He swallowed in a clear attempt to compose himself. 'So, what's your poison, Joe?'

Joe clung onto the rail behind him. An eerie laugh fell out of him, like something dark escaping from a dungeon somewhere inside of him. He was amazed he still had a laugh left in him. 'Crack,' he said, then continued to laugh, shaking his head at how ridiculous that sounded.

Ridiculous but true.

Ian looked at him and raised his eyebrows. Joe guessed the man wasn't judging him. Deep guilt coursed through him at the policeman's small, but thoughtful gesture.

'That's a tough one, Joe, but there are programmes for it. I can get you into one, or at the very least put you onto someone who can.'

Joe stopped laughing and shook his head, it was his turn to wipe his face. 'I don't think there would ever be a programme for my kind of addiction,' he replied. As he spoke, he looked around, searching for Helmet Man, he had been sure he would have been here for this.

He had been conspicuous in his absence of late.

Ian reached into an inside pocket of his motorbike jacket. 'Look at this,' he said, holding out a small scrap of paper. On it was a picture of a young blonde girl of about four years of age.

As Joe looked at it, a shiver coursed through his body. He recognised the little girl from the black wallet, the same wallet that now languished at the bottom of a deep cement pit, along with the badge and, of course, the owner.

'That's the reason I get up in the morning. If it wasn't for her, I'd be over there with you. Paula was my reason for living, then Paula and Sally.' He paused for a moment, looking at the small picture in his gloved hand. 'Now it's just Sally. Paula was supposed to become my wife.' He chuffed, it was just a small humourless noise that came out of his nose, but it spoke volumes about grief, about loss, and about helplessness. Joe hated him for it. 'Last week, actually. The day was all paid for. The dress, cake, band. Everything.' A distant look overtook his face as he tapped the picture against his hand. He offered the magnificent view a wistful look. 'Yup, she would have been my wife, but you know what? Do you want to know something stupid?'

Joe didn't want to hear what the policeman had to say. This was the worst kind of punishment for his crimes. He tried to shake his head—he really didn't want to know *anything* stupid right now; he'd had more than his fill of stupid. All he wanted was to either jump, and rid the world of him, and his fucking noise, or get off this bridge and make some sort of amends with his life, with his wife and his kids. All he managed to do was stare blankly at the man before him. The man he'd inadvertently ruined. His face was a mask of interest in what the policeman was about to say, but that's all it was, a mask. Behind his eyes was nothing but a hollow pit of regret and torment.

This man's misery, the misery he'd caused, touched him on a deep level.

'I went to pay for the dress. As I went inside, one of the girls wheeled it out from the back by accident, and I saw it. I saw the fucking dress before the wedding. Was it all doomed from that moment onwards? The woman in the shop told me. She said it was bad luck for the groom to see the dress before the event.' Tears were falling down his face in streams. 'She was right.' Without thinking about it, he wiped his face again as he looked at the little picture of Sally one more time. 'Do you have any photos of your wife and kids, Joe?'

Crack

Joe dropped his head. Real guilt was swelling through him. 'I do. They're in my wallet. I didn't bring it with me today.' He mustered up another snort of laughter. 'I didn't think I'd need it.'

Ian registered the small attempt at gallows humour and nodded, acknowledging it. 'Come on, what say we get out of here and maybe consider something that's going to make you feel a little better? Even if it's just for the short term; what do you say?'

Joe' eyes widened. *Why did he just use that term? Does he know something and is toying with me?*

'Come on. Maybe you can contact that family of yours tonight, eh? Just talk to them, let them know how you're feeling. Maybe, I don't know, tell them that you love them.'

Slowly, Joe began to nod. He never took his eyes from the policeman's face. Acting on autopilot, he ducked underneath the railing he was holding onto and clambered back onto the safety of the bridge.

Ian stood up and took his arm. 'Good man. You've done the right thing here. An ambulance is on the way. It'll take you to the hospital, and then wherever you need to be. Maybe get you some of that help for that stupid addiction, eh?'

Joe turned away from the police officer's gaze, towards the sounds of the approaching sirens. Once again, he felt hollow inside. *The fucking nerve of you,* a voice in his head shouted. It was a voice he recognised, only too well. *Only you, Joe. Only you could accept help from the man you ruined, who's life you have torn to pieces with your selfless action. You are a piece of work, Joe. You really are.*

'Thanks, Officer. I really want that help, and I do think it's my family who can provide it.'

'That's the spirit. Listen, don't call me Officer, though, my name's Ian, Ian Locke.'

With a contrite look, he offered the officer his hand, but he didn't want to know his name. It only emphasised the things he'd done. 'Thanks, Ian,' he mumbled, sounding like he meant it.

The kaleidoscope of thoughts running through Joe's head were making him dizzy. The consequences of one action here had dumbfounded him. How many people had been hurt by his selfishness? He thought about the other women, and the misery he'd brought to their families and friends. The enormity of it all made his head swirl.

He staggered a little as the world fell a little off kilter. Ian offered a hand to steady him, and Joe accepted it. Ian squeezed and grinned. The smile was tinged with more than just sadness. Joe could see the desperation of the man, hiding in plain sight, just below the surface. *He's not much different than me,* he thought.

'Just two sad old cases, you and me, yeah?' Ian offered, his smile as fake as Joe's.

Joe looked at him and returned the sad smile. For the sake of his own sanity, he had to look away from the man as he nodded. 'Maybe so.'

Ian gestured behind the crowd of onlookers on the bridge, towards the flashing lights. 'Here's your ride. Go make yourself better, Joe. Reconnect with your family. It's my bet they need you as much as you need them. Do it for yourself, even if it's just for the short term.'

CRACK!!!

~~~~

As Joe looked at him again, something passed over the man's face. Ian watched it happen, his head tilting for just a moment.

In that moment he though he recognised this man before him, Joe. He bit the inside of his cheek as he gripped the offered hand, squeezing it tightly.

The look was gone almost as fast as it had appeared. Ian shook his head, dismissing it, putting it all down to grief or guilt, or something closely passing for either.

Two police officers pushed through the applauding crowd, closely followed by two paramedics. The emergency service workers took the docile Joe from Ian's embrace and eased him into the back seat of their pre-assessment car.

The police officers spoke to Ian for a moment, both patting him on the back and offering him their hands. Nodding and smiling in his, now customary, gesture, Ian took their offered sympathy with

Crack

grace. He then looked over towards Joe sitting in the back of the car. He was looking at him out of the window. Both men kept eye contact until the car pulled away from the crowds, and off along the bridge.

There was something about that face looking out of the car window that Ian found... he didn't know if creepy was the right word to use, but he couldn't think of any other.

Passing the nasty feeling off as something akin to déjà vu, he watched the paramedics disappeared off into the distance.

'Good luck, Joe,' he whispered as he took his mobile phone out of his pocket and looked at the picture of him, Paula, and Sally on the screen. It was the same picture Paula carried in her warrant holder.

He dialled Joan.

She answered on the third ring. 'Hello, Ian. Is everything OK?' He could hear the tinge of panic in her voice.

'Yeah, everything's fine. I just wanted to hear Sally's voice. Is she about?'

Joan's tone calmed. 'Yeah, I'll just get her. Sally, your daddy wants to speak to you.'

He heard the thunder of his little girl's feet as she raced from wherever she was towards where her nanny was with the phone. It broke his heart that he couldn't see her.

'Hey, Daddy.' She gasped into the handset. 'I love you. Are you coming home soon?'

Tears were running down his cheeks again as he gripped the mobile device tightly.

She sounded so grown up.

'Yeah, honey. I'll be home very soon.'

EPILOGUE

IT WAS DARK, wet, and quiet. Joe was in a work van, his hands gripping the wheel as he regarded the almost empty street.

It was a seedy street, the kind he knew so well. The few streetlights dotted about cast dim yellow puddles of light that reflected from the puddles of water beneath. Inappropriately dressed women stood beneath these lights, huddled together for warmth, or protection, or maybe just for a sense of connection. Two of them noticed his van and began walking towards him, battling for who could get to him first.

Joe looked at Helmet Man sitting next to him. He caught his reflection in the cracked visor of his passenger's helmet. His face was pained, but it looked ready to do what needed to be done.

'Just for the short term, right?'

He picked up a cola bottle and gave it a little shake, watching the brown fizz rise to the top. A thin, white residue clung to the transparent plastic of the bottle.

'Yeah. Just for the short term!'

CRACK!!!

Crack

DE McCluskey

Author's Notes

I was driving home from work; it was mid/late afternoon. I'd been working in Oxford, and just escaped a traffic jam on the A34. I had taken me an hour and a half to do the thirty-five-minute journey to reach the M40. I wasn't feeling too frustrated, as I'd left work for the weekend and was looking forward to emptying my head for the rest of the three-hour journey.

The sun was shining, the traffic on the M40 was (unusually) light, and I had the CD playing.

I owned a CD (probably still do, somewhere in a box) called *California Highway*. It was a real driving mix, filled with The Doobie Brothers, The Eagles, John Cougar Mellencamp, to name just a few. 'One of these Nights' had just finished, and a one-hit-wonder band called Timbuk 3 had just started singing 'My Future's so Bright, I Gotta Wear Shades,' a song I absolutely love. Even though it wasn't featured in the film, it always reminds me of *Ferris Buller's Day Off*—but anyway, I digress.

I'm in the car, singing away, in rather a good mood. I move over to the outside lane, as the traffic is light, and put my foot down (not driving any faster than the speed limit, honest officer).

Then, from out of nowhere, and I mean nowhere, a motorbike zoomed up on me from the inside lane. It scared the bejesus out of me. He (or she, they were wearing a full motorcycle suit, so it was impossible to tell) then proceeded to swerve in front of my car, narrowly missing my wing mirror. I slammed on my brakes as the bike began to wobble.

I would say the bike was travelling at maybe one hundred mph, and it very nearly wiped out.

Crack

Everything happened in slow motion. I remember thinking, *if that bike goes, there's no way I'll be able to stop going over it, and the stupid rider.*

Luckily for everyone involved, the rider corrected themselves, opened the throttle and zoomed off up the motorway as if nothing had happened. They left me in their wake, dealing with the trauma of almost killing someone.

I composed myself, and after my initial anger subsided, I took a moment to reflect on what had just happened. Right there and then, the whole story of *CRACK* flittered into my head. Literally the start, the middle, and a good idea about an ending.

It really was that quick.

Sometimes inspiration comes from the strangest of places.

Once again, as with many of my tales, this was originally written to be a cool looking graphic novel, filled with exploding heads, a sinister looking Helmet Man, and an increasingly more psychotic looking Joe. But, as with *The Twelve*, it grew too large to be feasible. I imagined dark pages filled with woe, gore and bleak humour ... but all I could think of was the re-mortgage I'd have to get to pay for it all, not to mention the fifteen or so years I'd have to wait for the pages to be done.

So, I changed it about and made it into this novel.

I know this isn't an easy book to read; the subject matter, even though it's farfetched, can't be too far from people's subconscious, especially now where cars and motorbikes are getting faster, and people are getting stupider. Joe's scenario is one that could happen to any of us. Well, some of it, anyway.

This is the part where I like to give thanks to some of the fine, fine people who have helped make this book.

I have some excellent proof-readers who take their time looking for my mistakes (not in life, I'd need an army for that). These include, Annmarie Barrell, Clair Kabluczenko, Abigale Roylance, Stella Read (I spelt your name right this time), Natalie Anne Webb, Hannah Nicole Carleton Millar, Matt McCormick, and the best proof-reader of them all, Kelly Rickard. Also, I can't forget, Miss Lauren Irene Davies, partner extraordinaire.

A huge thanks goes out to Steve Barrell who helped with the police procedure information and the language they use over the radio. A huge shout out to Tony Higginson; his knowledge of books surpasses any that I have. Once again, one of my oldest mates came up trumps with the original artwork and fonts for the cover, Simon Green (rest in peace mate, I seriously do miss you). Paul Cave for the new artwork, go and check his stuff out, you won't be disappointed. And finally, Lisa Lee Tone, the best editor in the whole wide world. Seriously, this woman took an unedited book and transformed it from a piece of old rag into a fine, tailored suit. Thank you, Lisa.

And finally, to you guys for taking the time to read my odd book, about people's heads getting squished … you're the best! PS - Don't forget to drop me a review… Love ya.

Dave McCluskey
March 2018 (Jan 2024)
Liverpool.

**Thank you for reading CRACK.
Please find other works by DE McCluskey.**

The Twelve
In The Mood For Murder
Sing Sing Sing For Murder
Doppelgänger
The Contract
Z: A Love Story
Butterflies
Timeripper
Mutant Superhero Zombie Killing Disco Cheerleaders from Outer Space (with Uzis)
Glimmer
The City Of The Fireflies
The Throne of Glimm
Deathday Presents
The Grinkle Nonk
Zola
Cravings
The Special Stuff
The Stinky Stump
The Boyfriend
All Of These Kids Are Going To Die